The Judge's Daughter

RUTH HAMILTON is the bestselling author of eighteen previous novels set in the north-west of England. She was born in Bolton and now lives in Liverpool, and she writes about both places with realistic insight and dramatic imagery.

For more information on Ruth Hamilton and her books, see her website at:
www.ruth-hamilton.co.uk
www.panmacmillan.com

ALSO BY RUTH HAMILTON

A Whisper to the Living
With Love from Ma Maguire
Nest of Sorrows
Billy London's Girls
Spinning Jenny
The September Starlings
A Crooked Mile
Paradise Lane
The Bells of Scotland Road
The Dream Sellers
The Corner House
Miss Honoria West
Mulligan's Yard
Saturday's Child
Matthew & Son
Chandlers Green
The Bell House
Dorothy's War

Ruth Hamilton

The Judge's Daughter

PAN BOOKS

First published 2007 by Pan Books
an imprint of Pan Macmillan Ltd
Pan Macmillan, 20 New Wharf Road, London N1 9RR
Basingstoke and Oxford
Associated companies throughout the world
www.panmacmillan.com

ISBN 978-0-330-44522-1

3 5 7 9 8 6 4 2

A CIP catalogue record for this book is available from
the British Library.

Typeset by Set Systems Ltd, Saffron Walden, Essex
Printed and bound in Great Britain by
Mackays of Chatham plc, Chatham, Kent

Visit www.panmacmillan.com to read more about all our books
and to buy them. You will also find features, author interviews and
news of any author events, and you can sign up for e-newsletters
so that you're always first to hear about our new releases.

In loving memory of Lydia Carroll

Thanks to my grandson, Christopher,
for making me smile on dark days

Also:
My two sons for unswerving support
Their partners Sue and Liz for the same

Imogen Taylor and Trisha Jackson from
Pan Macmillan for faith and help

Sam and Fudge, older but no wiser Labradors
Oscar (ring-necked parakeet) for eating my words
– literally

Last, but never least, the readership

2004

Long after the man had finished pacing and calculating, his footfalls seemed to echo round the house, bouncing off walls that had heard no sound in many a year. He scratched an ear, shook his head, talked to himself for a few moments before going back to work all over again. He measured room after room, the instrument in his hand clicking with every metre he covered. There had to be something wrong with the new-fangled digital equipment. Three times, he had measured Briarswood; three times, the result had been ridiculous enough for a Walt Disney cartoon.

'According to this, the place should have fallen down years ago,' he muttered. But there were no huge cracks, no faults, no gaping wounds in the plasterwork or in the exterior stone and brick fascia. A place of this size had to have twelve-foot underpinnings – it needed a solid base. And nowhere on the architect's aged plan did a flatbed foundation get a mention. Anyway, why stabilize the back of the house and leave the front to chance and nature? The rear part was correct, each storey matching the one below right down to the basement, yet the front remained a mystery.

In a huge bay window, he paused and wondered, not for the first time, whether modern science represented any real improvement in his job. Sighing, he put away the newer tool of his trade and drew from a pocket that good old standby – a metal measure encased in bright orange plastic. He would start again. This time, he began in attics, moving down to bathrooms and sleeping quarters, finally tackling ground floor and cellar. The answer was the same. The cellar was smaller than the rest of the house and this fact presented something of an enigma for prospective purchasers. As surveyor, he had to hand in a sensible report and there was nothing sensible about Briarswood.

He sat on an abandoned kitchen chair and wrote down the bare bones of his findings. Never a fanciful man, he shivered and looked up, expecting to blame an open door for creating the draught, but he was still alone. The house was dark and reeked of emptiness. Could a place express loneliness? Could a house complain about solitude and neglect? A tap dripped. Jaundice-yellow emulsion was peeling itself away from walls. He wrote about slight roof damage, ancient rainwater goods and some broken tiling in a bathroom. He reported the need for damp-proofing, a suspicion about wall ties in a gable, a decaying perimeter fence in the rear garden. Lastly, he remarked on the impossible: the footings were smaller than the building. There was no dry rot, no wet rot, no decaying timber. But there was something amiss with the specifications.

Outside, he stared into a thousand eyes created by ornate leaded windows, many of whose panes were the imperfect products of primitive glassmakers. Normally, the faceted diamond effect would have pleased him, but this place reminded him of long-ago textbooks in which, as a child, he had studied magnified diagrams of insect eyes. Like a mature bluebottle, the large house owned a plethora of aspects through which it viewed the world.

2

It seemed alive, yet dead. And he needed a double whisky, his dinner, his family, his newspaper.

As he climbed back into the car, he felt as if the house were continuing to watch and analyse him. It was just the sinking sun, he told himself impatiently. He wasn't one for ghosts and ghouls, but even he had to admit that there was something strange about Briarswood. Almost laughing at himself, he pushed the gearstick into first and drew away. Did the house need an exorcist rather than a property surveyor?

At the gate, he braked and looked for traffic. Ah, well. He would commit the peculiarities to paper tonight, would hand in the work, then move on to the next project. No mention need be made of icy tingling in his spine, of hairs on arms standing to attention, of the feeling that he had been followed for two hours. It was just another house, a residence built of sandstone and imitation string courses designed to allow the house a relationship with Tudor mansions. 'I get dafter with age,' he mumbled. Nothing ever went bump in the night; most certainly not at four o'clock in the afternoon. The sun disappeared behind scudding cloud and every eye in the windows was suddenly closed.

Shadows appeared. Staring into his rear-view mirror, the man studied Briarswood. There was no one in the place, yet he imagined movement and felt sadness soaking through the building's fabric and right into his bones. 'Well, I wouldn't put my name down for a seance in there,' he told his notebook, which he had placed on the passenger seat. In a career that spanned some twenty years, he had never surveyed a property so creepy and odd. No wonder it had remained empty, he mused as the sun reappeared and woke the windows once more.

There had been rumours, stories of families leaving the place in a hurry, hints about disappearing objects and noises in the night. Lancashire had long been awash with such tales, many of which were aired and embellished by folk who had taken too much ale. The whole thing was crazy and he needed to pull his ideas together and stop talking to himself before going home.

But he found himself shivering anew until he turned out of the driveway and accelerated towards Wigan Road. Someone would have to get to the bottom of the equation, and he thanked God that his part in the business was now over.

Chapter One

1964

It was a tin of Barker's Lavender Polish this time. He picked it up, stared at it for several seconds, turned and left the shop with the container clasped tightly against his chest. As always, he looked like a man on a mission, not exactly in a hurry, but with no time for dawdling.

'Mr Grimshaw?' Eva Hargreaves moved very quickly for a woman of twenty stones and fifty years. 'Come on, Fred, you've not paid.' But he was yards ahead and the ironmonger dared not leave her business untended. The old chap wasn't in his right mind just now, and his daughter would bring the money. She always coughed up, did poor Agnes. Aye, she suffered in more ways than one, had done for years. Some folk endured very bad luck and some got away with murder. It was an eternal mystery and people cleverer than Eva would never find an answer to it. All the same, the theft was a damned nuisance and no mistake, but Glenys Timpson was entering the shop and would be waiting for her firewood, so the shopkeeper returned to her rightful place.

Glenys tutted when Eva came in. 'He wants putting away in the asylum,' she said, sour mouth even more down-turned than usual. 'Doesn't know what he's doing. There's no rhyme and no reason to his carryings-on. That Agnes Makepeace wants to stop at home and see to him. God knows he looked after her for long enough.'

Eva Hargreaves didn't want to lose a customer, yet she chose to reply. 'Agnes's husband isn't paid over-well by them in yon big house. Family needs her cleaning money. Her pop will get better – he's better already; it were only a small stroke. She's gone from the house nobbut three hours a day, and she looks after her grandparents for the other twenty-one hours. The old fellow walks in the night as well, you know. It's nobody's fault. Agnes has always done her best, and I dare say she'll carry on the same road.'

The customer sniffed. 'Two lots of firewood, Eva. I've company expected at the weekend, so I'll be wanting a parlour fire.' She inhaled again. 'For his own good, he wants putting somewhere safe. Mark my words, he'll be under a bus any day now. What price a little job in the pub when that happens, eh? She should know her duty – and not just to her kin, but to us as well.'

'It were only a tin of polish.' The shopkeeper placed two wired bundles of kindling on her counter. 'And he's miles better than he was. Takes time, getting over a stroke.'

'Happen it were only a tin of polish, but he'd not get away with it in town, would he? Then if the court says he's insane, which he is – a few raisins short of an Eccles cake if you ask me – he'll definitely get put away. Agnes'd be best doing it the right road, through her own doctor. No use sitting about waiting for a disaster. It wants sorting out now, before he goes from bad to bloody ridiculous.'

Eva offered no comment. She knew Agnes Make-peace and couldn't imagine her parting with the man she called Pop. Agnes was well aware of her duty and would see her elders through to the bitterest of ends. 'Anything else?' she asked her customer.

'Nay, just the firewood.' Glenys stalked to the door, then turned as an afterthought processed itself before pouring from her lips. 'Were he in his pyjama top?' she asked.

'Yes.' Eva was rearranging bottles of Lanry bleach. Fred Grimshaw was in his pyjama bottoms, too, though they were almost covered by a pair of tattered, unclean overalls.

'Nowt good'll come of it,' pronounced the redoubtable Glenys before striding homeward.

Eva sat on her stool for a few moments. She was getting too tired for this lark and her weight didn't help. Poor old Fred Grimshaw – what was he up to this time? Should she close her shop and dash along to the pub for Agnes? No, he'd be long gone by now. For a man with health problems, he could shift at a fair rate of knots. 'He is getting better,' she reminded herself through clenched teeth. 'And he deserves to get better, bless him. There's no man finer than Fred Grimshaw.'

She found herself praying to a God who would surely have mercy on a poorly gentleman, because Fred had been just that – one of Nature's better creatures. Then she stood up to measure paraffin into a container. Life had to go on; customers wanted their goods and homes needed to be heated, even in summer once the sun went down. Like Agnes Makepeace, Eva Hargreaves was completely powerless. Fred had likely gone missing again and there was nothing to be done.

Fred Grimshaw had never been late for work in his life. Even during this war, he still stuck to his tools, turning out ammunition instead of wrought-iron gates. His skills were required. All those railings wanted melting down and the place was full of women these days. Hard workers, all right, but they chattered a lot when his back was turned. A foreman needed eyes in the back of his head, that was a fact.

He stood outside the factory and blinked. Entwistle Motors? Ah, that must be a government thing, a way of hiding what really went on inside those sheds. Hitler was planning an invasion and he and his army needed to be confused. Entwistle Motors. Unimpressed by the new name, Fred entered his little kingdom.

Where was the furnace? Where was his lathe? The women had all gone home, curlers rattling beneath turbans made from headscarves. It wasn't home time. Bullets didn't make themselves, did they? How the hell could he carry on with no equipment and no work-force? Was he supposed to supply the army on his own?

He dropped the tin of polish and it rolled away across a flagged floor. The place was full of motor vehicles, some in one piece, others with their intestines spread out across floor and benches. His jaw dropped. How could things change overnight like this? Only yesterday, he had stood here making casings for bullets – he even remembered bandaging his thumb after he'd . . . There was no bandage on his thumb. He had made another mistake and another headache threatened.

Sam Entwistle raised himself out of a pit. 'Fred?' The unhappy wanderer was here once more, body intact, head nineteen years or more late. 'Come on, old lad. Let's be getting you home, shall we? Don't start upsetting yourself.'

Fred blinked. 'I've done it again, haven't I?'

'You have. Your mind's playing tricks because of your stroke. And I can't keep taking time off to drive you home, can I? These here apprentices get up to all sorts while I'm off the scene.' He shouted across to his second-in-command. 'Keep an eye on that crowd of buggers while I run Fred home.' Sam sighed. Fred was known far and wide as a man of opinions, a man who liked to speak his mind and shame the devil. He had even been labelled cantankerous and loud, yet he had been reduced to this in one cruel, fell swoop. 'Come on, Fred.'

Meek as a kitten, Fred allowed himself to be placed in the passenger seat of Sam Entwistle's van. 'I'm not right,' he said softly when Sam was seated beside him. 'I'm half here, half there and half no-bloody-where.'

'That's three halves.'

'I know. See what I mean?'

The fact that Fred had insight into his own condition was the biggest cruelty, Sam mused as he turned the vehicle into Derby Street. Yet there was hope, because this was not senile dementia – it was the aftermath of a bleed and the man would come good. 'See, Fred, you weren't well at all. You were a fighter, and you survived. Look – you've got your talking back and you can shift on your feet better than most your age. Another few months and you'll be right as rain in the memory department. It'll stop. I promise you – this carrying-on will stop.'

The passenger nodded. 'I blinking well hope so, son. I wait for our Agnes to come home from school – she's been working for years and she's married. I do daft things like this – going to work, getting on buses and throwing stuff out – I'm bloody puddled half the time.'

'But the other two halves of the time, you're all right. Takes a while, old son. My dad had a stroke and he never walked again. Be patient. You're doing all right, believe me.'

Fred was cross with himself. He knew full well what had happened – hadn't it all been explained in the hospital? A stroke meant all kinds of things and he could walk and talk well, could behave properly for most of the time. 'In me pyjamas again,' he pronounced morosely.

'At least you're not naked and frightening the horses.' Sam pulled up at Fred's front door. 'Now, listen to me. Find something to do with your hands – make toys or furniture or whatever you feel like. Your head's got a broken wire in – like a telephone that doesn't carry the message. There's things you've got to relearn, you see. And you're one of the lucky ones – you're not flat on your back or in a wheelchair. Get busy. Keep yourself occupied, that's my motto. It's the only way to stay out of the graveyard, old lad.'

Fred entered the house and inhaled deeply. It smelled of death. His good old girl was on her way out. He'd been married to Sadie forever, and she was leaving him. He should have been looking after her. He should have been looking at the card propped next to the clock, a white background bearing the numbers 1964 in large black print. Agnes had put that there to remind him of the year. There was a list somewhere – the Prime Minister and other stuff that didn't matter. Tory or Labour, they were all the bloody same, in it for what they could get out of it. He smiled wryly; some things were impossible to forget. Somewhere inside himself, Fred remained as angry and positive as ever.

Sadie was on morphine now. She didn't laugh any more, didn't talk to him; she just lay there till a nurse came to clean her up and try to get some fluids into her. Cancer. He hated that word. It meant crab, and crabs owned sharp claws. 'Sadie,' he whispered sadly.

His wife needed to die. That was another bit of sense he had retained – the ability to judge when a person had taken enough. And his Sadie had taken well more than enough.

She was in the downstairs front room. Denis and a neighbour had brought the bed down; Fred slept alone in a contraption that felt like an ex-army cot, just canvas stretched over a metal frame. 'But I'm alive,' he accused himself. 'And I have to learn...' Learn what? How to be a human being, how to get from morning till night? Hadn't he been doing that for over seventy years? Did he have to go back to Peter and Paul's nursery, start all over again?

Agnes would be home from school soon. No, that was wrong – she would be home from work. He had to behave himself, must make sure that he didn't ... Tin of polish. Had he paid for it? Where was it, anyway? He was stupid. Then he remembered Sam Entwistle pushing something into a pocket of the decaying over-alls and he plunged his hand inside. It was there. 'I remembered,' he breathed. He could go and pay for it, could complete the errand. They could call him daft if they wanted, but he was going to show them.

After looking in on his wife, he set forth to pay his debt to Eva Hargreaves. At the same time, he would buy a notebook. 'I'll write everything down,' he said to himself. 'That road, I'll have half a chance of remembering to be normal.'

Normal. What the blinking heck did that mean and who had decided? Normal was having no weak blood vessels in the brain, no cancer, a full memory. He could see the war all right – his war, the war to end all wars. Jimmy Macker blown into a thousand pieces, flesh and bone everywhere, corpses stacked beneath mud in

11

endless miles of trenches. But he couldn't remember the current days, weeks and months; was not *normal*.

Jimmy MacKenzie, usually known as Macker. Aye, he could see him now, cheeky grin, stolen silver cigarette case twinned with a silver matchbox, both taken from a body in a trench. That daft smile had been blown away with the rest of Jimmy and with a million others, all ploughed in now, all gone from mud to dust. *Alice in Wonderland.* He had read that to Agnes a few weeks – no – a few years back. Cheshire cat. The grin remained when tail, body and whiskers disappeared. Macker's grin had lodged itself into Fred's mind, clear as crystal . . . Poor Macker.

But what had Fred eaten for breakfast? Did it matter? Was breakfast important enough to be remembered? Yes, he would write everything in a notebook. Eva sold notebooks and pencils, didn't she? It was the only way to learn. He could copy the date from the newspaper at the top of a page. He would make a note of every damned thing he did, ate and said. Sadie needed him. She didn't talk, but he felt sure she knew when he was there. He must spend more time with his wife and less time wandering about in pyjamas. There was probably a law about pyjamas in the street. Blessed government – they all wanted shooting.

Glenys Timpson was cleaning her windows again. Oh, he remembered her all right. She stoned her steps and cleaned her outside paintwork several times a week, because she couldn't bear to miss anything. She was a curtain-twitcher and a gossip. That hatchet face was not something that could be forgotten.

'Fred Grimshaw?' There was an edge of flint to her tone.

He stopped, but offered no greeting.

12

'You pinched a tin of polish from Eva's shop before. I were there. I watched you pocket it and run.'

'And I'm going back to pay for it.' He was glad she had reminded him, as he still needed to acquire his memory notebook and the polish was not at the front of his mind any more.

'You should stop in the house,' she snapped.

He took a step closer to the woman. 'So should you. That scraggy neck's grown inches with you poking your head into everybody's doings. Mind your own business.' Another dim memory resurrected itself. 'You could try keeping your lads sober for a kick-off.' He marched away, head held high, the mantra 'Pay for polish' repeating in his head. But there was triumph in his heart, because he had remembered that nosy neighbour. One of these days, she'd end up flat on her face and with no one to help her up.

Glenys Timpson, who declared under her breath that she had never been so insulted in all her born days, retreated into her domain. Eva was right – the old man was getting better. Or worse, she mused, depending on a person's point of view. Some folk thought they were a cut above their neighbours and that there Agnes Makepeace was one of that breed. Aye, well – pride came before every fall.

Her lads weren't drunkards. They liked a drink – especially Harry, who was an amateur boxer – but they didn't go overboard unless it was a special occasion. Perhaps special occasions were becoming more frequent, but she wasn't having her lads tainted with the reputation of drunkards. She set the table angrily, throwing cutlery into place. Some folk didn't know when to keep their mouths shut. Some folk wanted teaching a lesson. It was time to have a word with Mrs Agnes Makepeace.

Fred entered the shop.

'Hello, love,' Eva began. She liked the man, had always had time for him and his loudly expressed opinions on most subjects. She could tell from his expression that he knew he had done something wrong and was struggling to remember the sin.

He held up a hand. 'I need help,' he said bluntly. 'Seems some of my memory got muddled while I was in the infirmary. I could do with a notebook and a pencil to help me make lists of stuff. My brain's got more holes than the cabbage strainer.'

Eva nodded. 'I've some coloured pencils. You could write about different things in separate colours. You could use both ends of the book as well – important business at the front and details at the back.'

'Good idea,' he said. 'And you can take pay for that tin of polish.' He had remembered the polish. This was a red-letter day, and he would mark it on the page in scarlet. 'Funny how you remember things,' he said. 'It's not the things themselves that come back right away – it's a smell or a sound or some bit of detail. Like Jimmy Macker's smile. I'll never forget his smile.'

Eva took money from his hand, counted it out, placed it in the till. 'Fred?'

'What?'

'Did you use that polish at all?'

He frowned. 'I don't think so.'

'Do you know whether your Agnes needs polish?'

He had no idea.

She looked at the tin. 'Tell you what – seeing as it's you, I'll take it back. That'll save you money and it'll save your Agnes worrying over where her new tin of Barker's came from. And you'll get your book and pencils for the same price as the polish.'

14

'Fair enough.' With his coloured pencils and his stiff-backed notebook, Fred went home. He intended to sit next to his dying wife and write the date in red at the top of the first page. Nothing was impossible. For the sake of his Sadie and his beloved granddaughter, Fred Grimshaw would carry on. There was life in the old dog yet.

The drain was blocked again.

Agnes, who had come to the end of her shortened tether, flung mop and bucket across the floor. Ernie Ramsden, nicknamed Ramrod by his staff, was too stingy to send for a plumber, so he would deal with this himself. He would uncover the outside drain, piece his rods together and riddle about until he had shifted the offending item. Derby Street was about to smell like a sewage works again, and the problem would return within days, but why should she worry? It was his pub, his stink, so he could get on with it, while she would clean elsewhere in the building.

In the bar, she picked up polish and duster and began to work on the tables. Ramsden came in. 'Have you done the men's already?' he asked.

'Blocked,' she answered tersely. If he wanted to go poking about in ancient drains, that was his privilege.

'Are you sure?'

Agnes shrugged. 'There's stuff all over the floor and nothing goes down. When I flushed, the place flooded. The women's isn't much better. So yes, it's happened again. You need a plumber.'

'Brewery wouldn't stand for that,' replied the landlord.

'And if something isn't done, your customers won't

stand for it, either. They won't be able to stand, because they'll be overcome by fumes. Every time you lift the pavement cover, folk start crossing over to the other side of the road. You're becoming a health hazard. Will the corporation not help with this mess before people start ending up in hospital?'

Ernie Ramsden shook his head. 'Nay. Trouble is, the blockage is here, under the pub. Not the town's property.'

Agnes stopped polishing. Several months, she'd worked here. It was part time and it was driving her part mad. But there was little she could do about it, because the hours suited her. Looking after aged grandparents meant that she couldn't take a full time job, so she came here every day and, at least once a week, needed her wellington boots so that she could wade through excrement and lavatory paper. 'Up to you,' she said before resuming her attack on a circular table. 'I can't do any more.'

Ernie stood for a few moments and watched Agnes at work. She was a corker, all right. Denis Makepeace was a lucky fellow, because his wife was built like a perfect sculpture – rounded, ripe and strong. She was a good worker, too. She did her job, invited and offered few confidences, then rushed home to see to her elders. 'How's the family?' he asked.

'All right,' came the dismissive response.

The landlord sighed before retreating to his living quarters.

They were a long way from all right, mused Agnes as she placed a pile of ashtrays on the counter. Nan was dying of cancer, while Pop, who had been the old lady's chief carer, was fighting for the right to return from a world all his own. Only last week, he had been marched

16

home by a bus conductor, a female whose vehicle had remained stationary for at least ten minutes at the top of Noble Street. Agnes could still hear the woman's shrill voice. 'Can you not keep him in? He's no right to be on a public vehicle in his dressing gown and carpet slippers. Said he were on his way to catch the train to Southport – and his train ticket were nobbut a label off a condensed milk tin. I can't be leaving the bus to bring him home all the while.'

Agnes swallowed hard while she wondered what Pop had got up to today. She'd locked the front door, but he needed to get out into the yard for the lavatory, so the back door was on the latch. Into the open drain beneath the tippler, he had thrown his lower denture, a week's worth of newspapers, one brown shoe and, she suspected, an antimacassar taken from the front room. It was probably Pop's fault that the area's drains were getting blocked. No, it couldn't be him. The stoppage was the sole property of Ernie Ramsden and the Dog and Ferret.

'I'll just have a go meself,' muttered Ernie as he struggled past with his rods. He was always having a go himself and he knew that the problem was way beyond the reach of his rods.

Agnes prayed that she had left no matches in the house. Pop needed to be separated from anything combustible or sharp. Knives were wrapped in sacking on the top shelf of her wardrobe. What a way to live. If she'd been one for visitors, she would have needed to excuse herself in order to fetch an implement with which to cut cake. But few people came to the Makepeace house. Denis's work took him away from home for many hours – and who wanted to sit with a poor old woman and a mad old man?

The familiar scent of human excrement insinuated its way into the pub. Almost automatically, Agnes took a small amount of cotton wool from her apron pocket and stuffed half into each nostril. The men's lavs were bad enough, but this smell was unbearable. Ramsden, fearful that the brewery might close him down, was trying with little success to keep the men's facilities in working condition, but he was losing the battle.

Voices floated through the open door. 'At it again, Ernie?' 'Somebody been passing bricks down yer lav?' 'Let us know when you strike gold, eh? Carry on this road and you'll hit Australia.'

She sat down for a few minutes. Even the mills were better than this, but she couldn't abandon the people who had reared her, could she? Agnes's mother had died two hours after giving birth to her only child, while the father was listed as unknown. Sadie and Fred Grimshaw, having cared for their own daughter, had been presented with her newborn baby girl and had simply continued with life. They had been firm, but kind, and Agnes owed her life to them.

A red-faced Ernie entered the arena. 'I reckon yon drain's collapsed,' he announced.

'Then you'll have to close down and tell the brewery,' she replied. She and Denis would struggle to manage. Pop could do a lot of damage in three hours, so Agnes needed to bite the bullet and quit. It wasn't going to be easy, but it had to be faced; she would soon need to stay at home all the time. Even five minutes was time enough for Pop to create disaster, and Nan was becoming too ill to be left to the poor old chap's mercies.

Ernie poured himself a double Irish. 'You're right,' he admitted gloomily. 'End of the road, Agnes.' He drained the glass. 'What'll you do? Mind, I'll take you on again like a shot if the brewery lets me carry on. You're the best cleaner I've ever had.'

She bit her lip and pondered. It seemed as if every other building on Derby Street was a pub. The Dog and Ferret, never truly popular, had lost more customers because of the drains, and its owners could well close it down or renovate it before putting someone younger in charge. There were too many pubs, and she disliked them, hated the smells, was afraid of what drinking did to people. She had taken enough. 'Nan's dying,' she said after a few moments. 'I was meaning to give notice soon, because she needs nursing round the clock. I won't have her spending her last days in hospital. I promised her she'd stop at home no matter what.'

'And is the owld chap still a bit daft?'

Everyone knew Fred, though few remembered the dedicated worker who had toiled for forty-odd years in the town's foundry. He had been a big man, but age had withered him and he was shorter, thinner and extremely frail. No, she told herself firmly – Pop was getting better. 'He's old,' she snapped. 'He's had a bit of a stroke – that's his only sin. None of us can fight the years – he's been a hard worker in his time.'

'I didn't mean to offend,' he said.

Agnes placed her box of tools on a table. 'I'm going.' She straightened and took one last look around her place of work. She would miss the thinking time more than anything, this island of relative solitude alongside which she had been allowed to moor herself for a few hours each day. At home, she had to face the reality that was Nan, the burden that was Pop, the same four walls day in and day out. If only that judge fellow weren't so selfish, Denis would be working regular hours for decent pay, but the judge represented rules in more ways than one. He interpreted the law of the land during working hours, then set regulations to suit himself and only himself when he got home. Judge Spencer was a tyrant, she supposed.

'I'll miss you, lass.' Ernie's expression said it all. He would probably lose his livelihood within days.

'They'll find you another pub,' she told him.

'I'm no spring chicken.' He left her and returned to his living quarters.

Agnes put on her coat and stepped outside. She removed the cotton wool from her nostrils and crossed the road, anxious to be away from the stench of human waste. Managing on Denis's income was not going to be easy. It would mean less meat, more vegetables and no new clothes for some time. She was twenty years old and she owned nothing, no record player, no transistor radio, no decent shoes. Denis, her husband of twelve months, was in possession of a weak chest and was unfit for anything approaching hard labour. Nan was dying; Pop ... Pop was walking down Noble Street with a package in his hands. 'Pop?' she cried. Oh, no. What had he done this time and who would be knocking at the door?

He turned, frowned because she had grown again. No, she hadn't. It would go in the notebook – Agnes was a woman and no longer went to school. Denis was her husband – that, too, would be recorded. Denis Makepeace, bad chest, huge heart.

'Where've you been?' she asked.

He had been sorting out his life, but the details were vague. 'Coloured pencils,' he told her. 'And a little book to help me remember.'

She grinned, recalled him swinging her in the air,

running round the duck pond with her, laughing at Laurel and Hardy at the local cinema. The Grimshaws had been good parents and Agnes had lacked for nothing during childhood. They could have abandoned her to an orphanage or to adoption, but they had given her a happy life and now she had to care for them. 'Oh, Pop.' She smiled. 'I hope you've been up to no mischief.'

'Me?' He was a picture of innocence. 'I can't remember,' he admitted eventually, 'but I think I went to work again. I'm worse in a morning, you know. By afternoon, I can nearly remember my own name.'

'The year's on the mantelpiece.'

'Aye.'

'I put it there for a reason.'

'Aye.'

'And if you say aye again, I'll clout you.'

'Aye.'

They walked down Noble Street until they reached Glenys Timpson's house. She was out in an instant, seeming to propel herself with the speed of a bullet from a gun. Thin arms folded themselves against a flat bosom. 'He's been thieving again.' Triumph shone in her eyes as she nodded in Fred's direction. 'Not fit to be out.'

Agnes stared at the irate creature. 'Mrs Timpson,' she began after an uncomfortable pause. 'Your sons, Harry, Bert and Jack – have I got their names right?'

The woman jerked her head in agreement.

'You'd best keep them in, missus.' Agnes moved closer to her adversary. 'I've heard talk. They'll have to start watching their step.'

'Eh?' Like many of her generation, Glenys wore a scarf turban-fashion, curlers peeping out from the edges.

21

She raised her eyebrows until they all but disappeared under pink and blue plastic rollers. 'You what? What are you incinerating?' She frowned, knowing that the word she had delivered was slightly inappropriate.

The younger woman lowered her voice until it became almost a whisper. 'Selling jewellery round the pubs. Probably from that safe job in Manchester. Remember? Wasn't your Harry in the army during his service? Perhaps he learned about explosives and a safe might be easy for him. He hangs around in the wrong company.'

'What are you saying?'

'I'm saying keep your mouth shut about Pop, or I'll open mine about a few cheap brooches and bracelets. I'm saying mind your own business. Pop forgets things. Your sons are just plain bad.'

Glenys fell against the front door, a hand over her heart.

'Don't forget – my husband works for a High Court judge.' Noting that the street's biggest gossip had gone into shock, Agnes took Pop's arm and marched him homeward. As she walked, she shook from head to foot, but she remained as straight as she could manage, because she didn't want Glenys Timpson to see how scared she was. At twenty, Agnes was female head of a household and it wasn't easy, especially with a man like Pop causing bother from time to time.

Gratefully, she closed her front door.

'Were that true?' Pop asked. 'Have her sons been stealing?'

Agnes studied her grandfather. 'You remembered that all right. Yes, it's true. She's so busy watching other folks' comings and goings that she misses what's under her nose. They've been chucked out of the Dog and

Ferret twice for trying to sell things. I've heard they're not welcome in the Lion and all. Now, I'll go and look at Nan.'

Sadie Grimshaw was curled into a position that was almost foetal. Her granddaughter cleaned bed and body, listened to shallow breathing and found herself praying for the poor woman to be released. This wasn't Nan, hadn't been Nan for weeks. It was a skeleton with yellowing flesh barely managing to cover bones, a curled-up creature with no life in it. Life had dealt some cruel blows to Sadie, who had suffered many miscarriages, whose only surviving child had died after Agnes's birth, who had raised Agnes and worked hard all her life.

Pop came in. 'She's in a terrible state,' he whispered.

'She needs to be in hospital – they could control the pain better.' The old lady was now too weak to groan or cry.

'They'd finish her off and she wants to be at home. We promised her, pet. Even if she doesn't talk, I reckon she knows where she is.'

Not for the first time today, Agnes realized that her old Pop was on his way back. Since the stroke, he had acted in a way Nan might have described as 'yonderly', a term invented to describe someone who was present in body, but not in mind. 'Would it be a bad thing if the hospital gave her a helping hand?' whispered Agnes.

He shrugged and asked if she knew where his baccy and pipe were. So his thoughts were still skipping slightly, though he seemed capable of concentrating for several seconds, at least. And he had remembered Glenys Timpson's sons for about two minutes, so that was a good sign. 'Behind the clock,' she answered.

Fred disappeared, came back almost immediately with the postcard that marked the year. 'What's this?'

'The year. Your pipe's behind the clock.'

'Right.' Off he went once more.

Agnes held a withered claw that had once been a hand, a hand that had fed and clothed her, a hand belonging to the only mother she had ever known. 'Please, please go,' she wept.

The front door opened and Nurse Ingram stepped into the room. She studied the scene for a few seconds, then stood behind Agnes, squeezing the young woman's shoulder in a way that was meant to be supportive and encouraging. 'Let me get the ambulance, love,' she begged.

'I promised she'd die here.' The words were fractured by sobs.

'I know that. But we want what's best for her, don't we?'

Agnes nodded.

After a pause of several seconds, the nurse spoke again. 'Get me a bowl of water while I wash her face.'

'I just did that.'

The nurse walked a few paces and stood eye to eye with Agnes. 'Get me a bowl of water and a towel. Go on. It's what I need.'

Agnes looked into the sorrow-filled eyes of a person she had come to know and trust in recent weeks. Although no words were spoken, she heard what the woman was not permitted to say. Unsteadily, she rose to her feet and dried her eyes. 'Thank you,' she said.

'She'll be all right,' said the nurse. 'Just let me see to her.'

Agnes filled the bowl and ordered Pop to follow her.

24

They re-entered the front room just as the nurse stamped a heavy foot onto a phial.

'I get clumsier all the time. Second piece of equipment I've lost today,' announced Alice Ingram, her eyes fixed on Agnes's face. 'She's going now. Stay with her.'

'Where's she going?' asked Fred.

'To Jesus,' Agnes replied.

So it came about that Sadie Grimshaw left her body and went to meet her Maker. The only evidence that she had been awarded an assisted passage was ground into a pegged rug beside the bed. With Fred on one side and her granddaughter on the other, Sadie breathed her last. Free from pain and all other earthly shackles, she floated away on a cloud of morphine, her ravaged features relaxed for the first time in months.

Nurse Alice Ingram wiped the patient's face. 'I'll get the doctor to sign the certificate,' she said, her voice shaky. She had done the right thing. Sadie would not have survived the journey to the infirmary, she told herself repeatedly. 'I'll lay her out myself.'

Fred looked at Agnes. 'Is that it? Has she gone?'

Agnes nodded.

His chin dropped and he stared at his dead wife. 'I'll have to pull myself together now, Sadie,' he said. 'I'm all our Agnes has left, aren't I?'

He left the room.

'How can I thank you?' Agnes asked.

'By saying nowt. I've done wrong, but it was right in my book.'

'And in mine. I know you're not supposed to . . . But sometimes, it can be a kindness.'

In the back living room, Pop was weeping quietly in the fireside rocker. Agnes squatted down and took his hand. 'It was time. Every day was worse than the one before. That wasn't Nan any more. She needed to go.'

He smiled through his grief. 'Your mam wasn't a bad girl, you know. And when she died, me and Sadie got you. Eeh, you were lovely. You kept us going, gave us something to fight for. Losing our Eileen were the worst thing that ever happened to me and my Sadie. But she wasn't bad, your mam. She didn't mess with all kinds of men.'

Agnes patted his hand. He could go back twenty years, but he struggled to remember yesterday. 'Is Sadie all right now?' he asked.

She swallowed hard. 'Nan died a few minutes ago.' This had been a long day. Nan was gone, the job was gone and Pop was on his way back.

He stared hard into the blue depths of his beloved little girl's eyes. 'I'm not that daft, lass. I know she's dead. I were there when she went. Nay, that'll stick.' Red-letter day. Why had this been a red-letter day? It was black now, dark, clouded over, miserable. He had pencils and a notebook; he had returned the polish; his wife was dead. This had become a black-letter day and he had to keep going for Agnes. It had always been for Agnes, because Agnes deserved the best. 'I wish we could have got you educated, love. You're cleverer than your friends, but you work in a mill.'

'No, I left the mill and went to clean the pub, but the pub's closing.'

'Closing time already?'

'Closing for good, Pop.' Like Nan, the Dog and Ferret was about to become just another piece of local history.

*

They waited for the hearse. Denis, who had been given a day off, was smart in his dark suit and white shirt. He paced about, uncomfortable in new shoes. Outside on the cobbles, Judge Spencer's Bentley gleamed in morning sunlight weakened by layers of dust and smoke from nearby mills. The judge had lent his precious motor so that Sadie's family could travel in style to church and graveyard.

Denis kept a keen eye on his calm wife. Agnes took things in her stride, but this stride had been a mile long, because she had adored her grandmother. She had no job, little money and the old man to care for. If only Denis had enjoyed health good enough for a proper job, things would have been different, but he was a manservant on low wages and he hated to see his beloved wife so poor. Her navy suit was clean and pressed, but shabby shoes told the world how impoverished Agnes was. The new shoes had been for him and should have been for her. His love was so strong that it hurt, especially now. 'All right, pet?' he asked for the third time. The judge had paid for Denis's shoes – they were part of the uniform.

She smiled at him. Here she sat, surrounded by Nan's furniture, Nan's rugs, Nan's memories expressed in photographs on the mantel. Every pot and pan in the place was Nan's, but that lovely woman was dead and Agnes felt numb and chilled right through to her bones. How could a person be cold on a nice June morning? Could she carry on here without the woman who had formed and nurtured her? Could she live among Nan's little treasures, those constant reminders of better days?

Pop was quiet. He was scribbling again in his little book, brow furrowed as he struggled with spelling, never one of his strong points. Since the death of Sadie, the notebook had been his constant companion. Every meal, every walk, every memory got space on the page. He was going to bury his beloved today, and each move would be recorded.

Denis sighed. He knew full well that Fred would make notes through the requiem and at the graveside, but that was the old fellow's way of coping. If the system worked, it must be employed. Agnes hadn't wept properly yet; Denis hoped that this would be her day for tears.

A sudden commotion in the street caused all three occupants of the room to move towards the front door. Hearses were quiet vehicles, but tyres screeched and someone ran quickly down towards Deane Road. They stood and watched as police dragged Harry Timpson into a car. His mother, turban dangling loose from curlered hair, was screaming and pulling at the nearest officer. 'Leave him,' she yelled. 'He's done nowt.'

The drama was over in seconds. As the police car drove off towards town, the hearse entered the other end of the street, moving slowly towards Sadie's house. It stopped and two men stepped out to collect the floral tributes and place them on the coffin.

Agnes felt a hand on her arm. She turned and saw a dishevelled Glenys Timpson with a bunch of flowers that had seen better days. The woman was weeping. 'For your nan. Sadie, God rest her,' she sobbed. Then, for the first time within living memory, Glenys apologized. 'They've took him away,' she added. 'He'll be in jail. Seems you were right.'

Agnes offered a weak smile. 'It's a bad day for all of us,' she said softly. 'I'll see you later.'

Fred and his granddaughter occupied the rear seat of the Bentley while Denis drove. Without the chauffeur's cap, he looked like any other car owner, but the vehicle had to be returned and garaged by this evening.

There was a large crowd outside the church of Saints Peter and Paul. Sadie Grimshaw had been loved, because she had been a caring, generous woman. The people parted and lined the path they had created while coffin and chief mourners entered the cool interior of the porch, then the large congregation of neighbours and friends filed quietly into the church. Catholics blessed themselves after dipping fingers in small fonts of water, Protestants split again into two types – those who tried to copy genuflection and the Sign of the Cross, and those who sat at the back.

It was in here that Agnes allowed everything to become real. In the arms of her loving husband, she poured out the grief she had contained for days made busy with arrangements, with the cashing of policies and the choosing of hymns. It was a long Mass and, at the end of it, a drained Agnes was helped outside by Fred and Denis. Her eyes moved away from the coffin for a moment and she saw Glenys Timpson, whose son had been arrested just an hour ago. This street gossip, although living through one of her own darker hours, had come to pay tribute to Sadie Grimshaw.

Glenys smiled through her tears.

Agnes leaned towards her. 'I didn't say anything to the police,' she whispered.

'I know you didn't, love.'

The cortège drove through the town into Tonge Cemetery, past the Protestant graves and to the Catholic side in which Fred and Sadie had bought their little bit of England. A gaping hole was blessed by the priest before Sadie's coffin was moved for the last time. It was done.

Fred had stopped his writing. He threw soil into the grave, mouthed a few indistinguishable words, then stepped away to make room for Agnes and Denis. The sun shone brilliantly, and happy birds flitted about in trees and bushes. 'We can go now,' said Fred. 'She'd want us to have a nice cup of tea and a butty.'

People came and went all day. The Noble Street house was filled with neighbours and friends; the priest came, as did a Methodist preacher and two nuns from the Catholic school.

When daylight began to dwindle, Denis took Judge Spencer's car back to its rightful owner. Sadie's chair was now occupied by Agnes, just as it had been all through the illness. Fred scribbled and dozed, Agnes stared into the fire and wondered about her future. Was it time to think about going for a proper job? Pop would recover completely before long, so Agnes would be free to choose the course of her own future. Her friends would be coming back to sit with her soon and she would discuss the matter with them. Lucy and Mags had got Agnes through this day.

No matter what, it would be lonely without Nan. But Nan would be up in heaven and expecting Agnes to do her best. And Nan always got her own way in the end.

Chapter Two

Helen Spencer, a spinster in her thirties, lived a monotonous life in a grand, colourless house that belonged to her father.

Judge Zachary Spencer was a mean-spirited man whose years in the courts had served only to make him bitter about his fellows, and age had not mellowed him. He listened to advocates, heard testimony, sat on his grand courtroom throne and said very little. Murderers, fraudsters and thieves were part and parcel of his daily grind, and he expected little of his daughter when he arrived home. She was not a son; she was, therefore, one of the more bitter disappointments in his self-absorbed life.

Control was something he prized above all things, so, apart from the booming works of Wagner and some of Beethoven's louder compositions, he enjoyed an uneventful life cocooned by domestic legislation invented and imposed by himself. He seldom spoke except to bark an order and made no attempt to conceal from his daughter the contempt he felt for the merely female. Servants had disappeared over the years, and the household was held together rather tenuously by one Kate Moores, who owned an admirable ability to ignore her employer.

Helen was lonely to the point of desperation, though she had been careful to hide her discontent with life.

Quietly resentful, she attended church, worked in the Bolton Central Library and, during breaks for coffee and tea, found herself virtually incapable of enjoying conversation with colleagues, so lunchtimes were spent in a quiet, sedate cafe away from crowds and noise. She feared people and did not trust her own ability to cope in any social situation. Of late, she had begun to quarrel with herself. The steady rock to which she had clung was suddenly embedded in quicksand, and self-control was becoming a luxury.

Why? was a question she asked herself repeatedly. Had her mother survived, would life have been different, better? Would siblings have cheered her, or had she been born different from the norm? Father didn't help, of course, all noisy music and imperious shouts, but surely other people survived such trials?

An avid reader, she screamed inwardly with Miss Catherine Earnshaw, allowed Heathcliff to break her heart, wept over Jane Eyre and her blinded master, allowed Dickens to place her in the company of Miss Havisham presiding over an uneaten and decayed wedding breakfast. Helen also laughed when she read, though she seldom even smiled in real life. Fiction had always been a place in which she might hide, a retreat from a stale, unattractive life.

Until now. He had slid noiselessly into her pale existence, had made her giggle and told her stories of his childhood, of his life at home, of his wife. His wife. Helen poured milk into her tea and stared blindly through the window. Today he was not here, because he was burying his wife's grandmother. Denis Makepeace was a quiet man, self-educated, willing and worthy of trust. Father had lent him the car and the good man was grateful for that. Like Helen, he had to make do with leavings from the top table. He was a servant and she was a woman. Both were treated by Zachary Spencer as peripheral characters – no, as part of a backdrop created to serve only the judge, who was the main figure on the canvas. Judge Spencer was Henry VIII all over again; Helen and Denis were two of the crowd to whom he occasionally threw a bone.

Helen Spencer, having never been in love, owned no yardstick against which she might measure her feelings for Denis. Love was in books; it had never figured on the pages of reality. Was the quickening of her heart a symptom, were the shameful dreams created by genuine affection for him or by the nagging frustrations of a lone, untouched female? Her cheeks were heated as she sipped her tea, and she wondered whether other women endured such night torments. Of course, she was younger and more beautiful when asleep. Awake, she was plain, ordinary and colourless. No one looked at her. She stamped books, collected fines, kept the reference section in order. Over the years, Helen had become part of the library, although she was not worth reading, so she remained on the shelf.

The mirror over the mantel told its familiar story – brown hair, hazel eyes, pale skin, nothing remarkable about the face. She was neither fat nor thin, yet her body had no real shape and she had never sought to embellish her physical self. Would she actually use the frivolous purchases she had made and could she change herself gradually in order to avoid comments from her father and work fellows? Suddenly giddy and young, she was about to embark on an adventure usually enjoyed by females half her age.

She took herself off to the privacy of her bedroom where, once seated on the bed, she began to unwrap the evidence of her folly. Silk slid through her fingers, soft, smooth undergarments in many shades – including black. Patent leather shoes and matching handbag were placed carefully in a wardrobe beneath a hanger bearing a fine wool suit in emerald green. Blouses and skirts remained in their packages, because she had more interesting objects to investigate.

Across the surface of the dressing table, Helen set out her stall. The girl in the department store had been patient and friendly, had shown the nervous customer how to attain a daytime 'natural' look, how to make herself up for the evenings. Evenings? Where on earth would she go and with whom? The Halle Orchestra in Manchester, perhaps? Concerts in the Free Trade Hall, a single ticket to the theatre, a lone seat in the cinema? There was nowhere to go, because she was nobody; perhaps, if she became a somebody, things might begin to happen.

Darnley's Liquid Satin foundation, compressed powder, four lipsticks, half a dozen eye shadows, an eyebrow pencil, mascara – did she dare? A small phial of Chanel No. 5 had taken a fortnight's wages, while the rest of the articles had cost a king's ransom. Did she dare? Would she ever obtain the courage required?

There was an anger in Helen, a deep resentment that, since childhood, had been forbidden to show its face at the surface. It had bubbled up recently in reaction to a small event, a comment made by a child in the library. The little girl had remarked to her mother that the lady had an unhappy face, and this same unhappy-faced lady had gone that very lunchtime for a make-up demonstration in a store. Perhaps she could not change her soul – no one had the power to alter the past – but she might make some attempt to reshape her future. Yet she had cleansed herself after the event, had removed from her face all evidence of the effort made by the gentle girl who had tried to help.

Now, she unveiled cleanser, moisturizer, a tiny pot of cream for delicate areas around the eyes. Pearl nail polishes in pink and white were lined up in front of other bottles and boxes. Like a man playing soldiers, Helen assembled her troops in preparation for battle. It would have to be done gradually, but she intended to make the most of her minimal assets. Other women wore make-up and perfume, so why should she be the exception?

The car purred its way into the drive and she leapt up. Father was away in London for a few days, yet Denis had been ordered to garage the vehicle after the funeral. Father did not trust the people of Noble Street to treat his precious Bentley with the reverence it warranted.

She peeped round the edge of a curtain and watched Denis. He was an excellent man, a reader, an interesting teller of tales. He was the one who had awoken her inner self, who had reminded her that she was a woman with real needs and desires. She could not have him; he belonged with another woman, but he might, perhaps, bring her out of herself and help her across stepping stones between her own silent world and normality. Denis listened. She had never been a great talker, but he encouraged her to speak out. One of Nature's gentlemen, Denis Makepeace was Helen's only friend.

Feeling very daring, she dabbed a small amount of perfume behind her ears before going downstairs. Apart from the ticking of clocks, the house was silent, Wagner-free and peaceful. She stepped out of a side door and made for the garage.

Denis was inspecting paintwork when she arrived. He looked up and smiled at her, trying hard to squash the small surge of panic that visited his chest. Miss Spencer was becoming dependent on him. At first, their conversations had been brief and infrequent, but lately he had come to realize that the woman waited for him. She had no life. Her father was a cold fish and her job was dull, but what was she expecting from a chauffeur-cum-handyman?

'How did it go?' she asked.

'All right.' He drew a soft cloth over the car's bonnet. 'Fred wrote in his memory book all through the service. Agnes cried. It's about time she cried. She took it too well.'

He was right, of course. People should show their feelings. 'Did her friends come?'

'Oh, yes. She had a good natter with them afterwards and they were very kind to Fred. Most folk treat him as if he has some kind of dementia, but he hasn't. He's getting better. Lucy and Mags talked to him as a normal person – he responds to that. Pity more folk don't understand that he's not on the slippery slope.' She was standing too near and was wearing perfume. This gauche woman had no experience with men and was behaving like a teenager. No, he was over-reacting, he reassured himself. He was just a servant and she knew he was married.

'Do you have time to look at my car?' she asked. 'It may be dirty petrol – I let the tank get very low yesterday – but it's not running smoothly.'

Would he take a look? This was happening too often – a drawer in her bedroom beginning to stick, the need for another shelf in her little dressing room, a squeaking floorboard. Helen Spencer presented as a good person, but she was isolated to the point of desperation. He feared her, feared himself, too – wasn't pity said to be akin to love?

He fiddled with the innards of the Morris Minor, drove it round the paddock, declared it to be as fit as a flea. 'It's running well,' he said after two circuits. 'Whatever was wrong must have cleared up. I've cleaned the plugs just in case.'

'Thank you.'

He closed the garage doors and declared his intention to go for the bus.

'I'll take you home.'

The calculated nonchalance in her tone startled him anew. Had her father been in residence, Helen Spencer would never have made such an offer. 'I'll be fine on the bus,' he answered. 'I'm used to it.'

'No, I insist. You must be tired after such a long day.'

God, what should he do? If Miss Spencer ran him home, he would have to ask her in for a cup of tea – to expect her to leave immediately would be churlish. Lucy Walsh and Mags Bradshaw would still be there, and Helen Spencer was no good with folk – hadn't she already confessed as much? Agnes might notice how she looked at him, how she hung on every word – he didn't know how to reply.

'Let me do this,' she was saying now. 'And I shan't intrude, not on the day of the funeral.'

Meek as a kitten, he got into the passenger seat of the Morris. Her hands on the steering wheel were the hands of a lady – long fingers, slender wrists. She played the piano – he had heard her during her afternoons off. Helen Spencer's music was not angry – the pieces she played sounded peaceful and melodic. He was out of his depth and he could feel the glow in his cheeks. She didn't even know that she was sending out signals, but he recognized them plainly enough. He was sitting next to a female animal anxious to breed before its time ran out. His collar was suddenly tight and he pushed a finger between it and his throat. There had to be a way out of this situation, yet he could not reject her, since she had made no definite move in his direction. It was coming. Helen Spencer was losing her balance and he would be expected to catch her when she fell.

'You look smart,' she said before starting the engine. He cut a fine figure. He was nearer in age to her than he was to his young wife. Agnes was twenty, Helen thirty-two, Denis twenty-nine. Father would hate it, of course, but divorce was becoming more commonplace these days. She chided herself inwardly. An honourable woman, she would make no attempt to spoil Denis's marriage. Would she? Her heart quickened and drummed in her ears. She was changing. The change was not connected to cosmetics or black underwear – she was losing her grip on the life she had made for herself.

She pulled onto Wigan Road and drove slowly towards one of the poorer ends of town. 'Perhaps you should move,' she suggested. 'There are cottages in Skirlaugh Fall and it would be easier for you, especially in winter. You'd need no buses.'

'We're settled where we are, Miss Spencer.'

'Helen. I've told you to call me Helen – except when Father is within earshot, of course. Wouldn't a change of address suit your wife and Mr Grimshaw?'

'I might think about it. Thanks.' He needed to change his job. He needed a change because Miss Helen Spencer needed a change, and he dared not figure in her calculations. She had never walked out with a man and Denis could not afford to be a participant in her delayed adolescence.

'Look at those girls.' She pointed to a small group at a bus stop. 'Father says they are asking for trouble by dressing like that. Miniskirts? I have a winter scarf broader than those. No wonder there's an increase in attacks on young women.'

Denis found no reply.

'What do you think?' she asked.

'People should dress the way they want to dress.'

'Does your wife wear such things?'

'No. She covers her knees.'

'Glad to hear it.'

Discomfort now bordered on pain, because Denis was acutely aware of Helen Spencer's dilemma. The judge was a pain in the backside, arrogant, stubborn, selfish and domineering. He treated Denis as an article, one of life's inanimate necessities. His daughter was guilty of not being a son, of not being bright enough for what he considered a true career. She was substandard in all departments, and he had no time to waste on her. Helen Spencer had never known love. 'Have you ever thought of leaving home?' Denis asked.

She turned briefly to look at him. 'I have money enough for a small house, yes, but I have never lived alone. It's a large step to take.'

Denis kept his thoughts to himself. Aloneness and loneliness were not the same. Living with her father, she was lonely; a person could be isolated in a city teeming with folk. She would be alone if she got out of her father's house, but loneliness would not necessarily be the result.

'I suppose I am afraid of change,' she said.

'We all are. Agnes is frightened of life without her grandma. Things alter even if you stay in one place – life happens no matter where we are.'

'Yes, I suppose so.'

He knew why she stayed at Lambert House. She stayed because she would automatically inherit property, land and money once her father died. If she angered him by moving on, he might very well cut her off without a penny. But some prices were too high to pay, thought Denis as the car pulled into Noble Street. The woman should clear off and start again; needed interests, hobbies and a place where she could be herself.

'I am grateful to you,' she said as she stopped the car. 'No one ever spent time with me before – unless nannies and governesses count. I scarcely remember my mother, and you know how Father is.'

'Yes.' He didn't need the gratitude, didn't want it. She was hungry and he dared not be the one to feed her. 'I still think you should find a life for yourself. Your father could last for a long time yet. Start going out; join – oh, I don't know. They have reading groups and poetry meetings at the library, don't they? And there's your music.' He sighed. 'Sorry, I shouldn't interfere.'

She placed a hand on his arm. 'You are a good friend. Thank you.'

He stood on the narrow pavement and watched as she drove away. It was silly, but his arm glowed from the touch of her hand. It was all nonsense. He loved Agnes, and that was all he needed to know.

The place was in chaos. Agnes, whose two friends had returned long after the main funeral party was over, was in the front room with Mags and Lucy. They were all shouting, and the reason for that was a great deal of noise coming from the back of the house.

Agnes smiled at her husband.

'What the blinking heck's going on?' he asked loudly.

She shrugged. 'Denis, Pop has started his new job.'

'Eh?'

'He's manufacturing.'

'Manufacturing? The neighbours will go crazy.'

'You tell him that. We've tried while we did some washing up, but he's got a bee in his bonnet and a hammer in his hand.'

Denis sighed and walked through to the back of the house. Fred was knocking bits of wood together. 'Fred?'

'Aye?'

'What are you up to?'

Fred stopped clattering for a moment. 'I'm going into doll's houses,' he pronounced.

Denis bit back a flippant remark about doll's houses being a tight squeeze for a grown man.

'Battery packs,' the old man continued, 'so there'll be lighting in every room. I can make furniture, paper the walls and carpet floors. Bathroom fittings'll have to be bought in from a toymaker, but I can do most of it by myself.'

Denis cast an eye over the scene. There was sawdust everywhere and tools were spread about the floor along with bits of wood, nails, screws and sandpaper. 'Agnes won't like it,' he said.

'I have to be useful. If I do more, I'll remember more.'

'Well, do it outside in the shed. We'll get a light put in. You can't mess the house up like this, Fred – we eat in here. You'll be having splinters in your dinner.'

Fred shook his head sadly. 'Shed's full. This is just the prototype. At the graveside, I promised my Sadie I'd start being useful as soon as I got home. I couldn't, because folk were brewing up and eating butties, but I started when most of them had gone. I shall be earning money.'

Denis sat at the table and scratched his head. What a day. Poor old Sadie gone to her rest, Helen Spencer clarting about like a kid, now Fred wrecking a house to make a house. Sometimes, life was a trial. 'You'd best clean up, old son, before Agnes starts on you. You know she's house-proud. Come on, I'll give you a hand.'

Fred was having none of it. He was experiencing difficulty with a gable end and a window, and he would clear the stuff away when he was good and ready, not before. 'They have to be strong,' he insisted. 'Little girls can be as destructive as boys. My hinges have to be childproof. And I've the wiring to work out.'

It was no good. Denis knew his grandfather-in-law and there was no point in pushing the old chap when he didn't want to be moved. Also, it was good to see him having a go at something, because he'd done very little since the stroke. 'I'll make a cuppa,' he said resignedly. He had no wish to enter into conversation with the mothers' meeting – a term he used for occasions when Agnes and her two best friends came together – so he would stay here and drink tea with Fred.

Fred laid out his plans on the table, explained several designs and how they would be priced. 'That lot up Heaton way with more money than sense will snap these up,' he declared. 'And I shall make some to specifications wanted by the buyer, so we've got to advertise.'

Denis warmed the pot. Agnes had lost her job, Judge Spencer was a skinflint and extra money was needed – but Fred? Was he up to this kind of thing? He turned and watched the old man working on his first roof. Fred was muttering about covering it with some kind of plastic with a pattern that looked like tiles. So far, so good. It had four walls, a roof and gaps for windows. Perhaps Fred was on to something? He was certainly making a mess, whatever the outcome.

'Denis?'

'What?'

'I can do it, you know.'

The younger man grinned. He nursed a strong suspicion that Fred Grimshaw could and would do it. Ah, well. Time would tell.

Lucy Walsh was describing her wedding outfit. She had just declared her intention to wear a minidress with knee-high white boots, and her mother wasn't pleased. 'It's my wedding,' she said, her pretty face creased by a frown. 'Mam says I'll look common. But if a girl ever deserves her own way, surely her wedding's the place to start?'

Agnes had stayed out of this discussion so far. She agreed with Lucy's mother, but she dared not say so. Mags, too, was keeping her counsel. The only one of the three to have remained completely solo, she was chief bridesmaid and had no intention of becoming a critic.

Lucy described the cake, the flowers, the invitations.

Like Agnes, she was marrying someone older than herself, a lawyer with good prospects and a very nice house. Agnes glanced at Mags, then decided to hang herself out to dry. This was the day on which she had buried her grandmother – surely she could make herself strong enough to put her foot through Lucy's mini?

'Lucy?'

'What?'

'George's colleagues will be there.'

'So what?'

Agnes raised her shoulders. 'I know minis are all the rage, but I can't see a load of crusty old lawyers approving of them.'

Lucy sighed heavily. 'I want to be fashionable.'

Mags took a sip of cold tea. She and Agnes – who was matron of honour – were already dismayed by Lucy's decision to dress them in watered black silk with dark red roses at the waists. But their clothes would cover their knees, at least. Lucy, always centre-stage and stunning, wanted to shock her audience. She had clearly begun to look upon her wedding as a stage production rather than a religious ceremony. The congregation would become an audience and Lucy would be the star turn on a stage rather than a bride at the altar.

Agnes took another huge stride into her friend's limelight. 'That Empire line dress – white watered silk – would look great with our black, wouldn't it, Mags? It's the same silk, but white. That's my opinion – for what it's worth.'

Mags nodded, though her lips remained closed.

'Lucy, don't wear the mini,' Agnes begged. 'It might look stunning, but every time you bend down some lecherous old lawyer will see your knickers. When they go home, they'll laugh at you.'

'If I wear any knickers.' Lucy swallowed cold tea and a facsimile of injured pride. 'All right,' she said resignedly and with an air of acute injury. Then she burst out laughing. 'Your faces!' she howled. 'Honestly, you looked like a couple of spectators at a public hanging. Did you really think I was going to walk up the aisle in knee-high boots and a lace mini?'

Mags, who had been swallowing her own cold tea, spluttered and coughed. Agnes hit her on the back till her airway cleared, then sat down again. 'Lucy, you'll be the death of us.'

The bride-to-be grinned broadly. 'Your nan would have laughed herself sick over that, Agnes. Remember? How she used to have those giggling fits? That's how we've got to think of her now. Her spirit, her silliness and how young she always was where it mattered.' Lucy tapped her skull with a finger. 'In here, Sadie never grew old.'

Agnes wiped a tear from her eye. 'Yes, she was funny. Except for the last few months, and they weren't amusing at all. But,' she jerked a thumb in the direction of the next room, 'look what she's left us to cope with. Wherever she is, she's smiling.'

The door burst inward to allow a red-faced Fred and a wooden item into the arena. 'See?' he said triumphantly. 'I've done half already.'

Agnes glanced at her friends. 'Well, half a house is better than none.'

When Pop had retreated, Agnes sat for a while and remembered her beloved grandmother. Denis looked in, saw her expression, noticed that the other two were quiet, and decided to leave well alone. Fred started to clear away his mess. Even his tidying was noisy, thought Agnes as she gazed into the near distance. But his half-house had seemed half-decent, so perhaps he was on to something profitable.

'I'm going to miss you, Nan,' she told the ceiling. But she had been missing Nan for months already. Only the body had been there at the end, and the body hadn't functioned. Should she have stayed at home instead of cleaning for a few shillings a week? To that question, she was never going to find an answer.

'You'll not find her up yon.' Lucy pointed to the upper half of the room. 'She's more likely to be making mischief with your granddad in the kitchen.'

Agnes lowered her eyes and looked at Lucy. Lucy Walsh, Mags Bradshaw and herself had been inseparable since nursery class. Mags, who had grown into a plain, quiet and dignified adult, had been a shy and frightened child. Lucy, on the other hand, remained capable of starting a riot in an empty room. She was the one who had guarded and guided Mags, and Agnes was the cement that had held the three of them together through their passage into adulthood. The vow had been that come boyfriends, husbands or children, Thursday nights would always be girls' nights. 'Thanks for being here,' said Agnes softly.

'Where else would we be?' Lucy began to stack cups and saucers. 'All for one and one for all, isn't it?' She moved quickly, had always been the first to dress, to clear up, to organize. Slim, dark and beautiful, she was sure of herself in mind and in body. 'We couldn't have let you go through it on your own,' she said when her task was completed. 'Anyway, your nan made the best jam cakes in the business. Didn't she, Mags?'

'She made the best of everything.' Mags stood up and prepared to carry the dishes away. 'Can't have been easy when her daughter died so young. But Sadie's generation never moaned. They just got on with what needed doing and that was that.' She left the room.

'What are we going to do about Mags?' Lucy whispered.

'Nothing.'

'What do you mean? There has to be someone who'll see beyond her quietness.'

'Some people don't need to be married.'

Lucy changed tactics. 'All right, so what are we going to do about you? Will you fill that form in? Isn't it time you pulled yourself together, Makepeace? The job in the pub was supposed to be a stop-gap – you've no excuse now. Your Pop will get better in time—'

'And the kitchen will be in bits—'

'So what? It's only a bloody kitchen. At least he's doing something. It's what you've always wanted and now's the time to do it.'

Agnes thought about Pop and wondered if he would manage. The hours of work would be long and varied, there would be exams, rules, a uniform . . .

'Well?'

Agnes sighed resignedly. 'For goodness' sake, Lucy. We buried Nan today. Does all the clearing up have to be done now?'

'You're the fastidious one,' replied Lucy. 'Get it done. You've always wanted to be a nurse and now's as good a time as any. You knew the mill was just for money till you got married, then the pub job came along and it fitted for a while. But are you going to be just a married woman? All that went out at the end of the war. Women work. They get decent jobs and keep house at the same time. What would your nan say?'

'She'd make me go for it.'

Lucy picked up her bag and gloves. 'Right, madam. I

want that form filled in or I wear a mini wedding dress. I mean it. George would be delighted – he says my legs go up all the way to Glasgow – so think on.'

After her friends had left, Agnes thought on. She peered into the kitchen, saw that Denis had been dragged into the business of house-building, took the form from the front room bureau. 'Bloody hell,' she cursed quietly. 'They want to know everything I've ever done. What have I done?' How might she fill all the naked spaces on the application form?

She had doffed spools at a mule, back soaked in sweat, feet aching, head banging because of noise and heat. She had cleaned lavatories, had cared for Pop and Nan, had even helped Nurse Ingram to see the old lady into the next world. Lucy and Mags, both legal secretaries, were pushing her towards a career, but what about Pops? With Nan dead, he was going to be at a loose end, and his mind was not yet fully healed.

Agnes stared through the window, saw a car edging its way past the house. She knew little about motors, as few in these parts owned vehicles, but the driver seemed familiar. Was it Miss Spencer? Why did she suddenly speed up after gazing into the house? Even Judge Spencer's Bentley caused discomfort to passengers when it moved at a snail's pace over cobbles – his daughter's smaller car might actually be shaken to bits. Oh well, it had been an odd day, an unhappy day, and Miss Helen Spencer was probably taking a short cut to somewhere or other.

'Agnes?' A hand touched her left shoulder.

'Miss Spencer just drove past.'

Denis felt the heat in his face. He coughed quietly. 'She brought me home.'

'Yes, you said. I wonder why she's still out there?'

He shrugged with deliberate nonchalance. 'No idea. She did seem concerned – asked about you.'

'Nothing like her dad, then.'

'No.' Helen Spencer bore not the slightest resemblance to her parent. She had a soft centre. She played Chopin and something called the Moonlight sonata – was that Beethoven? She had needs. Beautiful hands, desperate needs.

'Denis?'

'What?'

'Lucy threatened to get married in a crocheted mini.'

He relaxed. For now, the subject was changed. Yet the subject remained behind the wheel of a Morris with clean plugs and excellent timing. Denis shifted himself. There was sawdust to sweep, there were tools waiting to be tidied. 'I love you,' he advised his wife.

Agnes nodded. 'Make sure you pick up all the nails. And I pray to God that Pop hasn't got to the painting stage.' Doll's houses, indeed. Whatever next?

Imitating the process of osmosis, Helen Spencer was seeping via some invisible semi-permeable membrane right through the defences of Denis Makepeace. She booked her time off from the library, making sure that her holidays coincided with her father's absence on circuit business. While the judge covered his territory, she set up a stall on her own tiny piece of England. The campaign of which she was scarcely aware was plotted in her dressing room and completed in her bedroom.

She was now two people. There was the librarian – severe hair, sensible shoes, tweeds with kick-pleated skirts; there was also the strangely innocent siren. Transformation proved an interesting process. Her face was an almost blank canvas onto which she painted today's self. Eye shadows and liners emphasized her best features, and her skin glowed with brilliance borrowed from Max Factor. As the days wore on, Helen's confidence grew, bolstered by scaffolding acquired in department stores and chemist shops. She was finally a woman and he was watching her. When he watched, she tingled with anticipation, often blushing when suddenly aware of the full extent of her sins. She wanted him.

Denis, plodding through chores, pretended not to watch. But he was fully conscious of the dangerous game over which he had no control. There were no rules, no linesmen, no flags raised when play got out of hand. He washed the Bentley in which he had driven his employer to Trinity Street Station, pruned hedges, mended a gate, watered lawns. From open windows in the music room floated the accompaniment to his labours, as did a pair of muslin curtains through which he caught an occasional glimpse of the entertainer. For him, she had made herself beautiful; for him, she played brilliantly, windows flung wide, heart on a platter for the taking.

He had begun a frantic but futile search through the *Bolton Evening News*, eyes ripping down the jobs column in search of an occupation that might be managed by a man with a weak chest. Thus far, he had found nothing suitable and his main emotion had become that of dread. She had made up her mind. A poem about a fly invited into the parlour of a spider dashed through his head. He had to resist her because he was a decent man and he loved Agnes, yet he continued to harbour very mixed feelings. Helen Spencer needed someone and she had chosen him. 'Because I'm here, that's all,' he announced softly. 'Anybody would do for her, the state she's in.' And a married man should not stray, he told himself regularly. Even so, the pity he felt for the judge's spinster daughter remained.

He was flattered by the attentions of such a woman and that was normal – all men responded to this kind of courtship. Helen Spencer was gifted, knowledgeable, educated and, when encouraged, interesting. 'And rich,' he grumbled. She wasn't ugly, wasn't beautiful, but she certainly looked better in her new guise.

Denis continued to rake gravel on the driveway. The judge insisted on ordered pebbles and smooth grass with stripes rolled across its surface. He was a boring old bugger, and his daughter was delivering a pretty piece of Chopin – well, Denis thought it was Chopin. The gauze-like curtains parted anew, allowing him a brief glimpse of a handsome woman in a satin gown, probably something called a peignoir. 'Playing in her underwear now,' he muttered. There were no jobs in the papers. He was married to Agnes. Curtains came and went while Denis listened to a grand mixture of birdsong and nocturne.

She summoned him. He stood, face turned away from the house, heavy-duty rake clenched fiercely in his hands. He wanted to run, but his feet were welded to loose chippings. Ridiculous. He had to go inside, needed to tell her that he loved Agnes and only Agnes.

'Denis?'

Helen Spencer was not in her right mind just now. Running out of time, out of hope and patience, bored to death, in love, in this miserable house, she had set her sights on one of the few men within her limited orbit. What would happen when he told her he didn't want her? Would she fall apart, and would he feel guilty? Beautiful hands. She played like an angel, chose pieces that haunted, poured all her loneliness and despair onto piano keys.

'Denis?'

With excruciating slowness, he turned to face her, saw her standing in a frame of cloudy white muslin. On leaden feet, Denis Makepeace walked towards inevitability.

'Denis?' Her tone was quieter.

'What?'

'You enjoyed my playing?'

His heart was fluttering like a bird in a chimney, all fear and darkness and no points of reference. 'Yes, but I've a lot to do. Judge Spencer left a list and—'

'Have a rest.' She draped herself across a small sofa. Denis could imagine her practising such moves in bedroom mirrors. 'I like you.' Underneath the panstick, her cheeks glowed. 'I have grown fond of you.'

He opened his mouth, but no words emerged.

'You are a fine man. Even my father says so, and he hates just about everyone, as you probably know by now.'

Denis pulled at his collar, which was already open. 'I'm chauffeur and handyman, Miss Spencer.'

'Helen.'

'I work outside except for the odd mending job in the house. The judge would go mad if he knew I was taking time off to chatter. Sorry.' He turned to leave, but she went after him. The seconds that followed were a blur, but she managed to catch him, arms clasping tightly round his neck, tears hovering on the edges of blatantly false eyelashes. 'I think I've fallen in love with you,' she whispered.

His body, suddenly detached from brain and heart, responded automatically to soft skin, heady perfume and sad eyes. But he pushed her aside. 'No,' he said. 'No, Miss Spencer. This can't happen. You know it and I'm sure of it. You're a well-read woman, so you must know about infatuation. I was infatuated with Barbara Holt in my class when I was ten, but I got over it.'

She nodded. 'I am not ten years old.'

'Yes. But infatuation's nothing to do with age.'

Helen began to cry. Through loud sobs, she poured out a jumble of words relating to her ugliness, her loneliness, her love for Denis.

'You aren't ugly,' he told her. 'But I'm married and I love my wife. You're fishing in the wrong waters, Miss Spencer. You should be going for salmon or rainbow trout, not for plain tench.' He strode out of the house, picked up the rake and continued to work. But unsteady hands made a poor job of straightening shingle, so he went off to mend a fence. As he drove home a nail, he wondered whether his fences could ever be truly mended after today's tragic scene.

Eva Hargreaves stepped tentatively into the house. Even after knocking loudly and shouting at the top of her range, she had been unable to make herself heard. Into a brief silence, she called again. 'Agnes?'

Fred, hair full of sawdust, hands clutching hammer and nails, appeared in the kitchen doorway. 'How do?' he said politely, eyes blinking to rid lashes of wood shavings. 'She's gone into town – something to do with being a nurse.'

'Oh. Right.' Eva didn't blame Agnes for absenting herself from the factory that had once been her home. 'I've shut the shop.'

'You what?' The hammer landed at his feet, just half

an inch away from his toes. 'Shut the shop?' Eva never shut her shop. She was open from seven in the morning till nine at night, no excuses, no rest, food eaten at the counter, a stool the only perch she allowed herself. 'What's up?' he asked.

Eva dropped into an armchair. 'I've had enough,' she answered wearily. 'Everybody's beck and call, firewood, paraffin, nails, buckets – I shall be kicking the bucket meself if I don't slow down.'

'Nay, lass – you're not cut out for retirement.' Fred made some effort to shake dust from tattered overalls before joining Eva in the front room. 'You'd go daft in six months. And remember – I'm experienced in daft. Daft's making bullets for a war that's twenty years over and—'

'But you're all right now.'

'Aye, happen I am, but it's only through fettling with these doll's houses. I might branch out into railways – stations, trees and all that – but Eva, you've never been idle since your husband died.'

'I know.'

'What'll you do?'

She raised her shoulders in a gesture of near-despair. 'Little bungalow up Harwood, read some books, get a dog and walk it.'

'You'll not cope.'

'I'll cope. Other folk cope—'

'Yes, but . . . but you're—'

'That's why I'm here.' Eva took as deep a breath as cruel corsets would allow. 'Help me, Fred. If I get some help, I might just hang on a bit longer.'

'I've had a stroke, lass—'

'And you're turning this place into a right pigsty, aren't you? Yon shed's not big enough, but my air raid shelter is. They put it there in case of a bombing with a shopload of customers, so it's time it got used. Make you a good workshop, that would. Fred, you could serve a few customers while I rested – just a few hours a day.'

He leaned back and closed his eyes. If Eva would pay him, he could get better wood – he might even acquire nails in her shop for no price at all. And it was true – he was spoiling Sadie's house, making life difficult for his granddaughter. 'Is there electric in the air raid shelter?' he asked. 'Only I need to see what I'm doing.'

'There is now.'

'Let me think on it.'

While he was thinking, the back door opened.

'Bugger,' said Fred softly.

Eva squashed a grin.

'I'll be left out with the bins come Thursday,' groaned the old man. 'The dust cart'll take me away, just you wait and see.'

Agnes arrived in the doorway, arms tightly folded, lips clamped together, her expression promising some very bad weather. 'Hello, Mrs Hargreaves.' Agnes's eyes never left her grandfather's face. 'What the heck have you been doing, Pop? We can't live like this – I've a meal to make and baking to do.'

Fred scratched his head. 'We've been thinking,' he replied eventually. 'Me and Eva, I mean. She wants help in her shop and I could do with her air raid shelter.'

Agnes nodded. 'Yes, you'll need somewhere to hide if I find the place in this state again. Oh, and I could do with a kitchen table without a lathe stuck to it. Are you up to serving in a shop, though?'

He rose to his feet. 'Yes, I am up to serving in a shop and running me own business at the same time. There's still a bit of life in me, you know. And I would have tidied up, but—'

'But you didn't.' Agnes shook her head. 'He'll fill your shelter and spill into the house,' she told the ironmonger. 'He's all talk and screwdriver when it comes to straightening up after himself. Yes, you can have him, Mrs Hargreaves.' She grinned at her beloved Pop. 'You're well and that's all that matters. I love you, you old goat.'

An unhappy Denis had accidentally unleashed a woman of great passion and uncertain temperament. Freed from restraint, she followed him, played music for him, courted him. She would hear no argument. She wanted her way all the time and considered no one's feelings but her own.

'I'm a fool,' he told the pigswill bin as he emptied scraps into its depths. The daily, a woman from Skirlaugh Fall, was in the house and Denis was panicking. He had stepped out of his league all the way up to Lambert House, Skirlaugh Rise, and he had almost betrayed a beloved wife. Mrs Moores, the daily, had taken to looking at him sideways and Denis was sure that the whole village knew of his supposed crimes. 'I'm sorry, Agnes,' he breathed, his head leaning on cool stone. What was he going to do? What on earth could anyone do?

A light step bade him turn and he looked right into the angry eyes of his mistress.

'There you are,' snapped Helen. 'I want you to mend my bookcase upstairs.'

He placed the bucket on the ground. 'This has to stop,' he said.

'Why?'

Denis inhaled as deeply as he could. 'You're different. Everyone can see that you're different. They'll know. Your dad will find out, Agnes will find out.' There was a kind of madness in her eyes, a brightness that went beyond mere happiness or excitement. She didn't care about being discovered. 'It has to stop,' he said again.

'You have regrets.' Her tone was accusatory.

'Of course I do. I'm married. I love my wife. Your father's a judge with a lot of power. This should not be happening. I want things back the way they were. And that's just the start of the list.'

Helen Spencer nodded, turned on her heel and walked back into the house. Fury quickened her step as she ran up the stairs and into her bedroom. She dropped face down onto a chaise longue, balled fists beating pink velvet upholstery, mouth opened in a scream she managed to strangle at birth. He didn't love her. If an odd-job man could not love her . . . What was happening to her? Why did she occasionally lose herself and where had self-control gone for a holiday?

She had to have him, had to keep him for herself. He could get a divorce. Father would not approve, but Father seldom approved of anything. If Agnes Makepeace knew the full extent of her husband's supposedly bad behaviour, perhaps she would leave Denis. 'But I would be named,' she said aloud. Did it matter? Was any price too high when it came to the love of her life? She was unbalanced, yet she retained sufficient intelligence to allow insight into her own disorder. This was a clear route to madness.

She turned over, closed her eyes and imagined how he would be as a lover. He would treat her like precious porcelain, would be amazed and pleased by her responses. But no. He had no intention of indulging in an animal act, a business performed by any beast in field or stable yard. He was a good man in a world inhabited by the bad.

What could she do? Angrily, she rose and began to pace the floor, back and forth, hands rubbing together, forehead creased by a deep frown, ears on alert just in case he deigned to climb the stairs to mend her bookcase. Mother's money. Helen placed herself at the dressing table. She had come into a small inheritance at the age of twenty-one, and it had languished in a bank for all these years. Her own house. If she bought a place, he could visit her there ... but would she have any power if she moved out? His job was here, her father was his employer and she, daughter of the house, held some sway during her father's absences.

It was hopeless and she wanted to die if she could not have Denis. The library? She didn't care about her job any more, could take it or leave it. Mrs Moores knew what was going on, but that didn't bother Helen. Why should she care what a skivvy thought? And what was wrong with a few fashionable clothes and a bit of make-up?

He was walking across the lawn. Through narrowed eyes, Helen took in every single detail. Denis was carrying a canvas bag, a pair of work boots joined by laces hanging from a shoulder. 'He's leaving,' she whispered. 'He's walking out. And I am supposed to sit here like Little Miss Muffet.' She left the room and ran downstairs.

From the drawing room window, Kate Moores watched the scene as it unfolded before eyes that had seen too much in recent days. Helen Spencer had finally gone off her rocker. Kate knew Denis Makepeace well

58

enough to realize that he had been used by Madam. She also knew Madam, had often seen damped-down fury in pale hazel eyes. Lipstick and high heels? The reason for those articles was only too clear – Miss Helen Spencer had decided to indulge in sins of the flesh.

The view from the window was not pleasant. Denis was almost motionless while his companion stamped and ranted until she collapsed on the grass. 'Go,' urged Kate quietly. 'Get out now, lad, while the going's good.' He should stay away from Helen Spencer. Anyone who wanted the ordinary life should keep a fair distance from that woman. Kate dusted quickly. 'She was a sneaky kid and she's no better now she's grown.'

Applying beeswax to a side table, Kate Moores continued to pray inwardly. If Denis left today, he would get no reference; if he stayed, he would get no peace. The clock chimed, and Kate knew that her working day was almost over. She was also fully aware of Helen Spencer's quiet power, of her persuasive tongue. Only the judge had remained unmoved by his daughter's clever ways. 'Go home, Denis,' Kate begged inwardly. 'Dear God, make him go home.'

But he didn't go home. Helen Spencer returned to the house and ran upstairs once more, while Denis sat on a bench near the rockery. Kate dragged her coat from a hook in the laundry room, decided that the day was too warm to merit outdoor clothing, and left the house by the kitchen door, coat draped over an arm. As she rounded the corner, she met Denis on his way back. Dragging him along the side of the building, Kate tutted at him. 'You should have gone,' she said. 'What's the matter with you?'

He swallowed audibly. 'I don't know.'

'Well, I do. My Auntie Vi looked after Miss Spencer

for years back in the days when they had servants – before they closed off half the house.' She nodded furiously. 'From the age of about three, Miss Spencer had a way of getting her own road. Not where her dad's concerned – she gave up on him when she was a baby. Happen that's why she bends other folk to do her will – I'm not a head doctor, so I can't work it out. Get gone before it's too late, son.'

'She said she'll go and see Agnes. Nothing's happened, but she's going to pretend I've been to bed with her. She'll tell my wife.'

Kate Moores puffed up her cheeks and blew noisily. 'Will she heck as like. Come what may, she protects herself. That quiet woman in the dowdy clothes is just what she wants us to see – inside, she's all for number one. You're just another thing she wants. She'll do nowt that'll pain herself.'

He sighed. 'She's round the bloody twist and it's my fault.'

'No, it's not. Now, listen to me, Denis. Although she can't see it, she's her dad all over again – selfish, nasty, ill-tempered. I'll bet a year's wages she started it. Am I right?'

He nodded. 'It's my fault as much as hers – I should have told her to bugger off right from the start. I haven't even kissed her. I'm fed up.'

'And a bit flattered because she's Miss Spencer?'

'Aye, perhaps I was. Not now, though. She's dangerous.'

Kate gripped the young man's arm. 'Find yourself another job. This is just the start, Denis. You're like a fish on a hook – the more you struggle, the more she digs in. Look at me. There's none down the bottom know about this.' Her head bent in the direction of Skirlaugh Fall, the dip in which lay the village of her birth. 'I'll say nowt. But the longer you hang about round here, the more chance you have of getting caught out. You're a sitting duck, son. Bugger off home.'

Kate Moores was putting his own thoughts into words. He knew all the dangers, yet he feared that Helen would abide by her threat and tell Agnes a pack of lies if he left his job at Lambert House. 'He's bound to see the change in her when he gets home,' he said. 'She's walking about like a fourteen-year-old with a crush on some daft lad.'

Kate nodded in agreement. The judge said little except when giving orders, though he noticed everything and meted out punishments when life did not suit him. 'He'll hit the roof. I'd not like to be at the receiving end. All the lawyers hate him, you know. Prosecution or defence, they can't abide him.'

'If she's so clever, why can't she see sense?' Denis asked. 'She knows I don't want her and that I love Agnes – so why doesn't she leave me alone?'

Kate pondered a while before replying. 'Auntie Vi told me a few tales before she died. Too many for me to start telling now – my Albert'll be wanting feeding. But when she was a little lass, Helen Spencer stole and lied and played the angel all the while – butter wouldn't melt. She's sly and I'm going home. So think on. Remember – she's made in the image of her dad, not her mam, God rest that good soul.'

'I just don't know what to do. No matter what, I'm the one in trouble. Who'd believe me, Kate?'

'I would.'

'But everyone else?'

'Like I said, just think on before you do anything. And make sure the anything you do is not done with her.'

Denis thought on until it was time to go home. He toyed with his meal, found great difficulty in looking his wife in the eye, tried to feign interest when Fred rattled on about Eva and the shop. The thinking continued through evening and into the night, sleep punctuated by nightmares populated by silk and muslin and Chopin. This could not go on, yet Denis had not the slightest idea of how to make it stop.

'Are you all right?' asked Agnes sleepily.

'Yes. Go back to sleep, love.' There was nothing to be done. Unless ... Unless he could pluck up the courage to tell the judge.

Chapter Three

Talk to the judge? Denis struggled to remember a proper conversation with Zachary Spencer, realizing that there had been little true communication since the interview for his job. He tried to imagine himself asking for his employer's help in the current situation, and dismissed the idea before it had even taken root. But he shuddered at the thought of what might happen when the man returned in a few days to find his spinster daughter glowing with make-up and desire. Perhaps she would revert to normal?

'Denis?' Agnes was giving him one of her more searching looks.

'What?'

'There's folk in Africa would kill for that boiled egg.'

He finished his breakfast quickly, aware that his wife was troubled, knowing that he had to present himself at Lambert House within the hour, fearing the next move of a woman he now considered unbalanced. He could not hide from Agnes forever – she could read him like an open book.

'What's wrong?' Agnes asked. 'You've been like a cat on hot bricks since last week. Is the job too much? Could you not take it a bit easier if you're off-colour?'

Denis shrugged. 'I'm tired, love. It must be the heat. I'll do my best to slow down a bit.'

He left. While dusting, reading, shopping and washing,

she was worrying about Denis. It wasn't just his chest, not this time. He was walking about like a man with the whole world weighing him down and Agnes was troubled.

'We've always talked about stuff,' she advised the sink. Marriage was based on three things – love, trust and friendship. Those elements needed to run seamlessly through daily life, but Denis was holding something back. It wasn't like him. Any troubles, however small, had always been shared. Denis had got her through the months after Pop's stroke when she had worked at the pub. He had agreed happily about the nursing, had offered his support no matter what. If they had to eat less while she studied, that problem would be shared. The slightest thought was always meted out between the two of them so that a solution might be found before thought became difficulty. There was something wrong with Denis.

Agnes sat down. Pop was bringing in a wage, so things were not as bad as they might have been. Except. What a big word that was. Was it his job? Or was he trying to shield his wife from some terrible truth about his health? There wasn't another woman. 'I'd have known if it was that,' she whispered. 'But the lad's suffering.' If anything happened to Denis, she would be unable to continue alive.

She would deal with this tonight, after Pop had gone to bed. Whatever it took, Agnes Makepeace was going to get to the bottom of her husband's unhappiness.

Someone hammered on the front door and she ran to open it. A very flustered Glenys Timpson burst into tears as soon as she saw Agnes. 'It wasn't him,' she wailed repeatedly. 'He wouldn't. He was selling stuff, but . . . but he never did the shop. Oh, Agnes . . .' Loud wailing drowned the rest of her words.

Agnes produced tea and biscuits, waiting until Glenys had calmed before asking, 'Who and what? Slow down a bit, Glenys – I don't know what you're on about.'

'They've done something called referring him to Crown Court. He was handling stolen goods, but he never did the burglary and he won't say who did. He thinks he'll get beaten up or worse if he tells. There's some nasty folk about. He could get killed by the Manchester mafia.'

'This is Harry?'

The visitor nodded. 'Will you have a word with your Denis?'

'Eh? What for?'

'He can have a word with the judge. Even if he's not the judge on my Harry's case, he might say something to another judge.'

Agnes processed the odd request. 'So you want me to have a word with Denis about having a word with the judge about having a word with somebody else?'

'Summat on them lines, aye. I don't want Harry going down for years, do I? He's been in trouble afore, so it's not a first offence. I could lose him for good.'

'Were Jack and Bert involved?' Agnes asked.

'I don't know. I'd be lying if I said no and lying if I said yes. But they're not the ones in trouble. That Judge Spencer might listen to your Denis. You're the only chance I've got.'

Agnes shook her head. The judge never listened to anyone on the domestic front. 'It wouldn't make any difference, honestly. The judge is away at the moment, but he's not an approachable man, Glenys. And they're paid a lot of money so that they can't be bribed.'

'I'm not talking about bribery. Just a word in his ear. It won't do any harm to try.'

'He has to be impartial, love. You know the saying – justice must be done and must be seen to be done. The court'll look at it from the jeweller's point of view – his shop was wrecked and his stock was stolen.' She reached out and took the older woman's hand. 'I know it's horrible, love, but maybe your Harry will learn his lesson. Sometimes, it's the only way they do learn.'

Glenys closed her eyes and leaned back. 'He'll learn, all right. Last time, he learned just about every crime there is and how to break the law in a big way. Borstal near finished him. Prison'll only make him a lot worse. I'm frightened to bloody death. If he gets put away, it'll kill me and that's the top and tail of it.'

Agnes studied the woman in front of her. Glenys Timpson was near the edge of her chair and almost at the rim of reason. 'Glenys. Look at me. Go home, wash your hands and face, then come back. It's a nice day and we'll have a leisurely walk. We'll go up Skirlaugh Rise and see Denis while the judge is away. His daughter's off work at the moment. She might listen, but I can't promise that Judge Spencer will listen to her. It's worth a try, I suppose.'

Glenys awarded Agnes a weak smile. 'Thanks, love. Then at least I'll know I did everything I could. Even if it doesn't work, I'll have tried.' She left the house at top speed to prepare herself for the outing.

Agnes was not hopeful. The daughter was a pale, lifeless creature, while the judge was about as movable as the Rock of Gibraltar. Still, having made the offer to

Glenys, she knew that she had to carry it through. And it was a lovely day for a walk.

As Fred put it when speaking to his granddaughter, he and Eva Hargreaves got on 'like tongue and groove' from the very beginning. With no need for a timetable, they ran the shop between them, Fred disappearing into his shelter when he felt that Eva was up to scratch. A large woman, she needed frequent rests and was enjoying her business for the first time in years. She looked forward to Fred's arrival every morning, was pleased to have his company, was glad that he took to shop work like a duck to water.

'It's done me good, has this,' he told her one afternoon as they sat drinking tea outside the shop doorway. The pavement, covered in buckets, mops, brooms and other paraphernalia, was not exactly picnic territory, but both were content to bask in the sun during a lull in trade. 'I remember nearly everything now,' he said. 'Thanks, Eva. You've done me a lot of good, giving me this chance. There's not many that would take me on, the state I was in. I'm happy. You've made me happy. I'm grateful.'

'You're welcome.' She smoothed her apron. 'I saw your Agnes stepping out with Glenys about ten minutes ago. I wonder where they've gone?'

Fred nodded and took another gulp of stewed tea. 'Never holds a grudge, our Agnes. That battleaxe took to coming round after Sadie died, even made me a few meals. Not a bad cook, either – does a smashing corned beef hash. Everybody has a good side and Agnes always winkles it out. She's a grand lass.'

'She is.'

He studied his enamel mug for a moment. 'I might be holding them back, you know. Agnes and Denis, I mean. I don't like feeling as if I'm holding them back.'

'How come?'

'Well, they've been offered a peppercorn cottage in Skirlaugh Fall, just a stride away from his work. It's lovely up there – fresh air, good place to rear kiddies, plenty of places to play. It's dirty round these parts and Denis could do without breathing all these damned fumes. They stay because they think I can't manage by myself.'

'That's because you can't manage. When did you last cook a decent dinner, eh?' She grinned at him. 'You need them. Agnes feels she should look after you because you looked after her when her mam died. Just be glad you have a family that cares.'

'I don't want to be a burden,' he answered.

'It'll get sorted out.' Eva went into the shop to serve two newly arrived customers. A seed of an idea had planted itself in her brain, but she needed time to think about it, time on her own. She doled out paraffin and coal bricks, weighed some tacks, found a spanner for a man who needed to move a bed frame. The solution would arrive, she felt sure.

Fred wandered through the shop on his way to the air raid shelter. His doll's houses were coming on a treat and word was spreading. If he carried on this way, he would be hiring an assistant before the year was out. It was time to put an advert in the *Bolton Evening News*. Eva believed he deserved success after the work he had put into the enterprise.

Fred settled in his new workshop, proud eyes survey-ing shelves and cupboards – a place for everything and everything in its place. Agnes would be pleased when she saw this. Sadie would have been thrilled to bits. All he needed was a bit of advertising, and Eva had promised to see to that. He took a swig of cold tea before carpeting his tiny bedrooms. For the first time in months, Fred Grimshaw was a contented man.

It was a long walk and its duration gave Glenys the opportunity to unburden herself. She talked about her dead husband, about Eva Hargreaves, also a widow, with whom she had shared grief over premature deaths. 'We both married lads younger than ourselves and both lost them early. Very good to me and my boys, was Eva. Which is why I near flayed our Harry for breaking into her shop. He were only a kid, but I should have seen it then, Agnes. Three lads and I needed eyes in the back of my head – I still do. They've been trouble, but I love them all to bits. What the hell am I going to say to Miss Spencer if she sees me?'

Agnes didn't know. She'd come into contact with Helen Spencer in the big library, had even managed a bit of conversation with her once, but the woman seemed too quiet and shy to have any influence with her dad. 'You can only do your best – like you said earlier. Harry will have to take his chances, but your conscience will be clear.'

'Aye, let's hope so.'

During a quieter spell, Agnes wondered about the level of ferocity displayed by many women when one of their offspring was in trouble. It was clear that Glenys would rather do the time for Harry. 'I wonder if I'll be like you when I have a child?' she asked eventually.

'Like me?'

'Yes. Going to any lengths to help your son.'

'You will,' said Glenys with certainty. 'You'll be a good mam, Agnes Makepeace.'

'I hope so.'

They were in Skirlaugh Fall, a small village built in a cleft between moors. Glenys paused for a rest. 'I'll bet these places get flooded in heavy rain,' she pronounced, her eyes fastened to the big house at the top of Skirlaugh Rise. 'I mean, water runs downhill, doesn't it? They'll need wellies in their back kitchens if a storm comes.'

Agnes smiled. Her companion was trying to take her own mind off the task in hand. 'Denis has been offered one of the cottages,' she said. 'Small, but lovely – and look at that scenery.'

'Will you take it?'

'I would if Pop decided to come, but he's embedded down yonder.' She inclined her head in the direction of the town. 'He thinks Bolton'll come to bits if he's not there to supervise matters. And I'd have to travel to the infirmary every day, so I suppose we'll be stopping in Noble Street. Till they pull it all down, of course.'

Glenys grabbed Agnes's arm. 'This Manchester job were a big one. They'll need a whipping boy, and my Harry's been picked. It weren't him. I'd know. I always know. He were in on it, but he didn't blow that shop to bits.'

'And he knows who did?'

'Aye, he does, only he'd sooner be alive in prison than join his dad in Tonge Cemetery. His mouth's shut tighter than a prison door.'

When the two women walked through the gates of Lambert House, they scanned the front for a sign of Denis, but he was nowhere to be seen. 'Let's split up,' Agnes suggested. 'You look round the back, while I go over yonder.' She pointed to a nearby cluster of trees. 'I know Denis said something about thinning out branches, so he could be in the copse.'

'What's that when it's at home?'

Agnes grinned ruefully. 'Judge Spencer doesn't have anything ordinary like a wood or an orchard – he has to have a copse. I think Denis might be working in there, but he could be round the back, so you go and have a look.'

Glenys decided on a straight swap. 'I'll go in the corpse—'

Agnes laughed. 'Copse.'

'You know what I mean. I don't want to be poking about round the back of the house. At least you have Denis as an excuse – let me go to the woods.'

So it came about that Glenys Timpson unwittingly embarked on a course of action that would have repercussions for many years to come. Feeling relatively safe, she opted for the copse. Surely she would be all right in there? Surely no one would see her? She didn't mind being spotted by Denis, but the thought of being accused of trespass with a view to house-breaking was frightening. She was still on Spencer land, but the trees would hide her.

She entered the wooded area and looked for Denis Makepeace. He was a grand lad and he would help her. It occurred to her that she had never before been in a wood, had seldom seen dense foliage. It was dark and eerily beautiful, all dappled shadow and birdsong. 'Lovely,' she breathed softly. 'Scary, but lovely.' Birds rattled branches and a ladybird landed on a leaf. She might have been a thousand miles away from the centre of Bolton, because this place was truly beautiful.

Round the back of Lambert House, Agnes came into contact with Kate Moores, who was taking sheets from a washing line. 'I'm Denis's wife,' she told the red-faced female. 'Give me those. This weather's too hot for housework, isn't it? All I want to do is sleep, and I was hoping the walk up here would do me good. But this heat's turned me into a withered lettuce.'

Kate allowed Agnes to take some of the burden. 'I don't know where he is,' she lied. 'He's been doing all sorts today.' At the kitchen table, she studied Denis's wife. Why was she here? Did this young woman suspect that her husband was being pursued by Madam? And where the hell was Madam, anyway? 'I don't fancy ironing,' she added lamely. The washing had been baked dry by a relentless sun.

'It'll all want damping,' agreed Agnes.

'Have you come about anything in particular?' The daily set a kettle to boil, her face turned away from the visitor.

'Just fancied the walk. I might have enjoyed it if there'd been a bit of a breeze.' Agnes looked round the kitchen. It was bigger than the whole ground floor of the Noble Street house. 'Do you have to clean the whole place by yourself?'

Kate turned. 'No. Most of it's shut off. I don't know why he hangs on to it – they use four rooms at the most. A girl comes in sometimes to do the silver and a few other odd jobs.'

'What's the judge like to work for?'

'He's straight from hell,' came the swift answer. 'Never has a good word for anybody, never says much at all.'

'Oh.'

'I think your Denis is the only person he likes. But I'm guessing there and all. I've never heard him saying anything nasty about Denis, any road. But you really can't tell – he's shut faster than the cat's backside, is old Spencer.'

Agnes laughed out loud.

'Hey, you'd not find it funny if you worked here, lass. When was the last time you coped with oysters and bloody avocado? Smoked salmon has to be thin enough to see through. He likes his caviar chilled and on a bed of crushed ice – any melting and I'm for the high jump. Napkins have to be starched just right – too much or too little and I get the third degree. I reckon his wife died on purpose to get away from him. I'd sooner be in heaven than in this house, but we need his money.'

'Not a nice man, then?' Agnes smiled.

'He wants a bloody good hiding, and that's the truth of the matter. He'll be back in a few days, so expect rain.'

'I wouldn't mind a bit of rain.' Agnes added milk to her cup. 'I'll look for Denis in a minute,' she said.

Feeling reasonably safe, Kate chattered on about ironing shirts just right, about polishing antiques and trying to clean the drapes round a four-poster. The trouble was, you could never tell with folk these days. Denis's wife seemed calm enough, but there was no way to be sure. Kate clung fiercely to hope. When everything else failed, hope was all that remained.

A woman was weeping.

Glenys secreted herself behind a wide tree and listened. Denis was speaking now. 'I've told you to leave

73

me alone. What do you want from me? No, I'll take that back – I'm pretty sure of the answer. Have you no pride?'

The sobbing continued.

'I've enjoyed listening to your music this summer. But that's all there is to it. I'm married. You know I'm married – you've always known. I'll tell you what I think, shall I?'

'No.' The reply was almost strangled at birth.

'I think you need to see a doctor. This isn't normal behaviour. Running after a married bloke who hasn't had a proper education – that's not right, is it? What would your father say? What will he do when he gets home and finds you in this state? If I did anything wrong, I'm sorry. If I led you on, I apologize. I can hardly look Agnes in the eye – and what have I done? Nothing. Or, in the language I'm more used to, bugger all.'

Glenys remained frozen, though the heat of the day had penetrated dense branches and leaves. Her mind was far from still, though. Harry was her son and she loved him. No matter what, she loved her boys. Could she make use of this situation?

'I can't help loving you,' said Helen Spencer. It had to be Helen Spencer, thought Glenys. Who else round here talked through a gobful of plums? She listened while the invisible female ranted on about touching Denis's arm in her car on the day of the funeral, about him hovering near a window while she played the piano. 'You didn't exactly push me away or avoid me, did you?'

'I like music,' he said, his voice louder. 'Do I have to stop liking music? Look, get back to the house, for goodness' sake. Mrs Moores must be wondering what the hell's going on. Before you know it, we'll be the talk of the Fall and nothing's happened!'

Glenys held on to her courage and stepped forward. 'Hello, Denis,' she said, her voice sounding different, high-pitched and unsteady. 'Hello, Miss Spencer.'

'Who are you?' Helen's hand was suddenly at the base of her throat and her cheeks became ruddy. 'You are trespassing.'

'I'm with Agnes,' replied Glenys. 'Nice day, so we thought we'd have a walk and see how Denis is going on. I'm their neighbour.' She was here for her son and nothing else mattered. Whatever it took, she would have her say and to hell with the consequences. 'You all right, Denis?' she asked.

'It's hot,' came the reply.

It was hot, thought Glenys. In more ways than one, this was a situation near boiling point. She felt sure that she could feel steam rising from ground protected from direct sunlight, but still subjected to high temperature. Tropical jungles probably smelled the same. 'I'm Glenys Timpson and I'm here about our Harry,' she said boldly, voice strengthened by determination. 'Harry Timpson. He's up before a judge soon and I wanted to have a word with you, Miss Spencer.'

'Not a concern of mine,' replied Helen.

No trace of tears remained on Helen Spencer's face, and Glenys wondered whether the woman should be on the stage. 'I want you to talk to your father. Tell him our Harry's not a bad lad and he blew no safes in Manchester. Your dad might be the judge or one of his mates could be – I don't know.'

Helen waited for more, but nothing was forthcoming. 'Due process,' she said eventually. 'I have no say in any judgement made in court. Your son will have to take his chances along with anyone else who has broken the law.'

Glenys inhaled deeply. 'Aye, and you'll be forced to take yours if I know Agnes Grimshaw-as-was. She holds no prisoners, you know. It won't be a cell – you'll be six feet under if she gets her own road.'

'I'm not afraid of her.' Helen Spencer's voice trembled.

'Then you're daft,' spat Glenys. 'Agnes's nan used to say that their Agnes could start a war in a chip shop. She's put me and the rest of the neighbours in our places a time or two. A fighter, is Agnes. Well, just you listen to me, Miss Spencer. I stood there behind yon tree and I heard it all. Denis has no need to feel guilty, 'cos he's done nowt. But you? Huh!' The 'huh' arrived seasoned with more than a sprinkling of contempt. 'Your dad wouldn't be right pleased if he knew, eh?'

Helen blinked several times. If Father found out about her behaviour, it would be out in the open and . . . and Denis still wouldn't want her. Even if Agnes left him, he had no interest in his employer's daughter. Why bring it all out if she couldn't get what she wanted? On the other hand, why not bring it out into the open? She had nothing further to lose . . .

'I'm waiting,' snapped Glenys.

Helen sniffed. 'I shall think about it,' she said.

'Aye, you do that.' Glenys drew herself to full height. 'The name's Harold Timpson and he's up for a burglary in Manchester. He's frightened of saying who blew the safe, but he never did it, not in a million years. So, unless you want muck raking all over your name, think on and talk to your dad.' Glenys could not meet Denis's gaze. She was threatening him, too, but no other course

76

of action was available, so what was she supposed to do? Three decades of the rosary and hope for the best? Not likely – she hadn't come this far to end up on her knees.

Helen looked from one to the other, acutely conscious of her own misbehaviour, painfully aware that she had laid herself open to blackmail. She was expected to talk to her father, a man who had never listened to a mere woman in his life. 'I'll do what I can,' she said stiffly before walking away.

Denis closed his eyes and leaned back against the bole of a substantial oak. 'God, Glenys,' he breathed. 'What next, eh? What the bloody hell next?'

She placed a hand on his arm. 'You know, lad, as I'll say nowt to your Agnes, but happen you might have to in the end. I'd cut my own throat before I'd hurt your family now. How the hell did all that lot come about? What's Spencer's daughter doing sniffing round you?'

'No idea,' he replied wearily. 'I liked this job well enough till she came over all peculiar. I reckon she's desperate to get away from her dad and start a family of her own. I was the nearest.'

'And you're wed.'

'I know.'

'And she's a few slates short of a full roof.'

'Or several straws short of a thatch, as my old dad used to say, God rest him. What a pickle.'

Glenys told him how lucky he had been, how she had changed places with Agnes. 'She was going to come to this here copse, but I didn't want to be seen mooching about round the back of the house. If Agnes had heard what I heard . . .'

'I wish she had,' said Denis. 'Then she'd know what's

77

really gone on. If she finds out some other way … Mind you, there's nothing to find out. I've never looked at another woman – Agnes'll know that.'

Glenys nodded thoughtfully. 'Keep your mouth shut for now, Denis. Let Miss Silver-spoon talk to her dad before you have a word with Agnes. And when you do, I'll back you up. But while there's a chance of our Harry getting help, hold your tongue.'

Hold his tongue? He had no choice in the matter. How the heck was he going to explain this predicament to his wife? Who would believe that Miss Helen Spencer had made the only moves? 'Let's go and find Agnes,' he said. 'I think I've had enough for today.'

Helen peeled off the layers and placed them in a small heap on the bed. Father would be back tomorrow. Judge Zachary Spencer's return was imminent and his daughter had to … Had to what? Ah, yes. She had to become dowdy again. The exercise had been a failure, anyway, because Denis wasn't interested. No one was interested. She needed to return to her former self, unlovable, sad, the spinster and librarian.

In her dressing room, she rinsed Lux Flakes from underwear, wondering whether or when she would wear such luxurious items again. Bubbles disappeared down the drain, taking with them every drop of hope, every fleck of excitement. After cold cream had wiped off her make-up, Helen sat on her dressing stool and stared at the mirror's reflection until it disappeared into an almost amorphous lump of matter, a shapeless item in flat glass.

Then she heard them talking. Noiselessly, she positioned herself near the window, curtains concealing her from the happy people below. Denis was talking to the woman who had been in the copse. Was she Glenys? Denis and Glenys – how droll. But Denis was not the property of the older female. No. Denis was with a person of some beauty, owner of chestnut tresses, dark-lashed eyes and a pretty smile. 'I've seen her in the library,' mouthed Helen silently. She returned to her seat, her solitary position, her loneliness. She could still hear them chattering below. They were members and she was not. No matter what she did, she would never be able to join their exclusive club, because she was different, unloved and unlovable.

'I am no one,' she said just before the tears came. It was as if she had been parked in the margins of life, a shadow, a fleeting thing that would never be noticed. She hated who she was, what she had become. But above and beyond that, she despised her father, the one who had made and shaped her into an unattractive and self-absorbed creature with no idea of how to behave, of how to relate to others. It would be back to work, back to the little cafe where she ate her lunches, to filing systems, reference section, nice little love stories for nice little old ladies. In twenty years, she would become one of those old ladies, but she would never be nice because she was bitter to the core.

Kate Moores tapped on the bedroom door and announced her intention to go home.

'Very well,' Helen answered.

'I've left you some salad,' said the disembodied daily. 'Miss Spencer? Are you all right?'

Of course she was all right. In a few years, she might be chief librarian, bespectacled, respected, bored to tears. 'Thank you, I am very well.'

Footsteps faded, a door closed, gravel shifted under

the weight of the retreating Mrs Moores. The sigh that left Helen's body shuddered its way past quietening sobs. Six o'clock. What did normal people do at six o'clock? They probably ate in family groups, then talked, listened to the radio, played with their children. Occasionally, there would be an outing to a public house, a visit to relatives or to the cinema. There was television, of course, with its grim news programmes and silly games. The clock was ticking her life away. She did not want to watch TV, didn't relish the idea of an evening with her radio. She was losing her grip. Was she losing her mind?

'I want a family,' she informed the creature in her mirror. She wanted what most people had, needed to be ordinary, settled. But would she know how to behave at close quarters with others? Could she imagine herself as a wife and mother? And would any man fill the void left by the gentle, handsome creature known as Denis Makepeace? 'Infatuation,' she snapped. 'A childish fad, no more.' What on earth did she know of love, of normality?

The salad did not tempt Helen that night. Unfed and incomplete, she curled up on her virgin bed and cried herself to sleep. Tomorrow, she would think; tomorrow was the only certainty, and she had to content herself with that knowledge.

While Helen Spencer lay alone and disappointed, Agnes went about the business of getting to the bottom of her husband's misery. She talked and questioned and complained until he finally caved in. While he answered, she listened intently. 'I've no need to talk to Glenys,' she said when the tale had been told. 'I know you, Denis

Makepeace, and I trust you. Poor Miss Spencer. I suppose she just wants to fit in like anybody else.'

He should never have doubted his wife, should have confided in her from the very start. 'So, if she comes to you with tales of abuse, you won't listen to her.'

'Of course I won't. But if you think about the life she's had with that misery of a dad, it's understandable. Anyway, isn't it all a bit the other way round? Did you say Glenys threatened to tell me if Miss Spencer doesn't try to help their Harry?'

Denis nodded thoughtfully. 'She's not right, you know.'

'Glenys?'

'Don't be daft. Mind, thinking about Glenys, you may have something there. No. Helen Spencer. Sometimes, she has a wildness about her. She's very . . .'

'Intense?'

'Yes. Desperate. One minute she wants to tell the world that she loves me, then the next – oh, I don't know. Anyway, the old man's home tomorrow, so that'll cool her down a bit. And she'll be going back to her job soon enough. But I find myself half waiting for her to do something peculiar like drinking paint or ripping her hair out. She stares at me. Her eyes bore right through me – I feel as if she can read my mind.'

'Only a couple of paragraphs, then, so don't worry.' Agnes grinned, then shook her head pensively. 'So she threatened to tell me herself, then changed her mind. And when Glenys said she'd tell me, Miss Spencer ran off?'

Denis nodded.

'Doesn't know what she wants, does she?'

'No. I suppose this will sound daft, love, but it's as if she doesn't know who she is, who she ought to be, who she wants to be. I remember girls – and boys – very like her when I was at school: ready to grow up, but still kids. Oh, well. Where's our Pop?'

'Sorting out his batteries. He's putting torch bulbs in all his ceilings. Central heating next, I shouldn't wonder.'

'Shall I walk up and fetch him home?'

'No. Let me have you all to myself for a few minutes, Denis.' She kissed him. 'If we were all like you, we'd do.'

Denis, relieved of the larger burden, still managed to feel a pang of guilt. He remembered the music, the elegance of Helen's hands, the sadness in her eyes. Perhaps he had encouraged her on a level that lay just below full consciousness. But he hadn't done anything wrong and life, as the saying went, had to go on.

Glenys put in a sudden, belated appearance. 'I knew you'd come,' Denis said as soon as she stepped into the house. 'I knew you wouldn't leave me in a state.'

Glenys, flustered beyond measure, blurted out the tale. 'I said I wouldn't say anything, Agnes, but then I thought on and here I am.'

Agnes grinned. The arrival of her neighbour had not been completely unexpected. 'He told me,' she said. 'Don't worry – for your Harry's sake, I'll pretend I know nothing, then we'll see if Miss Spencer will have a word with her dad.'

'Might as well talk to the fireback,' muttered Denis before going to make hot cocoa.

Agnes studied her neighbour, the gossip, eyes and ears of the street, she who had always made everyone's business her own. Glenys had altered. Her face was thinner, there was more silver in her hair and her skin was lined. This was going to be a good friend.

'It's a hard life, all right,' Glenys was saying now. 'If he goes to jail, it'll kill me.'

It wouldn't kill her. Agnes, having grown up among strong women whose husbands were at war, recognized the steely quality that had kept machines turning and a country fed for six long years. Glenys would not die if her Harry went to prison; she would do what all females did in such circumstances – she would work and wait. 'We'll look after you, Glenys. Remember that.'

'Aye, I know you will, lass. Where is he with that cocoa? My throat's like the bottom of a parrot's cage.'

Sleep eluded Helen for the whole of the night. When she did drift for a few minutes, she was back in the copse with Glenys and Denis, whose rhyming names were no longer a source of amusement. Father was in the woods as well, his voice drowning hers, his presence crushing the very air from her lungs. There was another dream too, one she did not care to remember just yet. It was nasty and she was glad to be free of it. These days, it recurred more often and sleep had ceased to be a hiding place. There was noise in the second dream. And terror . . .

Awake, she stared into blackness and tried to curb her imagination, failing completely to control the circular motion of her thoughts. If people knew how she felt about Denis, Agnes Makepeace might leave her husband, but would he turn to Helen? If no one found out, might she persuade him to love her in secret? 'Why did I declare myself?' she asked the ceiling. 'What is happening to me?' Women in books didn't go around opening their hearts to all and sundry. Elizabeth Bennet, Jane Eyre – all the great heroines played their cards close to their hearts, never, ever wearing them on sleeves of transparent silken robes. 'I am sitting at my own wedding feast with no groom,' she whispered. 'Dickensian, over-dramatic and downright stupid. I should be shot, then I'd be released from everyone's misery.'

Sleep. She needed rest. Father had a cure for sleeplessness and Helen, desperate for some peace, descended the stairs and entered the sanctum of Judge Zachary Spencer in search of help. Rows of leather-bound books occupied polished mahogany shelves. His desk and blotter were pristine, no sign of work, no notes, no splashes of ink. The room displayed no character; it was a reflection of his severity and conservatism. Had he ever owned an imagination, had he suffered at all, had he loved her mother?

She removed a bottle of brandy from a cupboard, hoped he hadn't measured the contents. Instead of taking one of his sparkling crystal glasses, Helen went into the kitchen and chose a less ostentatious water tumbler before returning to her room.

The first mouthful made her cough, burning her throat like hot ashes. But the second went down easily and she felt calmer and almost carefree. Denis Makepeace? Why had she worried about a man so much lower than herself? Her father was a judge in the High Courts, for goodness' sake. She would find someone else, someone worthy of her attentions. Her body, limp from the effects of alcohol, began to relax. With the tumbler still in her hand, Helen fell asleep on the chaise. Everything would be all right. All she needed was a good night's rest.

If she had any nightmares, she did not remember them. Morning found her very well except for a slight headache that disappeared after several cups of tea and a light breakfast. But, when Denis arrived to do his job, her heart lurched in her chest as soon as she caught sight of him. Brandy was good for sleeplessness, but it did nothing to eradicate the cause of discomfort. It dealt with symptoms, not with cause. 'Like aspirin,' she muttered as she stood at her window. Denis looked handsome in his uniform. Shortly, he would leave to pick up Father from Trinity Street, and the house would once again be filled by the noise and bluster that always accompanied Judge Zachary Spencer. It was, thought Helen, time for a hair of the dog. A very little would suffice, as she sought waking peace rather than unconsciousness.

She ascended the stairs and prepared for the return of her only parent. He would dominate the house, would ignore her, would act the part of monarch again.

Brandy made it all much easier to bear.

Chapter Four

Lucy looked wonderful in her watered silk wedding dress. She would have looked gorgeous in a potato sack, Agnes thought as she took up her position as matron of honour. The bride turned just before preparing to leave the porch and enter the church. 'The old dragon's here,' she whispered, 'with his dragoness. I should have put garlic flowers in our bouquets. Grab a crucifix and don't look him in the eye.'

Agnes swallowed. Judge Zachary Spencer had begun his illustrious career in the chambers of Henshaw & Taylor, and he had apparently decided to grace the occasion with his surly presence. Helen Spencer, his 'dragoness', was the last person Agnes wished to see today, but the groom's side was wall-to-wall lawyers and it couldn't be helped. George's father was head of chambers and he had probably invited all his colleagues. Agnes drew back her shoulders, raised her chin and walked with Mags behind Lucy and her father. Aware that she looked her best, she intended to show Miss Helen Spencer that Denis was married to a fine specimen. She cast a sideways glance at the judge's daughter, who looked decent but unimaginative in a colourless suit that had probably cost an arm, a leg and a full dining room suite.

Helen watched the service, teeth biting down on lower lip, hands clenched around bag, gloves and hymn book, face deliberately cleansed of all expression. She could and would get through this. A half-bottle of Napoleon was secreted in a pocket of her bag hard against a quarter of Mint Imperials to shift the scent of alcohol from her breath. Father was huffing and puffing beside her. Father had no time for Catholics, foreigners, vagrants, criminals and daughters. The Latin Mass probably infuriated the bigoted old buffoon, and Helen was mildly pleased about that. He shifted his weight, sighed repeatedly and joined in none of the prayers.

During the hymn 'Love Divine', he bent his head and whispered to her. 'Chap over there, third row from the front – friend of the groom – you could do a lot worse.'

Helen followed his nod until her eyes alighted on a gaunt man with thinning hair and a very stiff collar. 'James Taylor,' mumbled the judge. 'Good man, big future. Time you settled.'

Icy fingers curled around her heart. She had seen Denis looking smart in his suit, had devoured the vision that was his wife and was now expected to pay full attention to a man with a neck thinner than Denis's wrist. She was exaggerating, she told herself sharply. James Taylor was probably no oil painting from the front; from the rear, he resembled an anxious-looking character from a Victorian novel, all starved and on the lookout for its next meal.

It was her turn to sigh. Why was she pretending to have a choice? There was no queue of suitors, no line of men waiting to meet the daughter of Judge Spencer. She remembered Charlotte Lucas from *Pride and Prejudice*, who had married a buffoon of a clergyman just to be safe in a comfortable home. Elizabeth Bennet was maid of honour in Helen's own story. Helen, halfway down the church and nowhere in anyone's opinion, was the plain and sensible woman who would have to settle for a Mr Collins. 'Just to be safe,' she whispered. Was that all there was going to be? Safety and a man uglier than sin?

'Did you say something?' asked her father.

Surprised beyond measure, she shook her head. When had he last been interested in any words emerging from her mouth? When had he last deigned to notice her? Noticed now, she felt threatened and decided that she could go through life more easily without the attention of her father. She wanted to run, but dared not follow so base an instinct. She did not want to be here, did not want to be anywhere, but she must endure.

The judge coughed his way through the nuptial Mass and proxy papal blessing. The whole thing was a bloody nonsense. Henshaw Senior refused to handle divorce because of his religious beliefs. Fortunately, his son, who was bridegroom, seemed more willing to accept lucrative cases. Divorce was about to become big business and sense needed to be employed when it came to litigation.

James Taylor, of a landed family, was a good prospect for Helen. He was already a senior partner and he showed great promise in spite of his lack of style. She was drab, as was he, and she would do well to marry him. If the union crumbled, any settlement would be large. 'Called to the bar before he hit thirty.' The words slid from a corner of his mouth towards his daughter. 'About your age, too.'

She suffered a renewed desire to run, but this time she felt like screaming while dashing from the church. As 'Love Divine' faded into the ether, Helen's first free-floating panic attack crashed into her chest like a ten-ton lorry. Oxygen suddenly became a luxury, and she grasped each breath, lungs stiffening, throat as dry as bone. She dropped bag, gloves and hymn book, sinking onto the pew bench just in time. Her heart was going too fast. Sweat gathered on forehead and upper lip, and she longed for brandy. Brandy was the answer. If she could take a drink, she would be all right. As soon as everyone else was seated, the judge, who had given his only child a withering look, forgot about her. She had sat down a second too early, that was all, and few had noticed, he hoped.

With a lace-edged handkerchief, Helen dried her face. Why had she suddenly become so frightened? It was like being in a darkened room with a wild animal, no chance of knowing where it was, just blind fear and a strong desire to be elsewhere. Was this her heart, would she die young? Her mother had died a premature death caused by a heart attack after some kind of accident. Would Helen suffer a similar fate? It didn't matter. The moment she ceased to fear death, her pulse slowed and she breathed evenly. If she died, it would be a release from the torture named life.

It was over. Bride and groom emerged from a side room in which they had signed legal documents attached to marriage. The main party left the church to the strains of a pleasant piece of Bach, then the congregation peeled itself row by row out of the pews.

Avoiding photographs at all costs, Helen stayed in the school playground, treating herself to a few drops of brandy before sucking on the necessary mint. 'Ah, there you are,' said a disembodied voice.

'Yes,' she replied, embarrassment staining her cheeks. Was there to be no peace at all today?

'I've seen you in the library,' added the owner of the

voice. 'I'm James Taylor. Your father suggested that I seek you out, as he will be in older company. You are Helen Spencer, I take it?'

'Yes.' Her vocabulary had shrunk, it seemed.

'Nice wedding.'

'Yes, it was. The bride looked lovely.' Agnes Makepeace had looked lovely, too.

'George is a lucky man. Shall we?' He crooked an arm.

Tentatively, she placed a very light hand on his sleeve and allowed him to lead her back to the large gathering at the church gates. He was definitely not a thing of beauty. Had she allowed herself to wear some of her new clothes and make-up, she would have outshone him with comparatively little effort. But Helen had come as her father's companion, and no one competed with Judge Zachary Spencer. The king of the beasts demanded pride of place. Pride among a pride, she pondered giddily, because most lawyers were bigger than their boots. The collective noun for lawyers should be 'pride' – and pride, as everyone knew, came just before a fall. She hoped with all her heart that the fall would be soon and that she could be there to witness the undoing of the super-king – her father.

A woman among the spectators was mouthing at Helen. It was Glenys Timpson, and the silent message was, 'Don't forget.'

'Are you coming to the reception?' James Taylor asked.

She nodded. Her father was studying her and she knew that she could not run away. The reception was to provide the setting for the mating ritual ordered by the judge. By the end of the month, she must be engaged. A winter wedding needed to be followed closely by pregnancy and trouble-free birth. Perhaps a grandson would placate Father, though he would doubtless have preferred a Spencer to a Taylor. That fact might well result in hyphenated surnames and she could not imagine herself sleeping in the same continent as her intended appendage, with or without hyphenation.

James drove her to the centre of Bolton, where the party was to be held. In a large ground floor room of the Pack Horse, tables formed three sides of a square, and Helen decided that the bride and groom must have been in on the plot, as she was seated next to James Taylor. From the rear, he had worn the air of a bird of prey; from the front, he was no less startling, as his nose resembled the beak of an eagle and he had a habit of staring unblinkingly at his companion. Any minute now, she would be snatched up and carried in talons back to his eyrie. Determined not to be cowed, she attacked her food with all the enthusiasm she could muster. It tasted like cardboard, but wine improved her palate.

He told her of cases in which he had triumphed, boasted about his prowess in court, declared himself to be quite the orator. His long-term intention was not the bar; he wanted to take his seat among the Conservative Party in Westminster. Before the meal was over, Helen had the full picture of his life, including attitudes to the work-shy, immigrants, miscreants and golf. The last saved a man's sanity after days spent in court. If rain stopped play, he joined his fellow damp players for a game of chess at the nineteenth. Did she play chess or golf? Oh, what a shame, but he would teach her both – it would be an honour. Golf would keep her physically fit, while chess would hone her brain to perfection. She hated him. Hating him was easy, but escaping him in this claustrophobic environment might prove difficult.

When the cake was cut, and speeches had been delivered, Helen excused herself and went to a powder room on the first floor, a quieter area well away from the wedding feast. In a cubicle, she gulped down another dose of her chosen medicine, remembering the Mint Imperial before emerging to stare at herself in an enormous mirror in the outer area of the women's rest room. 'What a mess,' she said aloud. In fawn and brown, she resembled a sixth-former from some Catholic grammar school run by over-protective nuns. She was not pretty, would never be pretty, yet she knew she could look better than this, though not in the company of the pride of the pride.

A cistern flushed, then a young woman emerged from the second stall.

'Sorry,' said Helen. 'Talking to myself again – I am the only audience that will tolerate me.'

Mags Bradshaw grinned ruefully. 'Did you come here to escape the madding crowd?'

Helen nodded.

'So did I. There's only so much beauty and happiness that can be digested in one day. I think my cup runneth over and I needeth a break.'

Helen found herself smiling. 'I'm Helen Spencer.'

'Mags Bradshaw, friend of the bride for my sins. As you can tell from the silly clothes, I am also bridesmaid.'

'Yes. You and Agnes Makepeace, isn't it?'

'She was matron of honour, because she has bagged her man. I am now the only singleton in the pack, and no sign of a man on the horizon.'

'I have had one thrust upon me.' Helen wondered why she was speaking so freely, remembering after a

92

second or two that this was a side-effect of her brandy. 'In the middle of a hymn, my father announced that I am to be sold to a balding eagle. Aforementioned balding eagle has been pecking away at me since we left the church. Any idea of how I might get away? These birds of prey are terribly persistent and I have no wish to be swallowed whole.'

Mags pointed to a green door. 'Fire escape? We could go and watch Donald Duck at the children's matinee. Or what about a manhunt? If we sit for long enough on the town hall steps, someone will pick us up. We'd do better there than here. I work with lawyers and they are a dry lot. Let's go and be discovered by a pair of lusty youths. We could repair to some nearby tavern and talk about football and stuff.'

Helen considered that. 'A balding eagle could find us. The eyesight of the species is legendary.'

'True.' Mags sat on a pink stool. 'Being unbeautiful isn't easy.'

'I know.'

'Lucy always says that my beauty lies within. I bet no one ever says that to Marilyn Monroe.'

Helen voiced the opinion that it was easy to hate Marilyn Monroe. 'Beautiful women have a special knowledge that precludes the need for actual brains. They always seem to know exactly what to do and say – it must be something that arrives with maturation and admiration. One minute, they are sitting at the back of the class with runny noses. The next they are at the Palais de Danse picking up every youth without spots.'

Mags agreed that the whole thing was sick-making. 'I had a boyfriend for six months. Then I found out he was only in it for the chips. My parents own a fish and chip shop and he got a free supper every time he took me out. A piece of bad cod put paid to that adventure, I'm afraid. Nearly put paid to him as well – terrible case of food poisoning.' She sighed. 'Alas, he survived. There is no true justice in this world.'

'So you are a friend of Agnes?'

'Yes.'

'Her husband works for my father.'

Mags nodded. 'Denis needs an easy job – he had TB when he was a child and it left a few scars. Even then, he and his family were well loved. Three mills set up a fund to send him off to Switzerland. He couldn't go till the war was over, so his lungs never fully recovered. He's lucky with his wife, though. Agnes has never been one for frills and flounces – and she adores him.'

'Good. He works hard. My father appreciates him.'

Mags raised an eyebrow and smiled broadly. 'Really?'

'Father approves of anyone who fights the odds, but there is no real affection in him.'

'Your mam died?'

Helen dusted a hair from her shoulder. 'I scarcely remember my mother, but I believe my birth was her undoing. She became unsteady and prone to accidents. Childbirth weakened her heart.'

'Sad.'

Emboldened by alcohol, Helen continued to open up to the stranger. 'I used to think he blamed me for her death, but nothing is as easy as that with him. He doesn't like women. I am a woman. Quod erat demonstrandum, as the theorem states. It's as if I'm not there. Or I wasn't until today.'

'Balding eagle?'

'Exactly.' Helen applied lipstick. 'We still haven't an answer. Where do we hide?'

'Give me five minutes.' Mags disappeared into the corridor.

Helen sat on the pink-padded stool and stared unseeing at the mirror. What on earth was she thinking of? First, she had tried in vain to have an affair with Agnes Makepeace's husband; second, she was currently engaged in conversation with one of that woman's closest friends. A nip of brandy put paid to misgivings. She was a thirty-two-year-old adult and she could do what she damned well pleased.

Mags returned, a key brandished in one hand. 'I got us a room for the day,' she crowed in triumph. 'Two beds, two chairs and our very own bottle of champagne.'

'But my father—'

'Your father can bugger off. If anyone questions you, I was taken ill and you were kind enough to cater for my needs. It's nearly true. I am allergic to lawyers and I need champagne. You can pour, thereby providing me with the medication I require.'

Helen blinked. Could all lies be turned into truth? Could she marry a man she had disliked on sight, could she go through a hyphenated life with a smile on her face? 'I won't marry him.' The announcement surprised her – she hadn't meant to say the words out loud.

'You tell 'em, matey. We've a similar article at work. He *is* articled – a mere clerk. He's as fat as two boars and the beer gut enters a room five minutes before the rest of him. He breathes.'

Helen giggled. 'Everyone breathes.'

'It's his main occupation. You can hear him from the other end of the building. Near me, he breathes more heavily and, to top it all, I get the impression that he expects me to be grateful for his attentions. Come on. We can manage an hour away from the chaos, but I'll have to go back eventually. Lucy and I have been friends since school.'

They drank the champagne, then laid themselves flat on the two beds. Helen, who had never before mixed her drinks, was decidedly befuddled, though she managed to remain alert while Mags told tales from a childhood she had shared with the bride and the matron of honour.

Then, while Mags Bradshaw snored gently, Helen considered her own childhood. It had not been normal, and she found herself resenting three girls who had played with skipping ropes, bats and balls, pieces of slate as hopscotch markers. They had been injured in the rubble of bomb sites, had gone to Saturday matinees armed with liquorice allsorts and sherbet dabs, had been dragged home by a constable after stealing apples from an orchard.

Helen's own childhood? A series of nannies, then a governess followed by some years in a select school for the privileged. Dance and music lessons while Father was in court, silence when he was at home. She had never been to the roller rink, to public parks, to the wild and wonderful moors. For her, Rivington Pike had been the name of a place; to Mags, Lucy and Agnes, the pike was for rolling eggs at Easter, for sliding down on an old tray in snow, for picnics on summer days.

'I hate him,' Helen advised the ceiling, which suddenly refused to keep still. 'It's not an earthquake,' she added, a barely contained mirth accompanying her words. But it wasn't just mirth – she felt like sobbing. The feelings were justified this time, though. The thing that had happened to her in church had been unattached to any particular fear and she hoped it would never return. She liked Mags Bradshaw. Would she be allowed to like Mags? Would she ever be allowed to choose anything or anyone?

Mags woke with a start and tried to work out where she was. Someone was talking. That someone lay in the other bed, and Mags remembered the strange turn of events that had led to her current situation. Downstairs, people were dancing and talking, celebrating Lucy's marriage to George Henshaw. She had to go.

'I hate him,' said the woman in the other bed.

Was she referring to her dad or to the balding eagle, Mags wondered.

'Nowhere to go, nowhere to go.' The words were accompanied by a few quiet sobs.

Mags sat up. 'Oh, my God,' she moaned. 'Remind me that champagne's off-limits for me, will you?'

But Helen continued to mumble, and Mags realized that the woman was now asleep, but still speaking.

As quietly as she could, Mags repaired damage to make-up, straightened her skirt, walked to the door. She had just spent an hour or so in the company of a very strange woman. No one loved Helen Spencer. She had travelled thus far without encouragement or affection. But Lucy and Agnes were downstairs and this was an important day.

Before leaving the room, Mags found hotel notepaper and scribbled a message for Helen. *Had to go back to the party, hope you are OK, Mags Bradshaw.* She placed it on the bedside cabinet and crept to the door. A strange feeling of guilt accompanied her all the way back to the reception. Helen Spencer was not fit to be left alone. Although Mags did not understand why, she continued to feel uneasy for the remainder of the day.

'Where've you been?' Agnes pulled Mags into a corner. 'You missed Pop having a go at the twist. He got stuck between Eva and the groom's mother – said he thought he'd need a bloody doctor to cut him out. Mind, he looked quite happy wedged between two pairs of enormous bosoms. So, where did you get to?'

'I found Helen Spencer in a bit of a state. So I put her in a room and sat with her till she fell asleep. It's her dad. He's found her some lawyer to marry and she's not best pleased.'

Agnes blinked rapidly. Had Miss Spencer mentioned anything about her misplaced affection for Denis? Probably not – Mags owned a face that gave away inner feelings, and she was looking her companion in the eye.

'Agnes?'

'What?'

'Have you ever met anyone really desperate?'

'My grandfather when he loses his rag with one of his blinking doll's houses. Lucy till she found the right wedding shoes. Oh, and you now. What's happened?'

Mags shook her head. 'I don't know. But she shouldn't be on her own. I feel as if she might do something horrible. She's living life right on the edge, Agnes. He never talks to her.' She nodded in the direction of Judge Spencer, who was holding court across the room. 'Now, he says she's got to marry somebody who looks like a starving hawk. I've never in my life met anyone so completely miserable. She's given up.'

'Stop worrying about other people and start thinking about yourself.'

'What's to think about? I look like the back of a bus stuck in mud.'

'You don't. You've lovely hair and—'

'Oh, shut up, Aggie. I know what I look like. Helen Spencer's the same – plain and resigned to spending the rest of her life as half a person. She looked at me and knew that I was in a similar boat. It takes one to know one.'

Agnes sighed and shook her head. If Mags would only add some colour to the thick, mouse-coloured waves, she would look so much better. Green eyes begged for blonde highlights, but Mags, who hated artifice, seemed determined not to make the best of herself. 'Right, you.' Agnes folded her arms. 'You are coming with me to the hairdresser's and I'll get you sorted out. Nothing drastic – don't worry. It's time somebody took you in hand, because you do nothing to help yourself.'

Mags blew out her cheeks. 'He'll breathe even louder!' She was referring to the articled clerk at her place of employment. 'It's bad enough now – if I go glamorous, he'll blow a fuse. I can't be doing with clerk articles puffing around my chair. And my nose will still be the same.'

'There's nothing wrong with your nose. God, are you determined to become a carbon copy of Helen Spencer? In ten years, you'll be exactly like her, dowdy and dull. If necessary, I'll get Lucy in on the act,' Agnes threatened. 'The minute she comes back from Paris, I'll beg her to help me frogmarch you to Bolton.'

'All right, I give in. But nothing spectacular – are you listening?'

'I'm listening. I'm always bloody listening. You're worse than the *Billy Cotton Band Show*, all noise and no sense. Mags, put your future in my hands. By the way – where's your locket?'

'Locket?'

'The one given to you by George – your bridesmaid's gift.'

'Bugger.'

'Let's be refined just for today. Buggery is off the menu.'

'I've left it upstairs. God, Lucy will kill me.' Mags left the scene at speed.

Helen was still unconscious, though the mumbling had ceased. After retrieving the silver locket from a dressing table, Mags stood over the sleeping woman. Agnes's words echoed through the whole building – if Mags wasn't careful, she might end up like the tormented and lonely soul in this characterless room. Mags swallowed. Agnes was probably right. In fact, Agnes had only skirted the edges of the problem.

On the landing, she fastened the locket round her neck, smiling as she remembered George's speech. For a lawyer, he was very funny. He had spoken of a queue of women wanting to marry him, of Lucy winning hands down because she told the muckiest jokes.

'Right,' breathed the bridesmaid. 'Might as well hang for the full sheep.' She had saved for long enough. It was time to bite the bullet and endure the knife. And the chisel. She swallowed hard. Margaret Marie Bradshaw was going to have a new nose.

Denis was relieved when Helen did her disappearing act, perturbed when Mags followed her. All through the service, he had imagined Helen's eyes boring into the back of his head like a pair of red-hot pokers. He hoped with all his heart that the judge's daughter would keep her mouth shut about a situation that existed only in her head. She was ill. Beyond a shadow of doubt, Helen Spencer was a sick woman, a time bomb preparing to explode.

But Mags was a sensible girl. Of the trio, Lucy Walsh had always been the fun, Mags Bradshaw the brains, Agnes a mixture of both. Of said trio, Agnes was the best by a mile and he didn't want her life made difficult by lies which would result in pity from her lifelong friends. Lucy would probably have dragged the screaming cat out of the bag; Mags, on the other hand, would always weigh pros and cons before wading in at the shallow end. He had to stop worrying.

The worry abated for about five minutes, then returned in the form of Fred, who had recently been rescued from the clutches of two inebriated and larger than life women.

'I were nearer death then than in any bloody trench,' cursed Fred, a grin widening his mouth. 'Stuck between two fine ladies – what a way to go, eh, Denis?'

Denis feigned displeasure. 'You're old enough to stop chasing the girls.' One of the 'girls' appeared behind Fred. 'Hello, Eva. Can't you keep him out of trouble?'

'No.' She lowered her bulk into a chair that looked too frail to bear such weight. 'I thought about locking him in my shed for the day, but he would have got out one road or another. I didn't know you could dance, Fred.'

'That weren't dancing,' came the swift response. 'That were hopping – you were stood on my other foot. It felt as if the coalman had dropped all his bags at once. Denis?'

'What?'

'Can we have a word?'

'I've never known you have less than five hundred words, but feel free.'

Fred placed himself in the chair next to Eva's. 'I want to ask you about Agnes,' he said.

'What about her?'

The older man inhaled deeply. 'I want to know how she'd feel if I got married again.'

'Married again,' echoed Eva.

Denis scratched his head. Was marriage infectious? Was this a germ picked up by Fred at the church this morning? 'Who'd have you?' he jested.

The 'She would' and the 'I would' arrived simultaneously.

Denis glanced from one to the other several times. 'Oh, I see,' was the best he could achieve.

'I've been thinking,' Fred said. 'I spend more time in Eva's place than I do in ours and we get on a treat – don't we, lass?'

The 'lass' nodded. 'House on fire,' she agreed.

This was a pantomime, thought Denis. Or perhaps a Laurel and Hardy film with a slightly altered cast. Fred, recently bereaved, stroke victim and doll's house builder, wanted to marry a shed. Was it right for a man to marry just for a damp-proof area in which he might work for a few years?

'We're suited,' chimed the chorus of two.

'Eva, you're a good twenty years younger than Fred.' Denis could think of nothing else to say.

'Companionship, mainly,' said Eva.

'And good meat and tatie pies,' added Fred. 'She's a better cook than our Agnes.'

Denis took a quick sip of beer. So, he was marrying

a shed and some pies. Oh, well – better two reasons than one, he supposed. And Eva was well respected by all who knew her. But how would Agnes feel? He had no idea whatsoever.

'There's a lot of reasons for getting wed.' Fred was clearly reading his son-in-law's thoughts. 'Eva here's been on her own for a fair while and she gets fed up.'

'Fed up,' she agreed.

'I know my Sadie's not long gone, but she thought a lot of Eva, and me and Eva think a lot of you and our Agnes. That's why we're going to clear a path for you. You'd be better off up Skirlaugh Fall with fresh air for that chest of yours. I'm holding you back.'

'Back,' chirped Eva.

Denis wished he hadn't drunk three pints plus champagne for toasts. He didn't want to be released to live in Skirlaugh Fall, right on the doorstep of a woman who was plainly suffering some kind of breakdown, a female who had set her sights on him. And how would Agnes react when she heard that Fred intended to remarry before Sadie was cold in her grave?

'What do you think?' Fred was staring hard at Denis. 'Will our Agnes throw a fit?'

'I don't know.'

'He doesn't know,' agreed Eva.

'It makes sense, though,' argued Fred. 'I am at one end of life, you and Agnes are at the other. Eva might be a few years younger than me, but we can keep each other company and run that shop. I can't have you two looking after me all the while, can I? Me and Eva will look after each other.'

Denis waited for the echo, but nothing came. 'I'll talk to her.'

'You talk to her.' Eva patted her rigid curls. 'Let us know what she says, like. We don't want to go upsetting her, but at our time of life, we can't be hanging about.'

'No,' agreed Fred. 'We can't hang about.'

This double act worked both ways, Denis realized. They were good people, lonely people who had found each other in spite of the odds against such a match. They talked in harmony, danced with difficulty and ran an excellent business between them. The doll's houses, recently advertised in the *Bolton Evening News*, promised to bring in a decent income – Fred was taking orders for Christmas and would soon have to close the book, as he had a full schedule for the foreseeable future.

'He's thinking,' said Eva, pointing at Denis.

'He is,' replied Fred. 'And it's a strain, because his brain cell's had a couple of pints – it's in danger of running out of steam.'

Denis found himself incapable of suppressing his mirth. 'I'll talk to you two later,' he threatened. 'And don't be getting into any mischief before the ink's dry on your marriage certificate, or Agnes will have your guts for garters and your bones for soup.'

Fred bowed comically at his intended before leading her to the dance floor for a sedate waltz. Denis watched. Eva had been an important ingredient in the recovery of a sick and confused man. She had given him space in her home, in her shop and in her heart. Fred could have done a lot worse. All that remained now was telling Agnes, and Denis had been selected to soften the blow.

It wasn't a blow, he told himself as he saw the couple laughing on the dance floor. It was a blessing. He would make sure that Agnes felt the same way. But Skirlaugh Fall? He shivered. Where was that bloody woman?

The judge arrived at Denis's side. 'Have you seen my daughter?'

'Erm . . . she left about an hour ago.'

'Her coat is on her chair.' The judge pointed to a table. 'She must be in the building, then.'

'I suppose she must,' agreed Denis.

Zachary Spencer lit a fat cigar. 'Find her,' he ordered before returning to continue a lecture on the anomalies of the British system of justice.

Denis gulped a large draught of air. He found Mags and asked the necessary questions. On leaden feet, the judge's servant made his way to the room booked for Helen Spencer. At the top of the stairs, he breathed deeply again. His master had issued an order and it must be obeyed. 'Three bags full, sir,' he muttered, touching the neb of an absent cap before knocking.

There was no reply. He knocked again, then entered the room. She was flat out on the bed, a half-bottle of brandy in one hand. The lid had not been replaced and she had a damp patch on her blouse. God, she was drinking. Because he had enjoyed her music and her conversation, she had turned to the bottle.

He shook her gently. 'Miss Spencer?'

Helen opened an eye. 'Denis? Where am I?'

'You're at a wedding. Pack Horse, Bolton. Your dad's downstairs looking for you.' She stank like a distillery. 'Can you stand up?'

'Of course I can.' She swung her legs over the edge of the bed, then fell backwards. 'Oops-a-daisy,' she said before righting herself.

Denis's mind shot into top gear. 'Listen to me. Listen!' He removed the brandy and screwed on its cap. 'You had better sober up. I don't need to tell you what your father's like about appearances – and disappearances, come to that.'

'Where's that young woman?'

'Mags? She's where she should be – with the wedding party. Look at me.' He had considered sending for Mags or bringing her to the room, but he knew Helen's vagaries too well. It was better to make sure that as few people as possible from his regular circle came into contact with Miss Spencer. 'Look at me,' he repeated.

She obeyed. 'You are so handsome.'

'And you, Miss Spencer, are drunk.' He picked up the phone and ordered black, strong coffee. 'Your story is this. A man bumped into you and spilled brandy all over your clothes, so you came up here to try to get yourself cleaned up. Do you understand?'

'Very handsome.'

Denis sighed. He had travelled from one comedic scenario to another, but this one was definitely a piece of black humour. 'Your father will ask questions.'

'He got me a balding eagle, you know.'

'What?'

'I am supposed to be courted by a man with little hair and a lot of nose. You must have noticed. His name's Pinocchio.'

Ah, so here was a second case of wedding fever, though this bride-to-be was not quite as happy as Eva. 'You must get downstairs before your father decides to have the whole hotel searched. Remember the brandy story.'

While she attempted to tidy herself, Denis received coffee delivered by a young man in braided uniform. He forced Helen to drink two cups, then began the business of persuading her to leave the room.

She studied him, following his every move. 'I expect

you think I'm a lunatic and a drunk,' she said eventually, words slightly blurred by the earlier bout of drinking. 'I'm neither. The brandy is a crutch to get me through occasions like this one – it isn't easy for a spinster to stand and watch others fulfilling their dreams.'

'We have to go soon.'

'Because he said so?' There was no need for a name.

'Yes. Like it or not, he's your dad and my boss. I hope you didn't say anything to Mags Bradshaw about . . .' About what?

'Of course I didn't. As for your neighbour at the church gate begging me to intercede on behalf of her son – what was I supposed to do about that? Does she know what an absolute monster my father is? When I was five years old, he locked me in my room for three whole days, food delivered on a tray, lectures delivered every evening. My crime?' She laughed mirthlessly. 'I stole a brooch of my mother's. I wanted something she had worn, something that would remind me that I was normal, that I had once had a mother.'

Denis dragged a weary hand through his hair.

'What does Glenys Timpson expect me to achieve for her son? Acquittal? A short sentence? A tap on the hand and advice to behave himself in the future? No one knows the life I have had with that man. He isn't normal.'

He began to wonder what 'normal' was. Agnes was probably the closest he could get to an embodied definition of the adjective. 'We'd better go.' At least her speech was improving. 'Remember – you came up here after someone spilled a drink on you.'

Helen shook her head. 'Mags booked this room for me and for herself. Like me, she is wallpaper. In a decade, she will be me. I just hope she doesn't fall in love as heavily as I did.'

'It wasn't love,' he protested. 'It was your loneliness and my liking for your piano playing.'

'I'm sorry,' she said quietly. 'But when a person falls in love, he or she has no choice in the object of their affections. You are a handsome man and I know you have feelings for me.'

He did have feelings for her. He pitied Helen Spencer, sympathized with her situation, wished with all his heart that he could do something to improve her lot. But Helen's predicament was not a matter in which he could intervene. He sat on a dressing stool. 'I love my Agnes so much it hurts,' he told her. 'I wouldn't swap her for a bank vault full of gold. You have been a friend to me, and your father is cold and unfeeling – I have to work for him, so I know that much. But I can't get you away from him.'

Helen gazed into her coffee cup. 'The balding eagle could,' she said.

Denis shrugged. 'All I can tell you is this – marry for love, not for money, not to please your father. Marriage is hard even if there's love in it. You have to make room for your partner's faults and needs. We're going to be a bit poorer while Agnes studies nursing – but we'll get there. We might have a few rows, but love sorts all that out. More important, Agnes is my best friend in the world. You have to find a friend you can love.'

'I love you,' she whispered, 'and I am a fool for telling you that.'

'We're friends and we'll get over it,' he replied.

'But not loving friends?'

'No.'

'I'm a silly woman?'

She was a frightened woman – Denis knew that. The prospect of living at Lambert House until her father's death was a terrifying one. Her only chances of escape thus far were to marry in accordance with her father's wishes, or to accept her daily escape into the dry and dusty embrace of the town library. 'Not silly.' No, she was more than silly – this poor woman teetered on the brink of reason. 'You did one daft thing. That doesn't make you altogether daft. Now. Go downstairs and I'll follow in a few minutes. Your dad sent me for you, but we don't want to set other tongues wagging, do we?'

She wanted tongues to wag like flags in a hurricane. She wanted to re-enter that big room on Denis's arm, wanted to fling abuse in her father's face, wanted the world to see that she had a man. But she had no man. Denis was immovable and she had to accept that. All her life, she had been accepting; all her life, she had been denied and ignored.

'Go,' he urged.

She went. As she walked down the corridor towards the stairs, she felt that she had left behind all hope. Even Pandora's box had contained some of that element, but she, Helen Spencer, was denied that one last straw. It wasn't fair, never had been fair. 'Abandon all hope ye who enter here,' she murmured under her breath before rejoining the party.

After explaining her absence to the judge, she found herself in the company of James Taylor, who stuck to her like an incubus. He must have had bad acne in his youth, she mused as she watched his mouth opening and closing. So busy was she studying the craters in his skin that she was surprised when his lips stopped moving.

After a moment or two, he asked, 'What do you think?'

Helen blinked. 'Sorry. I am too concerned about the way I must smell – brandy all over my clothes, I'm afraid. What did you say?'

He repeated a request that she would accompany him to a concert in Manchester.

'I'm afraid I can't go,' she said. 'I have been away from work for a while and will have to catch up. We have to list missing books and try to retrieve fines from those who have kept them. Another time, perhaps.'

He frowned, causing two pock marks above his nose to join in a miniature imitation of the Grand Canyon. 'Just one evening? Surely you can manage that?'

The man had a temper, she decided. Denied his wishes, he became another like Father, turned into a man who did not take rejection well. 'I must keep myself available,' she told him. 'It's like a massive audit and we all have to pull our weight.' She needed brandy.

'I shall telephone you,' he promised.

Feeling threatened, Helen declared her need to talk to a friend. She found Mags Bradshaw temporarily alone at the edge of the dance floor. 'Help me,' Helen begged. 'The balding eagle is back.'

Mags patted the chair next to hers. 'Sit down.' She giggled. The champagne had gone to her head, but this poor woman had taken in more than bubbles. 'How are you now?'

'Still running. Seated, but running.'

Mags told Helen of her plan for her nose. 'Agnes is determined to do something about me, but I am going to do something for myself. Harley Street. I've saved up. This is our secret, Helen. I am not telling anyone but you.'

Helen felt strangely pleased. As far as she could recall, no one had ever trusted her with a special confidence. She repaid the compliment. 'He asked me out. I made an excuse about working overtime. He's staring now – don't look just yet, but have a glance in a moment.'

Mags laughed again. 'I've seen better-looking road accidents,' she declared. 'Mind, I'm no raving beauty myself, so I should keep my mouth well and truly shut.'

'You've good hair and eyes,' said Helen.

'Have to get highlights – Agnes has spoken.'

'And your nose? What will happen to that?'

Mags shrugged. 'They use a hammer and chisel, I believe.'

'No!'

'Not a lump hammer, not a big chisel. But it's the same as a sculptor working with marble. For about three weeks, I'll look as if I've been in a boxing ring – black eyes and a nose like rising dough. Work has granted me extended leave – they let me save last year's holidays – so I'm doing what I always said I wouldn't: I'm trying to join the beautiful set.'

Helen wondered whether plastic surgery might improve her lot in life, but she did not air her thoughts. For the first time ever, she longed for her father to order her to accompany him home. Although she was enjoying the company of a potential friend, James Taylor stared constantly and the desire to scream and run was returning.

'Are you all right?' Mags asked.

'I'll go to the powder room.' Helen rose to her feet. 'He can't follow me there, can he?'

Mags blew out her cheeks. 'I have to talk to Agnes – see you later.'

Abandoned by Mags, Helen saw James Taylor embarking on a beeline in her direction, so she picked up her bag and fled the scene. This time, she remained on the same floor, locking herself in a cubicle before taking a few sips of brandy.

Cisterns flushed, taps ran, women chattered. 'He's a boring old bugger.'

'All judges are boring.'

A third voice chipped in. 'And that stuff about bringing back hanging – God, I wouldn't want to stand trial with that sitting on the bench in his flea-bitten wig. I bet he still has his bit of black cloth and I'll bet further he wishes he could use it.'

Helen fought a fit of giggles. She was separated only by a thin door from the wives of lawyers who had to contend regularly with the vagaries of Judge Zachary Spencer.

'My Peter gets in a terrible mood if Spencer's in court. He's always dishing out homilies on moral standards – but what about his own? Have you heard about his latest? A dancer. According to gossip in chambers, she can't possibly know her two times table, but she must have some good moves, eh?'

Helen's giggles subsided and she listened intently.

'They were seen in Chester last week. In a restaurant whispering sweet nothings, by all accounts. They say she looks like her clothes have been sprayed on. So how can he sit there telling criminals to stop sinning? Bloody old hypocrite.'

'His daughter looks like she's had a hard life. Librarian, isn't she?'

'Yes. I feel sorry for her. I feel sorry for anybody who has to live with that miserable monster. She's the one with the life sentence, isn't she? I wonder why she doesn't clear off and leave him to his mistresses? He could be charged with running a house of ill-repute if he brought home more than one at a time. You know how he'd look his best?'

'No,' chorused the rest.

'Six feet under with a nice headstone.'

The laughter rose, then died of its own accord. 'There'll be no real justice in Britain while that man lives,' said the one who had recommended a graveyard. 'According to Charlie Fairbanks, Spencer treats women criminals like aliens – he thinks only men should have the luxury of sinning. If a man steals a car, he gets his dues. A woman gets branded by his red-hot tongue. He's one of those who think women belong in kitchens and bedrooms. We're just another utility in his book.'

Helen swallowed. No, it wasn't just her. Other women hated him, too, while men didn't have a great deal of time for him either. How she wished she could have made a recording of the conversation. Hated and berated, the judge went through life crippling most in his path. Except for the dancer and her ilk. Jesus Christ, what a two-faced barbarian he was. Women? How many had there been in thirty years, she wondered.

Helen stood, flushed the lavatory and emerged to wash her hands.

Half a dozen women froze when they saw her. 'Miss Spencer?' said the nearest. 'Sorry about that. If we'd known you were there—'

'If you'd known I was there, your opinions would have remained the same.'

Bangles clattered on wrists while bags were grabbed.

'Don't worry,' Helen told her companions. 'I live with him and I know what he is. My sole regret is that I don't have the courage to tell him what I heard in here today. He's a bad man. None of us can choose our parents.'

A chorus of apologies echoed round the room after the women had rushed away. Helen dried her hands. A dancer? A dancer who was merely the latest in a long string of women? Yet his daughter was ashamed of admitting her feelings for a fine man who worked as hard as his disability allowed?

She sat on a stool for a long time. Women came, used the facilities, left. Some bothered to speak to her; others, seeing the expression on her face, or knowing who she was, left in clouds of perfume and heavy silence. Active hatred for her surviving parent was flooding her veins and increasing the rate of her heart. 'Why my mother and not him?' she asked of her reflection during a lull in traffic. 'It should have been him. I want him gone from my life.'

She fantasized for a few moments on the idea of a house all to herself, of an existence containing music, laughter and, above all, friends. There was Mags Bradshaw for a start. Helen could not imagine entertaining Mags while the judge was in the house. Even fellow school pupils had not visited Lambert House. A sad child, Helen Spencer had attracted few companions and, because of her father, had brought no one home.

But there was nothing she could do; there had never been an escape and she must continue, as always, to live in the shadow of her parent's sins. To do that, she would need her brandy.

Chapter Five

The wedding celebrations drifted to a halt as the sun began its descent across a flawless sky. Lucy and George left in a flurry of confetti and good wishes, a flustered Mags retrieving the bridal bouquet when Lucy tossed it over a shoulder. Mags, who had imbibed several glasses of champagne, held on to the flowers tightly – were they an omen foretelling the success of her planned hammer and chisel job?

Helen watched impassively as the bedecked Rolls-Royce pulled away towards Manchester Road and the airport. Mags didn't like the look of Helen Spencer. The woman appeared shocked, white-faced, and her fingers trembled. The others probably didn't notice, but Mags, even after so short an acquaintance, knew enough to feel concern for the librarian. Drinking was a terrible thing. It had taken an uncle and a great-uncle from Mags Bradshaw's family, and she didn't want Helen to suffer the same fate. Not that her dad would miss her, she mused as she joined with the rest and waved at the disappearing Rolls. He had a face like a clock stopped at midnight, two deep furrows above his nose announcing the time. The man was not smiling even now. He stood out among the happy throng and Mags, who knew what he was, shivered at the thought of such a father. Her own upbringing, while far from perfect, had been full of love. Love, batter, marrowfat peas and mounds of chips were Mags's foundation, and she pitied anyone who had not experienced the first on the list. Love was everything. It made even cod more palatable.

The judge frogmarched his daughter to the Bentley and prepared to motor homeward. Never the world's greatest driver, he missed Denis, but this was Denis's day off, and the man had to get his family back to that hovel in Noble Street. Denis Makepeace ought to take the cottage and be grateful, but he was fastened, via his wife, to her grandfather. It was nonsense. The cottages had two bedrooms, so there was space enough if she wanted to hang on to ancient emotional baggage. People were a mystery to Judge Spencer, as he did not make room for emotion.

Agnes, Denis, Eva and Fred walked to the station and climbed aboard the Derby Street bus. They sat on the lower deck, each tired and deep in thought, waiting for the stop nearest to Noble Street. Eva fiddled nervously with gloves and handbag; Fred stared through a window, outwardly absorbed in sights he had seen for seventy years.

As they walked to the shop after leaving the bus, Fred mouthed a message at Denis, a clear enough instruction regarding the approach to Agnes. Denis sighed. He had rescued Helen; now he had to contend with Agnes, who was sober, at least. Didn't Fred know his granddaughter well enough to approach her himself?

'Aren't you coming home, Pop?' Agnes asked.

'No. Me and Eva are going to have a drop of cocoa and Navy rum. We've things to talk about.' He winked at Denis. 'I won't be long. Go on – get yourselves sat down and have a rest.'

Agnes remained where she was, arms folded under her chest, a foot tapping the ground. The old couple disappeared into the shop before she spoke. 'What's going on, Denis? I know there's something brewing – I've felt it all day. I didn't arrive here with yesterday's Fleetwood catch, you know.'

He sighed again, wishing that his wife could be slightly less sensitive to atmosphere. 'I have to talk to you, but I'd rather we did it at home. Come on, shift yourself.'

She tapped the foot again. 'Is Miss Spencer still after your body? Has she asked you to elope with her?'

Denis forced a smile. 'As good as, yes – but that's nothing to do with what I have to say. Sad woman, that. The drink loosens her tongue – I've heard more words out of her this last couple of weeks than she's spoken in years. But there's nowt I can do about her.'

Agnes gritted her teeth during the short walk to the house. Secrets were things to be investigated, considered, dealt with. As soon as they were both inside, she spoke. 'Well? Come on, out with it.'

'Sit down,' he said.

'Why? Am I going to fall over with shock? Have you done something terrible?'

'I've done nothing,' he answered. 'Apart from trying to separate Helen Spencer from her brandy bottle. She's got that many sheets in the wind, she looks like Nelson's little trip to Trafalgar. No. It's not her this time. It's your granddad.'

'Oh?' Her face blanched. 'He's not ill again, is he? He looked well enough today, showing me up all over the Pack Horse. Don't tell me he's sick, Denis. I can't face any more, not after Nan.'

'He's not ill.'

'Good. What, then?'

'He's engaged.'

117

Agnes flopped into an armchair. 'He's what? He's seventy-bloody-two, Denis. He's not long recovered from a stroke and Nan's death – engaged? Don't talk so daft – he's having you on. Who's he engaged to? Helen Spencer and her brandy bottle? Or did he pick up a floozy outside Yates's Wine Lodge while I wasn't looking?'

Denis shook his head. 'No. He's engaged to Eva Hargreaves and her back yard air raid shelter. And tatie pies.'

'You what?'

'You heard me, Agnes. He's engaged to Eva. They're both happy, and he asked me to tell you about it. I suppose he doesn't want any scenes. He thought you might be upset because of your nan, you see. It's a bit quick after her death, and he's well aware of that. He's doing what he thinks best all round.'

Agnes tried to be upset, but could not manage it. She had watched her beloved grandfather blossoming in the company of Eva, had been relieved to hear his jokes and listen to tales about customers for firewood, customers for doll's houses, the price of paraffin and coal bricks going up. The old man was alive again, was laughing, remembering, was almost in charge of his own day-to-day existence. God love him, he was one hundred per cent better since starting to work with Eva.

'Agnes?'

'I'm thinking.'

He left her to it and went to make cocoa. She needed leaving alone when thinking deeply – that was one of the many traits they shared. Although there were few secrets in the marriage, each kept thoughts and feelings inside until ready to communicate. Denis knew that this was common sense, so he was willing to wait as long as necessary.

But he didn't need to wait.

She took the mug, enjoyed a sip of hot chocolate, then spoke. 'He does right,' she said. 'From that very first day with the notebooks – the day Nan died and we had that bit of bother with Glenys – Eva's been helping. She went out of her road to make sure Pop had a purpose in life, first with his notes in different colours, then with the shelter for his houses. Trusting him to work in the shop did him good, too, gave him a bit of responsibility and dignity. No, I'm all right about it. Run up and tell them it's OK – these new shoes are killing me. If I don't separate them from my feet, I'll have to separate my feet from the rest of me.'

While Agnes soaked her battered toes, Denis ran up to the shop to tell Fred that he didn't need a white flag to get back in the house.

Agnes leaned back and closed her eyes. It had been a funny sort of day. Nice – the wedding had been lovely – but Mags getting friendly with Helen Spencer had seemed rather strange, as had the information that Helen was on her way to alcoholism. Agnes hadn't mentioned Denis's predicament, but she hoped that Mags would not get too close to that sad woman. What if Helen Spencer had told Mags that she loved Denis? Oh, bugger.

Now, here she sat with her feet in hot water and her grandfather on his way to the altar. She raised her eyes to the ceiling. 'You always liked Eva, Nan. She'll look after him and he'll look after her. That doesn't mean he wouldn't want you back. You were the love of his life. We just need him to be safe and happy.'

Denis returned. 'He'll be back in half an hour,' he said.

Agnes stared at him with mock severity in her gaze. 'Just one thing, Makepeace.'

'Oh, aye? What's that, then?'

'I am not being a bloody bridesmaid or an anything of honour at Pop's wedding. I've had enough of watered silk and new shoes to last me a lifetime. I shall go to the church in me pinny.'

'All right.' He grinned. 'Better still, you can be the pretty little ring-bearer with a satin cushion and some rose petals. Hey!' he yelled when a missile hit him in the chest.

'There's your satin cushion,' she told him.

He tossed the weapon back to her. 'All right. Have it your own way, as per bloody usual.'

When he arrived home, Fred was the receiver of another of Agnes's famous 'looks'. This time, having achieved an air of patience layered over anger, she looked like a headmistress in the process of punishing a naughty child. 'I'm disgusted with you,' she began.

Denis fled to the scullery and stifled laughter with a tea towel.

'Seventy-two,' she went on. 'Seventy-two and still running after women. It's like living with a teenager, honestly. I mean, most folk grow old gracefully; you are doing it disgracefully. Thank goodness you've got a decent suit, you dirty old man.'

Fred beamed. He knew his Agnes of old. 'Second childhood?' he suggested tentatively. 'That does happen to old folk.'

'If it were second childhood, you'd be chewing

crayons. This is second adolescence. Chasing the girls, indeed.'

Fred sat down. 'Well, I was lucky for a while, because they outran me. Every bloody one of them was faster than me. But it'd take a mad bull to make Eva run – that's why I caught her. She just stood there. It's not my fault that she can't get any steam up.'

Agnes rose, removed dripping feet from the bowl, bent over and hugged one of her favourite men. 'Be happy,' she whispered. 'That's an order.'

'I will, lass. And it's no reflection on Sadie. If you look at it one road, I must have had a happy marriage – otherwise, I wouldn't try it again, eh? It's a compliment to a very good wife.' He dried a tear. 'And Eva can cook proper.'

She slapped his hand.

'Well, she can. She can do more with a potato than anyone else I've ever known.'

'She can stuff a pound of King Edwards in your gob and shut you up, then. That way, she'd be of service to the nation. The queen would give her an OBE for outstanding achievement as a peacemaker.'

Fred laughed. 'We'll look after each other, babe. You and Denis can take that nice little cottage without thinking about me. There's a bus. You'll still get to your training from up yon. Think of his chest, love. Up Skirlaugh, Denis would breathe better.'

In the scullery, Denis stood still as stone. Move nearer to madness? Be on hand every time the judge fancied a little ride out? Stand by helplessly and watch the decline of a woman for whom he had felt respect, a woman he had liked? But Skirlaugh Fall was pretty, and Agnes, who had always wanted a garden, deserved pretty.

He washed cocoa mugs and decided to let Nature take its course. In the absence of any other solution, it was the best he could do.

Zachary Spencer drifted into the kerb for a third time. 'Something wrong with the steering,' he said, also for the third time.

Helen, in the back of the car, replayed in her head all she had heard in the ladies' room. It wasn't just her. Even those who had to bow to his superiority in court disliked him. Their wives made fun of him; his daughter despised him; Denis Makepeace tolerated him for the sake of a pitifully small income.

'What did you think of James Taylor?' asked the judge.

He expected an answer? This was an unusual day. 'I scarcely know him.'

'Get to know him. He's a high flyer.'

She fought the need to cite as a mitigating circumstance an inbuilt fear of heights.

'Good barrister, good chap, has his sights set on government. Several of the Inns of Court have expressed an interest in him. Like me, he will go the whole hog – no pussyfooting around for that young man. Well thought of in the Masonic Lodge, too.'

Mixed metaphors. She wondered whether he used those in court. A hog and a cat's paw were hardly partners. Unless the cat was partial to bacon, of course. A giggle rose and she coughed it to one side.

'Did he ask you out?'

'Yes.'

He sighed impatiently. 'And?'

'He will telephone me.'

'Good. You should snap him up like a bargain. You'd want for nothing if you married him. Get yourself settled.'

Helen seethed. For some unknown reason, the balance of power had shifted slightly today. No, that was untrue, because she did recognize the reason: a catalyst had suddenly been poured into the mix. The chattering women had made her feel stronger, because, from this afternoon, she had not been alone. Would there be a hung parliament in Lambert House? Was she going to start arguing her own case from the back benches?

'You will go out with him,' ordered the driver.

As usual, she offered no reply.

'Did you hear me?'

'Yes.'

'Develop the friendship and let it take its course.'

Seething inwardly, Helen forced herself to imagine donating her virginity to a man whose face resembled the surface of the moon, whose nose was the upper half of a question mark, whose body was thin to the point of emaciation. Denis rushed unbidden into her thoughts. He had a frail chest, but his physique was excellent. Tanned from hours of working outdoors, his muscles had developed normally. That was the difference, then. Denis was normal, while James Taylor was a joke.

The rest of the journey was accomplished in complete silence, a fact that made Helen more comfortable, because silence was her father's preferred environment. It was hers, too, as she had been raised in a vacuum created by the selfish male who was biologically responsible for her existence. This was not a father; this was a mere robot with grandiose ideas and a liking for loud, dictatorial music, the kind of noise that had been much loved by Adolf Hitler.

He parked the Bentley, removed the keys and marched into his domain. She waited for a few seconds. When leaving the wedding, he had opened the rear door for her, had closed it after she had sat down. There was no one here for him to impress, so he reverted to type. He was a pig. No, she had met pigs, and they had been noisy, but pleasant.

She got out of the car, closed her door and walked inside, making straight for the staircase and her own room. Halfway up the flight, she paused. His eyes were boring into her spine. He ordered her into the study, then preceded her into it. Oh, no. Helen felt ill-prepared for further lectures on the virtues of James Taylor.

Her father was seated behind his desk, fingers steepled below his chin. 'Sit,' he said.

Feeling like one of his clerks, a mere minion provided to serve his every whim, she sat. He was ugly from a distance; close up, he was hideous. His face was lined, and none of Nature's tracks could be blamed on laughter, as he seldom smiled. She could not imagine him indulging in a good belly laugh when anecdotes were shared at his place of work. This was the face of a disappointed man, a man of ill-temper and personal indulgence. He was flabby, ill-defined, a glutton, a drinker. Helen swallowed. She, too, was a drinker, though she had yet to serve out her apprenticeship.

'There is a matter we must discuss,' he began.

Discuss? He would hold forth; she would be allowed little space for opinion or comment.

'I have remarried,' he stated baldly. 'My wife is currently collecting her belongings with a view to setting up home here, with me.'

A clock chimed. Outside, blackbirds fussed their way through evensong. Helen's spine was suddenly rigid. He had married without a word to her, his sole relative? Her flesh crawled. The thought of him touching a woman – any woman – was almost as repulsive as her earlier musings on the subject of James Taylor. Married? Living here? With me, not with us, he had said. Helen was anxious not to react, yet she could not quite manage to hold her fire in these circumstances. 'The dancer?' In spite of better judgement, she allowed her lip to curl.

The judge's face became a pleasant shade of purple. 'What?' he roared.

She was betraying nobody when she spoke again. 'The ladies' lavatories were alight with the news. It seems your colleagues cannot contain such secrets.' Her heart was banging like a steam hammer.

'The lavatories?' he roared. 'Today?'

She nodded.

'You should not listen to such drivel.'

'Contained in a stall, I had no option.' She could feel her moment travelling through her body. It was now; she could say much if she so chose. 'They were all agog about your many indiscretions – their words, not mine. I confess I was quite shocked when they spoke, but I heard a great deal.' The man was squirming, and she had a sudden urge to cheer.

He shifted his weight in the chair yet again. 'It's all nonsense,' he blustered. 'What else? What else was said?'

It had arrived. Her time was now and she must use it well. 'They were laughing at you and saying that their husbands often do the same. You are not popular among lawyers – that was the gist. At that point, I forced myself to put in an appearance and the gossip ceased.' Married? She could not believe it. He was going to bring home a wife?

'Who were these people?' The judge's skin had returned to its normal condition – grey and moist.

'I have no idea. They were married to the lawyers at the wedding – friends of the bridegroom.'

'Describe their clothing,' was the next order.

'There is no point,' Helen replied. 'I heard voices, but I could not attach any one voice to any one outfit. As I said, they stopped talking when I joined them at the washbasins. They know I am your daughter.'

Zachary Spencer banged both fists on his desk. 'I owe you no explanations,' he spat. 'As you just said, you are my daughter, no more than that. Yes, I have searched for a wife. I want a son.'

He wanted a son? God would surely need to come to the aid of any male child who might be raised in the image of such a man.

'To answer your earlier question – yes, Louisa has been a dancer, though she is also a qualified legal secretary. You might feel happier in another house – there is your mother's money to be used for that purpose.'

Helen simply stared at him.

'We shall need our privacy.'

She stood up and gathered all her strength around her, building a cage of anger and grief. 'This is a large house. I shall open up some of the far rooms, install a kitchen and live there until I choose to leave.' The glove had been cast onto the desk, and she waited for him to rise to her challenge. Never before had she denied or defied him. His discomfort was a joy she could scarcely contain. 'I can win the battle, but not the war,' her inner voice said.

Only his laboured breathing and the ticking of the clock pierced the ensuing silence. Unused to discussion,

Zachary found himself almost speechless. Helen's mother had possessed a backbone – it appeared that her daughter had inherited some of that wilfulness.

'Is that all, Father?' she asked.

The judge blinked. 'For the moment, yes. Louisa will arrive in a week or so. Perhaps you should remain here for a while – you can make yourself useful to her.'

Helen nodded. Her staying had to appear to be his idea, otherwise he would have failed to get his way. Had she owned a gun, she could have shot him quite cheerfully in that moment. 'Oh, another thing, Father. There is a young man named Harry Timpson – some nonsense about a jewel robbery in Manchester. He was involved, though just on the fringes of the crime. His mother is an acquaintance of mine – a great reader.' The lies slid glibly from her newly loosened tongue. 'She is not in good health. A long custodial sentence might well mean that she would never see her son again. You know the importance of sons in a family – he is the oldest.'

Colour rose in his cheeks once more.

Helen continued to stare in fascination. She had mentioned Harry Timpson not because she cared for him or his mother, not because she sought to conceal her silliness about Denis, but because she could. She owned an ounce of power and intended to build on it.

He cleared his throat.

Helen continued, pushing herself into an imitation of a caring daughter.

'Beard your lawyers in their own den, Father. They think you are too harsh and unfeeling. Alarm them by showing some compassion. Make fools of them. They will not speak badly of you again – I will not allow it. But you can help yourself. Change their opinion, make them worry. It will unseat those defence barristers for a while. If they are speaking so ill of you, make them uncomfortable. I should – most certainly.'

He tapped his fingers on the desk. With alarming suddenness, he finally understood that his daughter had a brain, an excellent brain. She might have made a good enough lawyer herself . . .

'I shall go now, Father. I need a bath – this blouse is saturated in brandy.'

Outside the study door, Helen found herself trembling. The palms of her hands were slick with sweat and, without thinking, she dried them on the jacket of her fifty-pound suit. He intended to father a son. That would mean . . . no. It did not bear thinking of. All the years she had served in silence, all the time she had spent in the presence of a cruel father, would come to nothing. Her reward for endurance was to have been sole ownership of this house and the large parcel of land that contained it. Her expectations would come to nothing if he sired a male child.

She sat on her bed and counted nosegays on wallpaper. She would lose the room, the corner that had been all her own. Since childhood, this had been her exclusive area, her bolt-hole. Now, she would be forced to remove herself and her furnishings to a neglected part of the house, while he moved in a dancer, a potential mother for his son. Try as she might, she could not imagine her father with a woman. He probably wanted Helen to move out in order to avoid having a witness to his silliness.

But she would not move out. Why was she staying? Because this was her setting and, like any other still life arrangement, she felt forced to remain where she had been placed more than three decades ago. She had neither the imagination nor the bravery to face a new beginning. And why should she go? Why should she move out for the sake of some cheap dancing girl?

A smile touched on her lips as she recalled her father's reaction to today's gossip. It had affected him – of that she was certain. Monarch of all he surveyed, he would perhaps look more closely now at those who worked below him, because they made fun of him. He would not like that at all. Nor would he be pleased about his daughter's refusal to move out of his house. As for her plea on behalf of Harry Timpson – that would leave him thoroughly flummoxed. Flummoxed was an expression she had borrowed from Denis. His father-in-law had been flummoxed after a bleed in his head.

Well, she could now tell Denis's neighbour that she had attempted to intervene on Harry's behalf. It would be interesting to see what happened, thought Helen. She would be in court on that day if her father was sitting; she would see whether she had had any effect on Judge Zachary Spencer. It was never too late to begin again, she advised herself. In some small areas, she must take the upper hand and manipulate him.

The biggest problem hung in the air like a low thundercloud. After thirty years as a single man, the blundering fool had married. Had she been challenged, Helen would have bet a month's salary that Louisa was under thirty, silly and impressionable. The woman was probably a fortune-hunter, too. How long would Father last with a young woman to satisfy? If he died, this house would pass to Louisa, and that was not fair.

She undressed and placed the suit on a chair in readiness for the dry cleaner. Brandy beckoned, but she refused to indulge. Her supper would be on a tray next to his – they never ate at the table – would that change?

No. Helen intended to have her own kitchen and her own life, though she would keep a close eye on those who shared her home. It was *her* home, not Louisa's. She didn't need servants, didn't require people on whom she might wipe her feet. 'I am not my father's daughter,' she told the flowers on her wallpaper. 'And I am certainly in no mood for a stepmother.'

Everything was about to change, and there wasn't anything to be done about that fact. But she had bearded him in his den, had pretended to support him. In truth, Helen Spencer's hatred for her father increased tenfold that evening. Had she possessed the smallest amount of courage, she would have packed up and left the house. But she needed to stay. She wanted to watch him closely. Helen Spencer prayed that he was sterile, even wished for his death. And guilt played no part in her musings.

Agnes Makepeace strolled through town, looking into shop windows, appearing engrossed in displays, her mind jumping about all over the place. It couldn't be true. It was true. No matter what she did, it would remain the truth.

She studied three-piece suites, clothing, shoes, even managed to feign interest in Thomas Cook's package holidays. But she did not want new dresses or footwear, had no interest in a week on the Costa Brava. Her life had changed with the suddenness of a lightning bolt and she was having trouble adjusting to the news. The nursing would have to lie in a pending tray, because Agnes was pregnant.

She should be pleased. The tiny life in her belly was a demonstration of the love that existed in her marriage.

130

They wanted children, but she needed a career. Nursing could be heavy work, though, and training in a lecture hall was only half of the course. The other half included bed-making, the lifting of patients, the laying out of the dead. She would have to give up her place, because pregnancy and heavy work were not ideal companions. Perhaps she would find a minder when the child was born, but would she be able to leave a baby? Raised by wonderful grandparents after her own mother's death, Agnes had developed a strong sense of family. A child needed a mother. Would she be granted another place next year? Would she be in a position to accept such a gift?

Feeling selfish and guilty, she rounded a corner and almost collided with Glenys Timpson. 'Sorry.' She smiled. 'I was in a world of my own.'

They drank coffee in the UCP, chatted about the forthcoming wedding between Fred and Eva. 'She'll look after him,' said Glenys. 'She's all right, is Eva Hargreaves. Speaking of all right, you don't look so clever yourself.'

'Bit of a summer cold,' replied Agnes. She could not yet confide in her neighbour, because Denis had not heard the news.

'When do you start your nursing?'

'September.'

'Good. That'll give you a proper job. I always wanted a proper job myself, but with three lads I had no chance. It's their turn to feed me now. I've done my share. So have you, love, but in a different direction. You looked after Sadie and Fred – grab your freedom while you can. You'll make a smashing nurse.'

Another pang of guilt stabbed at Agnes's chest. She had probably been looking forward to doing something for herself, for her own sake exclusively. But there would be no time, because babies required attention.

Glenys changed the subject. 'I went in the library and spoke to yon Miss Spencer. She's had a word with her dad. He didn't say much, but she planted the seed, said I wasn't well and I needed my eldest. Now, we just have to wait and see.'

'She tried, then.'

'She did. Give her her due, Agnes, she had a go. Our Harry's like a dog with two tails. I mean, he could still go down, because he's pleading guilty to receiving and handling, but not guilty to blowing up the jewellery shop. Seems there's enough evidence for him to be cleared of that, but he's admitting the rest. Fingers crossed, eh? Let's just hope the judge goes easy on him.'

'Fingers crossed, Glenys.'

They went their separate ways, Agnes to the Co-op, Glenys to meet her son at his solicitor's office.

When her purchases had been made, Agnes decided to walk home. The doctor had told her to keep active as long as she was fit, and she might as well take her exercise before she got a bump as big as Brazil. The timing of her pregnancy was not ideal, but God had dictated that she should have her first child in 1965. It would be a spring baby, a child born with all the blossom that was noticeable by its absence in Noble Street.

Oh, well. The decision had made itself. Agnes and Denis would be moving to Skirlaugh Fall, because a child would enjoy that blossom.

Louisa arrived in a cloud of perfume and fuss. She left Denis to bring in her expensive luggage while she greeted her husband. 'Darling Zach,' she exclaimed in a lightweight voice. 'How I have missed you.' After a pause, she spoke again. 'This place could do with brightening up a little.'

Helen, who had just arrived home from work, hid on the landing and listened to the canoodling. Father was whispering, while his wife giggled in a silly, childish way. 'She'll never fit in,' whispered Helen. Lambert House needed brightening up? For that to happen, its owner would need to put a great deal of space between himself and his home.

The reed-like voice made its way up the stairwell. 'But I must meet your daughter, Zach. We shall be like sisters.'

The judge muttered something about that being highly unlikely before positioning himself in the hall. 'Helen?'

The twin syllables sounded strange, as he had seldom spoken her name. Like a woodlouse, she was alive, an uninvited guest, usually invisible. Helen didn't know what to do. She crept hastily to a bathroom and locked herself inside. This was, she told herself sharply, very childish behaviour, yet she dreaded meeting the wonderful Louisa.

He was on the landing. 'Helen?'

'In the bath,' she lied.

'Oh. Very well. Louisa is anxious to meet you. We'll be in the main drawing room.' Heavy footfalls marked his retreat. He was angry. The speed of his movements betrayed inner fury.

Helen leaned on the door. Hurt and helpless, she felt much as she had just before declaring herself to Denis, upset and confused. The only time she felt sane was for an hour or two after a drink – and she needed a larger

133

dose these days. It happened quickly, then, the dependence on alcohol. Within a matter of weeks, her capacity for brandy had grown.

Softly, she opened the door, went into her bedroom, gulped some of the precious amber fluid. A mouthwash at the handbasin should chase away any fumes, she decided.

The staircase seemed to have shrunk, because she reached the hall in seconds. The judge and his wife were side by side on a sofa. Through the open door to the drawing room, Helen watched her father smiling. The whole world was standing on its head. He had listened to his daughter, had married, was smiling. Perhaps he would change; perhaps he would sire a son, then Helen would be out in the cold.

He rose to his feet, clearly embarrassed by the situation. 'Louisa, this is my daughter.'

Louisa leapt up. 'Hello!' she chirped.

Helen nodded and attempted a pleasant smile. Louisa was small, dark and beautifully turned out. This was a woman to whom she needed to become close, because the eleventh commandment was 'know thine enemy and guard him well'. She held out a hand and Louisa shook it warmly. 'You're a librarian, aren't you?'

'For my sins, yes.'

'I'm a big reader,' announced the young wife.

'So am I,' said Helen. 'I like Trollope and Galsworthy. You?'

Louisa reeled off a list of authors, some who produced trash, others who loitered on the hem of literature. This was not a stupid woman.

Zachary was pouring himself a drink. 'Louisa?' he asked.

She asked for a sweet sherry.

'Helen?' The name sounded rusty. He would need to practise it.

'Brandy for me, Father.' Helen placed herself next to her stepmother. He could sit elsewhere, as the sofa would not accommodate two women and his considerable bulk.

'When do you eat?' Louisa asked. 'I am famished after the journey.'

Helen became engrossed in a pattern on the rug. Her father cleared his throat. 'My daughter and I work strange hours. We usually eat separately. Mrs Moores makes up trays and we eat when we can.'

The new wife declared that this would not do, that they must be a family and eat together in the dining room. There were several changes to be made, it seemed. She wanted a horse, a dog and a proper dinner in the evening. 'Breakfasts on trays are all very well, Zach. But we must be civilized. Each evening, we shall eat together and talk about the day. That's the normal thing to do, I think.'

Helen finished her brandy, then excused herself, saying that she had a very important letter to write. Outside the rear door, she found Denis sweeping a path. He tried to smile. 'Well, he's gone and done it, then.'

'He has. Says he wants a son. If he gets one, I'll be left absolutely nothing but a bad temper.' She sat on a low wall. 'I don't know what's happened to me lately, Denis. Life seems to have got away from me – not that I ever had a life.'

'You're warm and fed,' he replied. 'Where I come from, that counts as a life. And, if you don't mind me saying, you should knock the drink on the head before it gets hold of you. I've seen too much of that in my time. I've known folk to starve their kids to feed the habit.'

She shrugged. 'Before brandy, I seldom spoke to anyone. With brandy, I talk to the wall – for want of better company, of course.'

Denis paused and leaned on his broom. 'She seems decent enough.'

'For a dancer, yes. But she isn't stepmother material.'

'No, you're right there. When he told me he had a new wife, I expected all peroxide and lipstick, but she's not loud. As for being your stepmother – I reckon she's younger than you. Oh, well. You'll just have to put up with it. You can't change anything.'

'Indeed, it's put up with that or a barrister with no hair and a hooked nose. Father's found me a bride-groom and told me to leave home. I'm not leaving. You are going to move me to the east wing. I'm not living with them, but I'm not leaving Lambert House. It's mine.'

A chill travelled the length of his spine. From the sound of Helen Spencer, she would stop at little to get what she considered her due.

She jumped down from the wall. 'Letters to write. See you tomorrow,' she said as she re-entered the house.

Denis finished his work. It was a rum do, all right. The old bugger had gone and got himself wed with never a word to anyone. His wife was about the same age as his daughter, and his daughter was going off her rocker via brandy and too much time spent on her own. Denis felt sorry for Helen, but he knew he had to keep his distance. He shouldn't be having conversations with her. She was like a boil ready to burst, and he wanted to be out of reach when she did finally explode. He would keep looking for another job.

He travelled home on buses, eager to tell Agnes. She would be amazed at the judge's behaviour, of that he felt sure. But when he reached Noble Street, he found his beloved doubled over the slop stone, her face as white as the blouse she wore. 'Agnes?'

'It's supposed to be mornings,' she groaned.

'You what?'

'Morning sickness. Not morning, noon and night sickness. Oh, Denis. I wanted to meet you with a smile and a nice meal, but I can't be anywhere near food.' She inhaled through her mouth in an attempt to quell the nausea. 'I'm not going to be Nurse Makepeace, love. I'm going to be a mother. Hello, Daddy.' She was in the very early stages, but her stomach was already a mess.

Denis's mouth hung open. He snapped it shut and picked up his wife. 'Don't you dare vomit on me,' he warned. Tears streamed down his face, but he was laughing at the same time. 'Lie down.' He placed her on the sofa. 'I'll make my own tea.'

She fell asleep almost immediately.

He sat and watched her, a silly smile on his face. He was going to be a dad. Agnes would be the best mother in the world. Noble Street was not a good place in which to rear a child. Fred would soon be settled in Eva's house. There was nothing standing in the way. Except for ... Except for his employer's daughter, who spoke to him as a friend, who wanted him as a lover. He longed for the days when she had seldom addressed him, because she was not a safe friend to have. But other matters had to come first, and at the top of his list was a pregnant wife.

The *Bolton Evening News* poked its way through the letterbox and landed on the doormat. Normally, he would have peeled away the pages until he found the jobs column, but there was no need, as the decision had been made. They would move to Skirlaugh Fall as soon as Fred had left this house. God must take care of the rest.

'I feel as if I've just escaped from the lunatic asylum.' Kate Moores hung up her raincoat and threw herself onto a sofa. 'Albert?'

Albert, who was semi-retired and taking his rest, opened one eye. 'What?'

'It's him – lord and bloody master. He's fetched a woman home, says she's his wife. No warning, mind. No meal ordered for her, nothing prepared, just one of them fate accomplishes.'

'Fait accompli,' grumbled Albert, who had read a few books in his time. 'What's she like, then, this new madam?'

Kate shrugged and lit a Woodbine. 'Smallish, darkish, prettyish and dressed to kill. Why has he waited this long, eh? Yon daughter of his could have done with a replacement mother when she were little, but she's thirty-odd now. Bit late in the day for him to be starting all over again.'

'First wife were never happy,' said Albert. 'Bonny lass, too good for him. I never could fathom what she saw in Spencer – she'd half of Lancashire chasing her for a date.' He went to put the kettle on. The conversation continued, as the lower storey of the house consisted of just living room and kitchen, so residents were never more than a few feet apart. 'How's Miss taken it?' he asked.

'That's another thing – dry as a bone, she was, till a few weeks back. Then she goes all daft, starts playing the piano with the window open, wears next to nowt and makes eyes at poor Denis. Lipstick and all. I'm telling you, nowt good'll come of that caper.'

'How did she take it?' he repeated.

'She ran out to Denis, of course. He's looked a bit easier since his missus come up with that neighbour – I think Mrs Makepeace sorted the bother. Any road, Miss Helen met the new wife – Louisa – then rushed outside to mither Denis again. She never used to have two words to grind together, now she can't shut up with him. She'll have took it badly, I'd say. She's a lot to lose and I don't trust her. She's sly.'

Albert returned with the tea. 'True – she has got a lot to lose. If he starts breeding again, she could be out on her ear come the day.'

Kate took a few sips of Black and Greens. 'I've not told you the best. His flaming lordship comes up to me just as I'm putting me coat on, tells me to find more servants on account of Mrs Spencer wanting the house nice. What am I supposed to do? Go to the village post office and order three maids and a partridge in a pear tree? I told him. Advertise in the paper, I said. He wanted locals, but he can find his own. I've not time for it and my energy's drained as it is. I wish I could afford to give up and let them get on with it. And I'll have to answer to the new upstart.'

Albert shook his head sadly. 'There's not many will want to work for that queer fellow. Denis Makepeace would have a better job and all but for his chest. The new Mrs Spencer's going to have her work cut out if she wants to live the high life.'

Kate agreed. 'Place is like a morgue till he starts with his music.'

'Do you think Miss will leave home, love?'

'Nay.' Kate poured some spillage from the saucer into her cup. 'Nay, she's opening up the other end of the house to get away from him and the new woman. Says she wants no servants and she'll do for herself.'

'It's him somebody should do for.' Albert shook open his paper. 'Anything tasty for tea, Kate?'

'I pinched a bit of ham and some eggs. Give me a minute and I'll get cracking.' She laughed. 'Cracking eggs, eh?' She paused for thought. 'You know, I've never heard anybody laugh in that house for years. I don't think I've seen a smile, either. Oh, well.' She stood up. 'Fried or scrambled?'

'Just get cracking,' said Albert. 'If the yolks break, scrambled. If not, fried.'

While Kate cooked the meal, she decided there was a lot in what Albert had said. Life was like eggs – to be taken as it came. See a problem, mend a problem, live and let live. He was deep, was her Albert, and she was a lucky woman. Kate didn't envy the new Mrs Spencer one little bit. The judge was just a big load of ear hole. And his daughter was going as cracked as Kate's stolen eggs.

The new Mrs Spencer sat on Helen's bed. Determined to make the best of things, she had decided to be a friend to her husband's daughter. 'We'll go shopping in Chester,' she said. 'I know Chester. Lovely shops, good clothes. I'll get you dressed to the nines in no time. You need brightening up a bit.'

Like the house, thought Helen. She worked hard to dislike Louisa, but it wasn't going to be easy. The new wife wasn't brainy, wasn't stupid, was astute enough to aim for peace in this fragmented household. The house was to be opened up. Helen should stay where she was. 'This has been your room for a while, hasn't it? Well, don't move on my account. If Zach wants to shift you, I'll fix him.'

'I would like a suite of my own,' said Helen. 'This one room and the dressing room – hardly enough for a grown woman.'

Louisa clapped her hands. 'What fun. All right, let's plan your move. We'll make you a boudoir, nice colours, plenty of space and light. Your own sitting room with a television, some bookcases, pretty rugs, nice pictures on the walls. The whole place could do with a bit of colour.'

Even the voice ceased to grate after a while. Did this woman know that she had been purchased as a breeding machine? Had she realized that she must produce a son for the great man in order to fulfil her function at Lambert House?

Louisa was suddenly serious. 'He says he's found a man for you.'

Helen frowned. 'Yes. He's found me a pock-marked beanpole with a face like the backside of a cow and a high opinion of himself.'

Louisa doubled over with glee. 'Oh, stop it. My God, I can see him – you should write a book, Helen. Have you never thought of writing? I mean, you're surrounded by books at work – you must know what people want to read. I'd love to write, but I haven't the brains or the patience. The way you described that poor bloke – hey, I hope he doesn't turn up here. I wouldn't be able to face him without laughing myself sick.'

'We met at a wedding,' Helen told her. 'I spent most of the reception – once the meal was over – hiding in lavatories and bedrooms. He even sat next to me at the table – talked with his mouth full, went on and on about himself. He seems to think he's God's finest gift to the world.'

Louisa laughed again. 'Put your foot down. I suppose you know how to handle your father.'

'I don't.' Though she was learning . . .

'He's a bully,' said Louisa. 'Like all bullies, he backs down if you stand up to him. It took me months to agree to marry him, and I did that only once I knew I could handle his moods. He can be very kind, you know. Zach's been good to me.'

Helen gritted her teeth. He could be kind, she supposed, if he wanted something. How would Louisa fare now that he had married her? Tempted to ask what on earth Louisa saw in such a man, Helen changed the subject. 'You're a legal secretary?'

'Yes. And I teach ballet and tap. I wanted to go into dance professionally, but I never made the grade. And I married young, but – anyway, it didn't work. Since then, I've done a few pantomimes, but more teaching than anything else. I'd like to open a school in Bolton, but Zach isn't keen.'

Helen walked to the window. No, Zach would not be keen, because the wife of a judge should not labour for money. How well did this young woman know the creature she had married?

'I'll get my way,' said the voice from the bed.

Perhaps she would. It promised to be an interesting episode, and Helen would watch it as closely as possible. Could this person really manage Father? Or would the honeymoon period come to a halt when he reverted to type? Something akin to pity for Louisa entered Helen's thoughts. She wasn't quite the expected floozy, was a decent enough soul. 'Let's get some coffee,' Helen suggested. Life promised to be improved by this newcomer. At last, there was someone to talk to. Things promised to go swimmingly. Until Louisa bore a son, at least . . .

Chapter Six

Excitement reigned during the next 'mothers' meeting' after Lucy came home from her honeymoon.

Repeated bouts of sickness had kept Agnes away from Mags: she couldn't visit the Bradshaws because of the smell of fish and chips; Mags had stayed away from Noble Street since her friend's closest companion had become a bowl over which she could hang her head while lying on the sofa. Agnes had managed, just about, to hang on to the contents of her stomach for the very small wedding of Fred and Eva, but had become increasingly fearful of leaving the house. She was not yet three months pregnant, and she had been warned that these symptoms might continue up to week sixteen.

'Have you chosen any names?' Lucy asked.

Agnes shook her head. 'At the moment, it doesn't answer to Bloody Nuisance. Denis calls it Bertie – no idea why – and it doesn't respond to that, either. The Bloody Nuisance was my idea, because I can't seem to keep down more than a cup of tea and a biscuit without starting World War Three. I'm living on dry cream crackers and arrowroot biscuits – can't walk past a bakery without coming over all unnecessary.'

'You be careful,' Mags warned. 'Don't be going all dehydrated on us. We don't want to arrive and find you curled like a crisp.'

'Desiccated, more like.' Agnes laughed. 'I knew

there'd be pain at the end, but I hadn't catered for this.'

'Tell me about the wedding,' Lucy begged.

The other two girls painted a vivid picture of Eva Hargreaves in full sail and powder blue. It had been a small wedding, they agreed, but the bride had made up for that, as she had practically filled the centre aisle by herself. They described her hat – a strange collection of netting, sequins and small feathers – Fred's new and squeaky shoes, the choice of hymns, one of which – 'Fight the Good Fight' – had been rejected by a very amused priest, and the post-nuptial feast of pasties and ale in a local hostelry. 'It wasn't anything like your do,' concluded Agnes. 'There was a game of darts in one corner, some old men fighting over dominoes next to the window, and the wedding in the middle. On top of all that, the brewery delivered and they had to fetch an ambulance when one of the brewer's men hurt his back.'

'Lively, then,' said Lucy.

'Lively?' Mags hooted with laughter. 'After four pints and a glass of bubbly wine, Mr Grimshaw had to be practically carried home by his new wife and Denis. He had no visible means of support apart from them.'

'Denis wants danger money if Pop ever marries again. It was good fun, though. Tell us about Paris.'

Lucy waxed enthusiastic about the city, which she had enjoyed hugely. 'But one thing I hadn't thought of – it's full of French people.'

'It would be,' said Agnes. 'It's in France.'

'They say the English have stiff upper lips.' Lucy was getting into her hilarious stride. 'You could park a double decker bus on a Frenchman's gob, and he wouldn't flinch. And we ate horse – we didn't know till afterwards. Sorry, Agnes – it would make anyone feel sick. George dared me to eat a snail, so I had five, then he had to eat frogs' legs. Tasted like strong chicken, according to him. The *Mona Lisa*'s horrible, the Eiffel Tower's a pile of rust-coloured girders, but the rest is stunning.' Thus she dismissed that wonderful city, adding only her opinion that the Arc de Triomphe was a bit good.

Mags cleared her throat. 'I'm off to London for a month soon,' she said as casually as she could. 'Time I took a break.'

'Why?' chorused the others. 'Why London?'

'It's there, we know it's there, but do we need to go?' added Lucy.

'We should enjoy our own cities first – what's the matter with London?'

'Southerners?' offered Lucy.

'Traffic?' suggested Agnes.

Mags shrugged. 'Victoria and Albert, Science Museum, Buck House, Tate, National, St Paul's – need I go on?'

'Pickpockets,' shouted Lucy.

'Thieves and vagabonds.' Agnes grinned.

'You've been reading Dickens again.' Mags smoothed her skirt. She wanted the whole thing to be a surprise, yet she feared the pain and worried about the outcome – what if they gave her the wrong nose? What if they gave her the right nose, thereby making the rest of her face wrong?

'She's hiding something.' Lucy folded her arms.

'She is.' Agnes stared hard at Mags. 'Out with it. Is it a man? Are you sneaking off for a dirty month with a married person?' She glanced at Lucy. 'George isn't going to London, is he?'

'No, he isn't. If he decides to go, I'll ground him with a couple of tent pegs.'

'Denis isn't going, either. Whose husband is she pinching, Lucy?'

'It'll be your Denis's judge. That should get her into the House of Lords. By a back door, of course.'

The judge. Agnes began to tell her friends about recent events at Lambert House, thus changing the subject for a relieved Mags. 'The wife's younger than Miss Spencer. Denis says the two women get along well enough together, so that makes life a bit easier. I feel sorry for Helen Spencer, you know.'

'She drinks,' said Mags. 'It's a damned shame, because it's all her dad's fault. Did you see the article she was sitting with at Lucy's reception? That's the husband chosen by his flaming lordship. Looked like the back of a mangled tram. That's why she ran off. Then I met her in the loos and booked her a room. I found her soaked in brandy later on. The judge sent Denis to find her.'

'I know.' Agnes chewed on a nail. 'We're going to live up there. Judge Spencer will like that, because he'll have Denis on the doorstep. We're to have a phone. If the old devil can't fasten his corsets, he'll be sending for poor Denis. I'm in two minds.'

'Does he wear corsets?' Lucy's perfect eyebrows almost disappeared under her fringe.

'He did the last time I saw him stripping off.' Agnes looked from one to the other. 'Joke,' she said. 'Anybody seeing him undressed probably needs to be under the influence of a strong tranquillizer. He's a mess. I hear he's to be the judge at Harry Timpson's trial. He's a hang-'em-high type, or so I'm told. Glenys spoke to

Miss Spencer, asked her to help, but I'm not holding my breath – unless I'm going to vomit, of course.'

'When will you be normal?' Mags asked.

'She was never normal.' Lucy drained her coffee cup. 'If she'd been normal, I wouldn't have wanted anything to do with her. Normal's boring.' She looked hard at Agnes. 'Is this vomiting going to carry on all through?'

'No idea. It could be temporary, could be hyperemesis.'

'Who?'

'Stop messing about, Lucy. If I've got hyperemesis, I could damage my brain, my liver and my child. I'd spend most of the time in hospital.'

Nobody liked the sound of that. 'Can I press you to a jelly?' asked Lucy, her stern expression surviving snorts of laughter. 'Look, some folk can hang on to that when all else fails – calf's foot, fruit jelly – it slides down. And,' she smiled again, 'if it comes back up, there's nothing to it – it slides like sugar off a shiny shovel.'

Cushions flew in the company of several impolite words.

They settled back eventually. 'London, though,' pondered Agnes aloud. 'You'll not need your bucket and spade or a phrase book, will you?'

Mags shrugged. 'I might need the phrase book – they talk a load of rubbish down there. And I draw the line at jellied eels and whelks. They don't even eat proper like what we do.'

'And we talk proper and all, don't we?' Lucy jumped to her feet. 'I've a hungry lawyer and three cats to feed. Look after yourself, Agnes.' She glared at her other friend. 'Don't go marrying any cockneys – I had enough of them with the *Billy Cotton Band Show* and his

"Wakey, wakey". Load of flaming numbskulls.' She swept out, leaving a sudden silence in the house, the word 'London' thrown over her shoulder as she closed the door.

'What's going on, Mags?'

'Eh?'

'You're up to something.'

Mags sighed. 'Don't tell anybody.'

'I won't.'

'Well, you know how I've never left home for a flat of my own?'

'Yes?'

'It was so I could save up for a new nose. If I decided not to have a nose, I could put a deposit on a house or a flat. But when I was sitting with that Miss Spencer at Lucy's wedding, I thought I might end up like her. She's plain, but not ugly. If I have a new nose, I might graduate to plain. With the right clothes and a good haircut, plain can pass as OK.'

Agnes bit her lip. 'God, that's scary. They break bones and stuff, don't they? And doesn't it take a few weeks for all the swellings to go down?' She shivered. 'It'll hurt.'

'Yes.'

'Aren't you scared?'

'Yes. Aren't you scared – all biscuits and bowls?'

'Yes.'

Mags reached out and grasped her dear friend's hands. 'Then we'll be scared together. I don't know what I'll look like; you don't know what Nuisance will look like. I'm sorry about your nursing, but we have to get on with life, haven't we? We only get the one chance.'

Agnes nodded. 'But a baby's a natural thing, Mags.

New noses interfere with nature. You've always been against make-up and hair dye – yet here you are, going for plastic surgery in London.'

'I am not walking behind this great big conk for the rest of my life. It comes into a room ten full minutes before the rest of me. There's no getting away from a nose like this. This is a nose you have to live up to. I'd do all right as one of the three witches in *Macbeth* – no greasepaint required. And I want to go to Carnaby Street for some daft clothes, get my hair done in the West End, see all those London markets. I'm doing it, Agnes. For better or worse, I'm doing it.'

Alone, Agnes thought about Mags's parting words. For better or worse sounded about right. You had to live with a nose before you understood its significance. The same might be said for marriage – for better or for worse, a partner, once chosen, was supposed to be there for life. Mags's nose was going to be a better or worse job, and everyone would have to take time to get to know it. 'Good luck, Magsy,' she whispered. Then she went to try a bit of toast.

She was still coming to terms with her bit of toast when love's young dream – as she had nominated Fred and Eva – burst into the house. 'Hello,' she said. 'Do come in. Oh, I see. You're already in.' Agnes noticed that Eva was breathless and that Pop was a strange shade of pink. Eva stood in front of the dresser.

'Tell her,' she ordered.

'They're coming,' he announced. 'With a great big van and stuff. You'll have to help me, Agnes – I don't know what to say.'

Thus far, the toast had sat well enough. But all Agnes needed was two confused senior citizens and she would lose calories, plus moisture, all over again. The pair shifted weight from foot to foot, putting her in mind of a couple of children kept in at playtime for bad behaviour. 'What are you on about?' she asked.

'Me doll's houses,' spluttered Fred.

'Doll's houses,' came the echo.

Agnes chewed, swallowed, took a sip of tea. 'Start at the beginning and finish at the end, please.'

Fred dropped into a chair. '*Coronation Street*,' he said.

'Them as makes it,' added Eva in an attempt to make matters clear. 'I've shut the shop. Your granddad's famous.'

Agnes glared at the personification of fame – dirty overalls with an off-the-shoulder touch of fashion at one side, hair full of sawdust, eyes as wide as a frightened rabbit's. 'Granada?'

He nodded, causing a shower of fine wood shavings to abandon his person. 'Making a series called *Man at Work*. It's about retired folk doing crafts and stuff. They say my houses are in a class of their own. Somebody up Chorley New Road ordered a Tudor mansion, then, after seeing the plans, went and phoned these here Granada folk. I'm going on the telly. They're doing an OB on me.'

'Isn't that a medal?' asked Agnes with feigned ignorance.

'That has an E fastened to it,' said Fred. 'OB is outside broadcast and they cost money. They want to see me in my natural wotsername.'

'Habit,' said Eva.

'Habitat, you daft lummox.' Fred sighed. 'We've even shut the shop to come and talk to you.'

'Yes, Eva said so before,' said Agnes.

'What'll I do?' Fred looked truly frightened.

'Nothing.' Agnes placed her cup on the table. 'They ask questions, film your houses, you just give answers. You don't know what they'll ask, so you can't practise for it.'

'Can't practise,' said Eva.

Fred jumped up. 'What are we doing here?' he asked his bemused wife. 'I've carpets to fit and lights to install. Come on.' He rushed out of the house. 'Where did I put that box of doorknockers?' The final words grew fainter as he marched up the street.

'I hope this doesn't make him ill again.' Eva walked to the door. 'He's getting all worked up.'

Agnes sighed and shook her head. 'For better or worse, Eva. Just let it all happen. It'll happen anyway. Enjoy it. He'll be all right. If he isn't, send him back. You've a twelve-month guarantee for parts and labour on that item.'

Alone at last, Agnes put her feet up and waited for her stomach to rise, but her indigestive system seemed to have made up its mind to take time off for good behaviour. She kept the bowl nearby, just in case, but minutes passed without the need to leave a deposit.

'Let's hope I'm finally on parole,' she told her feet. 'Because the three of us – not including toes – have to get moving – literally. Skirlaugh Fall, here I come.'

Skirlaugh Fall was a village consisting of a group of houses that clung together for support at the bottom of Skirlaugh Rise. The big house sat on top of the Rise, as if it oversaw movements among serfs condemned to live lower down both social and geographical scales. It was a pretty place and Agnes had always loved it. She was excited. Nuisance, too, seemed impressed, though it

152

was too soon for him to start kicking and Agnes put the flutters down to wind or imagination.

On all sides, moors swept towards every compass point, so the Fall could be a bit damp, but that fact made it all the greener. It was a fresh, wholesome place that made her think of the hymn 'All Things Bright and Beautiful'. The cottage was a bit small, but no one could have everything. There was no scullery, though the kitchen, which ran the full width of the building, was big enough to double up as a second living room. 'Nice,' she told her husband. It was more than nice. It was cosy, with wonderful views, clear air and decent neighbours in the form of Kate and Albert Moores. This was a splendid place in which to raise a child. There was a school within easy reach, there was clean oxygen to breathe, and there were playgrounds in the form of lush, green fields.

Inside the cottage, they had found a welcoming bunch of orange flowers in the grate. Agnes declared this to be a thoughtful gesture, as it gave colour without heat and made the place seem homely right from the start. 'They're from Mr and Mrs Moores,' she told her husband. 'That was a friendly thing to do, very thoughtful.'

'She's all right, is Kate Moores,' he declared. 'Solid as a rock and no nonsense. Her husband works the land, but he's semi-retired these days. She's run off her feet. Wife the Second up at the house wants more servants. Most round here would kill the judge before they'd work for him, so Kate's having to look further afield. It's all new curtains and rugs up yon. Mrs Spencer's a fresh broom, but she'll not do her own sweeping.'

'They never do. Denis?'

'What?'

153

'Come in the kitchen – Mrs Moores has left us new bread and butter, some cheese and a pot of home-made strawberry jam. She's got willow pattern plates. I've always wanted some of those.'

'And I grew the strawberries.' He came to stand by his wife at the kitchen window. The mock-Tudor mansion was clearly visible from this position. 'They're getting on too well for the old bugger's liking,' he said. 'Mrs and Miss are busy footling round Manchester, Chester and Liverpool, separating him from his brass, I shouldn't wonder. He's not saying much, but he's aged about ten years these past few weeks. Mrs is there just to produce a son and heir; Miss is staying put because she won't be shifted and I can't say I blame her. But the new wife's done her a lot of good, I must say. No, I can't blame either of them.'

'Me neither,' agreed Agnes. 'It's lovely here, Denis, but I don't like being near him. If there's a devil, he'll look just like Judge Spencer.'

'Well, I can't disagree with that. Now. Where are we putting all our stuff? The van'll be here in a minute, so we'd best decide.'

'I don't care,' she sighed happily. 'I'd sit on orange boxes if necessary. Nothing matters but this baby and that view. Not Lambert House – the rest of it out there.' She wished that they didn't have a view of her husband's place of employment, but it had to be accepted. 'Denis?'

'What?'

'Can we afford a television set? Just a small one?'

He smiled. 'We might be able to manage that. You want to see your granddad flummoxed in front of the nation, don't you?'

Agnes laughed. 'Flummoxed? He'll be in his element. As soon as he gets talking, they'll have trouble shutting him up. Camera shy? Not him. He'll be like a dog with five tails and a thigh bone to chew on. Yes, I want to see him on TV, bless him. That stroke and Nan dying – he deserves a good life, what's left of it. So does Eva, come to that.'

Denis chortled. 'She's getting herself painted and decorated all the way through – even the bedroom. The back bedroom's for storage, but she was going to empty that for painting till Fred put his foot down. He said he wasn't carrying that load of stuff downstairs, not even for bloody Granada. I wouldn't mind, but the TV folk'll be setting up in the shed. The only thing that'll bring them inside is tea and Eva's scones. Honestly, the way Pop's carrying on, you'd think it was going to be a Hollywood film.'

Leaving Denis to wait for the removal men, Agnes went for a short walk. These were proud cottages, each with a well-kept front garden and decent curtains. She found the post office, which doubled as a grocery, a tiny pub and cottage industries advertising eggs or bedding plants for sale.

She placed a hand on her belly. 'We'll be all right, Nuisance. You, me and your dad can make a fine life out here, just you wait and see.'

Two women were walking towards her, and she recognized one of them. Miss Spencer was in the company of a small, dark, attractive woman. This must be Wife the Second, then. Agnes stopped and pretended to study marigolds in a cottage garden.

'Is that Mrs Makepeace?'

Agnes turned. 'Hello, Miss Spencer.'

'This is Mrs Spencer – my stepmother.' Both women giggled. 'She's not old enough to be a wicked step-mother, is she? We're playing truant – we're supposed to be interviewing staff for the house, but we escaped. Kate will keep them in order – won't she, Louisa?'

'She keeps me in order.' The judge's wife smiled. 'She has a face that could stop a tram in its tracks. Mind, she does work hard.'

Agnes bid them a polite good day, then walked on. In her soul, she was chuckling, because those two ladies were in cahoots, if she wasn't greatly mistaken. From what Denis had said, Agnes knew that Spencer wanted the house to himself and his wife, that he longed for Helen to leave, but this unexpected friendship would leave his plans in tatters. Which was exactly what the old goat deserved, Agnes believed. He was always sending for Denis. Denis was expected to have no life beyond the judge and his needs. Well, with a new baby, things would have to be different.

She walked along tracks that bordered farmland, watched cows and sheep grazing, saw a donkey resting his head on a dry stone wall. It was another world altogether. No deposits from the Industrial Revolution were visible from here. Cotton mills? What were they? Yet the houses in the village had been built for one purpose only, to accommodate weavers and spinners before cottage cotton died.

At the top of a lane, she stopped and looked at Lambert House. It was massive. She would wager that three people could live in there for months without seeing each other. There was water nearby, so the house might have been the property of a fulling miller in the days of homespun yarn, but she doubted it. The mansion had been built to look old, was a pale imitation of Hall i' th' Wood, the place in which Crompton had invented the spinning mule. That had been a waste of a life, she mused, because the rights had been virtually stolen from him. Cotton and coal, she said inwardly, had been the two biggest killers in Lancashire since time immemorial.

It was time to go home. Home. She grinned broadly. Home was where the heart lived. Denis was her home. For the first time in weeks, her stomach was happy and she felt hungry. She wanted bacon and eggs followed by a nice custard tart. No – new potatoes with the bacon fat dripped onto them in the grill pan. Strawberry tart with thick clotted cream, a banana with ice cream, some Lancashire cheese on crackers. She smiled again. Greedy for food and hungry for life, she walked homeward to the man she loved.

Judge Spencer was not best pleased. Louisa – his Louisa – was spending all her spare time running to town and visiting Helen in the library, or carting Helen off all over the place to look for rugs and furniture. Like conjoined twins, they were welded fast together and he was not equipped to separate them.

Helen's suite of rooms was almost ready, as the two women had laboured most evenings and weekends in order to finish it. Louisa, who had turned out to be a compliant and dutiful wife, would not shift in this one area – Helen was her friend, and there was nothing he could do about it. He watched them ambling arm in arm up the drive, both grinning, no doubt sharing a joke. Was he the joke? Surely not. Louisa was affection-ate and pleasant, yet he was barred from membership of their exclusive club, and he would never become eligible, because he was male. They were females of similar age and seemed to be stuck one to the other like two pieces of iron soldered and shaped straight from the furnace.

He poured himself a large whisky, sat behind his desk and brooded. Since the day of George Henshaw's wedding to Lucy Walsh, Helen's demeanour had changed. She spoke to him at dinner, an institution ordered by his wife, was outwardly supportive of his views, seemed happy to chatter away with Louisa. It was her eyes, he decided. There was a look of damped-down challenge in their depths whenever she looked at him. Helen was clever. He should have noticed a long time ago that his daughter was a bright woman. She was thinking of writing a book. The hairs on his neck bristled when he wondered about the content of such a volume. She had not known a mother, while he had been too busy to pay much attention to her. Would she produce a Dickensian melodrama on the subject of lonely and motherless childhood? She might very well make him the villain, he supposed. Such a character would be veneered, yet all who knew him would recognize the model on which she had based her parody.

He could hear them in the drawing room. Helen would be dressed in some of the smart clothes chosen for her by Louisa. Their conversation was probably about fabrics or wallpaper, but he was excluded, as he had no opinion on such matters. Should he develop one? He was an old dog. New tricks had never been his forte, and he would probably not change now. About women's clothes he knew nothing, had no comment to offer on the height of heels or the breadth of a belt.

Louisa came in. 'There you are, darling. We had a nice walk. Now we are going to interview applicants for positions in the household.' Bequeathing him a dutiful peck on the cheek, his wife returned to her bosom ally. She almost danced away from him, feet patting the carpet lightly, face aglow in anticipation of another hour in the company of Helen.

He seethed inwardly. Louisa was planning an opening-up party to celebrate Lambert House's new lease of life. He could not fault her, was unable to nominate one single crime of which she might have been guilty. How could he berate her for becoming friendly with his only daughter? None of this had worked out in the way he had foretold. Helen was supposed to hate her step-mother for invading the domain, but Helen refused to play the Cinderella he had imagined. There was a deep unease within him; nothing good would come of the current situation.

He topped up his glass and scanned forthcoming lists. Harry Timpson's name cropped up among a dozen others. What had she said? Beard the lawyers in their den. Show some compassion and confuse them all. With a gold-plated pen, he tapped on his blotter. His colleagues despised him because of his conservative views. Was Helen on his side? Her words showed allegiance, but her eyes did not. It required thought, so he downed his drink in one swallow. Thought needed fuel and he needed sleep. The energy expended in trying to impregnate Louisa was taking its toll. He was not a young man; he should have remarried years earlier.

Ten minutes later, he was snoring, his head resting on a wing of the leather chair. Asleep, his dreams were of Louisa and Helen smiling at him, agreeing with him, stabbing him in the spine. On leaden legs, he tried to flee from these twin enemies, but he failed. As the knife pierced his innards, he heard their voices. One told him to alarm his fellow lawyers; the other pledged eternal love and loyalty. All the same, the knife twisted and he woke in a sweat. 'Nonsense,' he told himself aloud. Then he poured a third drink to chase away the nightmare.

Denis brought the invitation home. It was encased in a heavy cream envelope and the card it contained was gilded along its deckled edges. 'Bloody hell,' cursed Agnes after opening it. 'Do we have to go, love?'

'We do,' he replied resignedly. 'It's a bit like being invited to Buckingham Palace – a refusal is not acceptable unless accompanied by a doctor's note or, better still, a death certificate.'

She placed the card on the mantelpiece behind the clock. 'I don't want to look at it. I don't want it hanging over my head for weeks. Will you be working at the party?'

'No. They've drafted in a load of casual workers to pass the plates round. I know how you feel – I'm the same. I'd rather sit here with my cocoa and biscuit, thank you very much.' It could have been worse, he told himself inwardly. At least Wife the Second had distracted Helen Spencer – she was no longer looking at him all the time when she was at home.

'I'll need something to wear. I'd borrow from Lucy, but my waist's started to expand. Why do they want us there? You're a servant and I'm a servant's wife. It doesn't seem right.'

It didn't seem right to Kate Moores, either. She arrived a few minutes after Denis's return, another cream envelope held gingerly between forefinger and thumb of her left hand. She carried the item away from her body, as if she half expected to catch some contagious disease from its contents. 'This is her doing,' she announced. 'She's at the bottom of it – I'd wager my best shoes and a fortnight's wages.'

'Miss Spencer?' asked Agnes.

'No, the other one, the new one. She talked about egalitari summat or other.'

'Egalitarianism,' said Denis. 'And appreciation for loyal service.'

Kate blew out her cheeks. 'They expect me to get my Albert in a suit? That'll take an anaesthetic and five big lads. When we've been to weddings and funerals, he's always stood there with his finger down his collar doing an imitation of a goldfish out of water. I can't be doing with this. I'm the one who has to get him dressed. A corpse would be easier.'

'Say he's ill,' Denis suggested.

'Ill? He will be ill when he cops a look at this. And in this village, there's no point pretending to be poorly – they all know if somebody's poorly, because they start forming an orderly queue at the door with beef tea and home-made remedies.' She sat down. 'Denis – you'll have to break it to him. I've enough on with game pie and bloody caviar. Thank God they've got caterers for most of it. As if I hadn't enough to do already, up comes bloody caviar. And up's where it should stay – it tastes like cod liver oil.'

Denis smiled. 'All right, I'll tell Albert. But if he starts throwing things, I'll be out of there like a mouse in front of the cat.'

'Oh, he's not violent.' Kate cast her invitation onto a small table. 'Sometimes, I wish he would kick the walls or something. He sulks and moans. I can't be doing with sulking and moaning when I've pastry to manage. Picture the scene – me, you and Agnes lost among a heap of rich folk, and my Albert in a corner threatening to take his tie off. We need a committee, then we can take turns to stop him undoing his clothing.'

Denis started to laugh. He owned a deep laugh that seemed to travel through his whole body. Agnes grinned. Denis's humour was one of her reasons for marrying him. When he regained his composure, he came up with an idea. 'Mrs Spencer's getting her dog next week – a great big Alsatian. We can set that to guard Albert and his clothes.'

'Oh, he'd only sulk and moan at it. What I need is a small padlock. I could do up his top button, lock it and hide the key. Eeh, I don't want to go.'

None of them wanted to go, but they had to pay the price for being allowed to work for the Spencers.

'It's changed since she came,' pronounced Kate. 'His royal highness is not in the best of moods – I don't think he reckoned on his new missus and his daughter getting on so well. If he wanted another family, he should have wed years back – his lower storey might not be up to the job.'

Denis fell about again, enormous hoots of laughter deteriorating into a bout of coughing.

'Look what you've done.' Agnes wagged a finger at Kate. 'Next news, he'll be pulling at his collar. He'll be stuck in a corner with the other naughty boy. Denis?'

'What?' he managed.

'Pull yourself together. We're going to be forced to be dignified.'

Kate shook her head sadly. 'Nay, you'll not get dignified out of our Albert. He might produce wind – depends what he eats – but not dignified. He couldn't do dignified in a month of Thursdays. I can't say Sundays, because he doesn't do them, either. Says church is the opium or some such thing.'

'Opiate,' gasped Denis.

'You 'ope 'e ate? Not caviar. He'd definitely get wind with caviar.' She swept off the scene, offending envelope held well away from her chest.

Agnes wiped her face. 'There's no peace, is there? We've left love's young dream behind fretting over Granada, and we've gained another pair of flaming lunatics.'

Denis grinned. 'Yes. Good, isn't it?'

Helen tried on her new emerald green gown after lining up all the cosmetics she owned. Her stash had grown since the arrival of Louisa, whose opinion was that muted tones on the face were classy. She would help Helen when the big day arrived.

Helen hung up the dress, then lay on her bed for the last time. The new living quarters consisted of a large sitting room with TV and elegant furniture, bedroom, dressing room, kitchen and bathroom. This room was childhood, and she was leaving it behind. At the age of thirty-two, she would have her own apartment, but her feet would be wedged firmly in her father's door. He wasn't happy, so she was.

Louisa had made all the difference. Much as Helen wanted to dislike her, she found that impossible, because Louisa was fun. Fun had not featured in Helen's life thus far, so she embraced it with enthusiasm. But she had not forgotten her other friend, the one she had met at the wedding. She had sent the invitation to Mags's place of work. Mags, currently in London, would be back before the opening-up party.

Dinner, a trial at the start, had become a joy. Judge Zachary Spencer presided at the head of the table, while

163

Helen and Louisa, opposite each other, indulged in conversations of which he could never be a part. Louisa, a dutiful wife, occasionally threw him a lifebelt, but the friendship between her and his daughter was genuine, and it grew by the day while the man of the house remained out of his depth for much of the time. He seethed. While he seethed, Helen was triumphant.

Helen often wondered how Louisa bore the physical side of her relationship with Father. Lately, she had reached the fringe of understanding. Louisa had explained that life had not been easy, so she had developed into a pragmatic woman who could accept and make the best of any situation in which she found herself. Of one thing Helen was certain: Louisa was not in love. Remembering the Denis episode, Helen saw none of her own symptoms in her so-called stepmother. Louisa had tied her moorings at Father's berth, and that was an end of the matter. 'I'm glad she did,' whispered Helen. No matter what the cost, Louisa was worth every last penny.

When she thought about the longed-for son, Helen reached a grey area into which she dared not step. It was swamp and she might drown in its murky depths, so she lived for the moment and pushed all thoughts of half-sisterhood into a compartment well away from the main engine. Perhaps Louisa's common sense was rubbing off, because worry seemed to be a thing of the past. James Taylor, balding eagle, had telephoned several times, and been rejected. There was no more fear, because Louisa was on her side. Even the nightmares had lost some of their edge, though they continued to make regular visits.

Whatever the reasons, whatever the outcome, Helen was almost content. She lived with the idea that the bad dreams were nudging her to remember something, but her stepmother distracted her during the days and panic attacks were fewer.

Denis? The feelings remained, yet she managed to control herself. If she saw him, she spoke to him, but she never sought him out. There was no time. Helen's life was fully occupied with the library and with Louisian adventures. Helen smiled. The Louisian era was her favourite so far, and long should it reign.

When Mags Bradshaw returned from London, she did not go home. Having booked a room at the Pack Horse, she shut herself away and waited for the last of the bruising to subside. Over a period of days, she watched the butterfly emerging from its dark chrysalis. It was rather frightening in a sense, because she was looking at a stranger. All the time, it had been only her nose. She was no Marilyn Monroe, no Jane Russell, but she was almost pretty. Everyone in her position should have a new nose. It improved a person's outlook, her mental state, her whole life. She would never regret postponing the purchase of a house, because she had spent her money wisely on a whole new promise of adventure.

Margaret Bradshaw had new hair, new make-up, new shoes, new clothes. 'I am a reformed woman,' she said as she sat at the dressing table. It had been a painful road, and at times she had regretted the surgery, but the result was so stunning that she could not stop looking at herself. If this behaviour continued, she would become so self-absorbed that she might well imitate those she had always mocked, the look-at-me girls, the floozies, the good-time females. Although she wanted to show off to her friends, she dreaded the initial impact that would cause embarrassment at work, at home, in shops. But she would have to bite the bullet, and home was the place to begin.

After three nights, Mags made up her face, packed her bags and stood at the bus stop on Deansgate. It was time to face the world. No one stared, so that was the first hurdle cleared. The application of heavier make-up had concealed the last pale traces of multi-coloured damage. She was free. She would be able to walk into a room without her nose acting as usher. She was normal and she wanted to cry.

In the living quarters behind the shop known locally as Braddy's Chippy, Mags comforted her mother, who shed tears enough for both of them. 'You were lovely before, baby, but you are a stunner now.' It was clear that Mam had not realized how desperately Mags had hated her appearance. 'We thought you'd gone looking for work down yon,' she wailed, referring to the many days Mags had spent in London. 'We thought we'd lost you, sweetheart.'

Her dad was less emotional on the surface. He asked the usual questions about cost and pain, though he wiped a tear from his eye once he had gone back to his batter mix. Mags was beautiful. Like many fathers, he worried about the male of the species. His little girl was going to attract attention, and not all that attention would be welcome.

Work was the next hurdle. When she arrived on her first day, a receptionist looked at her quizzically, asked did she have an appointment; then, once Mags grinned, the girl leapt from her chair. 'It's you!' she yelled. She fled through the outer office and into the inner sanctum. 'It's her,' she shouted. 'Come and look.'

Animals in zoos probably got fed up, Mags decided

as secretaries, clerks and solicitors came to view. At one point, she made monkey noises and pretended to scratch her armpits before asking for coffee and a bun. 'For God's sake, bog off, will you? I feel like something in Tussaud's. Yes, I've had a nose job, yes, I had a deviated septum, so it was a good idea from a medical viewpoint, yes, I now cast a smaller shadow and no, I'm not going to tell you how it felt.' She marched to her desk, exclaimed over the heaps of post in her in tray, then carried on as usual. It would all calm down, she told herself. But she still had to face Lucy and Agnes.

An item in her tray provided her with the opportunity to plan the first meeting between her nose and her two confidantes. It was an invitation to celebrate the recent marriage between Zachary Spencer and a woman named Louisa. In handwriting at the bottom, someone – probably poor Helen Spencer – had appended a message containing the information that Lucy and Agnes would be there with their partners. Partners? Where could she get one of those within days? It was best to go alone anyway, because her nose would probably be the star, while she would play the part of a small attachment. She smiled to herself. After twenty years of being a mere appendage to a colossal proboscis, there had been no change – just a simple adjustment of parts to be played. Until people got used to her face, she would have to sit back and let the surgeon's triumph take the glory.

In her lunch hour she walked around Bolton, pretending to look at displays in shop windows while, in truth, she was looking at herself. She was an inch from pretty. When she passed some painters working on the frontage of Woolworth's, Mags Bradshaw was in receipt of her first ever wolf whistle. There had been times when she had almost used her savings on a deposit for a place of her own. That whistle told her that she had spent her money well. Now, all she had to do was find a truly stunning dress, because she wanted no complaints from this new, upstart nose. With a spring in her step, Mags Bradshaw began her search for suitable trappings.

Agnes answered the door. It was the twins, as Denis had begun to describe Miss and Mrs Spencer. 'Come in,' she said tentatively.

Louisa Spencer was an extremely pleasant woman with a high-pitched voice to which Agnes became attuned within minutes. Whatever the woman was – gold-digger or just plain silly – she had a genuine affection for and interest in her fellows. 'Was that your grandfather on TV last night? The doll's house man?'

Agnes laughed. 'It was.'

'You ask her.' Louisa was speaking to Helen. 'Go on.'

'Would he come to the party?' Helen asked. 'It would be nice to have someone famous – apart from my father, of course.'

'He's more notorious than famous,' said Louisa cheerfully. 'What a wonderful man your granddad is. He had Helen and me in pleats. I thought he'd never stop talking – I wanted him not to stop. He should have his own TV show. I laughed and laughed.'

'Me, too,' said Agnes. 'Though I'm used to it. He and Nan raised me – my mam died when I was born.'

'He's very witty.' Louisa laughed again. 'He treated the interviewer like an apprentice and I swear he could talk for ever. Those houses are extraordinary. He has actually made some real houses to scale, hasn't he?'

'He keeps busy.' Agnes smoothed her apron. 'Would you like some tea? It's ordinary Indian, I'm afraid.'

Louisa blew out her cheeks. 'Thank God for that. I'm not that keen on perfumed stuff. And I'm common – I take milk and sugar. Yes, I'd love a cuppa.'

While Agnes busied herself in the kitchen, Helen looked at Denis's home. It was small, but beautiful. Agnes was beautiful, too, but bigger than she used to be. A sharp pang of jealousy pierced Helen's chest, but its duration was short. She could manage without him. She had taken no brandy for days. Louisa, her friend and her prop, had shown her another way of life, had lent some of her own pragmatism to a woman whose life, thus far, had been filled by unattainable dreams. The nightmares continued, but every day was good and exciting and different from its predecessors.

Agnes brought in the tray.

'You're expecting,' announced Louisa.

'Yes.' Agnes poured. 'That's why we finally came up here. It's better for children and easier for Denis. Pop married Eva – she was the one who appeared on the programme by accident. Mind, she's a big woman, and she seems to get everywhere, so I'm not surprised. When Pop married, we didn't need to stay in Noble Street, so here we are.' She handed out cups and saucers.

'Will he come to the party?' asked Louisa. 'We haven't many older people on the list, and I'm sure he'd pick up some business. Not that he needs to. Didn't he say they were thinking of selling the shop?'

Agnes nodded. 'Eva says she'll do his soft furnishings. He's got so many orders, he'll have to take on a

169

man to help. God help that man. Pop's talking about buying Bamber Cottage, so we'll have him near us again. But they could change their minds – they often do. Eva's not one for quick decisions. She's not one for anything quick, come to that. Pop says she's built for endurance, not for speed.'

'But will they come?' Louisa begged. 'He has to come. I never had a doll's house as a child – perhaps I'll order one now.'

'He'll cause trouble. I mean, think about how he made that interviewer look daft. I can't see him fitting in with Judge Spencer and a load of lawyers.'

Louisa frowned. 'My husband isn't what people believe him to be. He may be a tough judge, but he's all right.'

Helen almost choked on her next sip of tea. All right? He was far from that. But Louisa had a knack of seeing the best in just about anyone. Helen envied her that. In spite of a past about which she would say little, Louisa Spencer looked on life as a glass half full rather than half empty. Above all, she was lively, unafraid and funny.

'I liked the bit where the man asked your granddad about material for the roofs.'

Agnes laughed. 'I know. When he said he'd stripped a church roof and cut all the slates into smithereens, I think they believed him for a minute. It's all wood and paint.'

'And electric lights. Very clever.' Louisa returned her cup to its saucer. 'Make him come.'

'I can't make him do anything. Nobody has ever been able to make him do anything – even Nan had a fifty per cent success rate at best. As for stopping him, you'd have a job. You should have seen my kitchen till he married Eva and her air raid shelter. Murder, it was.

Sawdust in the jam, chippings in my pastry, paint all over the ironing.'

'Then he definitely has to come.' Louisa stood, and Helen copied the movement.

In that split second, Agnes forgave Helen Spencer for chasing her husband. She had needed someone like Louisa, a pattern to follow, a friend – almost a sister. Louisa seemed to be a steadying influence, and that had to be a good thing.

'Promise you'll invite him,' Louisa pleaded.

'I promise.' Agnes suffered a temporary mental picture of two old men in a corner. Like Kate's Albert, Fred Grimshaw would tug at his collar, complain about the heat, hate the food, wish he could be normal in overalls. Perhaps they could keep one another company at the dreaded event.

'Goodbye,' chorused the two women as they left the house.

Agnes sank into a chair for a rest – the dishes could wait for half an hour. Pregnancy still failed to suit her, though the vomiting had stopped. She was tired all the time. Everything was an effort and she had to force herself to keep going. Nan would have shifted her, would have urged her on, but there was no more Nan.

She drifted into sleep, her mind filled with dreams of Pop making a doll's house in the middle of Judge Spencer's living room, of the judge bawling and his wig slipping. Miss Spencer had her arms round Denis's neck and he was bending to kiss her. Albert had stripped all the way down to vest and pants. Eva ate most of the food, leaving just a few scraps for a large dog.

Agnes woke with a start. What a stupid dream that had been. Everyone knew that judges didn't wear their daft wigs at home . . .

Chapter Seven

Zachary Spencer sat on the end of an oversized, custom-made bed. In his opinion, which was correct at all times, the situation within his own household had gone too far. Louisa, an excellent wife with many plus points on her check sheet, had upset the balance. The subject had to be addressed. It should have been dealt with earlier, but he had allowed things to slide because he needed to please Louisa. Now, he was going to put his foot down. A bride was required to learn her place in a household, and the shape and size of that position was the responsibility of the husband. There should be laws on statute books, then the whole business could be made clear from the start.

He fastened his waistcoat and waited for his wife to return. Where was she? She was at the other side of the house in her stepdaughter's rooms, was preparing Helen for this evening's party, was with her best friend. The fact that the atmosphere had changed shortly before Louisa's arrival had not escaped him, but his wife's support had allowed Helen to open up further, and he did not like the latter's attitude. Overtly supportive of and pleasant to her father, Helen was becoming talkative, was even daring to express opinions. While she invariably agreed with the few words he spoke at table, she continued to hold in her eyes an expression of challenge, as if she were taunting him and fooling him. He was nobody's fool. Fools did not become judges; judges seldom became fools unless senility overcame them after long service in the name of the Crown.

Inwardly, he seethed. He could not identify the game Helen was playing, but he had glimpsed the edge of her cleverness, had realized too late that she was bright as well as unpredictable. Her mother had been clever, yet not clever enough to conceal from her husband the fact that she disagreed with his politics and his attitudes. Helen had the brains to wear a thin gilding of good metal over her true self. She was brilliant, had inherited her father's brains and her mother's wilfulness. As time wore on, the veneer covering Helen's true core was beginning to erode. The result had to be dealt with immediately.

It was getting late. He glanced at a clock, imagined the two of them together in Helen's suite, all laughter and smiles. It was not natural. Most daughters would leave home if a parent brought home a new partner, but Helen was not a bolter. He had asked her to leave; she had stayed, had spent a great deal of money on creating her own apartment within his house, was even stealing the attention of his wife. It had to stop, he told himself for the thousandth time.

He fastened his shoes, pulled on a jacket, continued to wait. Unused to waiting, he tapped an impatient foot on the carpet. Louisa should be here with him. She was a good wife – that fact was undeniable. Always pleasant, always accepting of his attentions, never angry, she catered to his whims, yet stuck to Helen like glue.

She came in. 'Darling, you look smart,' she announced.

'Thank you. You were away a long time.'

'Helen's nervous,' she replied. 'She hasn't had much

of a social life, and I had to calm her. That's the problem with a girl who has been without a mother – she has no pattern to follow.'

He was surrounded by clever women.

'Let me fix your tie.' She stood over him and straightened the offending item. 'There. You'll be the best-dressed man in the room.'

'So I should be – this suit is hand-made by craftsmen.'

'Yes, dear.'

'I don't know why we need to have this damned party,' he complained. 'I can think of a thousand ways to spend an evening fruitfully, but this is not one of them. Damned fools coming into my house, eating my food, drinking my—'

'You'll enjoy it,' she promised.

'Will I?' His house would be full of lawyers, yet he could not be himself among his own colleagues, because Helen had put a stop to that. Had she really heard that gossip in the Pack Horse, or had it been an opening salvo, a warning shot to his stern? Whatever she had sought to achieve, she had been successful. 'Louisa?'

'Yes?'

'You spend too much time with my daughter.'

'Do I?' She sat at the dressing table. 'It is much better this way, my love. Imagine how hard life might have been had she hated me. I am fortunate. She likes me and I enjoy her company. Helen is very knowledgeable and interesting, you know.'

Life, he thought, would have been a great deal easier had Helen flounced out of the house in temper.

'I like your daughter, Zach. And she fills some of the hours during your absences. What am I expected to do? Sit at one end of the house while she is at the other? And she goes to work, so we are scarcely constant companions. We are the same age and we complement each other well. She needed help and I enjoy her companionship. She is coming out of her shell, probably for the first time in her life. Your daughter is lonely.'

He seethed. Presented by the defence, the argument for Helen's case was solid. In court, it would stand up to the most skilful cross-questioning from the best prosecutor on the planet. Louisa was talking sense and he felt like a boxer who had been knocked out in the first round. Yet he continued to cling to the ropes, refused to lie down for the count. 'She's devious,' he said.

'All women are devious, sweetheart. We are what men have made us.'

'Nonsense.'

'Yes.' She spun round on the stool. 'I'm sure you are right. I shall try to spend more time with you in the future, but you will need to be here. I can't go travelling from court to court, can I?'

He had lost. The jury would definitely come down on the side of the defence – there would be no sentence to impose. Sliding into his other simile, he was in the corner of the ring and the fight was lost. 'We shall have to go down shortly,' he said almost resignedly.

'Yes, dear. The food looks wonderful.'

'Good.' He looked at his watch again.

Louisa smiled brightly. 'Before we do go, I want you to know that you are going to be a father again.'

He simply nodded, though his eyes blazed with pleasure. That would be a nail in Helen's coffin. As soon as he had his son, the will would be changed. Of course, he would have to leave her something, but the boy would inherit the bulk. 'I am delighted to hear that,' he said. 'But should you be organizing an event in your condition? Don't you want to stay up here and rest? I can explain your absence if necessary.'

Louisa shook her head. 'No. I am well. Explain nothing, Zach. I always think it's tempting fate to announce a pregnancy too early. Let's keep this to ourselves for the time being. No one needs to know – except us and the doctor. This is our special secret.' A smile hovered on her lips. She could manage the man. Like many of his gender, he was a fool when it came to the machinations of females.

He kissed her on the cheek, then left the room.

When he had gone, Louisa stared at her reflection. The desire to scream had been with her for a while, but she would never indulge it. Zach was her safety and her future. The life she had left behind could be allowed no significance, because she had gained what she had sought – security and wealth. This was not a play in three acts, though; this was a charade she would need to perform well until the day he died. He was thirty years older than she was. All she required was patience, humour and one other important element – the distraction embodied by his daughter.

Scars from the past ached, and she pressed a palm into her right side. The disfigurement of her lower body was officially attributed to surgery. Before she had learned to compose herself and take silent charge, she had spoken her mind, had been battered and stabbed by a man who had supposedly loved her. Aware that she now lived with another man of uncertain temperament, she had laid her plans well. No longer a secretary, no longer the dancer, she was determined to make the best of Zachary Spencer. He was an unpleasant man. She would cope.

The door crashed inward. 'Denis? Are you there?' Kate drew breath before repeating the call.

Denis descended the stairs. 'I think I'm there,' he said. 'I was there when I looked a minute ago, but I'm here now, aren't I? Shall I go back there, then I'll be there?'

Kate tried to frown, but failed. 'Listen, you daft lummox. I can't do nothing with him. He's dug his heels in and won't fettle. It's like the horse and the water – he won't shift.'

Denis did not need the name of the 'him'. 'What's the matter?'

'Says he's not going, says he's no intention of wearing a suit, says the shirt I bought him's too tight at the neck. I'm going to kill him if he doesn't shape. Will you come and deal with him?'

'What can I do that you can't? You're his wife – I'm only a neighbour.'

Kate nodded several times. 'He'll listen to you. You're a man.'

'That still doesn't tell me what to do, though, does it? Shall I anaesthetize him? Knock him out? Fetch an ambulance? I know how he feels. I'd sooner sit knitting fog than spend three or four hours up yon. Send Agnes. She'll shift him. She's even shifted her granddad a few times, and that's like moving the Isle of Man.' He shouted up the stairwell. 'Agnes? Go and dress Albert, will you?'

Agnes appeared at the top of the flight. 'I've had trouble enough fastening my own frock – it fitted last week when I bought it. Anyway, I can't dress a man. It wouldn't be right.'

'I've got him into the trousers,' said Kate. 'You'll not see him naked. I wouldn't let that happen to my worst enemy. There's enough shocks in life without seeing my Albert in his birthday suit. Bad enough me having to put up with it. Just finish him off, Agnes,' she begged.

'What with?' asked Denis. 'Arsenic?'

Kate folded her arms. 'If necessary, yes. We can prop him up on a chair in a corner and say he's not well. We can order the gravestone tomorrow and I'll lay on a ham tea for the funeral. Stubborn as a mule, he is.'

Agnes sat on the top stair. 'Why don't we all go somewhere else? Please? I don't know which knife to use for what.'

'You don't need to,' said Kate. 'You'll be eating stood up. It's a buffet. Bits of stupid things on bits of stupid biscuits to start with, then salads and all kinds of meat – for God's sake, help me.'

Agnes rose to her feet. She was grinning broadly, because she was looking at herself and Denis in forty years' time. Kate and Albert were happy. They had celebrated their ruby anniversary and they were still happy. Until it came to suits. Dressing up was not Albert's idea of fun, and Denis was much the same. 'All right,' she said resignedly. 'But I'm promising nothing.'

'Fair enough.' Kate sank into a chair. 'I'm exhausted and we still haven't had the kick-off.'

After knocking, Agnes entered the cottage next door. Albert, in vest and trousers, was hiding behind the *Bolton Evening News*. 'Hey, you,' she began. 'Stand up, get rid of the reading matter and put your clothes on. You're driving Kate out of her mind.'

He folded the paper. 'Then she's not far to travel, has she?'

'If your wife's crackers, you've sent her that way. Now, get dressed or Denis'll do it for you. You've got five minutes. No use fighting it, Albert.'

He glared at her. 'I didn't ask for no bloody party, did I? I'm all right with me telly and the wireless. From the start, I told her I didn't want to go.'

'You'd let her go on her own, then? Four minutes and twenty seconds, you've got now.'

'She works there – she's used to it.'

Agnes sat down. 'Right. Remember my grandfather – he was on the telly with his houses?'

He nodded.

'He'll be there. Like you, he'll moan every inch of the way. Like you, he'll not want to go. And we have to put up with him all night, because he'll be sleeping over with his wife in our house.'

'What's that got to do with the price of fish?'

'Well, he's thinking of buying Bamber Cottage. If and when he does, he'll be looking for an apprentice.'

'And?'

'And you can apply. Get in first, get to know him and Eva, and you'll be working out of the weather and with my Pop.'

'I can't be an apprentice at my age.'

'You can. If Pop likes you, that is. He won't even meet you if you carry on sitting on the shelf like cheese at fourpence. What's up with you, anyway? Grown man, won't get dressed, carrying on like a five-year-old in a tantrum. Ridiculous.' She tapped a foot. 'Come on – the baby'll be due at this rate. Just do as you're told, because you are outnumbered.'

Sighing dramatically, Albert did as he was bidden. She tidied his collar, straightened the tie, examined his shoes. 'Right,' she said. 'You'll pass as human as long as you stay in the shade.'

The four friends made their reluctant way to the big house. Given a choice, each of them would have been otherwise engaged, but the judge had spoken. Or his wife had spoken. Whatever, they had to go.

Helen trembled, but the brandy remained in its container. She didn't need it, because Louisa would be there, and Louisa would look after her. James Taylor, the balding eagle, had also been invited to the party, but Helen had been prepared for him. Louisa had the answers; Louisa was Helen's prop.

'Tell him to bugger off,' Louisa had said. 'You're out of his league now. Time you started sticking up for yourself. You don't want him, you don't need him – just say so.'

From her bedroom window, Helen watched caterers carrying in the last of the food and drink. She didn't know how many people were coming, but she wasn't looking forward to the event. James Taylor had telephoned several times. Telephones were easier than face-to-face meetings. She had to get rid of him tonight, and he would probably run to Father with his tale of woe.

She sat down and thought about her stepmother. Married young to a man who had turned into a murderous monster, Louisa had escaped with her life, without a spleen and with one savable kidney. After four weeks in hospital, she had gone home, had sat, had made her decision. She had recently married a man who was worth divorcing. 'Only the very rich and the very poor can afford divorce,' she had advised Helen. 'The very rich don't miss a few thousand, while the poor have nothing to lose.'

She was wise. Zachary Spencer did not figure in his wife's emotions – he was just a piece of scaffolding designed to support her. If the marriage failed, there would be a decent settlement. As delicately as possible, Helen had asked about the intimate side of the marriage, had received the reply, 'I close my eyes and think of Gregory Peck.' Louisa was brave. She probably recognized Helen's vulnerability because it echoed her own past. 'But she is more Charlotte Lucas than I am,' Helen whispered. Austen's Charlotte had married a fool; Louisa had fastened herself to a bank balance; the fictional character and the living woman had both married for safety.

Was James Taylor to be Helen's safety? She thought not. As Louisa had said, if Helen didn't want him, he should be advised to bugger off. A smile tilted the corners of Helen's mouth. She would have loved to own the guts to scream those two words into a crowded room, but she would never get that far. Denis. A part of her still wanted and needed him. He continued to occupy her dreams, but she could never have him. Soon, Denis would be a father; Helen Spencer would probably be the eternal virgin.

The dreams about Denis came less frequently these days, but the other nightmare remained. She always woke in a sweat, always tried to piece together what she had seen while asleep, always failed. It was a noisy scenario, terrifying and intense. And she could remember no details. Louisa made up for the dreams, because Louisa had both feet planted squarely on terra firma. But Helen wished the night terrors would abate.

She stood and looked in the mirror. Underneath a deceptively simple dove grey dress, she wore the silk underwear she had bought during her silly phase. Her hair had been styled by Louisa, who had also applied cosmetics in muted tones. Helen knew that she had never looked as pretty as she did this evening, yet she feared company. An outer shell of acceptability would never completely shore up an injured soul. She did not possess Louisa's strength of character and she probably never would.

Cars began to arrive. Her father and stepmother would greet the guests, but Louisa had asked Helen to be present. 'This is your home, too. Let people know who you are.' Her home? According to her father, she deserved nothing, simply because she had failed to be male.

She touched up her lipstick, checked her hose for ladders, picked up a glittering evening bag. But she drank no brandy.

Dressed in their best, Eva and Fred were taking the opportunity to have a second look at Bamber Cottage. Detached, it stood in a large garden that would easily house a shed big enough for Fred's business. The house itself was not oversized; between them, they would be able to keep it in decent order. 'It's that quiet, I'll not know what to do with meself,' said Eva. 'No buses, one little shop, the same people every day.'

'If you don't want it, we won't have it,' Fred told her. 'It's your shop that'll be paying for it, so the decision's yours, too.'

'We'd live longer up here,' she said. 'And Agnes is near.'

'She is. She's near and she's bossy.'

Eva laughed. 'She can see straight past you, if that's what you mean. And I'm not going through what she went through – sawdust and paint. You get that shed built before we come. There's no room for your trankle-ments in the house – I don't want to see even one screwdriver. Do you hear?'

'Yes, miss.'

'And I'll want a proper washing line.' In her head, she carried a wonderful picture of snow-white sheets blowing freely against a background of greenery. 'I've never had country-aired clothes. We can plant flowers, too. Is there room for a greenhouse as well? I could grow me own tomatoes.'

Fred smiled. She had made up her mind and they both knew it.

The owner asked whether their mortgage was arranged. Eva, in a moment of pure pleasure, held her head high and her stomach as far in as she could manage without girders. 'We won't be having one of those,' she replied. 'We are already owners of property.'

The owners of property made their offer on the spot and it was accepted. They wandered off in the direction of Skirlaugh Rise, saw the house at the top and paused for thought. 'I'll never get there,' Eva moaned. 'It's too steep. By the time I get to that house, everybody else will be on their way home.'

'Take it slowly,' Fred advised. 'You'll get used to walking more once we live here. And we won't be going to Lambert House every day, will we?' Cars were passing them. 'Shall I thumb a lift?'

Eva shook her head. She was a big woman and there probably wasn't enough room in a normal-sized vehicle. 'No, we'll walk it. If it takes me till Christmas, I'll get there.' At snails' pace, the couple began the ascent to the top of the Rise. Fred wanted to kick himself – if he'd had an ounce of sense, he would have catered for this situation. When they were halfway up, they paused for a rest, though Eva, who was still forced to bear her own weight, got no benefit from stopping.

By the time they reached the front door of Lambert House, she was in a state of total disarray, face damped by sweat, skin reddened from exertion, ankles swollen like a pair of balloons.

Agnes flew to her side and ushered her into a downstairs bathroom. 'Sit,' she ordered, pointing to a wicker chair. She bathed the poor woman's face in cold water, pressed a damp towel against her neck, did her best to straighten Eva's powder blue wedding suit. It took over half an hour to achieve a condition in which Eva was sufficiently composed to join the party.

By that time, war had broken out.

At first, it was easy to keep away from the dreaded man. Helen, as deputy hostess, circulated and made the best she could of her conversational abilities. All the time, she could feel his eyes boring into her flesh, but she kept travelling about the room, since a moving target was reputed to be more difficult to hit. While she had improved in appearance, he had not. He was ungainly, ugly, disgusting. She could not embrace Louisa's theory of thinking about a film star – if this man touched her, she would scream.

The scream was meant to be silent, but it was far from that. When he stopped her for the third time, she eyed him sternly. 'Leave me alone,' she said quietly.

He blinked and swallowed, the protruding Adam's

apple moving like a buried mole beneath a stretch of sun-deadened lawn. Her flesh crawled with a million invisible ants and she stepped away from him. Unfortunately, she reversed into a waitress bearing platters. Food was spattered everywhere and she felt the colour rising in her cheeks. He had done this; why would he not leave her be?

The silliness happened then. She felt very much as she had during the Denis episode – detached from herself, yet deeply disturbed. Anger rose within her. It was a fury too hot to be contained and too strong for the current small crisis. The room disappeared and became silent. She was alone with the balding eagle. He had a great future, terrible skin and a horrible nose. He wanted her to be his biddable wife – grateful, obedient, unquestioning. He wanted to be her father all over again – another great dictator.

As her hand came up to slap his face into eternity, the waitress stopped scrabbling about on the floor, retreating to a safer area. The room became truly silent. Helen's slap, fuelled by emotions for which she would never account, reverberated around the large area. She was alone with him. Echoes from the bad dream bounced around in the caverns of her brain. Helen wasn't anywhere. She simply existed. As did James Taylor.

The man with the great future staggered back, a hand to his reddened cheek.

'Leave me alone,' she shouted. 'I don't want you near me, don't even like you.'

Louisa dashed to Helen's side, but although she tugged on her arm, she remained unnoticed.

'Father chose you for me. He thought I would be grateful. Now, bugger off out of my house and out of my life. My father never got one thing right in his life, but you are the ugliest of the man's mistakes.'

The mist began to clear. As if waking from sleep, Helen looked around at all the people in the room. Something had just happened. A burst of applause drifted through from the hallway where several lawyers had gathered to snort and chortle like honking geese. Why were they clapping? What had she missed?

Zachary arrived at her other side. 'Go to your room,' he snapped.

Helen began to laugh. She wasn't five years old, wasn't a child to be punished. 'No,' she answered clearly. By this time, she knew where she was. Something had happened, and she was at the core of it. What would people think? Did she care?

The gloves were off. Zachary Spencer, feet covered in caviar and face aglow with dismay, did not know what to do. Another ripple of offstage applause disturbed him even further. Who were those invisible chaps? Did they not realize that they were in the house of a judge?

James Taylor turned on his heel and left.

Louisa came to the rescue. 'Helen, there is food on your dress. Come with me and let's see what can be done.'

All the way upstairs, Helen whispered, 'Something happened. What happened? What did I do?' Yet she could only rejoice at the memory of her father's expression of confusion.

In the bedroom she shared with Helen's father, Louisa led her stepdaughter through recent events. 'You told him to bugger off, but you did it very loudly. Some sort of small riot exploded in the hall – your father's enemies were pleased. You blamed your father.'

Helen swallowed. 'I did what?'

'You said he had encouraged Taylor to court you. And you were very loud about the whole business.'

Helen's hands flew up to cover her face. What was happening to her? First, she had pursued the odd-job man; second, she had disgraced herself and her father in front of company. 'My secret world is breaking through,' she muttered. Part of her continued triumphant, yet the idea of being out of control made her panic. It was an attack of panic that had triggered the episode . . .

'What?'

'When I was a child, I lived in my head. That was the secret world. I used to act in front of the mirror and speak my lines out loud. I'm doing it now as an adult and without the mirror. Am I crazy?'

Louisa stared at her friend. She probably was slightly insane after a lifetime spent in the company of a cold father, no mother to soften the impact. 'You're tired,' she replied eventually. 'This event is probably too big for you and I apologize.'

'The room disappeared. The whole party melted away. There was just me and that horrible man. Father will force me to leave now.'

'Don't worry about that, petal. I can manage him, especially now – I'm pregnant.'

Helen blinked several times. This was the moment in which she should begin to hate Louisa and her child. Helen might live in the house for the rest of her life, but a son would inherit everything. 'It has to be a boy,' Helen said.

'I know.'

'Girls get locked in their room. Girls don't count.'

Louisa knew about that, too.

Whatever the situation, Helen could not manage to

hate this woman. For the first time, there was meaning to life, there was fun, there was conversation. 'We'll look after each other, Louisa.'

The pact was made there and then. No matter what happened in the future, Helen and Louisa were a team. There were two of them; there was only one of him. That special cleverness known only to women would need to be employed. Without any word on the subject, each knew that the other disliked Zachary Spencer. United by near-contempt, they intended to thrive in his shadow.

Louisa approached her husband. 'She is raving,' she said. 'If her temperature gets any worse, we must send for the doctor. She scarcely knows what happened, bless her. The fever made her act out of character, my love.'

Bless her? He could have killed her quite cheerfully. 'Did you hear what she said about me? Did you?'

Louisa nodded.

'I cannot allow her to stay under my roof when she slanders me in that fashion.'

His wife walked away and asked the string quartet to stop playing. Then she raised her voice and spoke to the gathering. 'Miss Spencer is not well,' she said. 'She has a fever, so I shall look in on her from time to time. She begs you all to forgive her bad behaviour, but she was not herself this evening. Carry on,' she told the musicians.

Albert and Fred, in a corner as predicted, complained to each other. How much longer would they be forced to listen to the wailing of cats? 'And this bloody collar's strangling me, as well,' moaned Albert.

Fred sympathized. 'They call that music? I'd sooner

listen to the BBC's hurry-up-and-get-to-work programme. When can we go home?'

'Not till Kate says so,' answered Albert. 'My Kate is
a force to be reckoned with. I'd sooner argue with
Winston Churchill, bless him.'

Fred studied the room. 'To make a doll's house of
this, I'd need a bloody plane hangar, let alone a shed.'

Albert grasped the cue. 'When you move to Bamber
Cottage, will you give me a try as assistant? I love
farming, but I'm getting on in years. I'm good with my
hands.' He held up fingers thicker than Cumberland
sausage. 'I might have big hands, but I'm good at
carpentry.'

'All right, you're on.' Fred spat on his right hand,
waited for Albert to do the same, and sealed their
gentlemen's agreement.

Lucy and Agnes were waiting for Mags. They had
prepared themselves for change, but were completely
taken aback by the confident and beautiful woman who
joined them just after nine o'clock. 'Oh, my God, oh,
my God, oh, my—'

'Shut up, Lucy,' said Mags. 'And close your mouth –
there's a bus coming.'

Agnes simply stared. The nose was right. Make-up
was perfect, because its wearer had been taught in London; the dress – black and sequined – fitted perfectly.
Apart from her nose, Mags's biggest transformation was
her hair. Feathered into her face, it remained shoulder-
length, and was now various shades of blonde and
brown. 'My God,' she whispered.

'Not you as well.' Mags laughed. 'Give God a rest
and get me some food – I am starving.'

While Agnes went to fill a plate, Lucy looked Mags
over. 'Definitely a desirable residence,' she declared after

her second tour. 'But still detached? Aren't you going to become a semi or a link-terraced?'

'No idea.'

'It's a miracle. Not that you were ugly before,' Lucy added hastily, 'only now, you're—'

'Stop lying. There was me and my nose and the nose was bigger than both of us. The town wasn't big enough for any of it, so one of us had to go. And it wasn't going to be me.' Mags took a glass of wine from a passing waiter. 'What's up with old Sourpuss? Looks like he lost a quid and found a tanner.'

Lucy glanced at the host. 'His daughter's what's up, that's what. She told that scrawny-necked Taylor to bog off, then blamed her father. You could have heard a feather drop, let alone a pin. She's gone upstairs, dragged there by her stepmother. That's the stepmother over there – winning smile, high heels, diamond jewellery.'

Mags looked. 'She's younger than his daughter.'

'Yup.'

'What's he up to?'

Lucy shrugged. 'What are any of them up to? They were cheering outside when Miss Spencer insulted her dad. I'm told that one fellow did handstands. When it was over, she looked round the room as if she'd been sleepwalking. There's something wrong with that woman. She could even be on mind-bending drugs. I don't trust her – don't ask me why.'

Mags wondered whether the something wrong might be brandy, but she held the thought inside. 'This isn't exactly San Francisco, Lucy. I don't think she's a pill-popper.'

Agnes returned and started all over again. She couldn't believe the transformation. Did they do plastic surgery on gobs, could they quieten Pop? How much did it cost and had it hurt? How long had Mags been bandaged and where had she bought the dress?

'Enough,' ordered Mags yet again. 'I've got this carry-on at work, at home, in the street, now here. I'm still me. However I look outwardly, I've got the same history as I had before London. The thing was, I could walk about in the street with a bandaged face and two black eyes there and nobody stared. London's like that – it doesn't care. I didn't dare get as far as Carnaby Street and I never saw a show, but I went for short walks and was ignored.'

'That's because they're hardened,' said Lucy. 'Everybody gets beaten up about once a month, so you'd have fit in well with all your cuts and bruises. But looking at you now, I'd say it's lock-up-your-husband time, because you are sensational.' She planted a kiss on her friend's cheek, then wiped away the damage bequeathed by Strawberry Glaze lipstick.

Agnes was looking at the judge. 'He's like a volcano preparing to erupt,' she said. 'No wonder everybody hates him. Imagine what it would be like to have that for a father. No wonder she kicked up a fuss.'

Lucy thought about it. 'She looked as if she didn't know where she was or what she was doing. Like I said before, she reminded me of a sleepwalker. There's something wrong with her.'

Mags swallowed a mouthful of caviar. 'Bloody hell,' she cursed. 'It's like do-yourself-good cod liver oil with no orange juice to follow. I can't imagine what all the fuss is about. Fish eggs? They can keep them.' She straightened her skirt. 'I'm going to find her,' she announced.

'You can't go wandering round Judge Spencer's house,' Lucy exclaimed.

Mags grinned. 'Watch me,' she said. 'Remember, there's a new girl in town and she follows her nose. She does what she damned well pleases.'

The two other girls eyed each other. 'She's letting her hair down,' said Lucy.

'Yes, but her hair's not letting *her* down,' answered Agnes. 'I think life's just beginning for Mags. She has unleashed a monster. Come on – let's get some more wine. And we'd better warn the men that Cinderella's looking for that glass slipper . . .'

There were many bedrooms, but Mags chose the one with double doors. After knocking gently, she turned one of the handles to find Helen Spencer staring into space. She was seated on a sofa near a window, clearly deep in thought. 'Louisa?' Helen asked as soon as the door was closed again. 'I feel awful.'

'No, I'm not Louisa. It's Mags. Remember? George and Lucy Henshaw's wedding reception at the Pack Horse in June? We were planning an escape route.'

Helen tilted her head. 'But you're not the same woman.'

'New nose.' Mags crossed the room and sat next to Helen. 'New nose, new hair, new clothes, new me. I'd saved for years and was thinking of buying myself a little house, but vanity prevailed. I had the operation.'

'You look wonderful.'

'Thank you.' This poor creature looked far from wonderful, thought Mags. She looked absolutely worn out and disappointed with life. 'Your dad remarried, then?'

'Yes. She's Louisa and she's already pregnant.'

'Ah.'

'But that's not why I became ... upset. I seem to have had some sort of episode – I think I've had one or two before. Were you there tonight?'

'No. I arrived late, but I heard about it.'

'I think I forgot where I was and gave James Taylor both barrels. Now, I can remember some of what I said, but I scarcely understood what had happened while I was downstairs. And I insulted my father. He is not a man who takes insults. Louisa is a good woman – she helped me up the stairs and said she'll take care of everything, including him.'

'Hardly a wicked stepmother, then?'

'The opposite. She's kind to me. I feel I have let her down, too. She so desperately wanted this party to be a success. I ruined it for her.'

Mags took Helen's hand. 'Please don't be offended – are you drinking?'

'No. I have scarcely touched a drop since Louisa came. She's fun. I don't want to lose her. He'll send me away, make me live elsewhere. You don't know him ...' The nightmare knew him. How could she not have realized that the dream contained her father? She remembered few details of the almost nightly torment, yet she knew he was part of the plot.

Mags didn't know what to say. It was suddenly apparent that her own solution to life's problems had proved an easy option; a new nose was not the answer for Helen Spencer. A new nose was easy. It was money and pain, no more. Helen's difficulties were more radical. How might a person acquire a new soul, a centre of self cleaned of scars from the past? How could anyone help in this case?

'I am so miserable, Mags.'

'I know.'

'He's quite nasty without being angry. Once he loses his temper, my father becomes one of Earth's elemental Forces – I swear the sky darkens. He may even be one of the four horsemen come to warn us of the end of the world.'

'Leave home.'

Helen shook her head. She was her father's daughter, and she recognized in herself the stubbornness displayed by him when he was cornered. He was going to have to force her out. Louisa would fight Helen's corner. But why should Louisa be upset, especially in her condition? 'I haven't the backbone to start all over again, Mags. In truth, I don't feel steady enough to live the isolated life.'

'These turns you have – what form do they take?' Mags chided herself inwardly – she sounded like a bloody doctor.

Helen shrugged. 'I am – well – I imagine myself in love with a married man. At the worst point in that scenario, I chased him, told him I loved him – I was all over the place. Tonight? Oh, I don't know.' Tonight had been much, much worse, because a piece of the bad dream had broken through. 'There was a noise,' she whispered. The noise had been a part of the dream. 'I don't know,' she repeated.

'Yes, you do,' Mags urged gently. 'Tell me. The noise was a waitress dropping plates and trays. Why did you turn on the balding eagle?'

After taking a deep breath, Helen relived all she remembered of her real world. She spoke of phone calls, of persistence, of politeness. 'After half a dozen refusals, any man should accept that a woman isn't interested. Tonight was his big chance – or so he believed.'

'And?'

'And he collared me. I avoided him successfully for well over half an hour, but he would not be denied. Then it happened.'

Mags waited.

'It was as if I were alone with him after the noise happened. I knew my father had chosen him for me, because he told me so at that wedding. James Taylor almost became my father tonight. He was yet another piece of damage inflicted by a man who has never forgiven me for being female. There are many witnesses to the rest of it. I screamed at him and I think I hit him. The thought of hitting him makes me sick, because I can't stand the idea of any physical contact with him. It isn't just his appearance. Inside, he's a damaged person – it takes one to know one. He bolsters himself, brags about a big future. He is his own favourite topic and that's my father all over again.'

Mags stroked Helen's hand.

'My biggest fear is that I, too, am my father all over again. I am so angry, Mags. Anger is all that sustains me. The only time I get anywhere near happiness is when I am with Louisa. If I lose control, then I lose everything. My small amount of control is all I have and I can't afford to have it disappear.'

'Helen?'

'What?'

'You need other friends close at hand.'

'There is no one.'

'But there is someone. There's Agnes. She is the best and most loyal person you could wish to meet. She's funny, clever, supportive and just at the bottom of the Rise.'

Helen dropped her chin. How could she be a friend

195

to someone whose husband she had tried to seduce? She continued to want Denis, although the feelings for him no longer consumed her. 'I don't know.'

'Think about it. You could do a lot worse than Agnes Makepeace. She hasn't had it easy, you know. Her mother died when Agnes was born, so the grandparents raised her. When they got old, she looked after them. Her nan died of cancer, her granddad is a handful – she nursed him after a stroke – yet Agnes manages to see the best in life. We're all hurt, Helen. A person would need the hide of a rhino to get through this world without pain.'

'I'll think about it.'

Forced to be content with a half-promise, Mags left Helen to her own devices. Descending the staircase deep in thought, she decided that Helen was probably ill. The self-effacing librarian had been kept down for too long, and the inner woman was fighting for her place in the world. It was understandable; it was also rather unnerving, because Helen was not thinking in a straight enough line.

Agnes joined her at the bottom of the stairs. 'Is she all right? I still can't get over how brilliant you look.'

'She needs a doctor. A head doctor. That bloody father of hers has messed her up to the point where she doesn't cope with life at all. Agnes, I want you to help her.'

Agnes swallowed. 'That's all I need. Thanks a lot, mate. If she needs a psychiatrist, what the hell can I do?'

'You can listen.'

Agnes thought about that. The woman upstairs had recently made a beeline for Denis. Denis worked at Lambert House – must Lambert House claim an even bigger portion of his life? There was a baby coming,

Pop and Eva would move into the village soon, and Denis had had quite enough of Miss Helen Spencer. Agnes decided to hang for the full sheep – Denis would understand. 'She's been making passes at my husband, Mags.'

'Ah.'

'What do you mean by "ah"? She's more than three sheets to the wind, is that one. Glenys Timpson heard her trying to get off with Denis – and you want me to help the damned woman? Not on your flaming nelly.'

'Agnes—'

'Sorry, love. She was walking round in a nightdress for days, windows wide open, playing the music he loves. He's fond of her, feels sorry for her, but she wanted more. A bloody sight more.'

'She can't help it, Agnes.'

'Can't she?'

'No.'

'Well, I can help it. I can help her stay away from my husband. You're asking too much of me, Mags.'

'She's aware that she's done wrong, but she's . . . Oh, I don't know. It's like she's two different people. Something triggers her and she changes. Take tonight. She lost herself. I can't explain it, but she becomes something else and all hell lets loose in her head. It's that bugger's fault.' She inclined her head in the direction of their host. 'Helen was born a girl, and to him that's unforgivable. He's a nasty creature.'

The nasty creature led his new wife into the office. Determined to be careful because of her condition, he sat her down before beginning his homily. Helen had never shown him any respect. He had supported her, sheltered, educated and housed her, but he had never received any thanks.

'All children take their parents for granted,' came her swift response. 'Every father in the world would agree with you, darling. But you must not throw her out. She is too frail to become a wanderer. Let me deal with it.'

He carried on passing sentence. His daughter had always been wilful and difficult. She had taken poor advantage of her education and was content to follow the lazy path via the library. She never spoke to him. She made up stories about other lawyers and how they hated him.

Louisa kept a poker face during this section of the monologue. The cheers in support of Helen still echoed in her mind; this was, indeed, a much despised man.

With fat fingers gripping lapels, he strutted up and down like the great prosecuting counsel trying to convince a jury. While she was the jury, Louisa would never be won over. 'She's lonely.'

'Her own fault,' he boomed. 'There's a perfectly decent and successful man chasing her, but is she satisfied? No, she is not.'

'She's lonely for friends, not for a husband.'

'Then she should make friends. God knows she meets enough people in her silly little job.'

Louisa groaned inwardly. Were it not for the likes of Helen Spencer, literature would be available only to the precious few. It was not a silly little job – it was a vital service. He rambled on, warming to his subject with every inch of the carpet he threatened to render threadbare.

She rose to her feet. 'I have no wish to be contentious, sweetheart, but if Helen is forced to leave this house, I shall have to accompany her and stay with her until she is settled. She is unwell.'

'What?' he roared. Had he made another huge mistake? Was this one going to be like the first wife, a moaner and a bolter? Not that the first had actually left, but she had threatened . . .

'She's in a state, Zach. She doesn't know whether she's coming or going – it's a nervous condition.'

'My family doesn't have nervous conditions.' He banged a fist on the desk. 'If she has a nervous illness, it's from her witch of a mother. Does she need to go into an asylum?'

'No.' Not yet, Louisa said inwardly. But if Helen ever did need a hospital, he would be the cause of it. It would be easy to dislike him. But she remembered the keywords – safety and wealth. 'A move might well destroy her. She would have nowhere to turn.'

'If she went into a mental hospital, it might quieten my colleagues in the wake of tonight's fiasco.'

'She hates the man,' said Louisa.

'Who is she to pick and choose?'

'She's human, not an animal to be mated with a chosen sire.'

Zachary Spencer glared at his wife. She was a good wife. She had never refused him, had never rejected him. The bad apple in this house was the one upstairs. 'I am not pleased with you, Louisa,' he said.

'I know and I am sorry. But that woman is your flesh and blood. She needs help and I will not turn my back on her. I look at her and I see you. To send her away would be unbearably cruel, and that is why I would have to go with her and help her to settle.'

His shoulders sagged, reminding her of a balloon

with the air escaping. She supposed that she was seeing a fair illustration of the saying about wind being taken from sails. No longer a galleon, he dropped into his leather chair. 'As you wish,' he said behind gritted teeth. 'But one more episode and she goes. I don't care where she goes, but I will not allow a madwoman to share a house with my son.'

Louisa nodded. She was an incubator, no more than that.

After escaping from the lion's den, Louisa fled upstairs to comfort her stepdaughter with the news.

But Helen astonished her. 'I think I want to leave,' she said.

'Helen – I have just been through hell and high water to—'

'I know, and I love you for it. But there are cottages in the village. I'd still be near you. You could visit me and I could come here while he's out. If he goes away, I'll stay with you.'

The idea of being alone with Zachary Spencer was not palatable. Panic seared through Louisa's body. She had known all along that Helen needed her; she now realized that the reverse was also true. 'Think before you act,' she advised.

'I will. Yes, I definitely will.'

'He's not been a good father, Helen. Some people are not cut out for parenthood.'

'He would have been good to a son.'

'Would he?'

The two women stared at each other. Had their relationship required a further application of cement, it would have arrived in this moment. The reject and the breeding machine were completely bound together.

'Cocoa?' asked Louisa.

'Yes, please. Louisa?'

'What?'

'Thanks. You are good to me.'

Louisa smiled and left the room. Life was not going to be easy in this house. The least troublesome option would have been to allow him his way, but Louisa feared for her stepdaughter. Helen needed a friend. As long as Louisa remained alive, she would have one.

Chapter Eight

Denis, a man of even temperament, slammed the front door.

Agnes ran through from the kitchen, a journey that required no more than four paces. 'Are you all right, love?'

Was he all right? Was he heck as all right. 'Put that kettle on, Agnes. It's been a foul weather day and there'll be more to come.' He threw down his canvas work bag and dropped into a chair. Anyone who knew Denis Makepeace was of the opinion that he was not easily riled; when he did lose his patience, the results could be almost meteorological.

Agnes did as she was asked, her eyes scanning a bright blue sky with just a few cotton wool clouds decorating its surface. There had been no rain and no thunder, but there had been Judge Zachary Spencer trying to save face after that disastrous party. Never a pleasant man, he had probably given her beloved husband one hell of a time. Poor Denis deserved better than this.

He took the tea. 'Thanks,' he sighed. 'Let me have ten minutes, then I'll tell you. My brain's all over the place.' He shook his head. 'Sometimes, I wonder whether there's any sanity left in this world.'

His head spun. Helen had paced through the day like a caged tiger, back and forth across lawns, round the outside of the house, in and out of the copse. She had popped up all over the place. Sometimes, he had wondered whether an identical twin had escaped from one of the attics. Officially, she had a summer cold and could not get in to work. In truth, she was a mixture of fear and fury, was every inch the caged wild animal.

Wife the Second was in a state, too. She had spent her day running between the judge and his daughter, clearly attempting to negotiate a treaty with more clauses than Utrecht. 'Bloody madhouse,' whispered Denis between sips of strong tea. 'They want their flaming daft heads knocking together.' But he couldn't be the one to do it. No one emerged unscathed from a confrontation with Judge Zachary Spencer.

It seemed that Helen Spencer had threatened to rent one of the Skirlaugh Fall cottages, an event that would surely unseat her dad. He probably wanted her well out of the way while he prepared his kingdom for a son and heir; the village was not far enough. The judge didn't want her on his doorstep, couldn't stand the idea of close neighbours accusing him of throwing his daughter out of Lambert House. Pride came before a fall? Had that been the case, the judge should have no intact bones in his whole body, because he had pride enough for ten.

The most panic-stricken of them all had been Louisa. On the odd occasion when Denis had got close to her, he had seen terror in her face. She was frightened of being alone with the old man. The judge's daughter had clearly proved to be a distraction for Louisa, and she dreaded losing the balm provided by this unexpected friendship. Denis, caught in the middle of hostilities, had washed cars, swept paths, weeded gardens. No one had spoken directly to him. Helen was possibly seeking to reinstate the necessary distance between employer and employee, a move for which Denis would be grateful beyond measure. As the day had matured, so had she. The walking had stopped and she had returned to the house.

Agnes sat down. 'Well?'

He sighed heavily. 'Just after dinner – lunch to that lot up yon – I was passing his office window with my wheelbarrow. The window was wide open. The boss was yelling like a madman. He was screaming at Helen, asking her why she wanted him to go easy on Harry Timpson. She gave him an answer, all right. She said, "Because I can" – just came out with it. I don't think she's even scared of you finding out about what never happened – she's well past that now. So she's doing it for devilment. Come to think, she's well past everything. She doesn't care – opens her gob without thinking first.'

Kate knocked and entered. 'Blood and stomach pills,' was her opening salvo, 'they want shooting, the lot of 'em. Miss Helen's riding high, told him he's made her ill, even invited him to bugger off and die. I'm surprised, because it looked like she was going out of her way to be nice to him for a while. Mrs Spencer can't cope – she'll be losing the kiddy if this carries on. I feel like packing it in, Denis. How was your day?'

'The same,' he answered.

Kate complained of untouched meals returning to the kitchen, said she had enough to feed Albert and herself for three days. She continued to moan, citing the noisiness and stupidity of her employers. 'It's a lunatic asylum, that's what. Miss Helen's off her rocker, her dad could do with hanging out to dry because of all the brandy, and Mrs Spencer deserves none of it.'

Denis agreed. 'But I can't pack the job in, Kate. Me and Agnes need to stay here because of our baby and my chest. You're right, though. They're madder than a bucket of frogs.'

Agnes listened intently. 'Is there an easy job I could do, Kate? I know you've been looking for folk. Something part time – I could clean the silver and do a bit of ironing.'

Denis tried to put his foot down. He wasn't having his wife in the same enclosure as Spencer and company. 'You're having a baby,' he informed her.

'Thanks for telling me, Denis. I'd never have realized. Look, Mags had a word with me at that party. She reckons Miss Spencer needs a friend nearby.'

'She's got her stepmother,' answered Denis. 'They're like twins.'

'Oh, be quiet.' Agnes frowned, obviously thinking.

'I could find you something light,' offered Kate. 'But she did make a play for your husband. She's a couple of halfpennies short of a bob. How would she treat you? I mean, she's at home a lot these days. I reckon she'll be leaving that library soon. At this rate, it won't be long before they all say she's unfit for work.'

'I don't want her living down here in the village.' Denis drained his cup. 'Bad enough being up at Lambert all day – I don't fancy falling over her every time I leave my own house. I'd feel hunted.'

'Then I'll work a couple of days starting tomorrow. Let's see if I can get near her and persuade her to stay at home.' Agnes glared at her beloved. 'Don't look at me like that – I still have a mind of my own, you know.

Being pregnant isn't a full time occupation. I can sit and peel veg, clean silver, polish shoes. I don't have to stop in this house all the while, and Kate could do with a bit of support. So could Miss Spencer.'

'But she's mad.' Denis stood up. 'You don't know what she's capable of – none of us knows yet. She has turns, Agnes. What if she has a turn and that turn's a turn against you?'

Agnes glanced at Kate. 'Hasn't he got a lovely way with words? Kate, you'll have to keep an eye on me, because it's plain I can't look after myself. Get a gun and a couple of silver bullets for when there's a full moon. Oh, and a few garlic flowers. I've got a crucifix somewhere – Nan bought it me last Christmas, God rest her.'

Denis gave up. 'I give up,' he announced.

'Knows when he's beaten,' Agnes advised her neighbour. 'You see, that's where Napoleon and Hitler went wrong – they didn't know when to quit. Marching on Moscow's not a good idea. Next time there's a war, they can have my husband in the planning department. He knows when to give up. I trained him myself.'

Denis shook his head before retreating to the kitchen. He washed lettuce and listened to the two women. They had a goal: Helen should stay where she was, because she had suffered enough and that was her own house, bought and paid for by years of misery. He sliced through corned beef while his wife and his co-worker stabbed at the judge. 'Too big for his boots,' declared Kate.

'Needs a good thump,' agreed Agnes.

Denis found cruet, cutlery and plates, and set two places at the table. Since Agnes would need all her strength, he poured a small bottle of stout into a glass.

She'd be wanting plenty of iron in her blood when she stepped into the valley of the cursed. He paused, then poured a pale ale for himself. It was a hard life and he must not weaken.

Louisa was afraid for Helen. The poor girl had clearly lost her sense of balance, was saying too much to her father and was in danger of becoming a certified lunatic if she didn't calm down. Not that it was a case of calming down at the moment, because Helen was calm. As long as she stayed away from her dad, she was almost rational.

'I'm going,' said Helen for what seemed like the fortieth time.

Louisa grabbed her hand. 'Wait a while,' she begged. There was selfishness in the request, and Louisa wondered how she would have managed without Zach's daughter. Having served her purpose by proving herself fertile, Louisa was now being ignored for much of the time. Her husband slept in his dressing room, using as excuse the opinion that Louisa needed her rest. He spoke infrequently, was distant and dismissive. Left here with only him, Louisa would surely go out of her mind. She and Helen might well finish up sharing a room in some private home for the terribly bewildered. 'Please, please stay. I need you, Helen. This baby will need you.'

'I can't.'

'Of course you can. There are no more shared meals to get through – you cook for yourself here in your own little apartment. You'll hardly see him. You don't need to see him at all if you don't want to.'

Helen turned her head slowly and faced her friend. 'And when I do see him, I'll kill him.'

A shiver ran the length of Louisa's backbone. She had married for security, no more, yet had clung to Helen like a drowning woman clutching a piece of frail flotsam. Helen had made the whole arrangement bearable. If she left . . . Louisa swallowed.

'It's difficult to explain,' Helen said. 'For years, I have avoided him. When I was a child I was ignored, and that neglect shaped me. It's strange. I am lonely, but I don't want anyone to come close. You are a very isolated exception. You are good to me and you make me feel better.'

'Then stay for me.'

Helen half smiled. 'Will you be there to take the knife out of my hand or out of his back?'

'It won't come to that.'

The room darkened. Helen frowned, tried to order her thoughts, failed yet again. There was something she knew, yet she didn't know it. Loud noises – like the clattering of the tray at the party – triggered a memory that was not a memory. Falling in love with Denis had produced a similar effect. There was in her a place she needed to visit, yet she dreaded reaching it. Nothing made sense. Helen, a clear enough thinker, was circling something big, something horrible. It came and went, while she simply became the space it occupied.

'Don't leave me, please.'

Helen looked at her fellow sufferer. Louisa was here in the now time, not in the nightmare, because she shared no history with the man she had married. 'You should have walked away from him. You can't possibly know what you have taken on.'

'He was to be my safety.'

'There is no safety while he breathes.'

Louisa gulped noisily. 'I would be here all by myself.

He doesn't want me, Helen. All he wants is a son. That son will have to follow in his father's footsteps, be successful in all he does.'

'And if you have a girl, you'll have to go through this again and again until he gets his boy.'

In spite of the heat, Louisa shuddered. 'You need to apologize to him.'

'Never.'

'I cannot stay if you go. I'll be homeless, with a child to rear. My first marriage left me with nothing.' She had finally painted in her backcloth, but only for Helen. The judge knew some of it, but Helen was now in full possession of the facts. 'You know what I went through.'

'This time, your scars will be mental. I don't know which is worse – physical damage or psychological destruction. He will wear you down and wear you out, Louisa. He chips away until you have no foundation, no steadiness. Come with me. I have my mother's money. I'll keep you safe.'

That was not the answer, either. Louisa did not feel equipped for yet another fresh start. Her first marriage had been a new beginning, as had the end of that marriage. The relief when her first husband had been carted off to prison had been boundless. Lack of money had driven her away from her secretarial job into the more lucrative area of club cabaret, but the shelf life of stage dancers was a short one, and she had become a teacher of dance. Zach was to have been the final new beginning. After marrying Zach, she should have been truly secure. She wasn't.

'Louisa?'

'Yes?'

'Imagine a life without him. I know you don't love him. My mother probably didn't love him, either. Even criminals often have one or two redeeming features, but my father?' She shrugged. 'He sits on his throne and sends men and women to jail and, because there are no feelings in him, he does it just to punish. He doesn't believe that a thief can reform himself through education and encouragement. My father would have every prisoner in a darkened room with just a mattress, a blanket and a bucket. Those judged as completely beyond the pale he would hang.'

'I know.'

'Then leave.'

'I can't.' An idea was forming in Louisa's tiring brain. 'We could compromise.'

'How?'

'We could stay till the baby is born, let him have the baby—'

'If it's a boy,' spat Helen.

'Yes, all right. Then, when he has what he wants, we can leave. He's a powerful man, Helen. I probably wouldn't get custody of the child anyway, not with the father being top of the legal tree. But don't leave me here while I am pregnant.'

Helen frowned deeply. 'You could give up your child?'

'I would fight to keep it, of course. But I can't go now. You must understand that. Oh, and there's another thing. If you move from the Rise to the Fall, could you bear the pity and concern of your neighbours?'

'I could bear his embarrassment very well.'

'Helen, there would be tongues wagging from here to the courts in Manchester. Yes, he would suffer. But so would you. I believe that you have been punished enough. Stay. Eat his food, use his furniture, let him pay all the bills.'

There followed a long pause before Helen responded. 'If he wants me not to move down the hill to sit on his doorstep like a boil on his nose, he must do one thing.' The one thing was no longer anything to do with Glenys Timpson or the Makepeaces – she was beyond such trivia – but simply to prove her power. 'I want a featherweight sentence for Harry Timpson.' The Timpson man had become a loaded gun for Helen. She needed to prove that she could encroach on her father's territory and even get her own way.

'Then you'll need to stay until after the trial.'

'Yes.'

With that, Louisa was forced to be content. Unhappily, she now faced the prospect of persuading her husband to go easy on a criminal. But she would try. If it meant that Helen would stay, Louisa would attempt the apparently impossible.

It was mayhem. Agnes, standing in the middle of it all, remembered reading about people throwing up their hands in despair, but it was too hot and she couldn't spare the energy. 'It's not a big house, Pop,' she said for the third time.

'Not a big house, love,' echoed Eva.

'I know it's detached and I know there's land, but you'd never get this lot in ten big sheds. I mean, what do you want with half a dozen paraffin heaters? Haven't you sold them on as stock, anyway? What are you planning?'

Fred sighed. 'The new owner of this here shop's

already minted. He won't miss a few heaters. I'll have to warm the shed, won't I? I can't risk good wood going dampish.'

Eva and Agnes stared at each other with near-despair in their eyes. Fred was in one of his squirrel moods and wanted to keep more than he could house. 'I'm going to see Glenys,' snapped Agnes. 'Because if I stay here, I'll wrap these bloody heaters round his neck.' She left the scene. Fred was stubborn, but so was she – it was best for them to be apart for the immediate future.

Glenys opened her door. 'Hello, love,' she said. 'You look like you need a wipe down with a damp cloth.' They sat in the kitchen. 'How's it going?'

Agnes told her ex-neighbour about developments at Lambert House, about Helen's continuing strangeness, about Wife the Second walking about with a face like ten wet Sundays. 'She's not happy.'

'Neither am I.'

Both knew the source of Glenys's unease, but the subject had been aired so often in recent months that it was beyond resurrection.

'It'll be all right,' said Agnes.

'I bloody well hope so.'

They sat with their cups, Agnes musing over her little job at Lambert House, Glenys praying silently for a son who probably didn't deserve to remain free.

'Kate Moores is good company,' offered Agnes to break the quiet.

'And the job gets you out. Are them two moving today?' She jerked her head in the direction of Eva's shop. 'I've seen some comings and goings. I'll miss them, you know.'

'Yes, it's today. That's why I'm here – I've escaped

from the shop. They're trying to get a whale to fit into a sardine tin. The stuff for his shed's already gone, but nobody will ever get past the vestibule in Bamber Cottage if he takes all he wants to take. I mean, who needs four clothes horses?'

'I wouldn't say no.' Glenys poured more tea. 'Have they not measured the house, then measured their furniture?'

'Have they heck as like. He's going off half-cocked as usual. And we can't blame his stroke – he's always been like this. Eva just agrees with everything he says, so she's as daft as he is. They'll never get up the stairs to bed tonight. Fully furnished? They'll be bursting at the seams and Denis will have to sort it all out.'

'I wish I could live up yon,' ventured Glenys.

'Stop where you are, that's my advice. You'd end up working at Lambert House – they can't get enough staff – and that would be a sure and certain way to insanity. I'm only there twice a week and that's plenty.' She replayed in her mind the slamming of doors, the grim atmosphere, the expression on Kate's face whenever the judge came home. 'None of them is happy. Miss Spencer has a face like a squeezed orange most days – nothing left in it, just a dry shell. Denis reckons she's heading straight for the mental hospital. I think he's right – she's not the same two days running. She talks to me, then ignores me. There's something very wrong with her.'

'That's a shame,' said Glenys. 'My Harry thinks the sun shines out of her, but we'd best wait for verdict and sentence, eh?'

Agnes agreed, then left to continue in her role as ignored supervisor.

Fred glanced at her. 'I'm taking two of them heaters.'

The tone was rebellious, putting her in mind of a young schoolboy after a telling-off. 'You never know – we could get a bad winter,' he added.

'Aye, a bad winter,' repeated Eva.

Agnes was past caring. They could leave their furniture on the front lawn if necessary, because he wouldn't listen to reason and, as ever, he needed to learn the hard way. 'I'm going for the bus,' she said, 'because I'm doing no good here. I'll get a bit of shopping in town, then I'll see you up yonder later on. God help Skirlaugh Fall. You'll be parking half your furniture with the neighbours and they won't be best pleased.'

Gratefully, Agnes sank into a seat on the Derby Street bus. Normally, she would have walked the short distance, but heat, pregnancy and Pop were against her. His furniture was stacked against the front of the shop, and it would shortly be stacked yet again all over the garden of Bamber Cottage, but she had tried her best.

After alighting from the bus, Agnes made her way towards the main shopping centre. Rounding a corner, she came face to face with a familiar figure, and she stopped in her tracks. She had taken a job in order to meet and help this woman but had scarcely seen her in the house, and now here was Helen Spencer, out of context and turning pink. 'It's warm,' Agnes said, inwardly kicking herself for stating the blatantly obvious.

'It is.'

'I was just going for a cup of tea,' lied Agnes. 'Would you like to join me?'

So Helen found herself in the company of a not-quite-rival. Already aware that she had never stood a chance with Denis, she now drank tea with his beautiful, pregnant wife.

'You are working at the house occasionally,' she said.

Agnes nodded. 'Mostly sitting down jobs. It's just to keep me occupied till Nuisance is born.' She patted her abdomen. 'I can't do much, but the work gets me out of the house a couple of times a week.'

Helen asked Agnes where she had been.

When the tale had been told, both women were laughing. 'What's going to happen?' Helen asked. 'And how will they cope?'

Agnes shook her head. 'I did my best, but my best wasn't good enough. They're bringing enough blankets to keep the Russian army warm and I never saw so many plates and cups.'

'And the shed?'

'That's for making his doll's houses in.' Agnes noticed that Helen's laughter was shrill, too loud. It came from a woman who probably cried just as easily. Did Helen Spencer live on the cusp, somewhere between hysteria and silent sadness? Did she swing from one to the other easily, because the two extremes were close neighbours? 'I'll have to be getting back. Somebody's going to have to make sense of the mess.'

Helen declared that she had finished for today, as the library was closed this afternoon. 'I'll give you a lift,' she said.

The lift developed into more cups of tea at Agnes's house, followed by the inevitable assault on Bamber Cottage and its soon-to-be occupants. For the first time, Helen had a glimpse of a normal family with its banter, small arguments and jokes. On her part, Agnes realized that Helen Spencer was a clever and humorous woman who was not insane. She was probably emotionally unstable, but she was not out of her mind.

By five o'clock, everyone was exhausted. Between

items of furniture, a small corridor to the kitchen had been achieved, but Eva was not built for small corridors. Agnes, hands on hips, stood in the kitchen doorway. 'You'll have to choose,' she advised her grandfather. 'It's you and Eva, or all the furniture. Get a tent. The weather's good, so you'll be all right in the back garden.'

Eva glanced from Fred to Agnes, then to Miss Spencer. Denis arrived, providing a fourth resting place for Eva's eyes. 'We don't know what to do,' she wailed. 'I can't get nowhere.'

'House is too small,' grumbled Fred.

'It's the same size as it always was.' Denis kept an eye on Helen Spencer. He still felt uncomfortable in her presence, but Agnes had stated her intention of helping the woman, so he had to accept that decision.

At the end of more lengthy discussions, Helen provided an answer. 'This won't do,' she declared unnecessarily. 'It won't go away, will it? There's far too much furniture to fit into a place of this size. You need to decide quickly what stays and what goes.'

Fred didn't want to part with anything of Eva's, but even he was forced to see sense in the end. 'Aye, we'll have to do something. We'll not fit a size nine foot into a size seven shoe.'

Agnes set the kettle to boil yet again. She felt as if she had been running a cafe all day. From the cluttered kitchen, she listened to Helen Spencer laying down the law. The woman was enjoying herself. All she wanted was to feel needed, to be part of a family, to be loved and respected. Agnes dashed a tear from her cheek; she had been lucky. Like Helen, she had lost a mother. Unlike Helen, she had been raised by grandparents in a caring environment. Money wasn't up to much, she thought as she poured tea. Money could not buy happiness for Miss Helen Spencer.

When the great plan had been finalized, Helen and Denis left together in order to begin the first phase. In Helen's car, they drove out to a farm and persuaded the tenant to bring horse and flat cart into the village. As they drove back to Bamber Cottage, Helen spoke. 'I'm sorry for what I put you through, Denis. Your wife's a lovely woman.'

'It's all right.'

She nodded. He had a generous nature and she was grateful for it. 'There's something wrong with me,' she continued. 'It's not madness. Sometimes, I lose control, but there's a reason. I have to find the reason.'

'I see.'

She smiled. 'No, you don't. I have a memory that I can't reach. It must be something that happened before I got to the age of reason. Whatever it was, it terrified me and has remained all through life. It's not diminished by the years, yet I seem no nearer to remembering what it is. I get panic attacks. They come from nowhere, yet there's something ... There's a big happening lodged somewhere in my brain and I can't get a hold on it.'

'Then how do you know it's there?'

'Because it's bigger than me, bigger than him, bigger than Lambert House.' She had no need to name the 'him'. 'Louisa has brought it back. Until Louisa, I thought I was just a quiet, uninteresting sort of person. But since she has been with us, I have come to realize that there is more to it than just that. There was a woman in my life thirty years ago.'

'Your mother?'

Helen nodded. 'And now, we have her replacement.

217

She's a trigger. And I like her. I like her very much. She may be a gold-digger, but she's not harsh, not unkind, not completely selfish. Louisa noticed me and is pleased to have me there. My mother was probably glad to have me there. So Louisa has taken me back to a place and a time where I was safe and happy. Because of that, the memory of whatever it was is digging at me, prompting me. I thank God for Louisa.'

'She probably reminds you of the mother you lost.'

'It's not so simple, but it is something like that, yes.'

With that, Denis had to be content.

They reached Bamber Cottage to find Agnes and Fred in another heated exchange. Helen looked at Denis and he looked at her. In that moment, both realized that the recent past could be laid to rest. They were good friends, and both felt comfortable about it.

Agnes was in full flood. 'I know what you're saying – I'm not deaf and I'm not daft. You've told me so often that it's probably printed through me like a stick of Blackpool rock. Eva makes your curtains. Yes, she needs her sewing machine and no, it can't stay down here. The spare bedroom can still be a bedroom – we can put the Singer in a corner.'

'That means she'll have to go upstairs to work. She can't do stairs all the while.'

'I can.'

Fred and Agnes turned and stared at Eva. Not since the wedding had she disagreed with her husband. She was of the generation that recognized the superiority of mankind over womankind, but she was putting her foot down with all her twenty stones behind it.

'Put it upstairs,' Eva said.

'Bloody women,' Fred cursed.

There followed an uneasy couple of hours during

which Fred and Eva were separated from half their worldly goods. Although Fred fought right down to the last picture of the Sacred Heart, he was forced to see sense. When the cart pulled away, the Grimshaws had a house in which it would be possible to live and move in a normal fashion.

Eva made the final cup of tea.

'Are them cellars dry?' asked Fred.

'Very,' replied Helen. 'The boiler's down there. It's a big one, because it heats a big house. Stop worrying, please, Mr Grimshaw. If you find you need something, it will be no trouble to have the item returned to you.'

Fred gulped a mouthful of hot tea. He studied Miss Helen Spencer. 'You're all right, you are,' was his stated opinion. 'Feel free to drop in for a cuppa whenever you've a mind.' He looked at Denis and Agnes. 'See? Not all rich folk are toffee-nosed.'

Helen Spencer went home a happier woman. Knowing that Louisa, the Makepeaces and the Grimshaws were her friends, she felt almost capable of coping.

Agnes phoned her two friends from the newly installed telephone in her cottage. Only if she canvassed their opinions could she make any changes to arrangements. 'Isn't she crackers?' was Lucy's typically direct response.

'She's lonely.' The line crackled while Agnes waited. 'Are you there, Lucy?'

'I'm here. Look, don't tell her it's a regular thing. If we don't get on, we can go back to the way it was before.'

Mags too agreed to the temporary admittance of Helen Spencer to their Thursday meetings. Agnes replaced the receiver, wondering whether she had done the right thing. She, Lucy and Mags had a long history and shared common ground, but Miss Spencer was very much the outsider. Would their evenings be spoiled? 'Somebody has to help her,' she told herself out loud. Agnes was no psychologist and no expert in any field connected to the behaviour of her fellows, but she knew need when it hit her in the face. Helen Spencer was needful and Agnes was there to help.

When Thursday arrived, she made a few scones and cakes, found Mags's favourite parkin at the shop, put crisps in a bowl for Lucy. Unsure of Helen's preferences, she threw together a few thinly cut sandwiches, removed the crusts and hoped for the best.

Lucy arrived in fine fettle. She and her new husband were selling their bungalow and buying a barn just a few miles from Agnes's house. 'It's huge,' she crowed. 'We can have visitors to stay and there's loads of land.' She paused. 'Where's Helen Wotsername?'

'Coming.'

'Remember the fit she threw at the party? Everybody in the legal community talked about it for weeks.'

'Then they'll be leaving some other poor soul out of the gossip while they deal with her.'

'What's the matter, Agnes?' Lucy sank into a chair. 'It seems ages since I saw you and you're in a mood.'

Agnes told the tale of the move to Bamber Cottage. 'It was hell,' she concluded. 'Hot day, pregnant, Pop on one of his hobby horses, Eva too big to get past the furniture – it was a farce. Helen Spencer sorted it.'

'Ah.'

Agnes dropped into the chair opposite her friend's. 'There's a terrible sadness in her. She spoke to Denis and he says she thinks it's something that happened, but she was too young to remember it. What's more, she seems to believe it was something too bad for a young child to cope with, so it's in a parcel at the back of her head.'

'Well, let's hope it's not in the lost property department at the post office.'

'It's not funny, Lucy. She's got a terrible life.'

Mags arrived. The other two were repeating their approval of her new face when Helen knocked.

'Come in,' said Agnes. 'Denis is at the pub with Pop. I don't know who to feel sorry for – Denis or the landlord.'

They settled into seats, picked at food, drank tea.

'I'm grateful to you,' Agnes told Helen. 'Goodness knows what we would have done without you.'

'Oh, it's nothing. We've huge cellars and Father's wines take up a very small part. I thought your grandfather was very amusing.'

Agnes snorted. 'You can say that when you've lived with him for twenty years. I love him to bits, but he would make a saint swear. Nan could manage him – she just gave him a certain look when he went too far. I've borrowed Nan's selection of looks, but he doesn't take much notice of me. Thank God he's over the stroke. If it wasn't for his funny walk, you'd hardly know he'd suffered. Now, everybody else suffers. Since he was on that Granada programme, he's decided he's in charge. Honestly, he couldn't run a bath, let alone a business. Thank God again for Eva's acumen – and Pop's near enough to us now, of course.'

A small silence hung over the room.

'I know,' said Mags eventually. 'It's a lovely evening – why don't we go for a walk?'

They left the house in two pairs, Lucy with Agnes,

Mags with Helen. At the top of the main street, Agnes got one of her ideas. She pointed to the pub. 'Let's go in.'

Helen looked at Mags. 'I've never been in a pub before.'

'Time you got educated, then,' Mags answered before grabbing her companion's arm and following the other two into the Farmer's Arms. 'You'll enjoy it,' Mags promised.

Denis and Pop were playing darts. The pub was about half full, and many of its occupants became silent on seeing Helen Spencer in their midst. Agnes marched up to her husband and her grandfather. 'Three teams,' she said. 'Two in each. You and Denis, me and Lucy, Helen and Mags. Lowest scorers buy the drinks.'

'I never played darts before, either,' Helen whispered to Mags.

'Just pretend the board's your dad. Don't kill any customers and watch Denis – he's silent but deadly when it comes to darts.'

It was a hilarious evening. Nobody died and Helen managed to hit the board on most occasions. There was a small contretemps when Fred was accused of overstepping the line before throwing, but all ended well. Mags and Helen, the losers, bought the drinks, then they all crowded round a table and argued about the game.

'I haven't had much experience,' said Mags.

'I've had none,' added Helen.

Fred guffawed and declared that darts was a game just for men. Agnes battered him about the head with his cap, Fred complained of ill-treatment by his own granddaughter, Lucy pretended to smile. There was in Lucy a reluctance to accept Helen Spencer, Agnes thought. Helen was older than the others, was quieter and less easily drawn into fun. But Agnes liked her. In spite of the Denis business, in spite of her reticence, the woman was all right in Agnes's book.

The women left the men to their drinking, Lucy driving Mags homeward as soon as they reached the Makepeace cottage. It was sad, Agnes thought, that Lucy could not even try to accept the new addition to their group. After waving off her friends, Agnes took Helen into the house. 'That's the last time I play darts in heat like this,' she declared.

Helen smiled in agreement. She felt strangely comfortable in the company of Denis's wife. She had expected Mags Bradshaw to be a closer friend, but there was in Agnes a dependable and supportive nature that was much admired by Helen. Agnes knew how to join in, where and when to have fun, how to speak up for herself. There was no fear in Mrs Makepeace, but there was respect for all around her.

'Do you like living here?' Helen asked.

'I do. We both do. I don't know how we'll go on with Pop so near – he's a caution. I love him dearly, but he can stretch my patience from here to Manchester and back. It's even worse since his stroke. I always knew we'd get him well again, because he'd the devil in his eyes even when he was flat out and unable to speak. He's the same, but different. Everything has to be done now and in a great hurry.'

'That's because he's looked Death in the face,' said Helen.

'Maybe.' Agnes sighed. 'If he carries on as he is, he'll die a rich man. There's a long queue for his houses and he's branching out into bigger things, Lord help us.'

'Oh? What's he doing?'

'Play houses for back gardens – Wendy houses, I

think they're called. Eva just says yes to everything he suggests. Meanwhile, the grass at the back of his house is dying, because he has bigger pieces of wood for the outside houses and he covers them in tarpaulin.'

'Oh, dear.'

'Yes. Eva's not been married to him for more than a few weeks and she's under his thumb already.'

Helen nodded thoughtfully. 'He must have a big thumb.'

Agnes laughed heartily. 'He likes large women. Nan was big till near the end. He says a big woman's the best hot water bottle available to man.'

Helen stared through the window at a darkening sky. 'You are so lucky, Agnes.'

'I know.'

'You love people.'

'Not all people.'

'But you approach them with an open mind and heart. I am . . . closed down, I suppose.'

'Your father.' This, from Agnes, was not a question.

'Yes. Lately, though, I have changed. In a sense, I appear to have woken up, yet in another I seem to be grabbing a childhood I never had. Control slips away from me at times.'

'Yes, I saw that at the party.'

Helen told the tale of the wedding reception, including the part played by Denis. 'I've stopped drinking,' she said. 'The expression on your husband's face on seeing me drunk would have stopped a bull smashing a gate.'

Agnes could almost taste the woman's misery. She wanted to jump up and shake her, wanted to drag her away from Lambert House and the man who had spoiled her life, but it wasn't her place. 'I'm always here, Helen,' she said. 'When it gets too much, come to me. Don't suffer by yourself, because you do have friends.'

Helen turned her head slowly and faced Agnes. 'There's Louisa. Louisa is the reason I am staying.'

'She married him with her eyes open,' said Agnes.

Helen nodded. 'The sighted make as many mistakes as the blind. She knows now that she is just an incubator. He wants a son.'

'Yes, Denis said.'

'Once he has his son, Louisa will be of no further use.'

Agnes wished that her visitor would cry, but it was clear that some of the hurt went beyond tears. No one liked Judge Spencer, and his daughter had travelled past dislike and was walking alongside hatred where her father was concerned. 'I'm sorry.'

'I've lived for over thirty years with my father, Agnes. Yet it's as if I was born again just recently. There's something . . .'

'What?'

'Just something. Tell me, Agnes – what's your earliest memory?'

Agnes pondered. 'I remember sitting outside the house – presumably in a pram. And being held over a tin bath in front of the fire while my hair was rinsed – I remember that. Don't know how old I was.'

Helen bit her lip. 'I have a not-quite memory. It's similar to a dream that's forgotten the instant you wake. Sometimes, I grab the edge of it, but it unravels like a badly knitted sleeve as soon as I try to concentrate. There was noise. I do know there was a great deal of unusual noise.'

'And then?'

'Nothing.' Helen looked down at her folded hands. 'Like Louisa, you make me feel better. Almost normal.'

'You are normal.'

'Am I? Is it normal to imagine yourself in love with a married man? Or to stand in the middle of a social gathering and decry the host – my own father? Is it normal for all those people at the party to disappear from my sight and slip beyond hearing while I have a tantrum worthy of a two-year-old?'

'You are not mad,' Agnes insisted. 'You are damaged. I know he's a tartar. I've seen and heard him for myself. Kate Moores, too, knows that life hasn't been easy for you – so does my Denis. Helen, look at me. I'll be here, Denis'll be here, Kate and Albert will be here – even my Pop and Eva will be here. You know where to run.'

'Thank you.' At last, the tears flowed.

Agnes, hanging on tightly to the tense body of Miss Helen Spencer, wondered whether she had bitten off more than she could chew. This lady had more than a chip on her shoulder – she carried a whole yard of lumber. What on earth had happened to reduce Helen to this? Why had she no friends and why didn't her father love her? And could Agnes be what Helen needed? Was a special doctor required?

Helen straightened. 'Thank you,' she said. 'I like you.'

'And I like you. Look after that stepmother of yours, but come to us if it all gets too much. We'll be here. We may not have much, but you're welcome any time.'

When Helen had left, Agnes sat very still in a chair by the window. Dusk was falling fast, but she didn't bother with any lighting. In her heart, she walked every weary and unwilling step of Helen Spencer's homeward journey. 'I'll do what I can,' she swore aloud. 'I'll try to make a difference.' Nan had always said that life was about making a difference, preferably for the better. Wisdom from the mouths of the uneducated was often raw and special. 'I'll try, Nan,' she repeated. Helen Spencer needed saving. She deserved to be saved.

Denis arrived home with Fred in tow and began to make cocoa. Pop was enthusing about his Wendy houses while Denis was quieter than usual. He left the older man to heat milk while he sat with Agnes. When he asked why she had been sitting in the dark, she replied, 'Helen Spencer lives in darkness, love. She thinks she's mad, but I think she isn't.'

'When did you pass doctor exams, sweetheart?'

She shrugged. 'She's not mad, Denis. I need to do something and I'll start with Kate.'

'You what?'

'There has to be somebody still alive who knew the judge and his first wife. They had more servants then. Whatever's in her head wants finding. Until she can get it out, she'll not cope. While she's not coping, she'll give her dad loads of excuses to lock her up. She'll not get better till she gets to the bottom of whatever it is.'

Denis swallowed. 'He won't go that far, will he? Locking her up, I mean. Madness in the family would reflect on him.'

But Agnes suspected that Judge Spencer would go to any lengths to rid himself of his difficult daughter. It would be relatively easy to lie, to say that Helen had gone abroad for a rest cure or was on an extended holiday in Europe. 'Judge Spencer will find a way to get what he wants. You know that, Denis.'

Fred entered. 'Nowt wrong with that lass except for the man who fathered her. She's nowhere near mad. I know what happened at the wedding and at the house party – I'm not as deaf or as daft as some folk want to believe. Helen Spencer's a gradely lass. You do right, our Agnes. Find out what you can, but don't get wore out. I don't want owt happening to that great-grandchild of mine.'

The back door rattled. Sighing, Agnes went into the kitchen. The miscreant had visited three times in one week, and Agnes was in several minds. 'Stay sitting down, or you'll be knocked over,' she ordered her menfolk before opening the door.

Louisa Spencer's puppy, Oscar, shot in like a furry missile from a powerful cannon. He jumped first on Fred, then on Denis, before launching himself at the woman of the house. A long-haired Alsatian, Oscar had a happy temperament and a bottomless appetite. He knew already that women meant food, so he concentrated on the female of this malleable species.

'Going to be a big bugger,' commented Fred after managing to save his cocoa. 'Feet like dinner plates.'

Denis simply laughed. When he was working, the dog was a companion, following him from garden to garden, task to task. Unfortunately, the animal knew little of the differences between weeds and legal residents of a garden, so Denis's life had taken on a new interest.

'Here.' Agnes threw a bone and the dog pounced on it. He settled in front of an empty grate and began to gnaw.

'He likes you,' Fred told Agnes.

'He likes her because she's soft,' Denis said. 'He hates the judge. The feeling's mutual – Judge Spencer would shoot the poor dog if he could get away with it.

Found a hair on his jacket on Tuesday. It had come off that tatty wig, I bet, but he insisted it was Oscar's fault. As far as I can see, Oscar has no white hair.'

'Animals have good taste,' Fred declared. 'No decent dog ever liked a bad human. Yon Oscar likely had the judge summed up in ten minutes flat.' He took a sip of cocoa. 'Hitler had dogs like that one,' he mumbled sleepily.

'Go home before you drop off,' advised Denis. 'Eva will be wondering where you are.'

Fred stood up, said his goodbyes and left the house.

Denis and Agnes stared at the dog. 'He'll have to go home,' Agnes said. 'If Louisa misses him, she might get upset.'

Denis found a length of rope and tied it to the puppy's collar. 'I'll come,' said Agnes. 'It's best if I exercise while I still can.'

They set off with dog and bone in the direction of Skirlaugh Rise. Oscar carried his meal proudly, wore the air of the triumphant hunter bringing back his kill. When they neared the house, the dog stopped, placed his bone on the ground and growled deep in his throat. A plume of smoke rising from a small circle of red advertised the judge's presence. He was having a final cigar before bedtime. Denis urged the dog onward, but Oscar refused to move until his mistress's husband had returned to the house.

'Oscar really doesn't like him, does he?' whispered Agnes.

'Hates the bloody sight of him, love. And he isn't on his own. Come on, let's get rid of Spencer's latest victim.' They put the pup in his kennel, tied the frayed tether to a ring in the floor, then walked home.

'We're all living in her nightmare,' said Denis when they were halfway between Rise and Fall.

Agnes gripped her husband's arm. Sometimes, he was very wise. She was grateful for that.

Chapter Nine

Agnes Makepeace was exhausted to the core. Her waist was thickening and her patience was shrivelling at a similar pace. Summer continued into September, which wasn't right in Agnes's book. Leaves had scarcely started to crisp and, apart from a slight nip in the air at dawn, the hot weather lingered. She spoke to Nuisance. 'No more summers with you attached, anyway. After a few more proddings by doctors and a bit of hard work on my part, you are out of there. You'd best look lively and get yourself a job in the pits, because you've been hard work up to now. It's payback time, mate.'

Had she bitten off more than she could chew? She had travelled the length and breadth of Skirlaugh Fall, which, though small, contained a couple of hundred people who might do well if gossip should become an Olympic sport. She knew who had slept with whom, could now nominate at least three people who were 'bad with their nerves', was custodian of confidences involving intricate surgical procedures performed on several men and women from here to the horizon. Oh, and there were a lot of folk suffering from piles. It had all been interesting, but not as productive as she had hoped.

The questions relating to the Spencers had been hidden within conversation – or so she trusted. The judge was clever; if he believed that Agnes was working to help the daughter for whom he had no love, repercussions might occur. Agnes had a husband and a baby to protect; should they become threatened, poor Helen would be on her own. Well, not quite on her own, but Louisa, too, was in a position of compromise. Agnes answered her own question. 'I have bitten off more than I can chew. Let's hope I never have to swallow any of it. Bloody man.'

One last chance lay with a married couple named Longsight, who lived in the larger village of Harwood. They had worked for the Spencers many years ago, so they had become the final target. What was Agnes seeking? She had no idea. Yet the feeling that Helen had suffered some kind of abuse in childhood remained strong. It had to be more than neglect. The neglect of a child was unforgivable, but Helen's unreachable memory was of one specific incident. The woman remembered well the occasions on which she had been deprived of space and company, could chatter away about days spent in her bedroom, yet the nightmare continued and Agnes was here to discover the eye of the storm. Or perhaps not – the eye of a storm was quiet and relatively peaceful. Whatever it was that made Helen so agitated was not in the eye – it was spinning around the edges in the company of a million particles of frantic dust. And the storm was no act of God; this was a tornado created by a man who was used to being king in his own arena. Judge Zachary Spencer had probably wounded his only child so badly that she could not allow herself to remember the incident. That was mental trauma, Agnes believed.

On the bus ride to Harwood, she wondered why she was doing this. Perhaps the discovery of the truth would injure Helen even further. Perhaps all this should be left to time and chance, because it was no one's business. Yet Helen was frail. It would do no harm for someone to be around when the memory came back. That someone should know as many of the facts as she could. That someone was going to be Agnes.

Denis's spine stiffened.

'So, you've given up your job? How on earth will you manage with no library books to stamp?' The judge's voice crashed through an open window. 'For God's sake, woman.'

Helen must have responded and the judge was quick to shout again. 'Louisa doesn't need you. If she required nursing, I'd hire somebody with nursing skills, not a woman who knows how to catalogue the reference section or find a stupid romantic novel for some elderly spinster. What will you do all day? James Taylor has left Bolton after your ill-treatment of him, so you won't be wasting his time any longer. He should sue for slander, as should I.'

A door crashed home. Denis tried to relax, but fury made his muscles taut. Now that the silly business was over, Denis considered Helen to be a friend, and a friend of his wife, too. That mean-minded and lily-livered Spencer needed his eye wiped, and Agnes was doing her best. There was something radically wrong in this household. Denis had begun to agree with Agnes that an event in Helen's childhood had shaped her and almost finished her. He shivered. Zachary Spencer was a fish cold enough to have perpetrated the worst of crimes; he was also sufficiently intelligent to clean up after himself. A bad but clever man was a dangerous enemy.

Oscar arrived and began to claw at a flower bed. Denis grinned. While Louisa was still suffering the nausea experienced by Agnes for just a few weeks, the dog had sought refuge with him. 'Leave the lobelia alone,' Denis advised, 'or I'll clobber you with my rake.' He wouldn't, though. Unlike Judge Spencer, he was incapable of damaging other people or animals.

Oscar fetched a stick and Denis threw it. Every job took twice as long these days, yet Denis would not have parted with the daft pup for all the tea in Asia. The dog returned, dropped his prize and panted hopefully.

Helen arrived and took over the job of throwing.

'Are you all right?' Denis asked. 'I heard.'

She shook her head. 'I keep telling myself that he can't hurt me any more, that I'm an adult and capable of answering back. Sometimes, I do answer back. Today I'm not up to it.' She fastened a lead to Oscar's collar. 'I'll walk him,' she said. 'Otherwise, we'll be throwing sticks and balls all day.'

Denis knew her probable destination. 'Here's my key. If Agnes is out, let yourself in and make a brew. There's a bone in the kitchen for Oscar.' He watched as she stumbled away behind Oscar, who dictated the pace of mobility. 'Find something, Agnes,' he begged inwardly. Somebody had to help Miss Helen Spencer, and that somebody could not be a member of her own family. Saddened, he returned to his weeding. The lobelia was safe. Were Helen and Agnes safe?

Agnes emerged almost unsatisfied from the Longsight house in Harwood. She could see the couple now, eyes darting away from her face, each looking at the other, a damped-down terror weakening their voices. They knew something. The judge had been a fair but firm boss, there had never been any trouble, the first Mrs Spencer had been a nice, pretty sort of woman. Helen was a difficult child sometimes, but she had improved with age. Yes, everyone had been sad when Mrs Spencer died; yes, Miss Helen had been upset for quite a long time and yes, there had been a big funeral.

The last hope sat in Agnes's handbag, a scrap of paper on which was written a name. This person was the one who had cared for Miss Helen during her early years. She was retired now and lived in a Blackpool rest home. Blackpool. It might as well have been the moon, because the chances of Agnes's getting to Blackpool were remote. She was pregnant, she suffered from the heat and Denis had little time for day trips and no money to afford such luxuries.

On the way home, she called in on Pop and Eva. The latter was making tea for 'them two'. 'Them two' were Fred Grimshaw and Albert Moores, who now held the grand position of superannuated apprentice. Agnes carried mugs to the shed.

'It's not seasoned,' Fred was yelling.

'Course it is. I got it from Jackson's Lumber and Jackson said it's well seasoned. Shall I fetch salt and pepper then you can give it another go?'

Agnes grinned. Had Pop met his Waterloo? Oh, how she hoped he had.

'Don't talk so daft.' Fred grabbed his tea. 'Hello, love.' Without pausing, he continued, 'I know seasoned wood like I know the back of my hand. This isn't for a doll's house – it's for a kiddies' play house. It'll likely be out in all weathers.'

Albert also knew his wood and he said so.

'My name has been built on things that don't fall to bits,' yelled Fred.

Agnes smiled. 'But his first chimneys were crooked.'

Fred glared at his granddaughter. 'That was deliberate,' he insisted. 'It was for that poem thingy – crooked man, crooked mile.'

'Rubbish,' she said sweetly.

Fred sank onto one of the work benches. 'Nearest and dearest?' he asked of no one in particular. 'I know what I'm talking about, but I can't get sense and I can't get good wood. Albert?'

'What?'

'Who's the boss?'

'You are, master.'

'Then take that bloody wood back and get summat as'll stand up to rain for a week or three. Then get down to the ironmongers in Bromley Cross and buy me a new drill – this one couldn't get through butter.'

'Yes, master.' Albert stalked out of the shed.

Agnes sat next to her grandfather. 'Go easy on him, Pop. He's a good man and a good worker.'

'I know. Worth his weight in gold – and he can take a joke.' He looked at her face. 'You're hot again. Any luck?'

She told him of the morning's events.

'Then you go to Blackpool.'

'How? When?'

Fred tapped the side of his nose. 'Leave all that to me,' he said darkly. 'I have ways of making things happen. Now, get you gone. Miss Spencer's in your house with yon daft dog. If you don't shape, he'll have eaten the sofa by the time you reach home.'

Agnes kissed him. 'You're a terrible man, but I love you.'

Eva arrived, a school bell in her hands. 'Oh,' she muttered.

'What's that for?' Agnes pointed to the instrument.

'It's for the end of the round,' replied Eva. 'When they get too loud, I send them back to their corners for a rub down with a wet cloth. Without this here bell, the authorities would be evacuating Skirlaugh Fall.'

Agnes went home with the distinct feeling that there was more to Eva than met the eye. As there was already quite a lot of Eva, this new version promised to be a remarkable phenomenon.

Helen was dozing in a chair, while Oscar, in his element, was crunching bone to reach the marrow. As soon as he saw Agnes, he dropped his prize and went to greet her.

Helen woke to joyous yapping. 'Sorry,' she said. 'I don't get much sleep these days.' The truth was that she was afraid of sleeping, because sleep brought dreams she could never piece together once she woke. 'Shall I make tea?'

'Yes, please.' Agnes reunited puppy and bone. 'Stay,' she ordered, though she expected little or no obedience from the young Alsatian. He needed training, and his owner was not well enough to spend time with him. She listened to sounds from the kitchen, the clatter of cup in saucer, the rattle of the spoon in the caddy, the decanting of milk from bottle to jug. This was what Helen needed – the ordinary, everyday things in life.

'Shall I pour?' Helen asked when she returned with the tray.

'Please. I'm hot.'

'Where have you been?'

'Oh – here and there – visiting, looking at shops.'

'You bought nothing?'

'No.'

'I'm trying to train him to walk to heel.' With a look of hopelessness on her face, Helen waved a hand at Oscar. 'He's going to be too big soon. We can't have a huge, frisky dog. Louisa loves him dearly, but he tires her and, like you, she is in no condition to be directing a determined self-guiding missile. He drags me from pillar to post.'

Oscar, tongue lolling, smiled at his womenfolk. They were talking about him and they wanted to slow him down, but the world was so exciting – all those sights and sounds, the wonderful smells, the inbuilt knowledge that he was born to annoy smaller creatures. He wagged hopefully, depending on his charm. Soon he would chase rabbits again.

'Any more dreams?' Agnes kept her tone in everyday mode.

'Yes, but I can't catch them.'

'Still no idea of what it might be?'

Helen shook her head. There was noise, a high-pitched sound followed by several crashes. After the crashes, she invariably woke and reached for pen and paper. But there was never anything to write, because she could not grasp the centre of the dream.

'Still writing?' asked Agnes.

'Yes. It seems to be a circular effort, since I appear to have begun in the middle. I suppose once I have written the middle, I should know the beginning.'

'And the end?'

The end was like the dream, full of noise and fear.

The end might come after the middle, or after the beginning – Helen wasn't sure. 'I thought I'd lived the dull life until I started to write about school. I expect most authors' early books lean towards personal experience. All of Austen's did, and she had a life as narrow as the ribbons she applied to her dresses when she needed something to look new. I think writing helps. Even if it's never published, it will be out of me. It's therapy.'

Agnes understood perfectly. For Helen, the writing was like going to confession or seeing a doctor. It was balm for the soul; it was also a search for truth, and Helen had to walk through a minefield to reach even the edge of that commodity.

'Like Austen, I write what I know. I didn't realize how much I had absorbed, because I have always kept it to myself.'

'You're a people-watcher.'

'Probably.'

Having said goodbye to Agnes, Helen left, the daft dog pulling her at considerable speed in the direction of Skirlaugh Rise. She tried to rein him in, failed, found herself chuckling as she was dragged along the lane.

'I am glad you have something to laugh about.'

Helen's flesh seemed to crawl. She looked through a gap in the hedge, saw her father's unwelcome sneer. 'The dog is silly,' she replied defensively.

'It'll have to go once the child's born.' He stared hard at her. What was she up to? Her attitudes ranged from the compliant to the argumentative with no visible warning of any impending change.

'I shall keep him in my apartment,' she replied. Father would not get rid of Oscar. She would not allow that. The power she owned was connected to ... it was

239

connected to . . . To what? The end of the book, the end of the dream? He was afraid of her. Why should he fear his own daughter?

'Keep the damned thing away from me,' he ordered before storming off in the direction of the house.

As soon as she was on home ground, Helen released Oscar and he dashed into the copse to annoy wildlife. She followed and leaned against the very tree behind which Glenys Timpson had concealed herself. 'Did I love Denis?' she asked herself in a whisper. 'Or was I merely imagining that I might have found someone who could take me away from here?'

Dappled light caressed the ground. A few leaves had followed the norm and were beginning to carpet the ground. It was a lazy day. She sat on damp moss, breathed the scent of earth, watched the pup as he leapt insanely from tree to tree. He was dragging a bough through a gap, was growling and panting as he fought to move the heavy object.

The world changed. Something in the sound made by the large branch cut into her head like a warm knife through butter. She was elsewhere. There was not much light, but there was noise and movement. Someone panted. Was that a scream? 'Come away.' The voice was female. There was not enough light. Backwards. She was pulled backwards into . . . Into the copse.

The dog, head leaning to the left, one ear cocked and the other remaining in Alsatian puppy mode, was panting in her face. His breath stank of marrowbone. 'I was dragged backwards,' she told him. 'There wasn't much light. Someone pulled me away from . . .'

Oscar grinned broadly before turning to display his huge find. He could not carry the whole piece home, so he began the business of stripping branches from the main stem. A happy woodsman, he became absorbed in the task.

Where? When? Who had said the words? She remembered half-light, a hefty tug, dragging, that panting sound. Had she been pulled away from something? Was she the something that was dragged? Quickly, she grabbed the dog and fastened lead to collar. She had to get home; there was the writing to be done.

Agnes picked up the receiver. 'Hello?'

'It's me – Lucy. Your granddad wants me to drive you to Blackpool. Will this Sunday do? Denis doesn't work Sundays, does he?'

'Erm – not usually, no.' Agnes feared that Lucy would not be happy if she knew the reason for the trip. 'I have to visit a nursing home,' she said.

'Oh?'

'I may have a lead on something I've been researching.'

There followed a short silence before Lucy spoke again. 'Mags tells me you've been trying to find out about Helen Spencer's childhood. May I ask why?'

'You can ask, but I don't know the answer.'

A long sigh preceded the words, 'Can't she do her own research?'

'No. She can't.'

'Why?'

How to explain that Miss Spencer was not crazy? How might Agnes convey her own feelings about this matter?

'The woman's had all the good things in life—'

'She's had no mother, Lucy. And her father is terrible to her. There's something she needs to remember, but I want to filter it and tell her gently. She's delicate.'

'She's crackers.'

'That isn't true. Lucy, don't bother yourself – we'll get a lift from someone eventually.'

'We'll do it. I'm sorry, Agnes, but you are on a hiding to nothing. George thinks the whole Spencer family is crazy.'

'Hmm. All two of them? Three if you count the new wife, I suppose. Why are you so much against Helen Spencer?'

Lucy sniffed. 'Madness frightens me.'

'Then don't drive us to Blackpool.'

'We are driving you to Blackpool and you are driving me mad.'

'Then you'll be in good company – sanity has never appealed to me. Much better to be happily mad than sanely unhappy.'

At last, Lucy giggled. 'How about unhappily mad? See you about ten on Sunday morning. 'Bye.'

Agnes sat down, a duster in her right hand. Absently, she cleaned the top of a small table as she thought about Sunday. Mabel Turnbull, the lady in the nursing home, was the last chance. According to the Longsights, she had been Helen's nanny, so she might be in a position to clarify some of the goings-on. A day out would do everyone good, she told herself. George and Lucy need not come into the nursing home – they could return to the Golden Mile for half an hour. Denis would be there. As long as Denis was there, Agnes could manage just about anything.

The man in question entered the house. He was laughing.

242

'What's funny?' she asked.

'That bloody dog dragging Helen all over my lawn.'

'The judge won't be pleased.'

Denis shook his head. 'He's never pleased unless he's punishing some poor bugger. You stay where you are – I'll brew up and see to the cooking.'

Agnes had always known that she had been lucky in love. During this seemingly eternal pregnancy, she had indeed been blessed. Her man thought nothing of doing a full day's work, only to come home and start all over again. His excuse was simple and beautiful – he hated a woman with swollen ankles. The truth remained that he loved and respected his wife. It was a pity that more men did not put family first.

'Are we having this liver?' he called.

'You are and Nuisance is. I am a mere third party – I just have to process the nasty stuff.' She sighed dramatically. 'Never mind, I'll get my own back when he's born.'

She hadn't realized that she could write, yet once she started her fingers flew over typewriter keys in a vain attempt to keep up with the speed of her thoughts. Sometimes, her poor typing skills were a good thing, as they slowed her down and made her consider what she was creating. There was an urgency in her, as if she believed her time to be limited, though there was no binding deadline to the unsolicited script.

Helen Spencer forced herself to stop. She leaned back in her chair and stared through the window at gathering dusk. Days were growing shorter. Autumn and winter would be bearable, she reminded herself, because the dog could be her excuse to leave Lambert

House several times a day. Should she have kept the job in the library?

He was out a lot these days. Summer recess stretched across several weeks and, unless there was a massive crime, Father could be around whenever he pleased. However, he seemed to prefer his Manchester club, often staying there for several nights in succession. Lodge meetings took up more of his time, and he played chess or bridge in town once a week.

Helen and Louisa were coping well with his neglect. They needed only each other, and both enjoyed being apart for a few hours each day. A rhythm developed and life became good as long as the head of the household was absent. The two women read, Helen wrote, Louisa was having a stab at tapestry work. The house hiccuped along under the watchful eye of Kate Moores, who supervised the comings and goings of three newly hired dailies. It was not a bad life. Helen knew that she ought to have been grateful, yet she continued to simmer and to suffer spells during which she was mentally removed from her environment. It was the dream. It was all tied up in that nightmare.

She left her desk and walked through the house towards Louisa's room. Life ticked on. As long as he wasn't in it, there was a degree of transient freedom.

Louisa opened her eyes. 'He phoned,' she announced. 'He's bought a yacht and he wants me to sail with him. I've told him I get seasick on a boating lake, but would he listen?'

'He never listens.'

Judge Spencer's wife nodded. 'He's getting sailing lessons. I'm going near no ships until this child is born. I've put my foot down.'

'Good for you.' Helen sat down and continued to

read aloud from *Great Expectations* while Louisa dozed. A yacht? She tried to imagine her father at the helm, failed miserably. He wasn't an outdoors type of person. Perhaps the sea was going to be his next conquest. A second Canute, he might well expect time and tide to work to his schedule. Never mind. With any luck, he would sink and drown. And *Great Expectations* deserved Helen's full attention.

Agnes replaced the receiver and looked at her husband. 'Miss Turnbull isn't in full possession of her faculties – that's what the matron said, anyway.'

Denis folded his newspaper. 'Who the hell's Miss Turnbull?'

'The nanny from thirty years ago. Blackpool – in a rest home.'

'Oh.'

She bit down hard on her lip. 'I might have to just give up. Lucy doesn't want anything to do with it, anyway – I wish Pop hadn't asked her to take us.'

'That doesn't sound like Lucy – she's usually game for anything.' Denis sighed. 'What's the matter with everybody these days? It's murder up at the house, Fred and Albert are always arguing—'

'No. They're being crusty old men. If you separated them, they'd wither a lot faster. People are just being themselves, that's all. The only one who needs help is Helen, and it's starting to look as if I can't do much for her. If the old lady's off her head, there's no point in me being car sick all the way to Blackpool, is there?'

'I suppose not.'

'And Lucy doesn't want to help Helen. Like you, I can't understand that.'

The phone rang a second time. Agnes, still unused to living alongside the instrument, jumped. She took the call, replied in a short series of yeses and nos, returned the receiver to its cradle. Triumphantly, she turned to Denis. 'There is something. That was Lucy's George. It all gets mysteriouser and mysteriouser. He told me to stay away from Miss Turnbull for my own good.'

'Eh?'

'Those were his exact words, love. "Stay away for your own good. There's nothing in Blackpool for you, and you need to be safe."'

'Bloody hell.'

'Bloody hell is right. George said the judge pays the rest home fees. He said he shouldn't be telling me that, but he had to say it because I'm Lucy's best friend. He said, "Look, Agnes, you're a clever enough woman. He pays the fees. Follow that train of thought and see where it leads. I can't say any more, because I am breaking contract by discussing a fellow lawyer's client." Those were his exact words, more or less, Denis. He's breaking some law or other to keep me safe. How can I follow that train? And should it be the Blackpool train out of Trinity Street?'

'No. George is a good lawyer and he's looking out for you.'

'Follow that train,' Agnes whispered.

Denis went to make a pot of tea. Judge Spencer was a rich man, but he didn't throw his money at the needy. He didn't like the needy; he believed that poor people were one of life's less savoury necessities, since they kept the wheels of manufacturing turning and cleaned up after the rich. The poor were often criminals, too. He was very harsh on penniless breakers of the law.

Agnes stood in the kitchen doorway. 'Don't pour a

cup for me, love. I've drunk enough tea just lately to refloat the *Titanic*.'

Denis went with her into the living room. 'Have you followed the train?'

She nodded.

'So have I. The matron said the old girl's doolally, right?'

'Yes.'

'He probably doesn't know she's gone senile. That's hush money, Agnes.'

'That's what I was thinking.'

'And George's firm – or George's friend's firm – handles the fees, I'll bet. No, I'll go further than that. I'd wager a pound to a penny that Miss Turnbull's been kept by Spencer since she left Lambert House. There has to be a reason for that. Another thing – what if the judge told the rest home to contact him if she got any visitors?'

A shiver ran the full length of Agnes's spine. 'Dear God,' she murmured. Then her face brightened slightly before she added, 'I don't think I gave the matron my name. I just said Nan had known Miss Turnbull and that Nan had died. She said nothing would register with the old lady and I rang off. I hope I didn't give my name.'

'I didn't hear you say who you are. Sit tight and try not to worry. But, Agnes . . .'

'What?'

The pause lengthened slightly before Denis spoke again. 'Miss Turnbull might have been paid to keep quiet because she could remember what Helen Spencer has forgotten. For all we know, the whole business could be tied up in the one knot.'

Agnes agreed.

'We don't need Lucy,' said Denis. 'I'll go to Blackpool and give a false name, see if I can get through to the old lady.'

'No, you won't.' Agnes shook her head vehemently. 'Unless you want to wear specs and a false moustache – and even then I'd say no.'

Denis sighed. 'Who wears the trousers in this house? No, don't answer that, because I know what you'll say. We wear one leg each – eh?'

'Too damned right, mate.'

'Mate is about correct,' he grumbled. 'Bloody stalemate or checkmate or whatever chess players say. We can't help her, sweetheart. At least you'll always know you did your best.'

But Agnes was far from satisfied. 'I'm taking her to Manchester.'

'Eh? Who?'

'Helen. I'm going to get her hypnotized.'

Denis almost choked on his tea. 'My leg of the trousers is planted, Agnes. You're having a baby. You've seen what happens to her when she nearly remembers. If one of those quacks can take her back to wherever she was when whatever it was happened, you could end up with a full-blown nervous breakdown in the middle of Manchester. Even I wouldn't take that on. You're not making yourself ill, and that's an end to it. There's nothing more to be said.'

Agnes, like Denis, knew when to concede defeat. He was right. There was no way of predicting what might happen if and when Helen remembered. 'All right,' she said.

'Promise me?'

'I don't need to. It was just a thought.'

'Right.'

They sat in silence until someone tapped at the door. Denis opened it to admit Lucy. 'Has he told you?' was Lucy's immediate question.

'George? Yes, he has,' Agnes replied.

Lucy sank into a chair. 'Thank God. Listen, both of you, and listen hard. Put as much space as you can between yourselves and the Spencers. Denis, you can help with the barn – we need to do a lot to make it fit to live in. When it's done, George will get you work in the fresh air. You have to leave the job.'

Denis stared steadily at the visitor.

Lucy turned her attention to Agnes. 'You, too. Let them clean their own bloody silver – you should be training for something better.'

'The judge pays half the rent on this house,' said Denis.

'I want to stay near Helen and Louisa,' added Agnes.

Lucy leapt to her feet. 'All I can say is this – a letter was witnessed thirty years ago. It's lodged with another firm, and we can only imagine the contents. The woman who wrote it is in that Blackpool home – that's why I didn't want to get involved. When the lady dies, Helen Spencer won't need to remember, because we think – we believe – that the whole mess is sealed in that envelope. The lawyer who witnessed it is dead – he went to pieces shortly after reading the contents. The woman asked him to check it to make sure she'd made her point clear. It's bad. It's sealed with wax and tied up with string, but we all know it's there.'

Agnes swallowed hard.

'Lawyers gossip, too,' said Lucy. 'And that judge is a much-hated man, so George and I have been on tenterhooks lately. When it happens, it'll be like World War Three, believe me.'

Denis stared through the window. Much as he would have loved to leave Lambert House a few weeks ago, he now needed to stay. Helen was a friend and someone needed to keep an eye on her ill-tempered father. Skirlaugh Fall was a good place; they had decent neighbours and Fred nearby. 'We'll let you know as soon as possible,' he told the visitor. 'I'm due back at work now. Thanks for coming, Lucy.'

Alone, Agnes and Lucy stared into separate near distances. Agnes, her eyes on the fireplace, was racking her brain for an idea that might enable her to help without putting herself in danger. Lucy, who had already said too much, looked through the front window. 'Pretty here,' she remarked eventually.

'Yes, it's lovely.'

'It's a big barn, Agnes, with a cottage at the back. It's every bit as nice as Skirlaugh Fall.'

'I know.'

'Will you leave?'

For answer, Agnes shrugged her shoulders.

'It's not a good idea to get too close to that family. You'll be dragged in when the day comes. Helen Spencer is unstable.'

'I know.'

'Then why stay?'

Agnes sighed deeply before replying. 'If you or Mags were in trouble, I'd swim to Timbuktu to help. Helen's become a friend.'

'Does that stop you listening to a longer-standing one? We've been together for ever, Agnes. If you only knew the whispering that's gone on in legal circles for thirty years, you'd buy a gun and lock yourself in.'

Slowly, Agnes turned and looked Lucy full in the face. 'He killed someone, didn't he?'

Lucy's face was stained by a sudden blush. 'There are crimes other than murder – serious ones.'

'Rape?'

'Agnes, leave it alone. The guy who handled all this became ill – he was getting on in years. But he never again spoke to Spencer, who was a leading barrister at the time. It all smells worse than the Tuesday fish market. Mabel Turnbull has senile dementia and can't talk in straight lines any more. Even so, her bills are paid. There has to be a reason.'

Agnes nodded thoughtfully. 'How come the judge has never heard about this letter? He seems to be the only one in ignorance.'

'Lawyers do gossip, as I said before, but no one cares enough to warn him. And it's thirty-year-old news. For all we know, this Miss Turnbull could live to be a hundred and the judge might die tomorrow. Whispers started up again when I told George about Blackpool. This time, Agnes, you had better ignore that stubbornness you inherited from Pop. You've a child to think about – and a husband. George has gone out on a limb for you and Denis, so think about George as well. If that limb snaps, my man will never work again.'

'So, if the rest home told the judge that Mabel Turnbull had had visitors ... Well, it doesn't bear thinking about. Even senile folk can often remember what happened decades earlier. Tell George not to worry.'

Lucy pleaded again, begging Agnes to walk away from Skirlaugh Fall with Denis. There would be work, a cottage and George nearby. It made sense, she insisted. Events from thirty years ago could catch up with the Spencers at any time, and Agnes should put herself away from the fallout area. 'Talk to Denis,' she insisted.

'I will.'

'Safety first, last and always. There's a wicked genius in Lambert House. When a clever mind turns bad, a psychopath is born. Think about him. He worries about no one but himself and he loves no one but himself. That's one dangerous man and his daughter could be cut from the same cloth.'

'No,' said Agnes. 'She isn't.'

Lucy picked up her bag. 'Don't be too sure of that. Even if she is sane, she's an emotional wreck. Don't be pulled down the plughole with her.'

When Lucy had left, a weary Agnes laid herself flat out on the sofa, her head spinning. A part of her wanted to pack up straight away and walk the three or four miles to Lucy's barn; the rest of Agnes needed to remain where it was, near Pop, near Helen, near Louisa. And the decision could not be made while Denis was at work. Tormented by dreams that were probably pale echoes of Helen Spencer's nightmare, Agnes slept.

She woke screaming. Trying to hang on to the tail end of the dream, Helen Spencer jumped from her bed and ran all the way across the long landing until she arrived at her old room. There was a small bed in a corner. Dolls sat on a shelf, fairytale books beside them. She was small. She could not reach the shelves, but adults could. 'Come away,' said the voice. There was urgency in the tone. 'Come away now.'

Helen blinked. Her mouth opened again and the child yelled at the top of its lungs. *I am not a child. This is all wrong.* The man came in, a woman behind him. They were from the other time, yet they stayed. She stared at her father. He was old. The woman was the wrong woman and the screaming would not stop.

He went out of the room. The child sat on a rug. The rug was made in the shape of a teddy bear. She wanted her . . . she wanted her mother. The woman was touching her. 'Helen, please stop this – he's getting the doctor.' But Helen heard another voice, the one that urged her to come away. It had happened. It was terrible. The child carried on screaming.

Louisa turned to the doctor the moment he arrived. 'Help her,' she pleaded. 'Can't you knock her out? She'll be all right after a sleep.'

Dragging. Banging. Someone else's scream. Two screams now.

A needle. Sharp. Silence.

By the time the ambulance arrived, Helen Spencer was unconscious. She was lifted onto a stretcher and carried down the long, winding staircase. Louisa, terrified, could only stand and watch while her best friend was removed from the house. Having pleaded with her husband and with the doctor, she knew that she had no chance of keeping Helen at home. She turned, saw triumph in her husband's eyes. 'She won't be away long,' she said.

Zach Spencer looked at his wife. 'She's crazy like her mother was,' he crowed. 'She'll be away for as long as it takes. If she doesn't buck up, she could be gone for the rest of her life.'

Louisa fled the tragic scene. Helen was not insane – he was. Pressing her hands against her belly, Louisa worried about the unborn child. Zachary Spencer had unseated his daughter – what would he do to her sibling? 'All I wanted was to be safe,' she told her abdomen.

'This isn't a safe place.' Nowhere was safe. Wherever she went, he would find her. He knew police, private detectives, lawyers by the score. There was no escape.

What about poor Helen? She had always known that there was no way to avoid the nightly torments – it was plain that something had upset the balance of her soul rather than her mind. Would she remember in hospital? Would the doctors help?

Louisa forced herself to return to her husband. The plan was a frail one, but it was the only idea she owned. 'Sweetheart?'

'Sweetheart' was looking very pleased with himself.

'Yes?' His lip curled. Louisa was no longer pretty; pregnancy did not suit her – she had a bloated face with dark patches near the eyes.

She inhaled deeply. 'It may be a good thing,' she ventured.

'What?'

'The hospital may get to the bottom of it all.'

He frowned. 'Ah. Yes, they might well do that.' Turnbull and Helen, the two biggest threats, had almost seemed to disappear in recent years. They knew nothing, surely?

Louisa continued. 'She dreams almost every night, Zach. It seems to be something from childhood, and she gets nearer to remembering it every day. Can you recall her being hurt?'

'No.'

'Are you sure?' Was Louisa sure? Was she now threatening Helen's very existence? Because she knew with blinding certainty that her stepdaughter's buried secrets involved this man. Might he hurt Helen all over again? Was he capable of killing her?

Zachary Spencer shifted weight from foot to foot.

He was unused to fear, was happy only when in full control of everyone around him. There was a danger that he had just painted himself into a corner. 'I'll get her home,' he declared. 'You are used to her and you probably need the companionship. I shall be sitting soon, when the courts reopen.' The mad should be left to their madness, he told himself firmly. Helen was insane, but psychiatry had advanced and she might very well respond to treatment. Was he in danger? No, no. Mabel Turnbull had seen nothing, his daughter had seen nothing. Or was he mistaken? He had kept Mabel Turnbull sweet just in case, but he had never considered his daughter to be a threat. Adults did not remember events that had taken place when they were twenty-eight months of age.

Louisa left him to his musings. As she walked away, the child kicked. It was as if the poor mite knew that trouble lay ahead. She closed her door and leaned against it for support. The beatings she had received from her first husband had been nothing compared to this. Even the stabbing and the surgery had left mere physical scars. Helen had been right. Judge Zachary Spencer was not a safe place for anyone. His daughter was now paying her dues and, at some stage, Louisa's turn would surely arrive.

Agnes refused to be moved. She stood at the desk in the ward sister's office, feet planted firmly, face set in a scowl. 'I'll wait,' she said. 'I've plenty of time today.'

'A first assessment can take several hours.' The crisply ironed female glanced at Agnes's abdomen. 'You should be taking better care of yourself in your condition.'

The unwelcome visitor seated herself in the corridor, took flask and box from her shopping bag, and began to eat her lunch. She wasn't going anywhere. The sister's eyes were still on her – even the eyes seemed fixed by starch – but Agnes munched stoically on her sandwich. She was not hungry, yet she refused to be beaten by a woman too big for any boots. Helen was here and Agnes had no intention of leaving before seeing her.

The woman in question emerged from her office. 'Follow me.'

Was it possible for vocal cords to be starched? 'Thank you.' Agnes repacked her lunch in its original place of residence. There followed a journey slowed by the unlocking and locking of doors. The fact that she was inside a mental hospital was underlined by the nurse's behaviour. In this place, those who failed to cope with life were condemned to exist. It was all cream and green, with fat radiators punctuating walls.

'She's in there.' The blue-and-white-clad woman walked away, turning as she reached yet another locked door. 'I'll come back for you shortly. Try not to tire her. If you have any trouble, press the red button.'

Agnes swallowed. Thus far, she had managed well enough, but now she was about to face grim reality. Helen was in that room. She had been hauled from her house by two big men, placed in an ambulance and driven to Manchester. She had not been certified. Had she been declared unfit for human company, Agnes would definitely have been turned away.

She turned the door knob. 'Here goes,' she whispered softly.

There were bars at a high window. A bed with a white quilt sat next to a nasty little locker that carried the scars of past assaults. Paint failed to hide completely scratch marks on a wall. Helen sat in a green chair, hands folded in her lap, eyes down-turned, lips slightly apart.

'Helen?' The eyes looked dim. 'Are you drugged?'

'Yes, I think so.'

Agnes sat on the bed. 'What happened? Denis ran home this morning to tell me about the ambulance arriving in the night. Louisa had a word with him. She wasn't well enough to visit you, so I took her place.'

'I'm glad you came. Thank you.'

'Has your father been?'

Helen smiled ruefully. 'No.'

'What happened?' Agnes asked again.

'The dream. This time, I woke screaming – please don't ask me why. I was little Helen all over again – dolls in my room, a teddy bear rug, fairytale books. I could hear and see him and Louisa, but I also heard another woman's voice telling me to come away.'

'Your mother?'

Helen shook her head. 'No. A servant of some kind. This time, I must have got very near to the truth, because I woke in terror. A doctor gave me an injection, I believe. Then I was brought here. I'm a voluntary patient, but, if I try to leave, I'll be certified for a month while they test me. I can't win, so I have bowed to the powers and promised not to attempt to escape. With so many locked doors, it would be a useless effort, anyway.'

Helen was a prisoner. Agnes held the woman's trembling hands. It was all she could do; no one on God's earth could change the minds of doctors.

'I've been assessed once,' Helen said. 'So far, so good. I think I passed my scholarship all over again. They looked very confused, as if they didn't know what to do with me. A peculiar set of people, I must say. If they are the ones who decide whether the rest of us are sane, God help the world. As for therapy – what good are they doing by shutting me in here without company or reading matter?'

Agnes smiled. 'They're watching us,' she said, her voice deliberately loud and clear. 'We are animals in a zoo, you and I. There's a camera in the corner, some sort of microphone, too, I expect. We are under scrutiny.' She rose and walked towards the corner. 'Hello, doctors,' she said. 'I am Agnes Makepeace. There's nothing wrong with this woman, but her father needs locking up. He's a vicious, nasty piece of near-human detritus. Save a room for him.'

'Good afternoon.'

Agnes froze, then turned slowly. Zachary Spencer, face stained a dark red, stood in the doorway. 'You are coming home,' he told his daughter.

'Am I?'

'Yes. They say there is nothing the matter with you.' His eyes remained on Agnes. 'I wish I could say the same for your friend. Meet me at the main entrance. Do you require a lift, Mrs Makepeace?'

'No, thank you.'

'Very well.' He turned on his heel and left.

Agnes crossed the room and perched on the edge of the bed. 'Jesus,' she said. 'He heard me.'

'Yes, he did.'

'Will he sack Denis? Only Denis has been offered another job, so we can escape if necessary.'

'Don't go. Please, don't go.'

'He'll punish Denis. He might even stop paying some of our rent. Helen, your father is one scary man.'

'He's afraid.' Helen's tone was quiet. 'I may be on

the receiving end of those little yellow pills, but I know why he's here. He wants to pull me out before doctors get to the bottom of me.' She stared hard at her visitor. Nothing must happen to Agnes, Denis, Louisa. Four friends, she had now. To the list of three, she added the name of Mags Bradshaw. Friends meant strength and support. 'He'll do nothing to you,' she said. 'He'll do nothing to Denis. Don't move away, please. I have his measure now.'

'And the dreams?' Agnes asked.

'Will be dealt with. I don't need to be in hospital to get help. I can visit a psychiatrist privately – Father need never know.'

Inwardly, Agnes shook. The judge knew her opinion of him. Denis worked for the judge. Helen lived with him, as did Louisa. Louisa's pregnancy was proving difficult. Inner instinct dictated that Agnes and Denis should leave Skirlaugh Fall and go to live near Lucy. The stubborn streak, along with concern for Helen, urged Agnes to remain exactly where she was. Then there was Pop. How would Pop manage without her and Denis?

As if reading her ally's thoughts, Helen asked, 'Did you know that your grandfather is commissioned to make a scale model of our house? It's to be a present for Louisa after her child is born. She never had a doll's house as a child. It will take months to make, but Father insisted and he's paying a good price.'

'Oh.' Agnes could find no sensible remark with which to punctuate the pause.

'He gathers all around him like a farmer bringing home the harvest. He pays Denis, he pays some of your rent, he pays the staff. Now, he goes for your grandfather. We exist only at the edge of his vision –

especially if we are female.' She sighed. 'Don't walk out on me just yet, Agnes, because you are a piece of my harvest.'

Agnes gazed at the floor. 'I can't help being afraid. He's so high and mighty, and I said what I said and he heard me and—'

'So did the microphone.' Helen strode to the corner and spoke to the box near the ceiling. 'You know I'm not mad,' she said clearly. 'My father is the cause of my temporary disarray. Keep your drugs and your electric cables for him. I am going home. Home is another word for hell. Goodbye.'

As if on cue, a nurse arrived with a sheet of yellow paper on a clipboard. 'You are released,' she said. 'Follow me.'

Helen laughed mirthlessly. 'I'll never be released, Nurse Jenkinson. Not until the day someone signs his death certificate.' On this note of high drama, Helen walked out of the room, Agnes hot on her heels. A key chain clattered, doors were unlocked, locked, unlocked, locked again in a seemingly endless walk to the outside. A woman screamed. Echoes of other doors slamming in other corridors flooded the air. Cream and green were the colours of the day, while the scent was pine disinfectant with a faint whiff of carbolic.

'God help all who stay here,' said Helen as they reached fresher air and open space. 'Come with me, Agnes – don't leave me alone with him.'

'You won't be alone – Denis is driving.' Agnes waved a hand at the Bentley. 'See?'

'Then you will cause more speculation by refusing a lift from your own husband. See? Whatever you do, my father enters the equation. So come along – let's go home.'

The drive started in complete silence. Helen, next to her father in the rear seat, saw nothing of the landscape throughout the journey. Agnes and Denis, in the front of the car, made mindless small talk about Pop, Eva and little domestic issues, but the conversation was strained. Agnes, dropped off at the cottage, thanked the judge with all the politeness she could muster.

Inside, she collapsed onto a sofa. How many times had she berated Pop for failing to hold his tongue? What had she done? That foolhardy business with the camera had given Judge Spencer further food for thought. 'Don't let him take it out on Helen or Louisa,' she begged God.

It was a long day. When Denis finally came home, he stood over his wife, one hand running repeatedly through his hair. 'He wants to know who you've been talking to,' he said.

'No comment.'

'Agnes, he demands to be told how you formed such a distorted view of him. We'd better clear off – we'll be safer with George and Lucy.'

'No.'

'What do you mean, no? He's boiling over in his study right now. Helen's shut herself in her flat, won't talk to anyone – even Louisa. He's banging about like a bull at a gate – why did you do it?'

'I didn't know he was there – what are you up to?' Denis had picked up the phone. 'Denis?'

'I'm phoning George.'

'No. We stay for now. He daren't touch me.'

Denis shook his head and walked into the kitchen. Much as he wanted to remain in the village, he needed his family to be safe. The phone rang. He answered it. 'Ah. Hello, sir. Right. Thank you very much.'

Denis replaced the receiver and spoke to his wife. 'He forgives you because of your condition and because he knows his daughter was out of sorts when she expressed her opinion of him.'

'Load of tripe,' was Agnes's reply.

'Very likely. We're keeping our options open, love. One more day like this one and we leave the village. All right?'

She nodded.

'I mean it, Agnes – I'm not messing about.'

'I know. He won't do anything to us, Denis. He's already in trouble up to his double chin. Helen is the only one in real danger. Please, love, let's wait a while.'

With that, Denis chose to be satisfied for the time being.

Chapter Ten

Stella Small, a woman of over six feet in height, saw private patients in a room that matched her name. For her own part, she had lived at peace with her surname, although, while growing at a rate of knots in childhood, she had needed to adjust her attitude at an early age. Having overcome her own giant status and silly name, she had equipped herself to help others through a life whose stone-punctuated and mud-spattered alleys marked Stella's clients in ways that went above and beyond feet and inches.

'I'm Helen Spencer.'

'Ah. Yes. Do sit down. My name is Stella and yes, I am Dr Small. If you are anxious or depressed, you will not wish to joke about my name. If, however, you are enjoying a good day, feel free to smile and we can get the business of my size out of the way.'

Helen chose to smile. 'You were recommended by my GP. Father had me locked away in a mental hospital for about sixteen hours, then decided that I had recovered. He fears my memory.'

'Right.' The doctor scanned Helen's notes, adjusted her spectacles to achieve better vision, then sighed heavily. 'These doctors can't write legibly. You are unhappy?'

Helen nodded.

'Which is not the same as depressed. But you have

had some panic attacks and have behaved unconventionally from time to time.' She closed the file. 'Happily, I am able to do two things at once and, while appearing to read your notes, I have been counting the number of times you have blinked. You are not neurotic.'

'Good.'

'Tell me everything.

Helen would never be able to explain why, but her whole life poured from her lips within half an hour. The doctor did not prompt, was not worried by short silences and, when Helen had finished, stood and walked to the window. 'When I pour tea into a cup, the tea takes on the shape of the cup.'

'Yes?'

'But you have no shape. You cannot measure yourself – no comments about my height, thanks – and you pour all over the place. There's no mould, you see, no cup to give you shape.'

'But that doesn't mean I am insane.'

Stella Small shook her head. The spectacles left her nose and dangled on a piece of braid just above her breasts. 'I must get some new glasses,' she remarked. 'No, you are not insane, but your father may be. You have had no love and no parents – that is his fault. Those dreams – that lost memory – he is a part of that.'

Helen waited for more.

'The brain is a clever beast. It will allow you to remember when remembering will do less harm than it might just now. Meanwhile, get out of your father's life.'

'But Louisa—'

'Will have to take her chances with the rest of us.' The doctor returned to her chair. 'Emotional retardation is completely divorced from intellect. You are a clever woman, but you have been through adolescence in your early thirties. You even chose a man who was safe, a man who would never carry you off on a white steed. Miss Spencer, you have only recently reached maturity. You don't need me or drugs or a straitjacket. You need a removal van and a fresh start. I repeat – get out of your father's life as soon as possible. You have my telephone number. If you need me again, I shall be here.'

A few minutes later, Helen found herself wandering aimlessly through the bustling streets of Bolton on a market day. She bought tomatoes, lettuce, cucumber and a large box of Milk Tray for her stepmother. The doctor's words echoed – 'Get out of your father's life.'

She sat on a bench and opened the chocolates. Louisa did not like coffee creams, so Helen rooted them out and chewed thoughtfully. Why should she do the moving? He was the miscreant, the sinner, the bad apple. 'Get out of his life?' she whispered. Oh, no. It would be far better if he got out of hers. How did a person get rid of a father? What plan might be employed to shift him from Skirlaugh Rise?

After finishing the coffee creams, Helen walked towards her car. There had to be a way. Because she was going nowhere, while he, the big man, should go to the devil in whose company he belonged.

Life settled into a routine of sorts after a while. Agnes continued to work part time at Lambert House, though she chose to be there only when the judge was absent. Through Denis, she was able to predict Zachary

Spencer's schedule, thus enabling her to appear at Kate's kitchen door when the chances of the man's putting in an appearance were minimal.

Louisa continued unwell while Helen, Agnes and Kate competed in an effort to find something she would eat, but the judge's wife seemed to have slipped into a state in which she cared little for herself. When reminded and bullied, she ate for the sake of her unborn child. Helen and Agnes watched the slow deterioration with concern – Louisa, the bright spark, the giggler, was no longer resident at Lambert House; in her place, a pale, listless creature lingered, all hope gone, the light in her pretty eyes extinguished, her lust for life diminished.

Under a cloud of gloom, the other three women sat in Kate's domain, a kitchen vast enough to house a whole family, beds included. 'I can do no more,' Kate grumbled. 'Scrambled eggs, beef tea, nice soups – I've tried the lot.'

Helen stared into her coffee cup. 'I warned her. It was already too late – they were married – but I told her what would happen.'

Kate nodded wisely. Forced by circumstance, Helen had found it necessary to include Kate Moores in her list of friends, because Kate needed to be aware of Louisa's needs and difficulties. The older woman blew on her coffee. 'She's not carrying well,' she pronounced. 'God help her if owt happens to that kiddy, because he's hung his hat on having a healthy lad.' She glanced at Helen. 'Your dad's a bad bugger.'

'I know.'

'We all know,' said Agnes. 'But the main problem for now is keeping Louisa in one piece. Like me, she'll be two pieces in a few months and she'll need to be strong to give birth and mind the baby.'

Kate stared into the near distance. 'You should beggar off, Miss Helen. Get gone and take her with you, because she's not the woman he brought home. You've that bit of money your mam left – get some out of the bank and use it.'

Helen half smiled. 'Where could we hide from him? No, he would seek us out even if we went to Mexico. Judges have long arms.'

Agnes blinked a few times. 'Look, if you could just get her away for a few weeks, it might make all the difference to her attitude and her health. Tell him you're definitely taking her away. He'll hardly notice anyway – too busy trying to learn to drive that damned boat.'

'Yacht,' said Helen. 'If you call it a boat, he goes purple.'

'We're serious, Miss Helen.' Kate patted her hairnet, pushing a stray strand of iron-grey hair into the mesh. 'Just go.'

'He'll bully you if I just disappear. I can't do that to you, Agnes and Denis.'

Kate snorted. 'I'm not frightened of that great lummox. I reckon if it came to the shove, my Albert and Agnes's granddad could give him a good hiding.'

'Never thump a judge.' Helen looked at her hands. She hadn't played the piano in weeks, hadn't written a syllable, had given up trying to read to Louisa, whose sole aim in life seemed to be constant sleep. 'If anyone hits him, he'll send that person down for twenty years. I've served thirty-two years of my sentence and—'

'Then give yourself time off for good behaviour.' Kate refilled Helen's cup. 'A month or two could make a big change to that poor girl up yon.' She pointed to the ceiling. 'Take a chance. Don't tell anyone where

267

you're going, then, if we are asked, we won't be lying if we say we've no idea.'

Agnes gazed steadily at Helen. There was something different about her, something new. 'The dream?' she asked.

'Gone,' was the reply. 'The whole situation has righted itself.'

Both women knew that Helen Spencer had spoken the truth. She was calm – almost cold. There was a new set to her shoulders – the slight roundness had disappeared, while her eyes no longer betrayed sleeplessness or troubled nights.

'Did that head doctor help?' Kate asked.

'Partly, yes. The pills from the hospital helped me to sleep at night. But Dr Small wasn't the whole answer. That came from a totally unexpected source.'

The housekeeper and Agnes waited, but no further information was forthcoming. Helen, her mouth set in a determined line, made up her mind there and then. 'I shall take Louisa to the sea and I shall tell him where we are. If it's for the good of her health and for the sake of his child, he will have to agree. Before you ask – yes, I am still afraid of him. But because of ... oh, never mind ... I am now in an even better position to stand my ground.'

Kate snorted. 'Good luck. You're going to need it.'

'If I am sure of your safety,' Helen told Agnes, 'then I can be stronger. We must all cease to show fear of him – keep it hidden, keep him guessing. If we can do that, he will leave us alone. He needs to be in charge, needs to translate fear into respect. His weakness is that he needs to believe himself to be respected in spite of ... in spite of all he has done.'

Agnes swallowed hard. It had happened. The dreams were no longer necessary, because Helen had the truth at last. From where, though? Had she travelled all the way in her sleep, had she woken with the full story in her head? Or had Mabel Turnbull died? To whom had that letter been addressed? 'I'll come with you,' she decided aloud. 'Denis won't mind. If I pay for my own food, then—'

'No.' Helen's face was alight with joy. 'No, you'll pay for nothing, my friend. I'll be so glad of your company – and a holiday will do you good. Denis will be glad for you, I'm sure.'

So it was decided that Kate would stand guard on the home front while Helen and Agnes looked after Louisa. Destinations were discussed before Agnes began the walk homeward. How cool Helen had been, how sure of herself. She was a new woman, remoulded and ready to take on the world. But would she really manage her father?

In the cottage, Agnes removed her coat and picked up the phone. As she had expected, Mabel Turnbull had died two weeks earlier. The letter, she concluded, was now in the possession of Helen. When asked by the matron for her name, Agnes terminated the call. It was over. Helen knew what her father had done and appeared to be dealing with it.

Denis agreed right away that a holiday would do Agnes good. 'But don't go too far,' he warned. 'I might get there for a weekend if it's not at the other end of the country.'

Agnes tried to imagine the scene at Helen's house, judge in his chair, defendant standing on the carpet, his face reddening, hers white with nerves. But it had to be done. Louisa's life was in danger, as was that of the child she carried. Away from Lambert House, there was a chance that she might thrive once more.

Had Agnes taken her imaginings to the ends of the earth, she could not possibly have pictured the reality of that meeting between father and daughter. When Helen had said her piece, Zachary Spencer, shaking from head to foot, could find no immediate reply.

'What's the matter, Father?' she asked. 'Did Oscar run off with your tongue? Don't worry – Denis and Fred will look after the dog while we're away. Oh, and remember my warning – it includes the dog. Miss Mabel Turnbull was brighter than you thought. In all honesty, I can't remember her face, but the letter convinced me that she had been a part of the household all those years ago. So.' She straightened her spine even further. 'So, I, too, have written a letter. It contains Miss Turnbull's letter to me and the whole bundle is in very safe hands. That letter could ruin you for ever – we both know that.'

He gulped noisily, reached for his brandy. The letter would be with George Henshaw, of course. Had anyone other than Helen read it?

'If I die, that envelope gets opened. Miss Turnbull's letter, too.'

So, Helen had been the sole reader. After clearing his throat, he finally spoke. 'Miss Turnbull was a nervous woman. She saw trouble where there was none.'

'Really? That explains how clearly her story resembles the dream that haunted me for months. I was there.'

'You were not three years of age when Mabel Turnbull ceased to be your nanny. She acted as housekeeper after that.'

'Yes, and after you had relieved her of her virginity.'

The judge took another hefty mouthful of brandy. 'That is neither here nor there. What else was in her letter? Not that anyone would believe her, of course.'

'Then why have you paid for her upkeep since she left? Why did you pay the fees at the home when she got old?'

He lowered his chin and said nothing. For the first time in his adult life, he was losing an argument. His daughter was the only person who had defeated him. He needed to know the contents of Mabel Turnbull's letter, but he realized that he dared not ask. 'Where will you go?'

'Somewhere between Blackpool and Morecambe – not too far away, as Louisa is unfit for long journeys. We shall travel in my car. You will continue here as usual, I suppose.'

'Don't tell me what I will do,' he snarled.

Helen clung to the edge of her courage. 'There was a name in that letter, Father. There were several, but I recognized one of them immediately. Need I go on?'

He hurled the brandy globe into the grate. 'Travel where the hell you like – summer is gone, anyway, so you have missed the best of the weather.'

She had never seen the best of the weather, because she had lived her whole life in the long, dark shadow of this man. Helen did not react to the smashing of the glass. 'Bracing winds might be just what Louisa needs. She did not enjoy the heat. A few weeks on the coast will do her the world of good.'

'Leave my office, please.'

She walked to the door, placed a light hand on the knob, turned to look at him. 'Isn't knowledge a wonderful thing, Father? It's power. All these years, you have presided over my life like some ugly ogre, ill-tempered, unpredictable, devoid of all decent human emotion. It's my turn now.' She opened the door. 'Go to hell,' she ended clearly. 'I am a match for you, because your blood runs in my veins, too.'

The trembling began as soon as she reached the main hall. Even now, she was terrified of him, because she knew that he was capable of acting beyond the reach of reason. It was all in the letter from Miss Turnbull, a message written decades earlier when the woman's mind had been young and clear. Judge Zachary Spencer was a self-created law. He embodied the book of rules, amended the contents to suit himself, assumed that he was beyond the reach of other mere mortals.

Helen closed the door of her apartment and sank to the floor. What was she going to do? Not about Louisa, not about the immediate future, but in the long term. Her father knew the true law of the land and might even escape the spectre of Miss Mabel Turnbull. But there were names in the letter. He had been a womanizer all his life and Miss Turnbull had watched the comings and goings in Lambert House for years before leaving. When his first wife's body had barely cooled, he had begun to share his bed with anyone who became available. After that, he had, for the most part, amused himself well away from the house.

The rest of the message? She shuddered anew. Two facts had emerged, one of them terrifying, the other a mixed blessing. There was a great deal to be absorbed and she could take her time over it while away by the sea. Helen now held her father's fate in her hands;

she was judge, prosecution and jury. His defence? There was none. Those twin facts from the nanny's letter were burned into Helen's brain like brands on the skin of farm animals; from two pieces of knowledge, she had gleaned insight into herself. She was her father all over again and she was the only person qualified to mete out his sentence. Judge Zachary Spencer was a marked man. And he knew it.

Lucy Henshaw, who still worked part time for her husband, looked up as a large shadow touched her desk. Irritated already by the complicated documents in her hands, she sighed heavily. People who wanted to play at litigation were silly and made a lot of work, so— It was Judge Spencer. 'Yes?' she asked.

'I need to talk to your husband.'

'He isn't here.'

He frowned. 'Then I shall wait.'

Lucy shrugged. She knew the probable reason for the man's visit – he would be looking for two letters, one written by his daughter, the other a legacy from Mabel Turnbull. Lucy knew nothing of their contents; neither did her husband, but the firm was responsible for the safekeeping of Helen Spencer's property. 'Please yourself, sir, but he won't be back for hours.'

Yet another woman was standing in his way – well, sitting in his way.

'Do you wish to make an appointment?' she asked sweetly. 'Or shall I get another of the partners?'

'No.'

'Is that a no to both suggestions?'

'Yes.' He walked out of the office, slamming the door in his wake. Lucy picked up her phone. George was

273

having a word with builders at the barn, where, according to him, the telephone was just about the only item in working order.

'George?'

'Yes?'

'The judge has been and gone.'

'Ah.'

'Is it lodged with the bank?'

'It is indeed. What was his mood?'

Lucy laughed, though there was no glee in the sound. 'The same as ever, love. Bright, breezy, cheerful – need I go on?'

'No. Tell me – what are we going to do about this damned fireplace?'

They talked about modifications to their new home, then Lucy returned to the original subject. 'Does this mean that Agnes is safe, George?'

'Safe as houses and a great deal safer than our barn.'

'Good.' She returned to her work, which embodied a silly quarrel about two feet of land at the rear of a pair of semis. Agnes was safe. Nothing else mattered. Two feet of land certainly failed to enter the equation.

They stayed outside Morecambe, Blackpool's poorer twin. It was quieter than Blackpool, with fewer shops and vehicles, but the sea was there, the air was clean and their accommodation, a rented semi-detached house, was comfortable. The only cloud on an otherwise clear horizon lay in the knowledge that Judge Spencer's yacht was moored well within driving distance. 'He won't come,' said Helen repeatedly.

Agnes kept a close eye on both her companions. Louisa, still quiet at the start of their holiday, was beginning to eat more regularly, while Helen was a strange mixture of calm and alertness. It was all tied up with the death of Mabel Turnbull – of that Agnes was certain. But she asked no questions, because the judge's daughter needed as much rest as anyone.

After three days, Louisa showed signs of her old self. As it was raining, she insisted on games of Monopoly and cards, even showing elation when she won. Away from her husband, she started to thrive, often cheating at dominoes and palming cards when she thought no one was watching. They were watching, each glancing at the other with relief in her eyes.

He came. Agnes saw the expression on Louisa's face when he kissed her on the cheek. It was as if a darkness had fallen over the woman's skin, a stain applied by the very man to whom she had entrusted her life.

Denis, who was on driving duty, followed his master into the house. If there was going to be any argument, he wanted to be there to protect his wife. The judge had damned and cursed his daughter for days, so there could well be a battle in the house.

Denis found the women seated in three chairs at a dining table across whose surface were scattered playing cards and dominoes. The judge had taken up a position of superiority near the fireplace, chest and stomach pushed outwards, hands clasped behind his back. There was a deafening silence in the room.

The big man cleared his throat. 'Are you improving, Louisa?'

'Yes, thank you, dear.'

Helen shook her head so slightly that the movement was scarcely noticeable.

'The air will do you good,' pronounced the embodiment of authority.

'We are all well, Father,' said Helen.

The judge did not look at his daughter. 'We have done a little sailing, Denis and I. It's quite easy once one grasps the basics. Denis?'

Denis hated the yacht. 'Yes, not as difficult as I thought.'

'We'll make a sailor of you yet,' promised Spencer.

There followed another silence. Helen folded her arms and stared hard at her father. 'We are better here than at Lambert House,' she said. 'There's been a dreadful atmosphere there just lately.'

The judge shifted his weight from foot to foot. Had she spoken to Louisa, to Denis's wife? Were these two women aware of the preposterous meanderings of Mabel Turnbull? What an ungrateful wretch that woman had been. He had kept her for years, had made sure that her dotage had been comfortable. Women were all the same – even when dead, they continued a torment.

'We shall be eating soon.' Helen's tone was soft. 'Unfortunately, we cannot ask you to stay, because we have not catered for company.' She glanced at Louisa, whose downcast eyes and sad expression spoke volumes about inner misery. 'Louisa needs to eat at regular intervals. In Morecambe, she will get well.'

He glowered. She was ordering him out of the house, was in charge of his every move. He needed those letters. A plan, half-formed thus far, was taking shape in his mind. There was always a way, he told himself. His treatment of Harry Timpson, which would be lenient, was going to pay off soundly. He could use a man capable of breaking and entering a well-locked jewellery store.

'Please go,' said Helen.

'You haven't won yet, madam,' mumbled her father.

Helen's cheeks glowed with anger. She wanted a blunt instrument and a chance to use it, needed to pound away at him until he died. The death sentence was still on the statute book in her personal legal system, and she was the only one qualified to apply it in this instance. The room was fading. She had promised herself that this would never happen again, but here it came, prompted by no dream, no sound, no warning. 'I know what you did,' she cried. 'I know all of it.'

He staggered back. 'Quiet, woman!'

But she saw him and only him. There was a long staircase, darkness, dragging, crashing. A woman bade her come away, but this time, she did not come away. 'Eileen Grimshaw,' she whispered.

He made for the door.

'How much did you pay to be rid of her? What contribution did you make to the upkeep of your other daughter?' Helen blinked, cleared her mind and focused on the present. 'Agnes, I am so sorry.'

Agnes had slid down in her chair. 'No,' she whispered.

It was too late. Helen, knowing that she was doing damage, had no way of taking back what she had said. At least she remembered the episode this time, but that was no compensation for the harm she had done to her half-sister. 'Meet your daughter, Father. I intended not to tell you until after the birth,' she said to Agnes.

Agnes shot out of her chair, reached the judge in two strides, raked her nails down both sides of his face. Denis grabbed his wife and pulled her away into a corner. 'Stop it, love,' he begged. 'Come on, this is doing you no good at all.'

'My mother died,' she screamed. 'And my Pop and

277

Nan were left to bring me up. They were poor. You left them poor. God, I'd rather have anyone but you as a father.' Did Pop know? Surely not. Surely, he would not be making a scaled-down copy of Lambert House if he knew that the customer was the one who had fathered his granddaughter? Silly little thoughts tumbled about in her mind, a million questions seasoned by fury and loathing.

Helen was sobbing. 'I wanted to protect you, Agnes. I've known about this for only just over a week.' She raised her head. 'And I know the rest, Father. There's enough there to send you to prison for life. Remember that. Remember and leave us alone.'

The judge wiped his bleeding face on a snowy hand-kerchief. 'Let's go, Denis,' he muttered.

But Denis held on to his wife. He placed her in the chair she had just vacated, strode across the floor and punched Zachary Spencer on the nose. The man fell back, his head striking a wall. Dazed, he struggled to his feet, eyes watering, face creased by fear.

Denis threw the keys on the floor. 'Drive yourself home,' he wheezed. 'Stay away from me and mine, or, God help me, I'll not be responsible for my own actions. Scarred lungs or not, I'll beat the living shit out of you.'

The unwanted guest opened his mouth as if to speak, snapped it closed almost immediately. His cheeks con-tinued to bleed, as did his nose. He retrieved the keys before continuing to mop his bloodied countenance. Unfit to drive, he stumbled from the house and sat in his car. She had won. The damned woman had won – unless he could retrieve the letters. If he could get his hands on those, Helen might be disposed of quite easily via the mental hospital – who would listen to her there?

Who would listen? The doctors would. No matter what, he was almost cornered, but he could, at least, make an effort to retrieve those papers from Henshaw & Taylor. Harry Timpson was his best chance. God, he hoped his face would heal before the session.

Inside the house, Agnes rocked back and forth in her chair. The baby, too, was mobile, as if the shock had affected the space in which he or she lived. She could not believe it, would not believe it. His skin was under her nails and his blood ran in her cold veins. Nan and Pop had laboured all those years to provide for a child whose father was one of the richest men in Lancashire. 'I have to wash my hands.' Agnes fled.

Denis's breathing righted itself after a few minutes. He was angrier than he had ever been in his whole life. That thing was Agnes's father. His knuckles ached from the blow he had delivered to the nose of a High Court judge. The job was gone. Agnes had to be cared for, as did the unborn child. Agnes needed more than money. He followed her path to the bathroom.

She was staring at herself in the mirrored front of a small cabinet over the basin. 'I don't look like him.'

'No, you are beautiful.'

Agnes turned. 'I hope my mother went with someone else as well as him. I hope my dad's out there somewhere sweeping up or weaving sheets. I'd rather be the daughter of a criminal . . .' She was the daughter of a criminal – Helen had just said so. Helen was her sister. 'I always wanted not to be an only child,' she said. 'But him? Why him? Why did my mother go with a brute like that one?'

'We'll never know, sweetheart.'

'Rape?' she asked.

'No way of finding out.'

279

'Nan and Pop always said my mam wasn't cheap, that she seldom went out of the house and seemed to have no boyfriend.'

Denis nodded.

'We have to look after Helen now, Denis. She's family. What will Pop say?' She sank onto the toilet seat. 'Pop doesn't deserve this.'

'He doesn't need to know. Remember the stroke? News like this would put his blood pressure at the top of Everest. You know what he's like, love. He gets himself worked up even when he's having fun – imagine what this could do to him.'

She nodded.

'I've got a feeling I lost my job today.'

Agnes stared into the near distance. 'Lucy was right. We should have kept away when she told us to.' She lifted hands reddened by scrubbing. 'I've nearly worn the nail brush out,' she said. 'But I can't rub him out. I'll never be able to rub him out, because he's in me.' She swallowed hard. 'I came from that pig.'

'So did Helen.'

'She's used to it.'

Denis perched on the edge of the bath. 'We haven't read the letter. I'm not saying that Helen is lying deliberately, but she does get confused.'

Agnes shook her head. 'Not any more, she doesn't. What she gets now is angry. She has his temper.'

'You don't, though. You're nothing like him.'

'No, but I am carrying his grandchild.'

'Agnes, you can't be sure of that.'

But she was sure. She continued sure for the rest of the day, even after questioning Helen very closely. 'It fits,' Helen informed her firmly. 'Miss Turnbull had nothing to gain by nominating your mother as one of his conquests. She herself was another victim, though she can't have borne a child or she would have mentioned it in an effort to secure some inheritance for it. No, she was simply recording the facts – it has to be true.'

Evening found them in the living room, all thoughts of board games abandoned. Louisa, who had eaten a good meal, was the first to speak. 'He's not hurting this baby,' she declared. 'I'm going to eat everything that gets put in front of me, because the child must be strong.'

Helen nodded. 'What do we do about you and Denis?' she asked her newly acquired sister. 'The half of your rent will be paid – I'll see to that.' She raised a hand to stop any argument. 'I'll see to it,' she repeated.

'I'll help with George's barn,' said Denis.

Agnes had little to say. Stunned, she merely sat, hardly hearing the conversation. She thought about her poor mother, knew that Eileen had gone right through a pregnancy with no husband and little financial support. Pregnancy was not much fun, but Eileen had been forced to endure it without the comfort of a partner. Agnes thanked God for Denis, for Pop and for Nan.

Denis, too, seemed lost in thought. He was chewing his nails – a habit he had lost in his teens. He had clouted a judge.

Helen was the one who brought sense to the situation. 'Look, none of this is new. Life is much the same as it was yesterday, except that we now have a little more knowledge. That can be said of any day – we learn as we grow. He didn't suddenly become your father, Agnes. Denis – you've never liked him. Louisa – you've lived with your mistake for months – what's changed? I have a sister and a brother-in-law – I shall be an aunt in the spring. We can't let him win. There is more to that letter than your mother's name, Agnes – a great deal more. But that's my problem – you all have enough of your own. Let's have our holiday. Denis – you phone George and tell him you'll take the job. Go by bus to work, or borrow my car. Agnes – just learn to live with it. Sorry to sound harsh, but nothing matters beyond your own family.'

'You're my family,' Agnes whispered.

Helen smiled. 'So it would seem. Louisa, do your best. You are the one who is forced to be close to him. For the baby, play your part. We'll rethink after the birth.'

No one slept well that night. But each realized that Helen was right – life had to continue alongside him and in spite of him. Helen rested better than the others. Her anger was too deep to be allowed near the surface, so she lay sleepless, though not in pain. Retribution had not yet begun . . .

He did not remember the journey, partly because he had been unfit to drive, mostly because his mind was filled by the dreadful scene in the house he had visited. What had that damned Turnbull woman written and what had she seen? Yes, he had known her in the biblical sense, but had the quiet, compliant woman been a witness to something he had sought to hide? That letter had to be retrieved from the offices in town.

Kate Moores was just leaving. She saw him, but asked no questions about his scarred face. It seemed that she was yet another member of his daughter's coven. How much did Helen know and what had she told the other witches?

Eileen Grimshaw. He threw his hat in the general direction of the coat stand. She had been about as much fun as a burning orphanage. He remembered her tears, recalled her coming to his office to speak of her pregnancy. He had dragged her outside, had told her to keep her mouth shut, as he would deny everything. Who would take the word of a mill girl over that of a rising lawyer? She must have come here, to the house, must have told her tale of woe to Mabel Turnbull. Mabel Turnbull had seen fit to record the incident along with ... The big man shivered.

He dropped into a chair. Bolton was the biggest town in England, yet the Makepeace woman had found her way to Skirlaugh Fall and into his house. Her grandfather's surname had not registered – it was not a common name, but there were too many Grimshaws in Lancashire to merit undue concern. In truth, he had forgotten about Eileen Grimshaw until today.

His face hurt from twin track marks made by an illegitimate daughter, while his nose, victim of his son-in-law's punch, throbbed with every beat of his heart. He had lost Denis. He realized that the loss of Denis was no small matter, because Denis had always listened, and seldom replied. He was a good gardener, an excellent driver and a man on whom the judge had come to depend.

He needed to find another chauffeur-cum-handyman, someone biddable, grateful and good-tempered. The nose continued to throb – even Denis Makepeace's patience did not last forever. The assaults would have to be ignored – Zachary knew he was in no position to have his assailants arrested. Helen had ensured their freedom from prosecution. She was a clever woman, had probably been a clever child – he should have noticed her. Clever women were a commodity much resented by him – they were unnecessary. But, had he kept her on his side, she might have turned into an asset rather than an adversary.

In the bathroom, he bathed his face, flinching when applying ointment to marks bequeathed by Mrs Agnes Makepeace. His hand stopped in mid-air. She was his daughter; she was carrying his grandchild. Louisa's chances of giving birth to a healthy son were not looking good. That wife of Denis's was a fine specimen – nothing like her downtrodden mother.

'Bloody hell,' he mumbled. 'Fine pickle, this is.' He felt his nose, assumed that it was not broken, went to bed. He lay there for half the night, his mind on one single track – he tried to imagine what was in the Turnbull letter. Helen had judged the contents to be enough to send him to jail – but no, that could not be right. No one had seen. He remained absolutely sure that there had been no witnesses to . . . It was better not to think about that particular event. Nothing could be proved, anyway. Yet he wanted to see both letters, needed to know the lies contained in those pages.

When he slept, he groaned and moaned his way through a dream that was new to him. A long staircase, noises, dragging. What was that? Had he heard the closing of a door? Had the sedatives failed? No, he was imagining the sound. The staircase grew longer. The nearer he got to the bottom, the more stairs it collected. He had to get there soon – had to move the evidence. That door again. No, no, they were fast asleep.

Morning found him in physical pain from yesterday's attacks. His mind, too, was disturbed by the troubled night. Women. This was all the fault of the female of the species, the mothers, wives, sisters and daughters inflicted by God as a punishment on mankind. It wasn't fair. And he had lost Denis.

October was passing. With enormous reluctance, Helen, Agnes and Louisa packed. Denis, who had visited most weekends, carried the baggage out to the car. It was time to go home.

Louisa, leaning for moral support on her stepdaughter, was returning to a man she had not seen since the day Helen had routed him. He had telephoned, had asked about the well-being of his wife and child, but he had not dared to come again to Morecambe. Louisa, in better health, had finally begun to bloom, but she showed signs of wilting when they left the house for the last time.

'Stay with us,' Agnes begged. 'We've got a spare room and you're welcome to it.'

'I can't.'

'I'll look after her,' said Helen. 'She will live with me in my apartment. There's nothing he can do, you see. I'd have fleeced him of all his money by now if I'd chosen to blackmail him. But I want him exactly where he is while I work out what to do with him.'

Agnes shivered. The weather was cold, but not as icy as the tone of Helen Spencer's voice. 'Don't do anything daft, Helen,' she begged.

'I won't.'

Agnes did not believe that. Helen seemed to have achieved a state in which she was calm to the point of madness – if such a thing were possible. The woman had a goal in life, and that goal was probably the destruction of Zachary Spencer. Agnes's own anger remained, but that was a healthy reaction, she believed, since she had only recently found out the name of the person who had impregnated and abandoned her own mother. Perhaps anger cooled over a period of months or years; perhaps she, too, would arrive at a place in which she wanted revenge. But she doubted that. The facts had to be accepted and dealt with – the rewriting of history was an impossibility.

'Agnes?'

She looked at her sister. 'What?'

'Don't worry.'

'I'll try.'

Helen climbed into the front passenger seat while Denis took the wheel. She was calm. But her main goal in life for now was to get past the two births – it was suddenly important that the expected children should be delivered in safety. Louisa, who had become a dear friend, must be guarded at all times; Agnes, Helen's new-found sister, should also be made secure. The babies were the priority for the time being. After the births, open season could begin.

Denis started the car. 'Are we set?' he asked.

'In stone,' replied Helen.

Louisa was weeping softly in the back of the car.

'Don't cry,' begged Agnes. 'Helen will look after you. Once she's made her mind up about something, there's no budging her. He's never hit you, has he?'

'His blows don't show on the surface.' Helen settled back in her seat. 'He's careful like that.' But so was she. Helen was, after all, her father's daughter.

The judge was away. Helen and Louisa settled into the apartment. Their prepared story was to be that Louisa needed a female at hand, because certain symptoms had begun to appear, and a man would not understand. He would fall for that, or so Helen believed. She could not imagine her father wanting to discuss the complicated arrangements of a woman's reproductive system.

Oscar had returned from his holiday with Fred and Denis, who had taken turns to mind him. The dog, who was twice the size he had been a month ago, yapped joyfully when he greeted them. Slightly older and wiser, he knew what he had to do. He had to be here; these women needed him.

They had been back for three days when Kate Moores knocked at their door. 'There's a young fellow to see you,' she told Helen. 'Wants to see you on your own. I'll sit with the missus while you go.'

Helen descended the back staircase slowly. Where was Father? And which young man had he sent to perpetrate some kind of revenge? No, no, he would not dare . . . Would he?

The young man stood in Kate's kitchen, flat cap squashed in nervous hands, a slight slick of sweat glistening on a handsome face. 'Miss Helen Spencer?' he asked timidly.

'For my sins, yes. But you have the advantage of me, because I don't know you at all. Or do I?'

'Harry Timpson, Miss Spencer. My mam asked you to help me and you did.' He moved forward, words tumbling from his lips. 'You've turned my life round. I couldn't have done prison again. It would have killed my mam. Your dad gave me probation – I expected a good three years. But I never blew the safe – I just took the jewellery to sell. Anyway, the long and short is this – I'm not the same person, honest. I have to behave now.'

'Please, it was nothing—'

'It was everything. I mean, I've no job and no money,

287

but I can walk about and meet my mates – as long as I don't break the law. Which is why—' He stopped abruptly.

Helen set the kettle to boil. 'Milk and sugar?' she asked.

He nodded, but remained silent.

She placed the pot on the table, asked him to sit, poured the tea. 'What's bothering you, Harry? May I call you Harry?'

'Aye, it's my name.'

'Well, Harry?'

He took a mouthful of tea. 'I'd be better off with whisky,' he managed.

'Shall I get some?'

'No.' Harry inhaled deeply. 'I'm in a bit of a pickle, as my mother would put it.'

'Oh?'

'Aye.' He drank more of the scalding tea, wiped his mouth on the back of a hand. 'There's this man,' he began lamely.

She decided to allow him to proceed at his own pace.

'He's asked me to do summat. It's a break-in at a lawyer's.'

Helen nodded. He scarcely needed to utter another syllable, but she let him continue.

'I'm to look for files under two names.' Harry bowed his head. 'I'm on probation. If I get caught, my feet won't touch the floor, because nobody would believe the name of the man who told me to do this. He's promised me a job, a proper job, if I do the robbery. He's high up, you see. I'd get years inside and he'd get away with it.'

'The names?' she asked.

He shook his head slowly.

'Do they begin with S and T?'

'Yes.'

'Then I know who has asked you to do that dreadful deed.' She stood up and paced about for a few minutes. 'The man who broke the safe in Manchester – do you know him?'

Harry nodded.

'I'll pay him to do this job in your place. Don't tell me his name – I have no need of it. I shall give him one thousand pounds.'

Harry swallowed. 'Eh?'

'One thousand. But wait until next Friday. Tell my— Tell your employer that it will be next Friday.' She needed time, needed to plant something in those offices – the safe-breaker should not leave empty-handed.

Harry's eyes were bright with a mixture of tears and adoration. She had saved him once and she was about to save him a second time. 'I don't know how to thank you,' he mumbled.

The boot was on a different foot, mused Helen after her grateful visitor had left. Her father was wasting his time by getting the offices raided, because both documents were sealed in an impenetrable vault below the pavement at a Bolton bank. There would be something to be found, though. She intended to hand another sealed letter to Lucy Henshaw. The contents could be quite amusing – she might write *Fooled you, Daddy* – no, she would not do that, because Harry Timpson needed to be in the clear.

A little note reminding George to confirm that her letters were in the bank would suffice. She had already received confirmation, but she could pretend that the letter had gone astray in the post. Life was interesting, she reminded herself as she returned to her rooms.

Revenge was sweet, but it needed to be served cold. There would be something for the burglar to find and, if he were arrested, no one would believe that a judge's daughter had initiated the crime. 'It works both ways, Father,' whispered Helen into the quiet of the hall. 'I can play the game, too.'

'What did he want?' Louisa asked when Helen returned.

'My father is thinking of giving him a job,' she said.

Kate was not pleased. 'I felt safer when Denis was here,' she grumbled.

'We all did.' Louisa went to lie on a sofa. Her back ached, her feet were swollen – and she had another five months to endure.

'That's right, you have a sleep,' advised Kate. 'I'll go and get on with me baking.'

Helen gazed into the flames. It seemed that Father had played right into her hands by asking for Harry Timpson's help. Harry was Helen's man. He was grateful to her and only to her. Harry would be an asset – she would make sure of that.

'What are you cooking up now?' asked a sleepy Louisa.

'Nothing of any consequence. Go to sleep. We'll need our wits about us when Father gets home. If he comes home.' Perhaps he was afraid. Perhaps he would move into his club for good.

'He'll come home,' sighed Louisa.

Helen made no effort to reply. Her father had no home, though his place in hell was booked and waiting. Nothing mattered now, because Helen held the biggest weapon available – she knew his darkest secrets. Let him come, let him go – she had the upper hand and would hold on tightly to the bitterest of ends.

Chapter Eleven

The thousand pounds, filtered through several minor representatives of the Lancashire bad boys, would never be traced back to Helen. When the story of the crime broke, it was given suitable prominence in local newspapers, but the reason for the burglary remained unclear. Several items of no particular import were stolen, and the job was generally believed to be the work of drunken amateurs.

Almost two weeks after the break-in, Judge Zachary Spencer returned to his own domain. He accepted the explanation for his wife's disappearance into Helen's part of the house; then, after a few days had passed, he sent Kate to fetch his daughter. Stalemate had been reached and he needed to clarify matters as quickly as possible.

She sat in a chair opposite his, noticed that his nose advertised his continued dependence on alcohol, thanked God that she had nipped her own problem in the bud. 'Here I am,' she said unnecessarily. 'What can I do for you, Father?'

He closed his eyes for a weary second. 'Look. I don't know what Mabel Turnbull wrote about me, but, whether it's right or wrong, it could do harm to this family.'

Helen nodded her head in agreement. 'It's my insurance policy,' she told him. 'To be used only in the direst of circumstances.'

'Quite. Thus far, we think alike.'

'Yes. Thus far and no further.'

She was more than a match for him now. He studied the set of her mouth, the erect shoulders, the quiet confidence in her face. 'Does anyone else know?' he asked.

'Agnes knows she is my sister – you were there at the time. I'm so glad the scars on your face healed, by the way. Beyond that, I have kept my counsel. There is no point in showing my hand before all betting has ceased. We are the only two players – you will have to take my word for that, since you have no other option. Even her grandfather does not know that you are the reason for Agnes's existence. Thus it will remain unless or until circumstances alter.'

'Good.'

'So now, we negotiate, Father. First, we want Denis back. Harry Timpson is a good worker – thank you for giving him that chance – but we are all used to Denis. I suggest you crawl on your belly and beg Denis to return – even on a part time basis if necessary.'

He blinked rapidly. 'He hit me.'

'Yes, he did.'

'But yours was the weight behind the blow.'

'Yes, it was.'

A short silence ensued. 'I shall give them the deeds to their house – the landlord will sell to me if I offer the right price. The grandfather, too, must be compensated—'

'No. Mr Grimshaw will be kept in the dark about Agnes's situation. He's had one stroke – a second could kill him. He is secure now, thanks to his second wife and his business.'

'I see. Any more conditions?'

'Leave Louisa with me until her confinement – as I told you already, there are complications best dealt with by the females of the species. After the child is born, she will make her own choices and decisions. Father, you have ruled for too long – I think it's time for another Regency period. You and I can be courteous in company, at least. As long as we understand each other, we'll cope. My documents will remain in a bank vault.'

'Ah.'

Helen tried not to smile – the burglary had been a waste of time, energy and money, yet she considered her thousand pounds to have been well spent. She watched while he processed the information, noticed that he did not flinch. 'We have each met our Waterloo,' she said sweetly, 'though I hold the bigger guns. Get Denis back.' After delivering the order for a second time, she left the room.

Judge Zachary Spencer walked to the window and gazed out on the land between Skirlaugh Rise and Skirlaugh Fall. He had to go down there now and prostrate himself before his illegitimate daughter and her husband. Unused to backing down, he watched Harry Timpson as he dragged a wash leather across the bonnet of the Bentley. Harry Timpson was a big man, but he was not suitable for manual work and held no driving licence. 'Bloody women,' cursed the judge as he turned and poured himself a drink. Two daughters, he had now. And he was in thrall to both.

After a large brandy, he decided to get the visit over. It promised not to be easy, yet it had to be done, because Miss Helen Spencer had spoken.

*

293

It was love at not quite first sight. Mags, who had been visiting Agnes, had been brought up to Lambert House in order to see Helen and Louisa. Full of stories about her new social life and about men who wanted to take her out and buy her gifts, Mags Bradshaw was rendered almost speechless by the sight of Harry Timpson. He was a seasoned if petty criminal; she was a legal secretary, but she fell hard.

She had seen him before, of course. He belonged in Noble Street, had lived for years a few houses along from Agnes, but Cupid had never loaded his bow until now. Harry was handsome, quieter than she remembered, polite to the point of shyness and she intended to ignore him.

Nevertheless, reasons for visiting Lambert House suddenly multiplied. She brought new-laid eggs to a village where they were always available, knew that she was carrying the proverbial coals to Newcastle. She bought baby clothes, blankets, a shawl for Louisa's expected baby. Sometimes, he wasn't there. Helen, who had been watching the situation with a degree of glee, decided to step in as ringmaster. She collared Harry one wet afternoon, brought him into the kitchen for a hot drink. Dripping wet, he huddled over the cup, steam rising from his person as he leaned towards the fire. Kate was elsewhere in the house, so Helen embarked on her matchmaking. 'Mags Bradshaw's looking well,' she began.

He nodded, causing a small shower of water to tumble from thick, dark locks. As ever, he hung on to every word uttered by his saviour and mentor. He adored Miss Spencer and it showed. 'She looks different,' he replied eventually.

'Pretty,' said Helen.

'Yes.'

'And she likes you.'

'Oh.' He swallowed the rest of his tea. 'I like her. She always stops and talks to me as if I'm an equal.'

'You are an equal.'

Harry laughed. 'What – me? The only qualification I've got is a life-saving certificate from the swimming baths. I had to sink to the bottom in my pyjamas, pick up a brick and save it from drowning. Oh, and I won the flat race at school once. I could have won again, only Bernard Short cheated. He used to copy my sums as well.'

Helen smiled. 'I notice that you're good with figures.'

'What? Oh, yes – I've always been like that, so Bernard Short got ten out of ten every time. Until the teacher moved him, then he fell flat on his face, but not flat in the flat race.'

Helen stood up and poured more tea. 'Then we'll send you to night school at the technical college. You can become an accountant.'

'But—'

'Leave butting to goats. And ask Mags Bradshaw to go to the cinema with you.'

'Eh?'

'You heard me, Harry. Mags could get any man she wants, but she's taken a liking to you. Look after her. She needs someone steady.'

He laughed joylessly. 'Steady? Aye, steady as a broken rock before I stopped drinking. It was the drink that got me in hot water, you see. I was always drunk when I went on the rob.'

'I gave up drinking, too,' she said. 'Take her out.'

He whistled softly. 'Are you sure?'

'Have I ever lied to you?'

'No. You're the best thing that's ever happened to me – apart from Mam. Mam was stuck with me, had to help me, but you chose.'

'I had my reasons.'

'I don't care.' He would have gone to the ends of the earth for Helen Spencer. 'You got me one last chance and I won't forget it. Mind you, I'm not so sure about working for your dad – sorry.'

'You're working for me, Harry.'

'OK.'

'And you're going to ask Mags out.'

Harry coughed. 'I'd feel daft.'

Helen sighed. 'You can't get all the way through life without feeling daft. It's daft to expect to get through without feeling daft.'

He understood her perfectly. He would always understand her perfectly.

By the time Judge Zachary Spencer arrived at the Makepeace cottage, its residents were already fully conversant with the plot. On the telephone, Helen had mithered, as had Louisa, until Denis had finally agreed to give the old swine a hearing. As for the deeds to the house – he would accept those without a quibble. Agnes had never received anything from her biological father – their child would get something, at least, in the form of a small, stone-built dwelling.

Agnes opened the door. She had not expected to feel embarrassed, yet she did. This was her dad. She didn't like him and would probably never like him, but he was related to her. 'Come in,' she said softly. He did not look at her as he walked into the house.

Zachary Spencer had always been a good public

speaker, which quality had taken him all the way to the top of the legal tree, but he had never been competent in a small setting. He needed to preach, to be heard by as many as possible; he needed the right setting and a big audience – here, he had neither.

Denis stood in front of the fire, his stance reminiscent of Judge Spencer's attitude on the day of reckoning in Morecambe, the day when Agnes and Denis had both injured him. 'Well?'

'The past,' began the judge, 'must be laid to rest. We have all been at fault. When the child is born, I shall set up a fund.' He waited for thanks, but received none.

Agnes was seated, hands folded in her lap. Her father, acutely aware that both his daughters were strong women, glanced sideways at her. 'I am sorry,' he said, his voice strained by the necessary apology. 'I was in the wrong.'

The Makepeaces nodded.

'Denis, I want you to come back to the house as chauffeur and handyman. Harry Timpson is a good enough sort, but he doesn't drive. He's learning, but he hasn't passed his test yet.'

Prepared by the Spencer women, who had dripped on him like water on stone, Denis made his reply. 'I have another job, sir, with a friend who is renovating a barn.'

'Ah.'

'I can't just walk out on him. Will you take a seat?'

The judge sat. 'There's a lot of that going on these days,' he offered in an effort to punctuate the weighty silence. 'Barns and so forth being made into houses. Sensible idea, I suppose. Though crops will always need storage . . .' His voice died.

'Yes.'

Two robins fought on a bush outside the front window. Robins, mused Agnes, were aggressive little buggers. Two angry robins outside, two inside. And who was she? Jenny Wren? Her supposed father spoke not to her, but to the man of the house. She didn't count, didn't matter, was only a woman. 'If my baby is female, will you still set up an account?'

At last, he looked at her. But his expression betrayed the impression that he had been interrupted from an unexpected source. 'Of course I will.'

Agnes leaned her head to one side. 'You know, Judge Spencer, you should have lived in Victorian times when women stayed at home and had vapours; when their dads could throw them out for no reason. Or maybe you'd be best off in one of those Eastern countries where wives and daughters stay several paces behind the men. You've used and abused women all your life, haven't you? Oh, and I'd better remind you – we have the vote these days.'

He simmered, but dared not explode.

'We sit on juries, some of us are doctors – even lawyers. Ah, but you know all about that, don't you?'

'Mrs Makepeace, I am here to make peace.'

Denis did not smile; neither did his wife. Their surname often brought forth puns and silly jokes.

'I'll do three days,' said Denis, anxious for the meeting to close. 'Thursday, Friday and Saturday, I'll help George.'

'George Henshaw?' The older man's face reddened. They were all in it together, of course.

'Yes,' replied Denis. 'That's the chap.'

The judge looked at his watch, remembered an appointment, made his excuses and left. Denis saw him off the premises, then dropped into a chair next to his wife. 'Well, Helen's certainly got him sorted out,' he observed. 'I wonder what else is in that letter? Being your dad isn't enough to reduce him to the state he's in. There's more, isn't there, love?'

There must be a lot more. Agnes wondered yet again about Judge Spencer's past misdeeds, tried to imagine anything bad enough to make the stubborn old man submit. 'It has to be either rape, massive theft, or murder,' she concluded out loud. 'For him, rape would scarcely be enough. It has to be worse than rape.' She shivered. The days were becoming shorter and colder, although pregnancy was easier in weather like this.

'Are you all right, love?' he asked.

'Something walked across my grave, Denis. It's bad enough thinking he might have raped my mam – but murder?'

'He didn't murder her. She died in bed, didn't she?'

Agnes nodded. He hadn't murdered Eileen Grimshaw, but he had taken the life from her, had probably removed her will to live. 'People kill people without actually murdering them,' she said softly. 'If someone stamps hard enough on your soul, you can die many times over.'

'Stop it, Agnes.'

'I'll be all right in a minute.'

Denis hoped so. For over twenty years, his wife had existed in the 'father unknown' category of life. That was difficult enough for anyone, but, for Agnes, the discovery of her father's identity had brought no relief. She was pregnant and tormented. She knew that the blood of Zachary Spencer ran through her own veins. She knew that her child would carry that same blood, albeit to a more diluted degree. 'Agnes?'

299

'What?'

'I have to go back to the house – you know that. They don't feel safe. Even Helen can't make them feel completely safe. Kate needs me there, too.'

'I know. They explained it enough times.'

'We have to get on with it.'

'I know that as well. It's just that . . .' She couldn't express how she felt, though a terrible feeling of dread had descended on her. Denis should not go back, yet he must. Her reluctance was all a part of being pregnant, she supposed.

'Just that what?' he asked.

'Nothing,' she said. 'It was nothing. Put the kettle on.'

The No Poultry Allowed party was the brainchild of Helen Spencer. 'I don't mean a political party,' she said in response to her half-sister's quizzical expression. 'Christmas evening. We'll all have eaten turkey, chicken or goose at lunchtime, so I vote we have anything except poultry. My father will be at his club with all the other lonely bachelors and widowers. So Louisa and I decided to have a bit of a gathering.'

They were with Louisa in Helen's apartment. She was looking well, was eating everything in her path and was even managing the odd quip. 'The rooster will be absent,' she remarked. 'He can crow in Manchester where we can't hear him.'

There had been little crowing from that source, thought Agnes as she accepted a cup of coffee. This was now Helen's house, with Helen's rules and Helen's style. The main rooms remained unaffected, but the flat used by her and Louisa was modern, all G-plan and teak, glass inserts in tables, rooms divided by open bookshelves, a light, airy feel to the place.

'Mags is head over heels,' Louisa remarked. 'And that young man of hers is doing very well at the college – his tutor says he's a natural accountant.'

Helen almost choked in her tea. 'There's nothing natural about accountants,' she spluttered. 'They're like lawyers – focused to the point of obsession. But he sailed through second year exams at the test, and he's only been there three months.' She was pleased with herself; she had found what her father might have begrudgingly termed a primitive genius. 'I'm glad for Mags,' she added.

'What about you, though?' Louisa asked.

Helen looked at her young stepmother. 'I have a different role to play. There can be no room for marriage in my life, Louisa. Like an accountant, I am completely focused.'

Sometimes, Helen frightened Agnes. A bright and amusing woman who had acquired her self-certainty almost at the cost of her sanity, Helen Spencer was an enigma. When she spoke of her father, her eyes seemed to darken, while the corners of her mouth dipped, as if she tasted something unpalatable. The calm she displayed was a cloak. It hid a turmoil too deep to be allowed space at the surface, yet it burned white-hot in her bones. To a mere onlooker, she was considerate, happy with immediate friends, capable of delivering a joke. Yet often, when companions spoke among themselves, she retreated into her shell, brow furrowing as she visited her own centre.

'Marriage is good,' Louisa said. 'I am so happy. Look at the daughter I acquired, look how she takes care of me.'

Agnes shook her head. Louisa wasn't married at all. She saw her husband a few times a month and spent the rest of her time with Helen and Oscar, who had calmed slightly now that his second lot of teeth had broken through. The new furniture had been bought only after his chewing phase had ended. He was a good dog. While the women talked, he lay at their feet, sometimes asleep, often glancing from one to another as if trying to understand their conversations.

'I have a list,' Helen announced.

'She likes lists,' said Louisa. 'Her whole life is planned in a locked drawer – isn't it, Helen?'

The dog scratched an ear.

'Not all of it, no,' Helen replied. 'But I shall be cooking on Christmas Day, so that's a big list. Kate will rest. She's on the guest list—'

'Another list.' Louisa laughed.

'Yes.' Undismayed, Helen continued. 'And we shall eat in the kitchen – I'm not keen on the dining room.'

The dog woofed.

'Yes, you'll get the leftovers.' Helen patted his head. 'This will be our last child-free Christmas – let's make the most of it.'

Agnes was certain that Helen Spencer was looking forward to the births of the two babies. Gone were the days when she feared being ousted by the new addition to her household, while the arrival of her niece or nephew was anticipated with pleasure displayed in the form of concern for Agnes and gifts for the nursery. But what was she up to this time? 'Are you sure he won't be here?'

'Our father who will never be in heaven?' Helen, who had stopped going to church, had got into the habit of referring to her father in biblical terms that were not far short of heresy. He would be Lazarus without resurrection, a shaven Samson, the stunned Goliath, Moses minus tablets, Judas at the feast – but not at this feast. 'He won't be here.'

'Are you really sure?'

Helen shrugged. 'We haven't done Christmas for years. When I was little, someone would stay in the house to give me my presents – a servant, a nanny – anyone who would agree to do it for a bit of money. Since I grew up, I have spent all my Christmases alone.'

A tear pricked Agnes's right eye. Christmas had always been magical for her. Stocking filled with tiny toys and nuts, always a surprise in the toe. One year, the surprise had been a little silver ring – she had out-grown it years ago. Downstairs, there would be a doll, or a toy sewing machine, several books. Dinner was chicken, as turkey could never be afforded. Her father would have had a good dinner, she supposed. But not with Helen, never with his own daughter. 'I had lovely Christmases, Helen. I wish you'd been there then. There wasn't a lot of money—'

'But there was love,' Helen finished for her.

'Yes.'

'Mr and Mrs Grimshaw will come, I hope. And Mags with Harry. We'll be merry if it kills us. Of course, we can't play cards, because my stepmother cheats.'

Louisa clouted Helen with a newspaper. 'I came up in the school of hard knocks.'

'As did I,' Helen said. 'Money, but no love. This party is for all of us, so that I can show my gratitude to those who have helped turn my life around. The loyal toast will be the Queen, the Duke of Lancaster and Mabel Turnbull. She knew loyalty.'

Agnes shivered. There was no point in asking Helen

to reveal in its entirety the document she had read, because such a request would receive no more than a polite refusal. The automatic response had been delivered many times – Helen remained as secretive as ever. 'Do we bring anything?' she asked.

'Just yourselves.' Helen smiled at her sister. She, too, wished that those long-ago Christmases could have been spent with Agnes. 'I wonder how many of us there are and whether we are all female,' she said, almost as if speaking to herself. 'There could be dozens of little Spencers spread across the northern circuit. He's a rake, but I am the shovel that will dispose of him.'

A heavy silence rested on the shoulders of Agnes and Louisa.

Helen laughed. 'Don't look so glum. I am speaking metaphorically, of course.'

Agnes was not sure, would never be sure. She changed the subject. 'Your doll's house is almost ready,' she told Louisa. 'Even the cellars are included. He's charging your husband a fortune for it, says it will allow him to charge less when it comes to ordinary folk.'

Louisa shook her head. The doll's house was not for her – it was for the proud owner of the house on which it had been modelled. 'It will be kept in the hall,' she said, 'so that everyone can see what a wonderful home the judge has.'

'He never has visitors,' said Agnes. 'It's for himself.'

'Isn't everything?' Helen stood and walked to the door. 'I declare this meeting of the NPA party closed. Unless there's any other business?'

Louisa raised a deliberately hesitant hand. 'Please, miss?'

'Yes?'

304

'Will somebody get Oscar off my foot? The toes have gone dead – he's cut off my circulation.'

Helen whistled and the dog dashed to her side.

'Thanks.' Louisa stretched her legs and counted her feet. 'I seem to have two,' she said.

'Don't brag,' quipped Helen. 'You'll soon have four.' She left the room.

'It's a big thing, isn't it?' Agnes asked. 'The thought of producing another human being, I mean. I'm not talking about the pain – it's the afterwards that frightens me. If a child is good and successful, they get the credit. If not, the blame is ours.'

Louisa was staring into the fire. 'I won't raise a child,' she said quietly.

'No. He'll get nannies and nurses, I suppose. The judge, I mean.'

After several seconds, Louisa replied. 'Yes. That's how it will be.' She leaned her head against the wing of her chair and dozed.

Agnes waited until Louisa was asleep, then crept from the room. Across the landing, Helen was seated at a bureau in her bedroom, head down, right shoulder moving. She was probably continuing with her book. Agnes left the author to the necessary privacy and silence.

Helen put down her pen, listened as her sister walked out of the apartment, looked down at the list she had made. Louisa was right – her stepdaughter was a maker of lists. The page she currently worked on was one no one must see. Its subject was retribution . . .

Christmas Day was fine, but cold. The party, due to begin at seven in the evening, was delayed slightly by

Helen's over-ambition in the area of cookery. Her philosophy was simple – if a person could read, he or she could cook. It did not run to plan. Six o'clock found her on the phone to her new sister. She refused to allow Agnes to fetch Kate, because Kate cooked frequently in the kitchen of Lambert House, and this was one of Kate's few holidays.

'What the heck have you done?' Agnes asked.

'Crème caramel is my first problem. It's in a bain marie and it's as stiff as the bread board.'

'Oh. Did you put water in your caramel?'

'What?'

'It's probably stuck. You've got melted sugar acting as glue. Start again.'

'There isn't time.'

'Cheese and biscuits?'

'That's the last course. We still need a pudding.'

'I've an apple pie, half a trifle and some mince tarts,' said Agnes.

'Bring them. Bring everything. Bring hammer and chisel for this crème caramel. Bring the fire brigade and bring Denis. I am in a mess.'

Agnes replaced the receiver and turned to her husband. 'Helen's in a mess.'

'Ah.'

'What do you mean, "Ah"?'

'She's bound to be in a mess. Her doings with ovens stop at warming up what Kate leaves. I thought she was taking too much on. Game pie? When she told me she was making that, I decided I wasn't game enough for her pie. Too ambitious, she is.'

'She needs us. Come on, shape yourself.'

He shaped himself and both entered the kitchen of Lambert House within half an hour. It was a war zone.

The table was littered with eggshells and implements; the floor was in a similar state. Helen was nowhere to be seen. Denis sighed. 'She's got herself in a right pickle this time, Agnes.'

The woman in question crawled out from beneath the large table. 'I've lost an onion,' she pronounced.

'Does she know her onions?' Denis asked.

Agnes shook her head. 'Probably not. She's likely lost a cauliflower. Perhaps she calls a cauliflower an onion—'

'A spade a lawnmower?' asked Denis helpfully.

The mistress of the house struggled to her feet. 'Shut up, both of you. My consommé is lumpy, the beef's still rare enough to be saying moo and you've got the pudding, I hope.'

'Yes.' Agnes placed a basket on the table. 'Right – stock cubes?'

Helen waved in the direction of a cupboard.

'I'll do imitation French onion soup – if you can find the onion. Denis – clean up and sort out the puddings.' She glared at Helen. 'You can just bugger off. Where's the game pie?'

'In the pigswill bucket.'

'Good. So it's pretend French onion soup, roast beef with Yorkshires and veg, then leftovers for pudding, followed by cheese.' Agnes cast an eye over Helen. 'You haven't managed to ruin the cheese, by any chance?'

'The cheese is fine,' said Helen before stalking out of the arena.

Agnes and Denis looked at each other and burst out laughing. It was one of those rare and precious moments in life when laughter takes over, when the body becomes too weak to fight hilarity. They cobbled together a meal of sorts, each working hard not to surrender to mirth all over again. It was an image worth remembering, thought Agnes. With flour on her nose and in her hair, Miss Helen Spencer had looked every inch the angry housewife. It had been fun.

The party started well. Eva, suitably impressed by her first taste of 'foreign' food, sipped politely from her soup spoon. Agnes, who had made the soup from half a dozen stock cubes and three onions, almost suffocated on her own spoonful. Helen pretended to glare at her. 'Careful,' she warned. 'You'll choke.'

Denis proved the worst. His silliness took him further than his wife was willing to travel. 'Helen?' he said.

'Yes?'

'You're a good cook. This is lovely soup.' The word 'soup' emerged slightly crippled, because Agnes kicked him under the table. With the air of an injured angel, he continued to enjoy his strange food. 'Are we having that game pie?' he asked, his face framed in innocence.

Agnes kicked him again.

'I decided on beef,' replied Helen.

'Good.' Fred Grimshaw slurped another mouthful of French onion. 'If I see another turkey butty, I'll scream.'

Agnes laid down her spoon. She had taken enough of her Oxo cube and onion. 'Shall I check the beef and Yorkshires, or will you, Helen?'

'Thank you. You do it.'

Agnes escaped to the far end of the room. Lucy and George, too polite to say much, were looking at each other in bewilderment. Mags and Harry had eyes only for each other, while Louisa, determined to eat anything and everything in sight, scooped up her soup without comment. It was Kate who broke the silence. 'This is nobbut Oxo with an onion in it,' she exclaimed.

Thus ended the charade. 'Out of the mouths of babes and servants,' Agnes muttered from the safer end of the room.

The story was told by Helen, who was prompted all the way by Denis. Kate hid her face in her napkin, her shaking back betraying uncontrollable glee.

George stood and pushed thumbs under his lapels, voice imitating that of the judge at whose table he was dining. 'The defendant must stand,' he ordered.

Helen stood.

'Before I pass sentence, may I say how dim a view I take of plagiarism. You have stolen the work of another woman and have passed it off as your own.'

'Yes, m'lud.' Helen's tone was suitably subdued.

'Have you anything to say before sentence is passed?'

'Yes, m'lud.'

'Very well.'

Helen inhaled deeply. 'I do not know my onions, m'lud. Nor do I know my bain marie from my elbow, if your lordship will permit so bold a statement. I am but a poor serving girl with no brain, no hope and no pudding.'

George smiled at Lucy, composed himself and carried on holding court. 'Your sentence will be three years in the Cordon Bleu Prison, Paris – which is in France.'

'Yes, m'lud.'

'This is one of the worst cases I have tried. Yes, it has been very trying. Compensation will be made to every person who has suffered as a result of your French onion soup and you will pay all costs pertaining to this case. Mrs Agnes Makepeace will no doubt take her own measures via litigation. All rise.'

309

They rose.

'This court is closed.'

They sat.

A shadow in the doorway became flesh. Judge Zachary Spencer walked into the kitchen. 'Very funny, Mr Henshaw,' he said.

Oscar, who had been sitting hopefully by the table, shot out of the room. He didn't like the big man. Nobody liked the big man.

George blushed, but made no reply. Lucy spoke in his defence. 'It was just a bit of fun.'

'Quite.' Judge Spencer looked at all the people in the room. A mixed bunch, they represented most levels of society, and they had been having fun at his expense. He had paid for the food; he was also the subject of mimicry. It occurred to him that he was the outsider, that he was condemned to look at life through tinted glass. He was alone, had always been alone.

His daughter – the real one – had managed to carve out a niche for herself. She sat among Henshaws, Makepeaces and others, seemed at ease with them and with herself. Well, she had been at ease before noticing her father. Now, she was staring at him with naked loathing in her eyes. He ignored her, walked into the kitchen, kissed his wife on the cheek, then left the room.

Silence reigned, the quiet interrupted only by the over-enthusiastic slamming of the vast front door. 'He's gone,' breathed Lucy. She no longer feared that Helen might be untrustworthy; Lucy realized at last the poor woman was the product of a brute and that Helen deserved better.

'I wonder what he wanted?' asked Louisa.

'A good kick up the backside.' Fred answered for

everyone present. 'Is that blinking beef ready yet? We're all dying of hunger.'

He drove at a furious rate in the direction of Manchester. After travelling so far just to visit his wife, he had found her ensconced with all kinds of idiots in the kitchen. In the kitchen? What on earth was Helen thinking of? There were servants at the feast, there was George Henshaw trying to be clever with his impertinent imitation of the man who owned the very table at which he was eating. 'Preposterous,' he spat.

The club was tedious. This year, only a handful of geriatric widowers and bachelors were in residence, most of them deaf, some in their delinquent dotage. There was no one to listen to tales of interesting cases, no one who was capable of enjoying a sermon on the legal system. He was bored.

Oh, well. There was nothing else for it – he would have to take an evening meal in the company of his peers. The conversation would involve symptoms of illnesses, requests for mustard, loud comments on the cardboard consistency of the meat. Some old beggar would break wind at table. Waiters would decide to ignore it, but Zachary Spencer would hear all, see all and say nothing.

At Lambert House, people were having fun. Zach did not believe in fun, as it wasted time that might be better spent in the furthering of one's career, yet he had a strong suspicion that he had been missing something. His daughter had looked happy. The other one, basting meat at the cooker, had ignored him. Happy? How happy would Helen be when a son turned up to deprive her of her inheritance?

He parked the car and entered the club. It smelled of old people, stale food and spilt drink. His own home had been taken from him by Helen, who had invited his other so-called daughter to share in the spoils. Well, it wasn't over yet. Soon, a son would be born.

Fred was rubbish at charades. Incapable of acting without speaking, he was sacked in the first round, thereby depriving his team of several points. He said it wasn't fair, he hadn't been ready and he'd never heard of the book whose title he had been trying to convey to team mates. 'What the hell's wuthering?' he asked. 'I can't wuther. Did she mean wither, that there Brontë woman? Or did she mean weather?'

'Or whether, or whither?' added George helpfully.

Fred glared at him. 'Shut up,' he ordered. 'For a lawyer, you're no bloody use at all. No wonder the court system costs too much. Where do you think you're going?' he asked Lucy, who was another member of his team.

'I'm just wuthering off to the bathroom,' she replied.

Fred retreated to his chair and grumbled softly about young people not being as they used to be. There was no respect any more and people were getting too big for their clogs.

Oscar, who had enjoyed many leftovers from the hastily prepared feast, stretched out on the rug in front of the drawing room fire. As the rug had been the stage, charades was abandoned while Helen and Agnes experimented with mulled wine. Fred poured himself a whisky, declaring that he had had enough of being a guinea pig for mulling, wuthering and culi-

312

nary disaster, so they could leave him out of the mixture.

Agnes, who was being disturbed by the movements of Nuisance, sat aside from the rest of the party. If Nuisance was going to practise cartwheels, she would need to be near the door in order to reach the bathroom when required. She watched her family – this was her family now. Pop, whom she had loved for a lifetime, continued to argue about wutherings and mullings. He was doing well in business, was content with his second wife, and was always at his most satisfied when involved in a dispute. He was involved at this moment, so he was as happy as a dog with two tails.

Eva, hoping that no one was watching, was fiddling with a tiny gold-coloured safety pin in an effort to fasten her blouse – a button had shot off into her food, an accident caused by hilarity during the meal. Once her blouse was fastened, Eva dozed by the fire. Pop was old, but happy; Eva was older because of her weight and all those years spent making a living at the top of Noble Street. They were a special breed and, Agnes hoped, not a dying one.

Helen, her new-found sister who had been the grey, listless librarian, was very much alive this evening. She had ousted her father, had humiliated him in front of many of the people here tonight. Only Pop and Eva remained unaware of the relationship between Helen and Agnes.

Lucy and George were still blissful. It was a good marriage, Agnes believed. No longer resistant to the approaches of Helen Spencer, Lucy had enjoyed herself this evening. George was quieter, because he was the one who had been caught by the judge while imitating him, yet even he seemed to know that Zachary Spencer's days were numbered. What would happen, Agnes wondered. When would Helen reveal the ace she held so close to her chest?

Mags, who had grown into her new nose, stared lovingly into the handsome face of Glenys Timpson's oldest lad. Agnes smiled to herself. Harry had always been a source of trouble to his mother, yet he had settled into his studies and showed great promise – which fact, Agnes thought, was sufficient to verify the saying about every dog having his day.

The canine dog was certainly having his day. Replete and exhausted by the effort of over-eating, Oscar lay at Eva's feet. They seemed to be indulging in synchronized snoring – the company was suddenly silent as each person became aware of the comic scene.

Oscar rolled over and broke the rhythm. 'Shame, that,' muttered Fred. 'I were going to accompany them two on me comb and paper.'

Kate and Albert laughed. They were the best neighbours in the world and Agnes was glad to know them.

Denis was joking with George. The scars left on Denis's lungs had not been too troublesome this winter, so that was another worry gone.

Only Louisa remained. Agnes cast an eye over the young woman who had married a man twice her age in order to secure a safe future for herself. But she had gained a good friend in her stepdaughter and motherhood would surely bring its own reward. Yet her husband remained in the house even though he was absent. It was as if he stained everything he touched, because each person here had been affected by him to a greater or lesser degree.

The thoughts came full circle. Agnes found herself

gazing at Helen yet again. Laughing and joking, she seemed to fool most people, though Agnes was not convinced by the act. Helen's anger was so deep that it had cooled all the way down to ice. She had a plan of some kind and it was tied up in the letters held by a Bolton bank under the instruction of George Henshaw. The judge seldom came home; he was threatened by his daughter and chose to keep a distance between himself and his own house.

Helen arrived at Agnes's side. 'You're quiet.'

'I'm tired – Nuisance is learning to dance.'

'He'll be born walking, then.'

'Probably. Helen?'

'What? Oh, not again, Agnes. Stop worrying. Nothing will happen. He'll simply disappear one day and we'll have peace.'

'Disappear?'

'Yes. Retire abroad – whatever.'

'And Louisa?'

Helen shrugged. 'Will stay with me.'

'The baby?'

'We haven't got there yet. Can't you just enjoy Christmas, Agnes? You're surrounded by friends and family, yet you still worry about Father. Forget him. He is a man of no importance.'

With that, Agnes had to be satisfied.

Chapter Twelve

As the date of Louisa's confinement drew near, Judge Spencer began to spend more time at Lambert House. Louisa, who was in better health, appointed herself peacekeeper during this stressful time. Helen, living in her own apartment, saw little of her father; Louisa, in search of a more tranquil household, divided her time between the two adversaries. She was a poor go-between, as she determinedly avoided conversations involving any controversy, and she realized that the relationship between father and daughter was not easily redeemable. She continued to eat well, using the latter part of her pregnancy as a cocoon inside which she was safe. But she dreaded the afterwards. The real trouble would begin once the baby had been delivered. For now, she was cushioned by her passenger, and she chose not to think too clearly about the birth and its aftermath.

Helen kept to herself, emerging only to visit Agnes. Mags and Lucy came each Thursday to the Makepeace cottage, and Helen was now part of the group. The subject of Helen's letter and the accompanying document from the deceased nanny had ceased to wear out telephone lines between the houses of Agnes, Mags and Lucy; the matter was no longer raised in the presence of Helen Spencer, and it seemed to die a natural death as the confinement of Agnes drew near.

'It's going to be a whopper,' declared Lucy, who, still slim as a reed, was munching on a chocolate bar.

'I hate you.' Agnes looked down, tried to see her feet, failed. She raised one leg to display a slightly swollen ankle. 'Ah, there you are,' she told the foot. 'But there should be two of you.'

Helen ate a sandwich. 'Louisa looks like a galleon in full sail. I'd swear she was carrying twins, but the doctors say not. It seems she's storing fluids. If she gets any bigger, we could rent her out as a petrol tanker.'

'Better a commercial vehicle than an object that stays in and waits,' Agnes grumbled. 'I'm a thing now – not a person. I'm just a building that's been placed around this child.' She patted her belly. 'I'm going to have a raffle when it's born. The winner gets the baby, three dozen nappies, a Silver Cross – second hand – and a good supply of clothing.'

'Green Shield stamps?' asked Lucy.

'Definitely not. I'm saving up for a coffee percolator.' Agnes winced. 'I didn't like that.'

'What?' asked Mags.

'Pain in my back.'

Helen sat up straight in her chair. She had read a book about labour and considered herself something of an expert. 'It can start there,' she advised cheerfully. 'The coccyx moves.'

'Does it?' Agnes shifted her weight. 'I'm not due. The coccyx can stay where it is or it'll be raffled off along with the rest.'

The three women stared hard at their friend.

'Stop it!' she yelled. 'Unless you paid to come in, you are not to look at the exhibits. Also, this zoo is closed until the spring. We are hibernating. Now, bugger off and let me get some sleep.'

Helen remained when the others had left. She declared her intention to stay until Denis got home. The book was in the car. A person who could read could deliver a child; a person who could read had failed to deliver a simple crème caramel . . . 'Any more pain?'

'No. The only discomfort I'm feeling comes from the expression on your face. I'm not due for a couple of weeks. Even if it does start, it can take days. God – can we not talk about something else?'

Helen grinned. 'Yes, we can. Your grandfather's work is on display in the main hall at Lambert House. It is brilliant, though. He did the immediate garden, and the house lifts off, section by section, until you reach the cellars. Father said – to Louisa, of course – that Mr Grimshaw can bring people in to look at his handiwork. The TV people are to be involved again, along with several newspapers. Your grandfather is a star.'

Agnes groaned.

'Are you all right?'

'No, I'm not all right. He's bad enough without being a bloody star. It'll all go to his head. He'll get himself excited, then he'll start going too fast for his own good. Poor Eva and Albert will bear the brunt. There'll be no living with him.'

'Oh, dear. Sorry.'

'Not your fault. He will push himself until he has another stroke, but that's his nature. Or he may prove too stubborn to have another attack – he could outlive us all. He will certainly brag about his house in your house.'

'Never mind.'

'Exactly.'

Helen smoothed her skirt. 'Our father who isn't in heaven is talking of retirement. According to Louisa, he

318

intends to spend much of his time on the yacht. I never saw her more pleased, because she won't take a baby to sea. We may survive despite him.'

Agnes looked at her visitor. She knew full well that Helen's brain seldom rested, that her thoughts were predominantly about her father and the damage he had done throughout his life. More specifically, there was one occasion in particular that had resurrected itself and Helen brooded about whatever it was. There was no point in asking; Agnes had stopped wasting time in that area months earlier. 'Denis will be home soon. Go back and make sure that Louisa is OK.'

'You're due before she is.'

'I know that, Helen, but babies are not trains – they don't run to a timetable.'

'Nor do trains. All right, all right, I shall go. Phone me if you need me. Promise?'

'Promise.'

Helen bent and planted a kiss on her sister's head. These babies would thrive in safety. Whatever it took, Helen Spencer would make sure of that.

'Helen, why don't you find yourself a nice man? Has there been no one since—'

'Since the balding eagle? No.'

'I was going to say since Denis.'

'Ah.' Helen blushed. 'Denis was one of my crazy times. I suppose I went through my teenage at thirty-two. No. My energies are directed elsewhere. Into writing, for a start.'

'For a start? I thought you'd stopped.'

Helen sighed. 'My dear, disabuse yourself of the mistaken concept that an author writes only with a pen or a typewriter. Every waking moment is spent writing. In here.' She tapped her head. 'It's a collection box.

When it gets full, I shall empty it, discard the dross and polish the good stuff.'

'But no man?'

'No.'

It was more than writing, mused Agnes when Helen had left. She was concentrating on something, and the something was a worry. Denis, too, had remarked on the preoccupation of Miss Helen Spencer. She was up to no good. But the room was warm and sleep beckoned. With her hands folded on the ever-increasing mound of her belly, Agnes slept the sleep of the very pregnant.

Denis came out of the pub. He was two quid better off after a game of dominoes and was looking forward to a brisk walk homeward. When he reached the bottom of the lane that led up to Skirlaugh Rise, he stopped. 'Judge Spencer? What are you doing here?'

'Waiting for you.'

'Ah.' What did the old beggar want at this time of night? 'I'm on my way home,' said Denis.

'I know. Just give me five minutes. It's about my daughter.'

Denis cleared his throat. 'Oh? Which one?'

'Helen.'

'Right. What do you want from me?'

Much as he hated to beg, Zachary knew that he had no alternative. 'Talk to her. Ask her whether she would thrive if she made public the contents of Mabel Turnbull's meanderings. Ask whether her expected sibling would thrive on the exposure of such lies. I just want . . .' What did he want?

'Yes?' asked Denis.

'I want things back to normal – family meals and so forth – the way Louisa had it when we were first married. My daughter hates me, but something must be done before my son is born.'

Denis did not ask how the judge would feel should the son turn out to be yet another daughter. 'I don't carry that much weight with Miss Helen, sir.'

'You carried enough to strike me a few months ago. Try. I want my house in some sort of order.' He placed a hand on Denis's arm. 'Tell me – how is Agnes?'

Denis blinked. Was the old bugger softening in his old age? 'She's OK, thanks. Getting a bit fed up with the weight and the swollen ankles, drinks a lot of bitter lemon – she's uncomfortable.'

'Give her my best wishes.' With that last unnerving request, the man disappeared into the blackness of the Rise. 'Blood and stomach pills,' mumbled Denis, 'he has to be going off his rocker.' Perhaps insanity ran in the family? Or was the judge genuinely interested in improving the lives of all around him? Probably not. He was more likely to be making an attempt to make his own existence more bearable.

Denis entered the house. His wife was asleep in a chair, feet propped on a padded footstool, hands folded across her swollen abdomen. Give her Judge Spencer's best wishes? Not likely – he wanted to keep her blood pressure at an acceptable level. He kissed her. 'Cocoa?'

Agnes opened an eye. 'Bitter lemon, please.'

'You don't like bitter lemon. You've always hated bitter lemon.'

She yawned. 'Tell that to the passenger on the lower deck. It's all his fault.'

Denis made his cocoa while Agnes chattered on about the visit of Mags, Lucy and Helen, complaining loudly about Lucy, who could eat sweets and chocolates with obvious impunity. 'I haven't had chocolate in six months,' she moaned.

'Have some cocoa – that's chocolate.'

But no, she had to have her bitter lemon. They sat in front of the fire like an old married couple, each too tired to talk or move. Agnes knew that this was a precious time, that the marriage would change once there were three of them. 'I love you, kid,' she told her husband. 'I'm saying it now before the dynamics get bewildered, before I become all nappies and feeds and walks with a pram.'

Denis grinned. She would be the best mam in the world. And he couldn't wait to be a dad.

He woke sweating again. As far as he could remember, Zachary had never suffered from nightmares. Even after . . . after that business many years ago, he had slept the sleep of the just.

He switched on a lamp and struggled into a sitting position. The room was cool, yet his skin seemed to be heated by the fires of hell. Some medics were of the opinion that everyone had dreams and that they were often forgotten, but Zachary had not been aware of dreaming. Until now. Until now, when his daughter occupied the witness stand, the judge's seat and every space along the jury's benches. Almost every night during his sleep, she appeared and screamed out his sins for the world to hear. Journalists dashed in all directions, each needing to be the first to break the story of a corrupt judge.

When he poured the brandy, decanter and glass

shook in uncertain hands. He could do nothing, because Helen had protected herself. Even were she to die of natural causes, the documents would be opened. Brandy burned in his throat, dragging into his digestive tract any vestige of heat that had been present in his sweat-slicked body. The shivering began, so he staggered to a wardrobe, found an extra blanket and placed it on his bed. Denis Makepeace? Forced to beg the help of one of his two manservants, he hated his daughter all the more. He should have made an ally of her, because she was proving to be a formidable enemy. Women were stealing positions of authority, were called to the bar, were becoming hospital consultants and managers of industry. He should have noticed, should have encouraged her.

It was too late for that. But it was never too late to paper over cracks. He, Louisa, Helen and the expected child should cobble together an outwardly happy picture of domesticity. Denis, nearer in age to Helen, might just be able to plead the cause on his master's behalf. But even Denis had little time for his employer. He did his duty and no more, was always keen to return to his wife or to his other job. It all boiled down to those damned letters in the vault of some damned bank, contents to be revealed in the event of Helen's demise.

Retirement beckoned. Many judges continued into their dotage, but this judge was standing – or sitting – on rocky ground. He had his yacht and could disappear whenever he chose, but first, he had to be here for the birth of Louisa's child. Another brandy slipped down into his stomach and he leaned back against the pillows. He needed sleep, dreaded the dream, hoped that the brandy would preclude it. It wasn't fair. Life had never been fair. Pitying himself for his gross misfortunes, Judge Spencer fell asleep for a second time. And the dream came again.

For the sake of Louisa, Helen agreed to the terms put forward via Denis. An uneasy truce ensued, with all three Spencers eating together in the main dining room when the judge was at home. When he was away, the two women returned to Helen's apartment to experiment with Helen's faith in reading as a basis for cookery. She improved, though meals created by Kate Moores remained superior to Helen's efforts.

A rhythm developed. Breakfast was taken in Helen's part of the house, as was lunch; then, if the judge was at home, a later meal was served at the dining table downstairs. The women read, watched television, became addicted to *The Archers* on the radio. While Louisa napped, Helen dealt with Oscar. It was the happiest time in Helen's life thus far. She had her family at last – Louisa, Agnes and the dog.

The dog, walked by Helen every day, always made a beeline for the Makepeace cottage. He had three homes, and he made determined use of every one of them. Agnes and Fred usually kept scraps for him; he was having an excellent life – as long as he stayed away from the big man.

On the day of the second visit by Granada, Helen and Oscar returned, with Agnes, to a house of turmoil. Cameras and boom microphones took up most of the space. Kate, who was still running around like a cat on hot bricks, had polished to within an inch of its life anything that failed to move – the hall sparkled. In its centre sat a large table on which was displayed Fred's latest work of art. Even his granddaughter gasped in wonderment when she saw the model. Pop was gifted. If he could learn to keep quiet, he would go far.

But he didn't keep quiet. Fred delivered a lecture on life's never being over until the lid settled on the coffin; he berated all who retired to idleness and argued with the interviewer that tiredness and ill-health were no excuse for inactivity. 'Everybody should be doing,' he said fiercely. 'There's no excuse for sitting and doing nowt.'

'But what about disability?' asked the poor newsman.

'I'm disabled. I've had a stroke and was as daft as a brush for a while. No excuse. You have to keep at it.'

Agnes hid her face in one of Denis's handkerchiefs. She knew her Pop inside out, knew he wasn't one to change his mind even when in the wrong.

When cameras and microphones were switched off, the interviewer collared Agnes. 'How do you put up with him?' he asked.

'I don't. I sold him to the highest bidder and she sold her shop to afford him. He's a kind man in his way. He just wants to encourage folk to be useful.'

'Yes, and he'll have several of them depressed. Some people really can't do anything. But his work is brilliant. He'll be doing models of all the big houses soon.'

'He won't. He's booked up for two years. So if you want a house for your daughter, you'll have to wait.'

The man grinned. 'I ordered mine months ago. I could tell then that he was unusual.' He walked away.

Unusual? Fred was a one-off, a treasure, a pest and a wonderful man. He was now tackling the judge, who had come home to bask in the reflected glory of Fred's model of Lambert House. 'You can't retire,' said Fred. 'Judges don't retire – they die with their wigs on.'

Judge Spencer was not used to such bluntness. 'I've served my country,' he answered stiffly.

'Aye, so have I, but that's no excuse. Will you go travelling on yon yacht?'

'Probably.'

Fred was quietened by that single word. 'That's all right, then. You're doing summat different – sailing. If you can afford it, you do it, lad.' Thus spoke the father of Eileen Grimshaw, mother to Agnes, victim of Judge Spencer. Having granted permission to retire, Fred went off to irritate others. Helen grinned broadly. Her father was taking advice from his chauffeur, the grandfather of an illegitimate daughter and from his one and only recognized child. At table, he often asked Helen's opinion. It was a charade, but it would do for now, she supposed. Louisa was better, there were just a couple of months to go, and all was well thus far.

Agnes tugged at Helen's sleeve. 'Did you hear Pop talking to your dad?'

'I did. Our father's being kept in his rightful place, exactly where I can see him.' She shook her head. 'Agnes, stop looking at me like that. I don't know what will happen in the future any more than you do. Leave him to me. He'll get what's coming to him.'

Agnes sat and gazed again at Pop's handiwork. She wished Nan could have seen it, though she would not have denied Eva the opportunity to wear her wedding outfit for a third time. Eva was as proud as Punch of her husband. There was no one like Fred in her book. There was no one like Pop, full stop, thought Agnes.

Denis joined her. 'Are you all right?'

'Eh?'

He pointed to the floor beneath her chair. 'I think your waters just broke.'

'Oh.'

Denis pushed a hand through his hair. That 'Oh' was typical of Agnes. She took life as it came, didn't seem to panic, wasn't one for the vapours. He grabbed Helen. 'Please get your car. Agnes is going into labour and I don't want to put a wet wife into your dad's Bentley. We can collect her bag on the way to Townleys.'

Helen gasped. 'It's not due yet, is it?'

'No, but this is Agnes we're dealing with. She's got a lot of her granddad in her, so she doesn't work to any timetable. Please hurry.'

Agnes was bundled into the car and driven to the cottage to wait while Denis got her case. She sat in the back seat and sucked a mint.

'Any pain?' asked Helen anxiously.

'No.'

'Are you sure?'

'Yes. When the pain starts, you'll be the third to know. Me first, then Denis, then you. OK?'

Helen shook her head. She wished she could boast such pragmatism, but she never would. According to Father, Helen's mother had been difficult; Eileen Grimshaw had probably been compliant, though there was little of that quality in Agnes. Agnes just got on with life, Helen supposed, as Denis jumped back into the driving seat.

They reached the hospital within twenty minutes, Agnes complaining not of pain, but of dampness. 'I can't remember the last time I wet my knickers,' she complained as she was led towards Maternity.

When Agnes had been taken away for examination,

Denis and Helen sat nervously under a poster about inoculations. There was clearly a lot of complicated stuff involved in the production and rearing of a child. 'Denis?'

'What?'

'Have you thought about names?'

'Oh. Yes, we have. A boy will be David and a girl Sally.' He drummed his fingers on a knee. 'They've been a long time.'

'They've been three minutes, Denis.'

'Oh.'

Agnes returned eventually. She wore a nightdress, a dressing gown and a disappointed air. 'Can't go home because the waters have gone. Can't get on with it – nothing's happening. The baby is happy where it is and we just have to wait.'

'You can go home,' Denis advised Helen. 'Tell Fred and Eva what's happening.'

'What's not happening.' Agnes's tone was gloomy. 'And get me some bitter lemon, please. And keep Pop away from here – he'll be telling everybody how to do their job and I won't cope with him.'

Helen left.

Agnes paced up and down the corridor until her husband thought her in danger of wearing out the tiles. She counted doors, posters, other pregnant walkers, teacups and saucers on a trolley. Finally, she counted her blessings. There were girls here with no company, no husband, mother or father. Denis intended to be present throughout – she was very lucky.

By evening, the corridor was packed as tightly as a children's matinee at the Odeon. Eva had arrived in full sail – including wedding outfit, as she had not had time to change – with Fred in tow. Helen sat with Lucy and

Mags; Harry Timpson came to keep Mags company. He was followed closely by Albert and Kate Moores, who wanted to know if Agnes needed anything. When George put in an appearance, Agnes had gone off the idea of a quorum. 'Will you all beggar off home?' she pleaded.

A midwife arrived to take Agnes's blood pressure. 'There's ten of you,' she exclaimed. Agnes, who had taken to counting anything and everything in order to relieve boredom, put the midwife right. 'There are twelve if you include parents and lower deck passenger.'

Agnes sat while the monitor did its work, was told that the reading was acceptable, then she waded in. 'Will you get rid of this lot? I'm beginning to feel like a spectator sport at Olympic level. There should be two of us, three if you count Nuisance – but no more. Evacuate this corridor, please, or I am going home.'

The midwife did better than that by removing the patient from the scene. 'She's going on a ward until labour starts,' she explained to the audience. 'We won't move her to the labour room until she's further on. Please go home – we haven't room for a crowd.'

Agnes didn't move further on until the next morning, when she was delivered of a healthy boy weighing almost nine pounds. When he was handed to her, she nodded and spoke to him. 'I've a bone to pick with you,' she said before giving him to his dad.

Denis wiped away a tear as he passed the child over to the team for cleaning and checking. 'You did well,' he told his wife. 'No swearing, no screaming.'

'I couldn't let him win the last round, could I?' She took a cup and drank from it. 'Yuk,' she exclaimed. 'What's this rubbish?'

'Bitter lemon.' He took it away. 'I did warn you – you've never liked bitter lemon.'

Agnes smiled at all around her. She had a son, a wonderful husband and a nurse bending over her. 'Your dad phoned,' said the latter.

'I haven't got a dad.'

'Oh. Right.' The young woman left the bedside.

Exhausted, Agnes leaned on her pillows. Judge Spencer had no claim on her son, no proof that he was the grandfather. If he thought he was going to get his sticky paws on David Makepeace, he had another think coming. Helen would sort him out, she told herself. Helen had him by the scruff of the neck, didn't she?

Denis returned. 'I'll come in tomorrow,' he promised. 'Oh – the midwife said well done, because if our lad had gone full term he would have been an eleven-pounder.'

Agnes winced. It had been like launching a battleship, but if the pregnancy had gone full term it would have been the *Queen Mary*, plus all hands on and below decks. 'It's over,' she said unnecessarily. 'And I'm not doing it again, so enjoy your little lad.' She lowered her voice. 'My father phoned.'

'Eh?'

She nodded. 'Tell Helen to get him to back off. And bring me a quarter of Keiller's butterscotch and some proper lemonade.'

'Right.'

'I love you, Denis Makepeace. Fetch me that noisy child while I learn how to feed him.'

Denis handed over the baby, kissed his wife and left the hospital. Helen was waiting at the door. 'Is she all right?'

'Course she is – you know our Agnes.'

'And the baby?'

'Screaming fit to bust – she's going to try feeding him. Are you giving me a lift?'

She nodded and led him to the car. On the way back to the village, Denis told her about the phone call. 'Said he was her dad.'

Helen grimaced. He couldn't do anything and wouldn't do anything. The bombshell under the Midland Bank was for emergencies only, but, if necessary, Helen would use it now. 'Don't worry. He daren't move a muscle without asking me first.' She smiled. 'I'm going to be a good aunt. I shall teach him to read, take him to the zoo and to the seaside. I could help him play the piano, get him taught to swim, buy him books.'

'Hang on.' Denis laughed. 'Let's change his nappy first, eh?'

Agnes had heard all about post-natal depression, but she didn't agree with it. A lot of new-fangled illnesses didn't make sense, and that was one of them. She loved being a mother, even when it didn't quite work. David was, she supposed, an easy baby. He took his nourishment, brought up wind and soon learned to play with anything within reach. The child laughed a lot, and Agnes found herself wondering about the joke she had missed. Was he remembering stuff from before he was born? That was possible, because he was particularly amused by certain words, one of them 'nuisance'. 'You've been here before,' she told him with monotonous frequency.

With pride in every step, she pushed her second-hand Silver Cross through the village and allowed all comers to coo over him. He liked an audience; oh, God – was he going to turn out like Pop? Pop had gone all posh and was going into marketing strategies. Marketing strategies involved a big sign in his garden – *POP'S HAPPY HOUSES* – a great deal of advertising and the employment of a small sales team. He was probably going to be a millionaire and that would make him thoroughly rumbustious. Rumbustious – that had been one of Nan's words. Sometimes, when she remembered Nan, Agnes cried because the old lady had never seen her great-grandson. Perhaps that was post-natal depression? If it was, then she was in step with everyone else, so that was all right.

Denis rushed home every night from Lambert House or from Lucy and George's barn, always ready to fight about who should bath the baby, always willing to do battle with Napisan, terry towelling and water. They managed to buy a washing machine and Pop paid for a tumble dryer, so life was a great deal easier than it might have been.

Helen, Lucy and Mags visited. They, too, fought over the child and who should hold him. Agnes borrowed a stopwatch and turned the whole thing into a farce, but David adored it all. He was loved; everybody wanted him, everybody sang and read to him, so he embraced his correct place as centre of the universe and thrived.

Helen borrowed David when he was six weeks old. She took him to visit Louisa while the judge was safely out of the way. Louisa broke down in tears when she saw the little boy. 'He's gorgeous,' she declared. 'There's the son he wanted.' Her own baby had not moved in the womb all day, and the midwife was expected at any moment. 'Don't let him get near little David, Helen.'

'He has no chance. Come on, buck up.'

The midwife arrived and exclaimed over the thriving baby boy before listening to Louisa's abdomen. 'Is your case packed?' she asked.

'Yes.' Louisa was to have her child in a private hospital at the other side of Blackburn. 'Will you phone the Manse?' she asked of Helen.

'No time,' said the midwife. 'Townleys is nearer. I think we need to get this child out today.'

So Louisa was rushed by her stepdaughter into the hospital in which young David had been born. The surgeon was waiting, as was the anaesthetist. They asked questions about when Louisa had last eaten, placed her on a trolley and dashed away in the direction of the theatre.

Helen paced about like an expectant father. The real father was away in some court or other, far too busy to be in attendance at the birth of his long-awaited son. When an hour had passed, the double doors at the end of the corridor were pushed aside to reveal the surgeon. Very slowly, he walked towards Helen. She waited. The journey could have taken no more than a few seconds, yet it seemed to continue forever.

He reached her side. 'Are you related to Louisa Spencer?'

Helen nodded. 'Stepdaughter.'

He took her arm. 'I am very sorry, but she suffered a pulmonary embolism and we couldn't save her.'

She stumbled. The man steadied her and placed her in a chair. 'Deep breaths,' he advised. 'She didn't suffer.'

Helen shook from head to toe. 'Did she see her baby?'

'No.'

'Is the baby ill?'

'She's small, but there's nothing wrong apart from

low birth weight and the need for a little help with her lungs.'

A girl. Helen swallowed. Father's wrong-side-of-the-blanket daughter had birthed a son, but his second wife had failed him. 'Millicent,' she whispered. 'That was the name Louisa chose. Millicent. Millie for short.'

'Can I get anyone for you?'

Helen shook her head. Denis and Agnes would be here soon. Kate was going to mind David while they came to the hospital. 'Can I see Louisa?'

'Soon, yes. They are preparing her now.'

Alone in the well-scrubbed, green-and-cream-dis-infected silence, Helen wept. She mourned a stepmother who had been a sister, cried for the motherless baby girl, sobbed because she knew that her father would never accept little Millie. Agnes and Denis did what they could, but she was still weeping when they all visited Louisa in the chapel of rest.

'God,' whispered Agnes. It could have happened to her and little David. Fiercely, she clung to her husband's arm.

'She looks pretty again,' said Helen.

'Does your father know?' Denis asked.

Helen shrugged listlessly. 'It won't matter. Meals at the table will stop, but that's all the effect Louisa's death will have on him.' A light dawned in her head. 'She'll have to be mine,' she murmured. 'Millie will have to be mine.'

They said their goodbyes to the cooling corpse, then set off in the direction of Maternity. Millie was in an incubator, small hands closed like sleeping flower heads, little chest moving with each quick breath she took.

'She's perfect,' said Helen. 'Not all creased and squashed.'

'Caesars are pretty. They don't have to fight to get out, you see.' Agnes squeezed her sister's hand. 'We'll help. Denis and I will do all we can, and I'm sure Kate will, too.'

'She's lost her mother.' Helen's tone was soft. 'She has lost a wonderful woman. And she'll never have a father, because she's just another bloody woman in the making. I have to make her life special. I shall make her life an adventure.'

Agnes and Denis were in no two minds about that. Helen had suffered and she would ensure that Louisa's baby had a childhood better than her own had been.

'He has to be told,' murmured Agnes.

Helen took a deep breath. 'I'll tell him,' she announced. 'It's my place to do that, isn't it? Then he can bury his second wife and ignore his second daughter.' She glanced at Agnes. 'His third daughter, I mean.'

Agnes grasped Helen's hand. 'I know this is horrible, love. I can't think of anything worse, but you have a daughter and a little sister all in the one package. If you can't bear to live in the house, move in with us for a while. Eva's lovely – she'd help. And you know Kate Moores would.'

'She doesn't like me. I've heard her saying I was sly as a child.'

'And now she knows why.'

Helen's eyes brimmed over. 'No, she doesn't. No one does. Mabel Turnbull and I are the only ones who know the full truth – and she's gone. No. Millie will live in her own house – our house. David will be her friend. We can rear them between us.'

In that moment, the rest of Helen Spencer's life was laid out for all to read. She would be a mother who was not a mother; she would stand between her father and Millie, would devote every waking hour to the child. Agnes dashed from her heart a stab of fear about David – was he Judge Spencer's only male descendant? Now was not the time for such selfish worries; now was the time to support Helen and this newborn girl.

A nurse came and opened a small door in the side of the incubator. 'Put your hand in,' she told Helen.

Small fingers curled around Helen's thumb. But the sudden, vice-like grip on her heart was an unexpected reaction. Her brain had already accepted responsibility for rearing the child, but this was different – this was emotion. Maternal love bloomed in a soul who had never been a mother, who would probably not give birth to a child of her own. Tears stopped flowing down her cheeks as she felt the tightening of tiny digits. Here was her goal in life, and it had nothing to do with writing books or getting the better of her father. This baby owned Helen Spencer. She would never again be the sad and lonely spinster. All the same, she grieved for her friend and close companion. Louisa had left yet another gaping hole in the fabric of life. No amount of patchwork or darning would close the gap.

He seethed. Helen stood at the other side of his desk. She had said all the right things, had expressed her sadness and her worry about the premature child, had told him that she would miss her stepmother.

The judge took a mouthful of brandy. 'Another girl, then?'

'Yes. And your lovely wife is dead.' He reminded her of Henry VIII, a man who had gone through many women in order to father a son. And then the sickly

336

boy had reigned for a mere six years before making way for his sisters: first Mary, and then Elizabeth I, a queen with the heart of a lion, had taken the reins. 'I shall arrange the funeral,' Helen said.

'Good. I have a busy schedule.'

'When will you visit the hospital?'

'I shall leave all that to you.'

Furious, she stamped out of the room. A son would have had him resident in the hospital; a male child would have wanted for nothing. Millie, who fought for life on a daily basis, was unimportant. 'Be strong,' Helen whispered. 'Get to the right weight, then I shall bring you home. As for him – he doesn't count.'

When the post-mortem had been completed, the body of Louisa Spencer was brought home. She lay in the hall next to Fred Grimshaw's model of the house, her stepdaughter a constant companion, her husband elsewhere at sessions. When the undertaker arrived to place the lid on the casket, Helen had to be led away by Agnes. 'Why her?' she sobbed. 'Why not him, Agnes? It should have been him. If you only knew . . .'

The church was packed. Zachary Spencer, who had managed at great personal cost to squeeze his wife's funeral into a hectic list, left after throwing a few crumbs of earth into a gaping maw in the churchyard. Mourners returned to Lambert House, where Kate Moores served sandwiches and many cups of tea and coffee.

Lucy arrived at Helen's side. 'If there's anything we can do, Helen—'

'Just keep that letter safe.' Underneath the tear-stained skin, an expression of cold determination was fighting to reach the surface. 'Those documents are the future for me and Millie. I cannot emphasize enough the importance of that package.'

'George and the bank will make sure. God love you.'
Lucy fled in tears.

Harry Timpson appointed himself guardian of his saviour. He followed her constantly, made sure that visitors did not overtire her, brought her tea, gave her several clean handkerchiefs. Occasionally, he nodded and smiled at Mags, who was taking care of Agnes. Mags was now Mrs Timpson, though no one except their parents knew. Harry loved his Mags and worshipped Helen Spencer – he was a lucky man.

When everyone had eaten, Helen got Harry to silence the gathering. She stood near a window and addressed them. 'If Louisa had been here, she would have enjoyed today. That may sound silly, but she preferred the uncomplicated life, which is why we chose to have plain fare.

'There are some of you here who remember me as a child and who thought me unpleasant. I hope most of you realize by now that I was the product of a miserable excuse for a father and a dead mother. I scarcely remember her, you know. But I'll never ... I'll never forget my wonderful stepmother.' She paused for a while, a cloud seeming to pass over her features.

'When she died, Louisa had been delivered of another disappointment – a girl.'

A murmur spread across the drawing room.

'Millie is improving. She's still a bit small, but I shall be bringing her home soon. Many here have visited her; her father has not been near the hospital. So I stand here now, a spinster with no experience, and I beg your help. Millie will not be sly or bitter – she will not need to lie or steal in order to compensate for lack of love. To that end, I ask all my friends here to advise and guide me while I rear my sister.'

'He should be bloody shot at dawn,' shouted Fred from the back.

Eva thumped him and Agnes told him to be quiet, wondering how he would react were he to discover his relationship with the object of his indignation.

Helen smiled. 'I'll put that one on the list, Fred. Any further suggestions should be made anonymously on postcards and sent to my solicitor. Thank you all for coming. Louisa was special and I shall miss her for the rest of my days.'

Harry pulled her into his arms and allowed her to sob on his shoulder. That bloody judge wanted a boot up the backside; he might have helped save Harry from prison, but he was as bent as a nine-bob note. Judges shouldn't be bent – their reliability and moral strength were the reasons for their very existence. This woman in his arms was the one to whom Harry owed everything. He whispered into her hair. 'Hey – I've got a secret.'

She looked up at him. 'Oh?'

'Me and Mags got wed the same day that . . . The day the baby was born.'

'The day Louisa died.'

'Yes. It was family and witnesses only – Mags hates fuss.'

Helen nodded. 'Congratulations, Harry. Louisa would have approved of that. She would have wanted us all to go on in a fashion as near to normal as possible.'

'Don't tell anyone. We're going to have a party, but we'll wait a while now. My mam's like a dog with two tails – thinks I've landed a gradely catch.'

'So has Mags,' Helen whispered. 'You will make a brilliant accountant one of these days.'

'I'm always here for you, no matter what. Remember that. No matter what.'

'I'll remember,' she promised.

A fortnight later, Millicent Louisa Spencer was released into the care of her sister. She came home not in the majestic Bentley, but in a very small Morris. A beautiful nursery had been prepared, all pastel colours, teddy bears and pretty pictures on the walls. The crib was next to Helen's bed, because she intended not to allow Millie out of her sight until she had gained weight and strength.

After three days, the baby, almost a month old, met her father for the first time. He looked her over, grunted, poured a brandy.

'Would you like to hold her?' Helen asked.

'Not at the moment.'

'Her name's Millicent.'

'Yes, I believe you mentioned that.'

Helen lowered her tone. 'Not a boy, though, eh? You'll have to work fast to find another wife, you know. After all, you left all this business very late, didn't you?'

He offered no reply.

'And you could carry on forever having girls. The father dictates the gender, or so I am told. You might take four or five wives in some countries and still have only daughters.'

'Go away,' he said.

She sat down, the child clasped to her chest. 'You know what's in Mabel Turnbull's letter, don't you, Pater?'

His face was suddenly deep crimson. 'I do not.'

'You know. Had you not known, you would have kicked me out months ago. So. You are in a delicate position. And I shall rear this child. You will pay me. Then bugger off to your yacht – I hope you drown.'

340

He maintained eye contact with her, but remained silent.

'You will leave this house, not I, certainly not Millie. Try sailing round the Cape – that should shorten your life by a year or two. You've a stroke coming – your face is a dreadful colour.' Helen stood up and carried her precious bundle out of the office. She walked through the house until she reached her own area, locked herself in and gave Millie her bottle. Sometimes, her father seemed beyond the reach of reason, and when he was in such a state, she believed him capable of doing harm. In a blind rage, he might forget about letters and threats.

The baby finished her feed and was congratulated for consuming three whole ounces. Back in her crib, she slept, one hand on her face, the other clutching a blanket. This child would hang on – she had no intention of giving up on life.

Helen herself drifted in and out of sleep. Nights were fractured by Millie, who needed feeding little and often, so her guardian had to snatch rest whenever the opportunity arose. In her dream, she opened the package and read the contents to a gathering of people in the drawing room. A little girl in the corner began to cry – was that Millie?

Her eyes flew open. It was strange how often sense arrived during sleep. The letters would hurt Millie. He knew that. With her heart beating wildly, Helen Spencer leaned over the sleeping child. Father was not a stupid man. He was rash, but not deficient. Even if he had not already spotted his oldest daughter's Achilles heel, it would come to him. The whole family would suffer once the secret became public. 'We are still vulnerable,' she told the baby.

Had she been the only one involved, Helen could have carried the burden of truth, but Millie had her whole life ahead of her and the sheet needed to be clean. Why on earth should a small child suffer because of the sins of her father? 'I have to talk to someone,' Helen whispered. The weight was suddenly too great for one person to bear; it needed to be shared. There was just one name on Helen's list of possibles. It had to be done and it had to be done today.

Pop was fuller than ever of his own importance. Granada Television had taken his plans for Lambert House, framed them, and placed them on a wall between studios. Anyone might have believed that his name was lit up in Piccadilly Circus, thought Agnes. She was pleased for him, yet worried about him. Fred Grimshaw needed an aim in life, but he also needed to take things at a slower pace. He and Eva had taken David in his pram for a walk through Skirlaugh Fall. Here was an opportunity for vacuuming without waking the baby, but Agnes simply sat and flicked through a magazine. House-proud was one thing; obsessive was another.

Helen arrived. It occurred to Agnes that she had simply swapped one baby for another, but she smiled and greeted her visitors gladly. Helen needed help and Agnes had made a promise.

Oscar bounded in first. He did three circuits of the living room, then a lap of honour at a slower pace.

'He misses Louisa,' said Helen. 'Even though she seldom fed him or took him out, he knew who his mistress was.' She sat down.

Agnes noted the expression on Helen's face and waited for her to speak again. To fill the gap, she went into the kitchen to fetch coffee and biscuits. Oscar, hearing the noise of dishes and cutlery, performed another circuit of the room in the hope of winning a treat. He accepted a few morsels, then went to claim his customary place on the hearthrug in the living room.

Agnes placed a tray on the coffee table. 'Well?' she asked.

'Let me sort my head out. I'll tell you in a minute.'

They drank coffee while Millie slept.

Suddenly, Helen leapt to her feet. 'I'll be back,' she promised.

Agnes scratched her head. 'You were going to tell me something—'

'Yes. I'll be back.' She rushed out of the house, leaving Agnes standing in her doorway and staring stupidly at the disappearing woman, baby and dog. Perhaps she would do the vacuuming after all.

Chapter Thirteen

Agnes answered the phone. 'Lucy? Whatever's the matter?'

Breathlessly, Lucy tripped over the words. 'She's gone wild-eyed again – Helen Spencer, I mean. George went to the bank with her – he's nominated second key-holder for the box. She's bringing her letters to you. Agnes, she's got Louisa's baby with her – she isn't fit to mind the dog. I thought I'd better let you know. I thought she'd got over all the nonsense.'

Agnes dropped into a chair. 'She was here earlier on, said she wanted to talk to me, then disappeared in a rush.' Poor Helen Spencer seemed to have crammed a whole life into the past few months. She had travelled through teenage fixation, had attempted to grow up and cope with her father, was now in charge of a baby girl. But to remove from a vault items she considered beyond value? There was something afoot once more. Helen had been wrong with Denis, wrong at Lucy's wedding, wrong at the Lambert House party. Was she off the tracks once more? 'Thanks for letting me know.'

'Be ready, love – she's off her head again. I'd better go – don't want anyone to overhear me. Be careful.'

Agnes replaced the receiver and waited. She knew all about waiting, realized that it could become an active occupation – she'd studied it before going into proper labour with David. But she didn't feel like counting

344

flowers on the wallpaper, so she brought in her washing from the line and was engaged in folding nappies when Helen arrived. She was, indeed, wild-eyed.

'Sit down.' Agnes took the baby. 'What's the matter, Helen?'

Helen remained silent for a while. She remembered the therapist's words – 'get out of your father's life' – but would it not be better to get him to leave? What must be done to make him go?

'Helen? I asked you a question. What's up?'

'I don't know. Well, I do know, but I could be mistaken. Millie has taken away my insurance.'

'Ah.' After waiting again, Agnes asked, 'How?'

'By being born.'

'Right.'

'It could ruin her life.'

'I see.' Agnes couldn't see, but she decided to agree with everything while Helen was in this state.

'Read them and hide them.' She placed a package on a small table.

Agnes swallowed hard.

'They're possibly useless now. That letter of Mabel Turnbull's could ruin Millie's chances in life. If I went public with that stuff, my sister could be pointed at and bullied. It wouldn't be fair. I have to manufacture a different plan.'

Agnes followed her to the door. 'Take the edge off for me,' she begged. Denis had gone to the yacht with Judge Spencer and would not be back until quite late. 'Tell me what it's about. I want to hear it before I read it.'

Helen looked at Agnes as if Agnes were the crazy one. 'The murder, of course. Hadn't you worked it out? He killed my mother. After killing her, he carried on womanizing instead of remarrying. When he got older and ugly, no one wanted him. Until Louisa, who had her reasons.'

Agnes closed her gaping mouth with an audible clash of incisors. A judge who sentenced lesser mortals was a murderer himself? 'Are you all right to look after Millie?' was all she managed to say.

'What? Of course I am. And if anyone tries to take her away from me – ever – I shall follow the same path as my father. She's mine and I'll kill anyone who makes a move on her.'

As if the threat might be an immediate one, Agnes stepped back.

Helen looked her half-sister up and down, ordered her not to be upset, reclaimed Millie and left the house.

The car drove off. Agnes stared at the sealed envelope. It was a huge brown packet with an old-fashioned seal set in red wax. Although the seal was already broken, she was wary of opening so fierce-looking a bundle. It was a legal thing: it contained the thoughts, memories and feelings of a nanny who was dead. 'Nothing to do with me,' she mumbled nervously. Her Catholic upbringing had taught her that the confessional was sacred, that no secrets could be divulged by the priest – wasn't the law similar? No, because this was Helen's property and she had opted to share it. Even so, it didn't seem right.

David woke and demanded attention. When he was fed, loved, cleaned and bedded, Oscar arrived. Agnes played with the dog in her back garden, but she stayed near the door. David had to be minded, as did that flaming package. She half wished that someone would come along and steal it, but she knew she would be unable to live with that.

The phone sounded again, its shrill bell almost making Agnes jump out of her skin. 'Ah, Lucy,' she said nervously.

'What happened?' asked the disembodied voice.

'Nothing.'

'Did she come?'

'Yes.'

'Have you read it? What did it say? I won't tell anyone, honestly.'

Agnes took a couple of deep breaths. 'I've no idea. It's still sitting on the table where she left it. Denis is at the yacht, so he'll be late, and I don't feel like looking at it while I'm by myself.'

'I'll come.'

'No, Lucy. It wouldn't be right. Remember hearing about the old lawyer who checked Mabel's letter for spelling mistakes? Remember how everyone thought that was what made him ill? The fewer people who handle this, the better. Sorry.' Agnes could not repeat the words of Helen Spencer, would not tell anyone about the supposed murder. Denis would be the sole exception.

Lucy was not pleased. After replacing the receiver, Agnes stared at it for several seconds, as if expecting Lucy to continue berating her even after the connection had been severed. The packet was still on the table. It was only seven o'clock. Oscar was demolishing a small dinner of chicken skin and dog biscuit. One minute past seven. The man who had fathered her was a murderer. The murderer was a judge. That thought had consumed ten more seconds. Her bones felt cold; having a murderer for a father was truly chilling.

Pop entered the arena. He was still full of Granada and his blueprints for Lambert House, which items were now on display in a corridor leading to the *Coronation Street* studio. Eva came in behind him, and said she would go quietly upstairs to see the baby. Nothing Eva did was quiet, so Agnes was forced to bring down the disturbed and crying David. She was grateful, because the moment of the grand opening had been postponed yet again.

She made tea. Pop played with his great-grandson while Eva waited for *Coronation Street* to begin.

'All them stars'll be looking at my blueprints,' bragged Pop. 'I'll be getting orders from them next – they've plenty of money.'

The baby slept while Eva watched a fight between two women near a viaduct on an imaginary street. Some people came along and separated the warring females; Agnes made more tea during the advertisements. After the break, there was louder shouting, some smoking and a bit of a story about two young girls wanting the same unkempt and totally undesirable man with red hair and bad skin.

The music played. Eva, who seemed to think that the programme was fact rather than fiction, waxed on about Ena Sharples being rude and Annie Walker being too big for her slippers. 'She wants shifting,' she declared. 'They should put her in a posh pub over in Cheshire, bring her down a peg or three. She pretends she's posh, but she's not.'

Pop snored. 'Well.' Agnes plumped up her cushion. 'That's both babies asleep.'

Eva smiled. 'What's happened, love? I've known you since you were knee-high to a cotton spool and I can tell when summat's up.'

Agnes sighed and shook her head. 'Just stuff, Eva.

'Stuff I can't talk about, because it's someone else's secret.' That wasn't true. She would have to talk to Denis, because she couldn't go through this business all by herself. 'It'll rinse out with the whites, as Nan used to say. I never realized how wise she was till she'd gone. She was always at the back of me, always showed me what to do.'

Eva's eyes narrowed. 'She did a good job, lass. You're the most sensible one I know out of your generation. Look at Mags Bradshaw – all that pain for a new nose, head over heels for a wrong 'un, married in secret, party next week. And that there Lucy carries on like a bloody teenager – skirts halfway up her bum, false eyelashes thicker than your yard brush.'

Agnes laughed in spite of her tension. Eva had a way of summing people up in a couple of sentences. 'Perhaps I'm too sensible?'

'Nay.' Eva heaved her bulk out of the chair. 'Eeh, love, if I put any more weight on, we'll be needing a tin opener to get me off the furniture. Fred?' The final word was shouted. David woke, Agnes grabbed him from her grandfather's arms, and Eva went about the business of shifting her husband.

'Come on,' she chided.

'I'll be there in a minute.' The voice was sleepy.

'There in a minute? Last time I gave you a minute, you nodded off in the shed with a hammer in one hand, nails in the other. Come on. Now.'

He stood up, rubbed his eyes and glared at Eva. 'All right, boss,' he said before a yawn overcame him.

Eva ushered him out of the house, leaving Agnes alone once more with twin burdens – one a small child, the other a quantity she wished could remain unknown.

It was ten minutes past eight and, though the days were getting longer, the light was diminishing fast. Denis had to be home soon.

With the baby settled once more, Agnes picked up the envelope and weighed it in her hand. It looked heavy, but it wasn't. Its contents were going to be heavy, though. Where was Denis when she needed him most? He hated the yacht, only went aboard if the judge had too small a crew to help with his latest toy. The big man was talking about retirement. Well, if he thought Denis would traipse around the seven seas with a murderer he had another think coming.

She looked inside. There were two smaller envelopes, one off-white and flimsy, the other buff-coloured and brand new. 'Come home, Denis,' she mouthed. 'I can't do this.' The washing was folded and the house was clean. She should start ironing. The trouble with being a housewife was that most jobs were automatic and didn't prevent the mind from working. She had books. But she couldn't imagine concentrating on the written word while she was in her current state.

The phone sounded again and she picked it up quickly in case it woke the baby. It was Helen. No, she hadn't read the letters. She was waiting for Denis. Helen didn't want Denis to read the letters. 'We have no secrets,' Agnes said. 'Don't you trust him?'

She did trust him, but Agnes was her sister and this needed to be kept in the family for now.

'Then come and take the damned things away, Helen. Anyway, he's my family. You've told me already that your dad killed your mother – I expect he killed mine, too, though not as directly. I'm sorry – it's me and Denis or neither of us. Whether I read this lot or not, my husband will know what you told me earlier.'

Helen expressed the fear that Denis might walk out of the job if he knew the full truth. 'Neither Millie nor I will feel safe if Denis isn't here for half the week.'

It was stalemate. In the end, Helen had to grant permission for Denis to see the letters, because, no matter what, Agnes would tell him what she already knew. 'As I just said, I'll be telling him about the murder anyway. We lead a shared life, Helen. It's the only way to stay married.'

At last, he came home. Still on tenterhooks, Agnes served his meal and waited until he had finished and the table was cleared. They drank coffee in the living room, Denis describing his time in Morecambe Bay, Agnes listening while he went through seasickness and his employer's attitude to the crew. After five or so minutes, Denis finally noticed his wife's silence. 'What's going on?' he asked.

She nodded in the direction of the offending item. 'Helen dragged George to the bank and pulled the letters from the vault. She brought them here for me to read. Denis?'

'What?'

Agnes swallowed. 'She says he killed the first Mrs Spencer – Helen's mam. The proof's in that package. I couldn't read it on my own.'

He placed his cup and saucer on the windowsill. 'Killed her? By making her life a misery? Aye, I've heard people saying she died on purpose just to get away from him.'

Agnes shook her head. 'No. Murder. Real, actual murder.'

A heavy silence hung over the room while they both stared at Helen Spencer's property. 'How long's it been here?' Denis asked.

'Hours. Helen phoned, because she thought I'd have read them. Lucy phoned and asked what was in them. Pop and Eva came – that killed half an hour or so. I'm worried about Millie in case Helen isn't up to the job. It's not easy work.'

'No.' He stood up. 'Shall I read it out?'

Agnes closed her eyes for a moment. 'No. Read a sheet, then hand it to me. I don't think I want to hear the words from you. This is none of our doing, so it's best if the words stay flat on the page.'

He opened the main envelope and removed the contents. 'Right,' he said, 'that's the first incision.'

It took over an hour. Agnes wept, while Denis determinedly held back his own tears. At the end, he folded everything and placed both letters, each in its separate envelope, back inside the outer cover. 'I don't want that stuff in my house,' he said gruffly.

'Neither do I.'

'Why did she bring it?' he asked.

Agnes had an insubstantial answer. 'Millie's father is a killer. Helen holds those letters over him like the sword of Damocles. But if she is forced to reveal their contents, she will be tainting Millie's life for ever. Millie would have to go through school in the company of people who might be aware of her family's skeletons. Helen knows her father will be thinking along the same lines, so I suppose she just wanted someone else to have seen the contents. She said Millie has taken away her insurance policy. Denis, she's running round like a blindfolded cat, all confusion and desperation.'

Denis sat quietly for a few seconds. 'I could take it out of her hands now. I could carry Mabel Turnbull's letter to a police station and get the bloody business over and done with.'

352

'But you won't.'

'No. It could destroy Helen, too. She'd be so worried about the baby that she'd lose her marbles again. What a mess.'

'She wants you to promise not to give up working part time for her dad. She'd be scared if you left.'

Agnes could not get to sleep that night. She tossed and turned alongside her husband, tried to relax, failed miserably. In the end, she abandoned the attempt and, at three in the morning, she reread the close, tiny handwriting of Mabel Turnbull. It was no less shocking the second time, but Agnes needed to make an effort to digest it fully.

With a cup of tea at her elbow, she started again.

My name is Mabel Anne Turnbull. I was employed by Mr and Mrs Spencer in 1932, when their daughter (Helen) was a few months old. Mr Spencer was away quite often. His work took him all over the place and he stayed at his club a lot. He seemed to be keener on his friends and colleagues than on his family and was anxious to be invited to join the Freemasons. He was one of the youngest ever lawyers to be called to the bar and was always determined to become a judge. His wife was frail. I was left to look after her and Helen during his absences.

I am ashamed to say that I was one of the many women to be seduced by Zachary Spencer. He was very attractive and charming and he gave me a job in his household. My head was turned – I was a silly girl. From the day I began working at Lambert House, my sympathies and loyalties were with Mrs Spencer and her young daughter, Helen. I made it

plain to my employer that there would be no further
intimacy between us and he was unconcerned, as he
had many lady friends all over the country. He came
home from time to time, but not on a regular basis,
as he was far too selfish to consider the needs of
anyone but himself.

Not that he was any use when he was there. Mrs
Spencer had a bad heart, but he yelled at her a lot
and got her worked up. She gave as good as she got
sometimes, but would be ill afterwards. He kept
screaming at her because she hadn't managed to give
him a son and was too ill to try again. Sometimes,
I wanted to hit him. He ignored Miss Helen most of
the time. She was all right at first, because she had
her mummy as well as me to play with, but her
father made her feel unhappy when he shouted.
I loathed and despised Zachary Spencer and my
feelings towards him remain the same, but I swear I
am telling the truth rather than seeking vengeance.

It got worse. He was bad when he drank and he
drank too much. I used to keep Miss Helen upstairs
a lot of the time because she was safer away from
him and his noise. But there wasn't much I could do
for her poor mother. She stood up to him and got
weaker all the time.

The weakness took the form of turns – like
fainting fits – and she would lie very still and hardly
breathing. There were tablets to put under her
tongue. She always had them with her and I always
carried some just to be safe. I begged her to stop
facing up to him, but she wouldn't listen. If her
health had been good, she would have divorced him,
I'm sure. He was and is a cruel man. He hates his

daughter and she likely hates him, with good reason on her part.

Things went on the same with him away a lot and his wife not well. We had some nice times when there were just the three of us. Helen seemed shy and frightened, but that was his fault, because she was all right with her mother and me. (After her mother died, she got naughty, but that was understandable.)

His absences became less frequent. Most people in normal families would have been glad, but we weren't, because we dreaded him being back full time and we were better off without him. He stayed for longer periods at the house. The mistress, Miss Helen and I kept out of his way whenever possible, but there was no way of avoiding him altogether.

He started telling the mistress to get out of his house because she was useless. I remember her laughing at him – not amused laughing, more sneering. She said she would leave Lambert House in a box and he said that could be arranged. I could hear from the top of the stairs – they were really screaming at one another.

When I got to bed that night, my cocoa was already waiting for me. Old Mrs Battersby, who slept in an attic, was the live-in cook in those days and she was very good to me and to Miss Helen and she always made my cocoa before going up to her own room under the eaves at the other side of the house. I drank my cocoa and must have fallen asleep straight away. The next thing I knew, Miss Helen was tugging and pulling at me. I got out of bed and I felt very strange. Ever since, I have been sure that he must have drugged my cocoa after Mrs Battersby left it by my bed.

They were fighting again. Mrs Spencer was calling him all kinds of names and her language was very strong for a lady, but I didn't blame her. I pulled open the door a crack and he had her at the top of the stairs. He pushed her. I swear on a hill of Bibles that I saw Zachary Spencer kill his wife that night. The drugs dulled my mind, but I know what I saw.

He made her fall down the stairs. She had tumbled down before – one of her fainting fits on the stairs – the doctor knew about it and had told her to sleep on the ground floor, but she was never one for doing as she was ordered. She was weak in body but determined in mind and her husband did not like anyone who argued with him. Anyway, I saw him push her. Where the stairs turn near the bottom, she was lying like a rag doll. I think she was already dead before he went near her again. He walked downstairs and pulled her down the rest of the steps into the hall and I could hear her head banging on each of the treads.

He stood over her and told her she would be leaving in a box. I saw him bend and feel for a pulse. Then I noticed Miss Helen clinging to my nightdress. I don't know what she had seen, but I told her to come away. We went back into the bedroom. Miss Helen didn't say a word. I sat with her till she fell asleep, then I opened the door again and he was still standing over Mrs Spencer. As I closed the door, he looked up, but I didn't think he had seen me.

The ambulance came. Mrs Spencer was taken away and he went with her. He was shouting and pretending to be upset. I drank a lot of water to get the drugs out of me. The little girl slept. I sat all night in a chair and I heard him come back. The next morning, he told us his wife had suffered a heart attack and broken her neck on the stairs. He was staring at me.

I handed in my notice after the funeral. Mr Spencer begged me to stay as housekeeper for a lot more money. I did stay, but more for the sake of the child. I was frightened all the time, yet I worried about Miss Helen and stayed for her sake. But he got her a governess and I didn't have a lot to do with Miss Helen after that. From the age of three, she was given lessons and she read like an adult at a very young age. She had a good brain. The first governess said she was the cleverest child she had taught so far. But she did become very quiet and rather underhand and naughty at times. I was the only one who understood why, but I could not talk to such a small child about what had happened before her third birthday.

He continued to behave atrociously to women. I remember clearly one occasion just before the end of the war. A young girl called Eileen Grimshaw came to the house. She was pregnant and he would not help her in any way. He had thrown her out of his office and denied his involvement with her. She came to me and there was nothing I could do for her.

I left the house in 1944. He got me a good job and continued to send me money. When I was still relatively young, I became disabled with the arthritis. He still sent me money and paid for me to have residential care.

I have nothing to gain by writing this letter. I don't know how much time I have left, but I am leaving what I have written in the care of a solicitor. It is for Miss Helen Spencer, daughter of Judge Zachary Spencer and Elizabeth Spencer, deceased. He should not get away with it. A man in his high position is supposed to be decent and law-abiding. He killed his wife. Please accept this as the statement of a dying woman. I don't know when I will die, but I have to write this while my hands still work.

Helen may remember that night. She has not spoken of it as far as I know, but she may have seen some of what happened. When she became naughty, I truly believed that what she knew had affected her, but I am not a clever woman and I can't say for sure.

Miss Helen, if you read this, please know that I did all I could for you. When I became housekeeper, I saw less of you, but at least I was there. Sometimes, he would look at me and I could tell he was wondering what I knew of the night when your mother died. He was never sure of me, which is why he has kept me in comfort.

I wish you well in your life and hope you grow strong in spite of your father and his wickedness. My only regret is that I did not prevent your mother's murder. She would not have lasted long, but her death should have been natural and not assisted by the creature she had married. If he had been putting her out of her misery, I might have

358

understood, but he killed her because she disappointed him and answered him back.

Should Miss Helen Spencer predecease me, this will be read by the lawyers into whose hands I have placed it. Sirs, Judge Zachary Spencer is a murderer and he should be tried for his crime. I swear by Almighty God that everything I have written here is the truth. My education is limited, but I am well read and I know right from wrong. Please have him arrested.

Yours sincerely, M. Turnbull (Miss)

Agnes took a sip of water. There was a ring of honesty to the letter and she did not doubt the contents for one moment. The handwriting was shaky, because the author had suffered pain in her joints, yet she had laboured, possibly over a period of days, to get the letter finished. It was the absolute truth – of that Agnes was certain. The bit about her mother had cut her to the quick.

There was no need to reread the few lines appended by Helen in the other envelope. Helen had confirmed Mabel's statement and had explained about the nightmares and the amnesia brought on by shock. But now Helen was afraid of these letters. She had depended on them for her own safety and security, but she now felt that their very existence threatened the well-being of an innocent baby girl.

Birds began to sing. Agnes drew back the curtains and watched the dawn as it started to break. This was a time of day when wakefulness could be a burden, because the person who did not sleep felt truly isolated and out of step. It would be a difficult day, since she was bound to be tired and edgy. But no – it was a George-and-Lucy day, so Denis could make his apologies, stay at home and help with the baby, because George knew that Agnes had the letters and would be in some kind of shock. Agnes and Denis needed time together, as there was a decision to be made. Should they go to the police and risk Helen's wrath? Or should they keep quiet, just as Mabel Turnbull had kept quiet?

Sometimes, there was a very hazy line between right and wrong, Agnes thought. Pure right could be a terrible thing with dreadful consequences; wrong was often the kinder choice. A man who abused his position should be punished, yet his punishment might affect the lives of people who did not deserve to be hurt. Denis wanted to go to the police. Agnes did not. The decision would be hers, because Helen Spencer was probably her half-sister. But what was the right thing? Nobody wanted Millie to become the butt of jokes and snide remarks because her father had been the infamous and murderous judge.

'Agnes?'

She turned to her husband. 'She's right, Denis. Millie could suffer if all this came out. Poor old Mabel Turnbull was wasting her time, too, it seems.'

'So we do nothing?'

Agnes nodded. 'We can only make things worse by interfering.' The charade had to continue. 'Don't go to work, sweetheart. Phone George – he'll understand.'

'Spencer should be in jail, Agnes.'

'I know.'

'And the house is like a time bomb – something has to give. She'll crack. He's made her brittle and frail. God, what is the right thing to do?'

Agnes shrugged and smiled weakly. 'The wrong thing

360

is sometimes the right thing. This is one of the sometimes.'

The house had been built very cleverly, each room a section that slotted onto the room beneath. Even the ground floor lifted off to show cellars with boiler, coal store, miniature wine racks and bottles. Fred was very proud of his achievement, though his delight was tinged with sadness, because the house had been made for Louisa, who had died giving birth to a daughter. 'Just like our Eileen,' he whispered as he put some finishing touches to his work. The house would belong now to little Millie, so it needed to be strong and durable. He was examining pegs and slots when the row began.

The replica of Lambert House, now in its permanent place of residence in the hall, looked wonderful. Absorbed in his work, Fred fought not to hear the raised voices of the judge and his daughter. All families had differences that needed airing from time to time, and he was wondering whether to change the carpet in one of his rooms, since the real floor covering in Lambert House's library was in a lighter colour than the one he had used. It was hard to concentrate.

The volume increased. It was a pity that folk didn't own wireless knobs, because they needed to be turned down a bit when a bloke was trying to do a job of work. The judge was yelling about his retirement and his intention to spend time at sea. His daughter was urging him to stay at sea, as he would not be welcome here. She was also advising him to leave all lifebelts at the moorings – she had quite a temper, it seemed.

If he varnished the tiny door handles, the brass would stay bright. Fred wrote that in his notebook. He was still waiting for a pair of lions couchant to arrive for the top of the front steps. He had explained on television that he had been let down by a maker of miniatures – he wasn't having folk think he did half a job. There were sets of moulds he might buy – rubber contraptions into which plaster of Paris could be poured – perhaps he could make his own garden ornaments? Trees were easy – train set manufacturers made good trees and hedges.

'This is my house!'

The old bugger was in danger of blowing a fuse, Fred thought. Like a pressure cooker, Zachary Spencer could do with a valve on the top of his head for the letting off of steam.

'You're not wanted here.'

Perhaps his daughter might benefit from similar equipment – she was more like her dad than she chose to believe.

'I shall do as I please.'

It happened then. As clear as any church bell, Helen Spencer's voice travelled through the hall to Fred's ears. 'You have three daughters. Me, you ignored to the point of neglect. Agnes was raised by grandparents and Millie will be raised by me.'

'Better if I had her adopted,' shouted the judge.

'No! Millie will stay with me.'

Fred stood as still as one of the stone lions. He blinked stupidly, then leaned for support on the huge table that bore the weight of his model. Agnes. Eileen. Sadie, God rest her. Spencer, bloody Spencer. Dear Lord, let this be a lie.

'Agnes knows,' Helen was saying now. 'She knows everything.'

Fred pulled himself together and left the house by

the front door. He would not have another stroke; he would not weaken to the point of illness. Had anyone asked him about the walk from Skirlaugh Rise to Skirlaugh Fall that day, he would not have had anything to say. Seeing and hearing little, he simply placed one foot in front of the other, all senses dulled by shock.

Without knocking, he walked into his granddaughter's cottage.

Denis, who had taken the day off to think about Helen's famous letters, stood up as soon as Fred came in. There was no need for the old man to speak, because the whole mess showed in his face. 'Fred?'

'Where's our Agnes?'

'Hanging nappies on the line.'

Fred, whose legs were threatening to buckle, dropped onto the sofa. 'How long has she known that yon bugger's her dad?'

Denis swallowed. 'Long enough.'

'I'll kill him,' snarled Fred. 'I might be old and weak, but I can wait till he's asleep and—'

'Stop it, Pop.' Agnes, washing basket balanced on a hip, stood in the doorway between living room and kitchen. 'Don't make things worse than they already are,' she said. 'There's more to it – a lot more. He's given us this house and Helen will make sure we are OK.'

'OK?' yelled Fred. 'OK? Your mam wasn't OK when she bled to death, was she? Three dead women – that's some track record for a judge, eh? And what's this house worth – a couple of hundred quid? What about your shoes and your clothes when you were growing, eh? What about the times when my Sadie had to do magic with a few bob a week?'

'Stop this, or you'll be in hospital again,' advised

Denis calmly. 'Take my word – there's stuff you don't know, stuff you're better off not knowing.'

'I know what he did to my daughter, and that's enough.' Fred stood up and walked out of the house. In Eva's fleshy arms, he wept until he felt weak, weary and dry to the core. 'Bastard,' he cursed.

'You'll make yourself ill, love.'

He pulled away from his wife. 'Nay, I won't. Ill's stuck in a trench with your best mate's blood on your face.' He pulled from a pocket Macker's stolen lighter. 'Ill's not knowing what you're doing, or having no control over what happens. Ill's cursing your officers for sending you up front, then finding the same officers as dead as the rank and file. I'm thinking, Eva. I'm thinking and I'm grieving and yes, I'm bloody furious. But I'll do nowt till I've thought on it. This time, I'm in charge. It's my bloody turn now.'

He sat in the same chair for the rest of the day, stirring only when food and drink were carried to him. Eva watched, waited, said nothing. Agnes called, but was told by her grandfather to go home. He loved her and he told her that, but he was busy thinking. The sun began its descent and Fred walked to the bathroom. He completed his toilet with a shave; then, when dusk thickened, he left the house.

Eva ran as quickly as she could to Agnes's cottage. 'He's got the big axe,' she mumbled through tears. 'And his dander's up. I know he's a noisy old bugger, but this time it's different, because he's quiet. I've never known him like this.'

'Silent?' Agnes asked.

Eva nodded.

Silent was dangerous. Agnes pushed her husband out

of the house. 'Be quick,' she said. 'He'll kill him. Make sure Helen and the baby are all right, too.'

Eva and Agnes stared at one another for what seemed like hours. The clock was on a go-slow, its hands moving reluctantly to mark each passing moment. Eva sobbed quietly; Agnes trapped nervous hands between her knees and prayed. Pop was lethal when truly angry. He had almost belted a teacher for giving Agnes the cane, and he had been very subdued and menacing on that occasion, too. 'Mark our Agnes again,' he had said softly, 'and I'll have you skinned at yon Walker's Tannery – your hide's thick enough.' Oh, God, please don't let him kill anyone, Agnes pleaded inwardly.

'How long now?' asked Eva.

'Twenty minutes.'

'Is that all?'

Agnes nodded. Denis would catch him and stop him – wouldn't he?

Fuelled by anger, Fred Grimshaw took the short cut across the fields. Denis would be hot on his heels, but nothing could stop Fred now. He remembered Macker, remembered also the lads who had fought in the second half, as he termed the later war. A country fit for heroes? A country in which a barrister, soon to become a High Court judge, could impregnate an innocent girl and get away with it? 'We didn't lay down our lives for this,' he told his inanimate companion, a weighty axe that was suddenly as light as a feather.

Denis was there before him. He was hanging around at the front of the house, so Fred took a detour through the copse and entered the building by a rear door. The place was as quiet as a graveyard. With no one to impede his progress, Fred walked through the mansion until he reached the hall. 'Sorry, Millie,' he said before delivering the first blow.

Now, the axe was suddenly heavy, but he dragged it over his shoulder and into the model until the table below, too, began to buckle.

Denis ran in and tried to stop the destruction, but Fred ignored him. Yet he saw the judge plainly enough, mouth opened wide, feet planted halfway down the stairs, hand gripping the banister rail. 'Stop this foolishness,' Zachary Spencer called, but Fred was beyond retrieval.

When his work was completely destroyed, the grandfather of Agnes Makepeace paused for breath. Then he raised the weapon once more and addressed the man on the stairs. 'This should have been planted in your head.' He nodded at the blade. 'Agnes's father? You? Our lovely Eileen made dirty by a man who was never a man? Missed the second war, didn't you? You sat at home and kept the legal wheels turning, soft job, soft chair, soft life.'

'Be quiet, man,' spat the judge.

Fred took from his pocket a handful of coins. Macker had died for this creep and for governments who still failed to make sense. Macker, twice the man that Spencer would ever be, was just a cigarette case, a lighter and a remembered smile. 'You big shit,' said Fred, his voice unnaturally low. 'Here you are, Iscariot – count them.' He cast the coins into the debris that had been the model of Lambert House. 'Judas,' he spat before walking out of the house, thirty shillings left behind for the traitor's pay.

Denis said nothing. He simply followed his grandfather-in-law down the hill to Skirlaugh Fall, made sure that he went into Bamber Cottage, then turned to go home to Agnes. Eva, who had fastened herself to Agnes's window, left and pursued her husband homeward. It was going to be a difficult night, but Eva would cope, because Eva loved her husband.

'Don't go,' Agnes begged the next morning.

Denis shook his head. 'Sorry, love. The judge will be like a tiger on fire – I can't leave Helen and the baby to his tender mercies.'

'There'll be repercussions. You're related to Pop by marriage. The man's a killer, Denis.'

But he would not be persuaded. He left the house by the front door, turned and waved to his wife and child.

Agnes felt a chill in her spine. She wanted to run after him, to plead with him to stay at home, but she knew he had made up his mind. She watched as he moved towards the big house, her heart filled by fear, her mind scarcely working.

In years to come, she would speak sometimes of the dread she felt that day. After Denis had disappeared into Skirlaugh Rise, Agnes never saw him again.

Chapter Fourteen

2004

Ian Harte stepped out of his car and locked the door. The house known as Briarswood, formerly Lambert House, was still on the books, but a keen client had emerged and it had fallen to the surveyor to discover, as cheaply as possible, why the house conformed to no law of architecture, gravity or simple common sense. The front of the building should sag, but it did not, so an explanation had become flavour of the moment. Alterations to the cellars were the probable cause of the dilemma, but proof was needed in order to furnish the prospective purchaser with a proper report.

A Mrs Agnes Makepeace was caretaker and key-holder, so he sought to discuss the matter with her, but no one responded to repeated knocking at the door of her cottage. After a couple of fruitless minutes, he moved to the house next door. A young woman answered. She was done up like someone preparing to have tea with the queen, but that was normal these days, because the long-ago weavers' homes had become the bijou residences of the up-and-coming. 'Yes?' she asked.

He cleared his throat. 'Do you know where Mrs Makepeace is?'

'Morecambe,' she replied. 'She goes once a year to remember.' The woman looked over her visitor, deciding that he seemed of decent enough professional standing before allowing him into her overstated home. The windows were dressed in knickers, as Ian Harte had come to name foolish looping draperies with lace and broderie anglaise trimming their edges. Dried flowers in terracotta cones hung each side of the fireplace, while the mandatory pot pourri acted as centre piece on a coffee table.

After an invitation to be seated, he placed himself in a cream leather chair. The room was stuffy and over-perfumed. Imitation antiques lined the walls – a bureau, a chesterfield, some deliberately distressed bookshelves that housed, among others, Barbara Cartland, Mills & Boon and, to add a little class to the establishment, a few tomes in imitation leather. *Lancashire Life* and *Ideal Home* flanked the pot pourri with a set of silver-plated coasters completing the piece. This was the stage on which actors acted day-to-day parts in their make-believe lives. The setting was a much-loved disaster, its owner proud to show it off. 'Morecambe?' he asked.

'Would you care for a cup of tea or coffee?'

He saw the desperation in her face, recognized lone-liness, opted for coffee. While she made the drinks, he sat feeling sad. Why? Because this village, once bustling with life and a sense of community, had become a waiting room for the ambitious young who clung by the skin of their teeth to the first rung of the property ladder. Gardens had been replaced by slabs on which cars could be parked, while almost every house boasted a burglar alarm colourful enough to catch the eye of any would-be thief. The residents of Skirlaugh Fall were in hiding, each holding on desperately to pos-sessions and position, every man for himself, lottery ticket in a drawer, the pub continuing to serve chicken in a basket and Black Forest gateau, post office gone, new dormer bungalows in hideous pink or yellow brick hiding in dips behind the original stone-built dwellings.

'How long have you lived here?' he asked. Had she not heard that minimalism was now in vogue, that dado rails were no longer the fashion?

'A few months. We stand to make a killing and move on pretty soon. This house isn't big enough for a family, and I am expecting our first. You were looking for Mrs Makepeace?'

'Yes.'

She poured coffee from a steel-and-glass jug, said she hoped he liked Kenya blend, offered him a bourbon cream. 'She'll be in Morecambe. That's where he died, you see.'

'Oh?' He swallowed a mouthful of biscuit. 'Who died?'

'Her husband. It must be going on forty years ago now, but my mother remembers it. They died at sea.'

'They?'

She nodded. 'Him – Mr Makepeace – and a judge who used to live at Briarswood – they were the only two on board. No crew that night, my mother said. It was all over the papers. Anyway, Mrs Makepeace never remarried. She must be sixty now, but she's still pretty.'

'So is her garden.' The Makepeace house was one of the few to have survived the invasion.

'She does it all herself. Not that I know her, you understand. We keep ourselves to ourselves. Anyway, the yacht exploded and both men died. They'd been putting some sort of fuel in the kitchen – the galley – and something went wrong. Mrs Makepeace was left with a small baby and no husband. Very sad.'

'Terrible. When will she be back?'

The woman raised her shoulders. 'No idea. I believe

she rents a house for a few weeks, but, like I said, we don't mix.'

Nobody mixed any more, because there was nowhere to go. The pubs in towns were crammed with kids, the bulk of whom appeared to be below the age of reason. Cars disappeared with monotonous regularity, many burned and exploded in an effort to destroy all evidence when petrol tanks ran dry. Life was lived these days in secure units that had once been proper homes. Keeping people out was the main aim in life as man entered the twenty-first century.

The town centre was dying, its murderers sitting in municipal offices to plan the rerouting of a river, the destruction of beautiful commercial properties, the reduction of Bolton to a town like any other, building societies, fast food, fast shopping, layered car parks. Social life was arranged these days around fortresses occupied by friends – so it was dinner parties, bridge, garden barbecues. No one borrowed a cup of sugar any more; no one took sugar any more, he thought as he dropped a sweetener into his cup.

'If you leave a card, I'll get Mrs Makepeace to phone you when she gets back.'

'No need,' he answered. 'I shall put a note through the door. Thank you for your help.' He took a last sip of coffee and decided that he didn't like Kenya blend.

Outside once more, he unlocked his car, climbed into the passenger seat and sat for a few moments outside the Makepeace house. He now knew the recent history of Briarswood and was coming close to believing in ghosts. Over several decades, the building had been rented out to various people, but no one had stayed beyond a few months. As for the construction, there was an extra wall in the cellar – that was the only explanation for the anomaly. To investigate, he needed the permission of the current owners. The owners were Helen Spencer, Millicent Spencer and Agnes Makepeace.

Briarswood was supposed to be haunted, and Ian Harte understood why tenants had quit. It was a very odd place. He remembered his last visit and had no desire to return to the house, but, as the one elected to get a builder to sort out the footings, he was forced to become involved. Because Briarswood, once Lambert House, was to become a health farm. 'Another slide into bloody stupidity,' he muttered. The country was going to the dogs and he was forced to play a part in the sin.

It would be a simple case of taking out a few bricks to ensure that the building was stable, but permission was required. He sighed, wrote his note for Mrs Makepeace, delivered it and returned to his vehicle. As he turned the key in the ignition and pulled away, he found himself wishing that someone else could take charge of this job. Briarswood was crazy, and he wanted nothing more to do with it.

Agnes gazed out to sea, her eyes fixed on the area in which her beloved husband had last drawn breath. There had been no funerals, because the yacht, reduced to matchsticks, had taken with it two people whose bodies had never been found. She recalled the inquest, remembered a man from the Lifeboat Association stating baldly that any persons on board would have ended up as fish food.

For at least two years after the accident, Agnes had been a robot. She had functioned, had fed and clothed her child, had scarcely noticed when Helen had left with Millie, Mags and Harry to live in the south of England.

'Just me and Lucy now,' she breathed. George had lasted longer than poor Denis, but a single coronary occlusion had eventually taken him away from his wife and children.

She said her goodbye to the grey water, picked up the handle of her wheeled suitcase and dragged it towards the station. Home. She was going home to an existence that held few pleasures now that David was gone. She was proud of her son. He was a consultant who specialized in childhood cancers at Great Ormond Street hospital. He was married, Agnes was a grandmother, and she lived for infrequent visits. Everyone was so busy these days, seeming to live at the speed of light, with no time for anyone or anything.

Mags, Harry and Helen were becoming distant memories. The geographical space between them was a factor, though separation had begun before they had left Lambert House. It was probably because of the accident. Harry, who had passed his driving test just before the explosion, could have been the driver, but Denis had taken the judge to Morecambe Bay and Denis had died. That was not Harry's fault, though he had shouldered a form of guilt, and, probably for that reason, he and Mags had followed Helen to Hastings.

In spite of his position in the legal world, Judge Zachary Spencer had died intestate, so all property and monies had gone by default to Helen and Millie. Helen, in typical fashion, had managed to divide everything into three parts, for herself, Millie and Agnes. Should Lambert House be sold, that money, too, would be split in a similar fashion.

But no one had wanted the house. Agnes could not understand why. She had spent nights there, had experienced nothing, yet she had been forced to listen to complaints from tenant after tenant while wild stories were told. No, they hadn't actually seen or heard anything, yet stuff moved. The furniture remained in situ, but smaller, personal items disappeared all the time, only to turn up later in improbable places. The house was dark and often chilly, they said. Agnes had never found it to be dark. One tenant pointed out that the place became lighter and warmer every time Agnes entered it, but that was foolishness, surely?

She played with a crossword, read the headlines, then fell asleep. Morecambe was miles behind her when she woke. Oh, Denis. How could the pain continue after thirty-nine years? Why did his raincoat still hang from the hall stand with that ancient brown-and-black-checked scarf? She had never let go, had never said goodbye, had remained half a woman. Perhaps the burial of a body might have made things easier to accept, though she doubted that, too. He had been her soulmate and she had lived nearly two-thirds of her life without him to keep her warm and safe.

The bus dropped her outside the house and she entered by the front door. There was no one to greet her, no human, no animal, no sound. The television filled the void and she sat, still wearing her coat, to stare at a bouncy young woman making garden features. The young woman was not wearing a bra and her hair kept falling over her face. She spoke loudly and dragged bits of grey, dried wood hither and thither, her plan to make a Chinese garden in an English suburb achieved within five heavily edited minutes.

His photograph was on the mantelpiece. Pop and Nan were there, too, along with Pop and Eva, then Albert and Kate, who had lived next door. They were all gone now, of course. Agnes had inherited Bamber

Cottage, had sold it and was living comfortably on her savings. What was this card about? She stared at the item she had picked up on her way in, fished out reading glasses and saw Ian Harte's name and telephone number with a message. He was a surveyor and he wanted to talk to her about selling Briarswood. Agnes sighed. She had changed the name and the decor, yet still no tenant had endured beyond six months. Haunted, indeed. Oh, well, she would phone the man in a day or so.

As if reading her thoughts, the instrument rang out. It was Lucy. She was going round the bend with boredom and stated her intention to visit the next day. 'Heard from Mags?' she asked.

'No,' replied Agnes.

'I'd never have believed she'd stay out of touch,' Lucy complained. 'We were all so close, weren't we?'

Agnes sighed. A lifetime ago, she had married the sweetest man in the world, and Lucy had married her George, who had been the second sweetest. Mags and her new nose had been joined in wedlock to Harry Timpson, who had become a very successful accountant. Then, suddenly, it had all gone awry. 'Morecambe was cold again,' she said.

'Isn't it time you stopped going, Agnes?'

'No. You can put flowers on George's grave, but the sea is all I have when it comes to Denis. Yes, get your old bones round here tomorrow. I'll go mad, butter some bread and open a tin of soup.'

She decided to unpack in the morning, made her way upstairs and, after the necessary preparations, climbed into a bed that had seen better days. She would never part with it. On Denis's side, the old pillow remained. She had worn out several of her own and had replaced them, but she kept his and changed its cover twice a week. For a while after he had gone, the scent of him had lingered, but he was all swallowed up now, obliterated by time and by the fact that few of the current neighbours remembered him.

'It just goes on, come what may,' she told the luminous dial of her alarm clock. The ticking and the turning of pages in a calendar continued, no matter what. She remembered the day, felt the baby in her arms and the chill travelling the length of her spine. He should not have gone to work, should have stayed at home after the previous day's troubles. But he had gone and nothing would ever bring him back.

Denis remained the same as ever, young and handsome in various frames around the house. Agnes, still straight and fairly strong, had silver in her hair and lines on her face. She was not afraid of ageing, was not afraid of death. All she feared was this continuing emptiness, the silence, the isolation. All she wanted was to be part of a family, but David was too far away and Denis was long gone.

Never mind. Lucy would be here tomorrow.

Lucy bustled in with fish and chips. 'I didn't get any mushy peas for me,' she said, 'they give me wind in the willows.'

They sat at the kitchen table, each leaving many chips uneaten. 'One portion between two next time,' said Lucy. 'Never mind – it saved you opening a tin and buttering bread.'

In the living room, they played Scrabble for a couple of hours. Lucy, who had become an addict, manufactured some improbable words. When challenged by her partner, she came up with the inevitable Chambers dictionary and proved herself right. 'Shall we go to the pub?' Agnes asked as dusk fell.

'No. It's full of thirty-year-olds with prospects.'

'And credit cards.'

'Exactly. I can't recall the last time I was in there. Remember Helen's first game of darts? I reckon they had to plaster three walls after that. Anyway, I have come with a cunning plan.'

'Ah.' A cunning plan was typical of Lucy, who still continued to be the naughty child. 'What is it this time?'

Lucy grinned. 'It's time we had another Hastings adventure. We won't tell them we're coming, eh? I can book us into a hotel and we'll get fed and watered with our own money. Then we just turn up at the house and surprise them.'

'I'm not sure that's a good idea.'

Lucy sighed heavily. 'Look, we were the three graces for long enough – brought one another up, we did.'

It was Agnes's turn to sigh. 'I just feel we're not wanted. Helen said she would do what she saw as her duty by me, then that was that. I even had the DNA done to prove that we share blood, which took ages – it's harder to prove siblinghood than parenthood. But I had to do it before accepting all that money and a share of the house. She's stubborn, but so am I. I had to hang on until DNA technology had been refined before accepting the money, but she never touched my share. She waited for the test, then made me a rich woman, and that was the end of it. If they wanted us there, we would have been invited, Lucy.'

The visitor scowled. 'Time we had it out with Mags, then. She just buggered off without so much as a by-your-leave – we hadn't done anything to deserve that, had we?'

'I suppose she knew we were surprised when she married Harry. He turned out OK and we all like him. But we're not wanted.'

'Why, though?'

'I don't know. I've told you for years that I don't know.'

But Lucy had made up her mind. Agnes, who knew that Lucy could be rather direct and indiscreet, had to agree to the plan. She wasn't going to allow Lucy to barge in and start a war – Hastings had seen enough of that in 1066. 'All right, but you'll have to behave.'

Lucy pretended to pout. 'You mean I can't wear my crocheted wedding dress and high boots? Do I have to be sensible?'

'Yes, you do.'

They parted company just before the six o'clock news. Lucy returned to her converted barn, while Agnes stared at trouble in the Middle East and decided that religion was a bad thing. Wars had been fought in the name of Jesus Christ; now people quarrelled over another prophet. Even the Jews, whose Messiah was still awaited, couldn't sit still and behave themselves for five minutes. She shook a fist at the television and turned to a cable channel. It was chewing gum for the mind, but it got her through another evening spent in the company of soup, sandwiches and silence. Broadcast sound made the house seem occupied, and she was fast becoming a fan of soaps and comedy series. But such luxuries were a poor substitute for a family. Yes, she would go to Hastings, because time, the great enemy, needed to be filled. And she must remember to phone that surveyor.

*

'What did you say?' Mags leaned over the bed and waited for an answer.

'The parcel. As soon as I go – post it.'

Mags blinked away yet more tears, wondered how much more saline she could possibly produce. 'Are you sure?' What good would it do? What was the point, after all this time? Helen was fast losing her hold on life, and Mags was her sole attendant. This stubborn patient had refused admittance to hospital and had banned all visiting nurses. The doctor who handled Helen's drugs was allowed begrudgingly to attend the bedside when the drip needed checking. All other callers were turned away from the door. Helen, having been given little choice in the early years of her life, was taking full control of the end. 'Try not to think about it,' Mags urged.

A travesty of a smile stretched parchment-thin skin. 'What else would I think about?' She often thought about Millie, although she didn't want to, as Millie had been spoiled to a point where she considered herself to be the centre of the universe. Helen's sister, who, because of the age difference, had been more like a daughter, was not here to support the woman who had guided her through life. Millie was on the point of divorcing a second husband and had no time for visits while chasing a third. 'I was not a good guardian,' said the woman in the bed.

'You did your best. No one can do more than that.'

'She's selfish.'

'So are my sons. Don't dwell on it. And yes, I shall post your parcel when the time comes.'

'Thank you.'

When Helen had succumbed once again to morphine-induced stupor, Mags crept out of the room and descended the stairs. Away from Helen, she managed not to cry, choosing instead to tackle stained bedlinen and other daily chores. The cancer had travelled at lightning speed through the poor woman's body; she had days to live and Millie didn't seem to care.

As she filled the washing machine, Mags thought about the Helen she had met almost forty years ago at Lucy and George's wedding, remembered her pain, her brief flirtation with alcohol, her vulnerability. Thought skipped ahead to Harley Street, the new nose, her own marriage to Harry Timpson. Harry had made a good job of himself, though his nerves had never been in top condition. Mags knew why. The knowing why had brought her here, to Hastings, had separated her from Agnes and Lucy, the two people who had been her constant companions through childhood, adolescence and into adulthood.

Helen had forbidden Mags to inform Agnes of her illness and imminent death. Mags, having returned to work after her sons had grown, had now retired, but caring for Helen had become a full time job. She no longer went home at night; Harry, too, slept at Helen's house. His blind loyalty to Helen Spencer would stay with him until the day she died.

Mags was bone weary. Although Helen had become slight after the ravages of disease, the task of moving and changing her was taking its toll on her carer's health. 'I'm too old for this,' Mags told the wall. 'I should be knitting for my grandchildren.' She should also be up north. Hastings was a good place, but it wasn't home. Living on the hem of the sector known as Bohemia, she had made friends among writers and artists, many of whom were interesting, some of whom were precious posers and unloved. Now in her fourth decade as a resident, Mags knew every house, every fishing boat, every spire, castle and battleground within ten miles of the town. But she still wanted to go home.

Harry appeared. 'How is she?' were his first words.

'The same.'

He banged a briefcase onto a side table. 'If she were a dog, she'd be humanely destroyed.'

'But she isn't a dog. What we did for Oscar can't possibly be done for Helen.'

'No.' He studied his wife. 'I'm going to take a few weeks off work. Let's face it – I should have retired by now. I'll help you. You look like you need a rest.'

'I can't rest. And you know why. None of us can rest while we know what's coming.' She shook her head. Harry was already on the highest permitted dose of an anti-depressant. He would probably have fared better at work, but there was no point in arguing and she was too tired, anyway, to start a discussion on a subject that was already worn thin. 'I'll make some tea,' she said.

But he was up and out of his chair before she had finished speaking. The kettle clattered and cups were banged onto a tray. Mags simply stared at the wall. It was all going to happen and she dreaded the outcome. Helen Spencer was on the brink of death and Mags, acutely aware of the promise she had made, would abide by her word. It would be a repeat of the Battle of Hastings, but nothing could be done about that.

A picture of Agnes and Lucy suddenly insinuated its way into Mags's exhausted brain. Oh, for the chance to talk to Agnes, to prepare her for what was about to happen. She sat with her head in her hands, elbows on the table, mind in turmoil. For Helen, death was going to mean an end to all troubles; for those she would leave behind . . .

'Shall I take some tea upstairs?' Harry asked.

Mags sat up straight. 'She won't drink it. I've been wetting her lips with a bit of ice. She'll be needing no more tea, love.'

He sat opposite his wife. 'Not long, then?'

'No. Could be today, tonight, tomorrow – I've no idea.'

'And Millie?'

Mags shrugged. 'Mucking about in London as far as I know. She dumped the dentist and she's chasing a stockbroker. I think she'll become one of those serial monogamists.'

Harry attempted a joke. 'I thought she was a physiotherapist.'

Mags shook her head. 'She's a bloody pest, that's for sure.'

'Aye, she is. Oh, I bought a bit of fish for a change.'

Mags pretended to frown. 'That's unusual, isn't it? Fish in a fishing port?'

'It is,' he replied. 'Especially when ninety per cent of it goes to Captain Birds Eye or some such frozen person. Do you not fancy fish?'

She closed her eyes. She fancied fish and chips Lancashire style, nice, smooth batter beaten by her dad, chips fried by her mam at Bradshaw's chippy. She fancied eating from newspaper on the moors, drinking dandelion and burdock from the bottle, wiping her hands on grass. 'I want to go home,' she said quietly. Mam and Dad weren't there any more, but she still needed to be in Lancashire with Agnes and Lucy. 'Retire, Harry. We'll go home and face the brass band.'

His face was ashen. 'I'm scared.'

'So am I.'

'I did what I did for Helen.'

'Yes.'

'But it was wrong.'

'I know. At the time, there seemed little choice.'

They drank tea in silence, then Mags went to prepare the fish for supper. She was worried about her husband, about the poor soul upstairs, was still homesick after going on forty years in the south. Someone rang the front doorbell, and she heard Harry walking down the hall. When he returned, he was not alone. Mags dropped a knife. 'Agnes,' she whispered. 'Lucy – when did you get here?'

'Yesterday,' answered Lucy. 'We've done all the compulsory things, just as we did last time we came. We've done Battle, the Shipwreck Centre and the Fishermen's Museum. I still say we would have won if King Harold hadn't been worn out after York.'

Agnes saw the expression on Mags's face. 'Mags?'

'Hello.'

'What are you doing in Helen's house? Is she all right?'

'No,' replied Harry. 'She's on her last legs.'

Mags dried her hands on a tea towel. 'She hasn't been on her legs for weeks, Harry.' She turned her attention to her two friends. 'She's got cancer. It's a nasty one. It travels express and takes no prisoners. There's nothing to be done apart from palliative care. She refused to go into hospital or into a hospice, so I look after her. Harry helps all he can.'

Agnes leaned against a wall. 'How long?' she asked.

'Any minute now.' Mags sat on a straight-backed chair. 'Helen forbade me to contact you. She said you'd suffered enough and she didn't want to put you through this.' Mags could not mention other difficulties that would surely arise in the very near future.

Agnes's jaw hung open. She could not think of anything to say.

Lucy waded in, of course. 'Agnes is her sister. She should have been told.'

For once, Mags stood up to Lucy. 'When a dying woman expresses a wish, I listen. Isn't it time you did the same – time you listened, I mean? Hear yourself, Lucy. Think about what you're saying before allowing the words out of your mouth. There – I've waited years to say that.'

It was Lucy's turn to have a slack jaw.

Agnes left the room and made for the stairs. Apart from her son, she owned but one living relative, and her sister was about to die. There was Millie, of course, but Millie was too busy crossing the pond to buy shoes on Park Avenue, or, when she was in London, chasing someone else's husband, to count. Panic fluttered in Agnes's chest. Poor Helen. She had never married, yet she had been a mother to the ungrateful Millie, had devoted her life to the child.

Lucy stared at Mags. Mags had changed. 'So, you're standing up for yourself at last, are you? I'll go and look at Helen—'

'No you won't. As you just said, they're sisters. They haven't seen one another for God alone knows how long – let Agnes have some time with Helen alone.'

'I never realized how much you dislike me,' said Lucy.

Mags smiled grimly. 'I don't dislike you. It's just that you've always been the centre of attention and it's time we all grew up. Try some sensitivity. Think about other people for a change.' Lucy put Mags in mind of Millie, who had always been precocious and spoiled. The small, neat woman who had been married to George Henshaw continued to act the clown, the beautiful, forgivable girl. It didn't work any more. Like body parts, the personality should age as gracefully as possible. Naughty children in their sixties were not charming.

When Agnes walked into Helen's bedroom, a silly, disjointed thought entered her head. She had forgotten to phone that surveyor. Helen, who had wanted to retain Briarswood for rental only, had been outvoted by her two half-sisters. Millie demanded the money, while Agnes, tired of being caretaker to an empty pile, simply needed to be rid of the house.

All thoughts of surveyors left her when she saw what time and cancer had done to Helen Spencer. Limp, grey hair hung in clumps, punctuating baldness resulting from chemotherapy. The neck was more than thin, while the shape beneath the blankets was horribly emaciated. She was awake, at least.

'Hello, love.' Agnes sat down by the bed, afraid of touching a hand that was almost transparent.

The skull on the pillows smiled. 'Hello.'

'Don't tire yourself,' Agnes begged.

'No point in saving energy,' came the reply. 'I'm on borrowed seconds now.'

Agnes swallowed.

'I'm sorry.'

'For what?'

'It's all there for you – in the book I never published. Let me die first.'

'I don't want you to die.'

'You can't choose. Is the house sold?'

'No. But a man wants to survey it properly.'

'When I'm dead. Wait, please.'

'All right.'

Helen took a deep, rasping breath. 'The haunting began before we left. Millie's toys would be moved, my watch disappeared more than once. He's there, you see.'

'Your dad?'

'And yours. Agnes – get Mags.'

Agnes descended the stairs and gave Mags the message.

'She's too weak now to deal with the morphine,' said Mags, drying her hands.

Lucy and Agnes waited in the drawing room. They listened as Harry followed his wife to Helen's bedroom, sat in silence among Helen's treasured antiques. A grandmother clock chimed the quarter-hour as Mags entered the room. 'She's gone.'

It was Lucy who cried, Lucy who said it wasn't fair. Agnes simply sat and allowed the message to be absorbed by her soul. She was glad. No one should be forced to continue alive in such condition.

'She didn't suffer,' said Mags. 'She just closed her eyes and fell asleep. You helped her, Agnes. It's as if she knew you would come. I think she was waiting, but she wouldn't let me fetch you.'

Lucy turned her face to the wall and stifled the sobs.

'The funeral will be at Skirlaugh,' Mags announced. 'I have detailed instructions – she is to be buried with her mother.'

Agnes nodded, sighed, looked down the long road she had travelled in the company of Helen. The further back she went, the narrower the track became, because the beginning had been so unreal – Helen trying to seduce Denis, Denis resisting, Helen turning on her father – on the man who was Agnes's father, too. There were those letters, there was an unpublished book, a funeral to arrange. 'We'll go home and get ready for you,' she told Mags.

'Thank you.'

Agnes and Lucy went to say their final goodbyes to Helen. The face on white linen was as pale as the pillowcase, but pain seemed to be lifting itself out of features in which it had become ingrained. 'She's all right now,' Agnes told her weeping companion. 'Don't cry. You never trusted her, anyway.'

'I did. Once all had been explained, I even liked her.'

'How fortunate for her.'

Lucy, unused to sarcasm from her friend, had nothing else to say.

They left for the north the next day. A Hastings undertaker would take the body, then it was to be transported home and delivered to a funeral parlour in Bolton. For Agnes and Lucy, the rest was vague, though they had been instructed to arrange a buffet at Briarswood. The will would be read in a Bolton office and Agnes hoped against hope that Millie would at least come to the funeral of the woman who had been a loving mother.

'What about that surveyor?' Lucy asked as the train pulled into Trinity Street Station. 'The one you forgot to ring?'

'He can wait till it's all over.' The selling of the house was no longer at the top of the list, because Helen Spencer was coming home.

Chapter Fifteen

It was over. Agnes, feeling like a limp dishcloth, returned with Lucy from the reading of the will. Lucy, pleased to have been left pearls she had always coveted, expressed her concern about deserting Agnes in her hour of need. 'I have to get home,' she grumbled. 'The decorator's going to do an estimate today. I could put him off—'

'No. Go and get it over with.'

'Phone me if you need me.' Lucy left. Agnes, glad of her own company, sat and studied the fireplace. Lucy had had an ulterior motive for wanting to stay, because Agnes was in possession of the sole copy of Helen Spencer's unpublished typescript. Lucy always wanted to be the first to know just about anything – she had been the same since childhood.

'No Millie, of course,' Agnes whispered into the silence. 'After all Helen gave up for her, she couldn't even be bothered to put in an appearance now.' It had been a very quiet funeral. The village that had known Helen no longer existed. After almost forty years, the residents of Skirlaugh Fall had forgotten the Spencer family of Lambert House, now Briarswood, Skirlaugh Rise. People came, people went, life went on. 'Just as well,' said Agnes as she removed her shoes and pushed her feet into a pair of old, well-loved slippers. 'Or we'd still be mourning Adam and Eve.'

She looked at the parcel, recalled another package left here many years earlier, remembered with clarity the day she had read how Judge Spencer, after murdering one woman, had impregnated another, her own mother. More reading to be done – more discoveries to be made, she supposed. A long time ago, Mabel, Helen's nanny, had left a letter; Helen had left several hundred thousand words.

The doorbell sounded. Agnes hauled suddenly heavy bones from their resting place, opened the door and was shocked to find Millie on the step. 'Yes?' Agnes had little time for her devious and rather decorative half-sister. She was wearing well for her age, but plastic surgery had become a necessity, clothes a fixation, make-up an absolute must-have. Her surname seemed to change with the seasons – few remembered whether she was married or to whom. This woman seemed to be as ruthless as her dead father had been; she cared only for herself.

Millie pushed her way into the house. 'I missed the reading of the will,' she said as she placed herself in front of the over-mantel mirror. A hand strayed to her throat. Did she need a little more work in that area?

Agnes closed the door. 'You aren't welcome here,' she snapped.

Millie, unused to being addressed in such fashion by Agnes, turned away from her own precious image and glared at the owner of this tiny house. 'Why is that?' she asked. 'I haven't seen you for years – what on earth has happened to make you so nasty? I'm sure I don't know what I am supposed to have done.'

'You missed the reading of the will? Bugger the will – you missed the funeral. Helen gave up her whole life for you.'

The visitor shrugged. 'No one asked her to. Anyway, what sort of life would she have had? No man wanted her. I was the only reason for her to get out of bed every morning.'

'That's not the point.' Helen had indulged the child, had made excuses for the teenager, had lost the woman who stood here now. 'Your father didn't want you. He threatened to have you adopted.'

'Good job he died when he did, then.'

'And you know about the will – half to you, half to me.'

'But you aren't a proper sister.'

Agnes lowered her chin. 'I didn't see much of Helen after she left for Hastings, but I was a better sister than you were.' She raised her head. 'What did you ever do for her – for anyone other than yourself? Go and contest the will – I don't give two hoots about the money. My grandfather – his work now sells second hand for a small fortune – left me very comfortable. And Helen made sure I was safe. Do as you please, but leave my house.'

Millie's jaw hung for a split second. 'I couldn't make the funeral – I was in hospital in San Francisco. What was I supposed to do? Get on a plane and let my wounds become infected?'

Agnes half smiled and shook her head. 'What was it this time? Liposuction? Another implant, a bit of collagen? You want to be careful – the skin of your face is stretched so tight you look like something out of Tussaud's.'

'Nonsense. I like to make the best of myself. What's wrong with that?'

'Look at that skin-bleached pop star – the one whose nose seems to be parting company with his face. You can go too far with that particular addiction. Anyway, I have something to do straight away, so leave now. Oh, and if you were going to ask yet again about the house – a surveyor is looking at it. You'll get your share.'

Millie opened her mouth to speak, thought better of it, and left the house in a cloud of expensive and rather overpowering perfume.

Agnes set the kettle to boil, then stood and leaned against the kitchen sink. Through the window, she had a clear enough view of the big house. It wasn't as easy to see as it had been forty years ago, because trees had grown thicker, but it remained visible. Briarswood had become a thorn in her side. It had been impossible to let and was even proving difficult to sell. Briarswood had been a suitable name for a thorn in her flesh, she mused for a second or two. She had just shown another spiky problem out of the house – how dared Millie turn up at this late stage?

She settled in front of the television with toast and tea. Whatever was in Helen's book would still be there tomorrow. But no programme suited her tonight, and she found herself thinking about Mags, who had already returned to Hastings with Harry. Mags knew about the house and its weirdness. She had stayed in it with Helen and Harry after the explosion that had taken Denis and the judge. It was creepy, she had said.

Agnes chewed thoughtfully. Bangles, beads, watches, cufflinks, wallets and purses had all disappeared, only to turn up an hour or a day later in rooms that had been unused. Mags didn't lie. Therefore, it was probably right to believe the stories of tenants, most of whom had left the house within a few months of failing to settle into it. Had the surveyor noticed anything odd? Was that why he needed to speak to the owners?

Her eyes strayed once again to the parcel. According to Helen, the book was her own life story, but all names had been changed. The haunting was probably mentioned in there – perhaps she should read a little of it tonight.

She finished her simple supper, checked locks and windows, picked up the package and carried it upstairs. It was unlikely to be suitable bedtime reading, but Agnes wanted Helen's view of the so-called spirits who were said to inhabit Briarswood. After preparing herself for sleep, she switched on her reading lamp before settling in bed with the large envelope. Poor Helen. Did she want Agnes to try to get the story published?

The accompanying note said nothing about selling the script. It simply drew Agnes's attention to chapter seven.

The rest is just a piece of self-pity and an account of the devil who was our father. I ask your forgiveness before you begin to read. This story will help you understand why I left the north for Hastings. It will also explain my over-lenient attitude towards Millie, who has grown into a person of whom I find it impossible to be proud. In trying to make her happy, I spoiled her beyond retrieval.

My dear Agnes, I thank you for your friendship and forbearance. I have loved receiving your letters and I love you for the time and trouble you took to keep in touch with me.

I beg you to forgive me.

Your loving sister, Helen

Forgive? Forgive what? Agnes turned immediately to chapter seven. From the start, she was riveted to the script. Oh, God, this could not be true. But it was true, it had to be true. She got no sleep that night.

Ian Harte knocked on the door of the only decent-looking cottage in the terrace. Mrs Makepeace had never got back to him, so he was making a renewed effort to solve the riddle of Briarswood. It was a valuable property, and his employers were keen to get it sold so that they could reap their statutory percentage.

The door opened to reveal a dishevelled woman who did not seem to fit with the neat house and garden. She was in dressing gown and old slippers, but it was the expression on her face that dismayed him. The woman looked ill and worn out.

'Yes?' she said.

'Ian Harte, Mrs Makepeace. I'm the one trying to do a full survey on Briarswood. You are one of the key-holders, I take it?'

'I am.'

He hesitated. 'Is this a bad time?'

'I just buried my sister.'

'Ah. I'm sorry. Would you like me to come back in a few days? I've no wish to intrude on your grief.'

It was Agnes's turn to dither. Should she wade in and get the business over and done with? Or did she need some more thinking time? 'There are complications,' she said slowly. 'My sister who died was part-owner, as is another sister. There were three of us,' she added lamely.

He gave her an encouraging smile. 'I see. Well, if you want to leave it for now, I'll—'

'Come back on Wednesday,' she said. 'Sorry to mess

you about, but I have some legal business to finish and . . . erm . . . I'm not feeling too well.'

'Is there anything I can do?'

Agnes smiled at him. He reminded her of Denis. Denis would have become a gentle, thoughtful soul – no – he had always owned those qualities. 'No, thank you. This is something I have to do by myself. Family and lawyers – I'm sure you understand.'

'Of course.' He turned, then swivelled back to face her. 'Look after yourself, Mrs Makepeace. You have my phone number.'

Lucy phoned. 'Have you read it?'

Agnes was transported backwards in time to the day when Lucy had asked the same question about testimony bequeathed by an ex-nanny. 'Some of it, yes.'

'What did it say?'

Lucy had always been so full-on, so direct and challenging. 'I can't talk about it. Lucy, please don't ask.'

'But—'

'I told you not to ask. Mags lost patience with you in Hastings – it takes a hell of a lot for Mags to lose patience. Sometimes, people need to be left alone to digest information. Not all knowledge needs to be broadcast immediately, you know. I have to come to terms with this on my own. When I am ready to talk, you will not be the first to hear – I am sorry about that. Things need to be done now in the correct order. I shall give them their airing when my own head is clear.'

'Oh. Right. Shall I stay away for a while, then?'

'Good idea. I'll call you once the show is on the road.' It would be a show, too, she thought. A three-ringed circus was about to pitch its big tops in the grounds of the village named Skirlaugh.

Agnes sat all day in her dressing gown and slippers. She drank what seemed to be a gallon of tea, ate arrowroot biscuits and half an apple. The typescript remained upstairs, because she did not want it in the same room as herself. Its current place of residence was at the bottom of a blanket box underneath one of Denis's cable-knit jumpers. Denis. Oh, Denis. At last, the tears came. There was no need to cry quietly, because this was a proper house, its walls inches thick and made of stone.

The truth of which she had just become proprietor weighed heavily. It was not something she could keep to herself, yet she scarcely knew where to begin. Was there a right way? Who would be hurt?

She dried her eyes and phoned Hastings. 'Mags?'

'Yes?'

'You were expecting me to call.'

'I was, yes.'

'Is it the truth – this chapter seven?'

'I never read it, Agnes, but I think I know what it says.'

'And Harry really did do that?'

'He did. He would have done anything for her. It's been difficult. Their relationship had a passion I never shared with him.'

A few beats of time passed. 'Did they sleep together?' Agnes asked.

'It was the price I had to pay to keep the man I loved. And, no matter what, I could not have resented Helen Spencer. I cared for her in my own way, you see.'

Agnes replaced the receiver. Everyone had paid, it

395

seemed. The judge was the rot in the fruit's flesh. He had caused pain to all in his path, and Helen had suffered the most. It was ten o'clock, almost time for bed. She did not want to go upstairs. Still unwashed and bedraggled, Agnes Makepeace curled herself on the sofa, head propped on cushions. She leaned over and pushed *Pride and Prejudice* into the DVD player, pretending to watch a story told in a time that was difficult, but clear-cut. Jane Austen knew all about the small life, the ribbons, the gowns, the carriages. Yet she said nothing real about men, was a mere observer of their functions and a listener to their pronouncements.

Jane Austen had never attempted to climb into the mind and soul of the human male. It was plain that she knew nothing of true evil. If Wickham was the wicked-est creature that writer could imagine, her life had been blessed indeed.

Agnes rose at nine o'clock, went upstairs and took a hot shower. She dressed soberly in black skirt, white blouse, grey cardigan and a small amount of make-up. It had to be done today, and Ian Harte had seemed a decent enough man. After telephoning to ask him to come today instead of on Wednesday, she busied herself with chores in an attempt to fill in time. He would help her. With unwavering certainty, she knew that she had found the best compromise.

He came, as arranged, at two o'clock. Agnes provided tea and biscuits, then sat for a few minutes arranging her thoughts into a semblance of order. It had to be done; things could not be left as they were.

'In 1965,' she began, 'my husband and Judge Zachary

Spencer died. Judge Spencer and his daughter, Helen, lived at Lambert House – Briarswood, as it's called now. There was an explosion on the judge's yacht in Morecambe Bay – something to do with fuel in the galley – and the yacht was blown to smithereens.'

'Yes, I know. It must have been a very sad time for you.'

Agnes inhaled deeply. 'It never happened.'

'I beg your—'

'It was a lie, a sham. Helen Spencer murdered her father and killed my Denis by accident. Helen's father had done away with her mother thirty years earlier – that's why she murdered him. There was written evidence of his crime and Helen had witnessed it herself, though she was very young at the time and needed her memory jogging. She wrote her life story in the form of a novel – the names are changed – and she waited until after her own death to let me know. I don't blame her for that – she had trouble enough in her life. Now, I have to bear the weight for her.'

'So – where are the bodies?' He knew the answer before the question was fully aired. 'They're in the cellar, aren't they? That's why the specifications have gone awry.'

Agnes nodded. 'It was arsenic. Denis never touched brandy, but he must have taken a drink of it on that particular evening.' Hardly surprising, she thought, after the trouble of the previous day. 'The yacht was blown up by some man from Wythenshawe – I suspect he had played a part in a robbery at a Manchester jeweller's in the previous year. Someone drove the judge's Bentley to Morecambe, Helen followed in her car and brought the driver back. The Bentley was found by police in

Morecambe. They assumed that Denis had driven the judge to his yacht. The crew of the lifeboat said no remains would be found, as the yacht was in splinters.'

'Bloody hell.' Ian Harte pushed a hand through his hair.

'My Denis hated that bloody yacht.' Agnes shook her head. 'We need the police,' she said, her voice steady. 'A wall was built in the cellar with both bodies behind it. The cellar was plastered over – Helen wrote all the details – and those two souls – one good, one evil – have haunted that place ever since.'

'More evil than good,' he said. 'I've never had faith in such things, but the house is definitely creepy.'

Agnes smiled wanly. 'Not evil when I'm there, though. If I go into the house, Denis looks after me.' It all sounded silly in broad daylight, yet she now believed in those two spirits. 'The police will have to deal with this, Mr Harte. Your client must step back for a while – the house cannot be sold just yet.'

'Quite.' He shivered. 'You want me to do this for you?'

She nodded and handed him chapter seven. 'It's all in there. I know full well what needs to be done, yet I find myself incapable of doing it.' Harry would be implicated. 'You came along at just the right time, Mr Harte.'

He lowered his chin. 'We've both been through the mill, Mrs Makepeace. I lost my mother to cancer just weeks ago, so I know what grief is. Yes, of course I'll help.' He scribbled on a scrap of paper. 'That's my home number and my mobile – call any time. Joyce – that's my missus – is a good listener, too. Don't be alone, please.'

Agnes stood at the window and watched as Ian Harte drove away to instigate enormous trouble. When the car had disappeared, she pulled on a coat, picked up the keys to Briarswood, and left the house. She was going to say goodbye to Denis. This would probably be the last day of sanity for some time to come, and the big house was going to be out of bounds.

When she opened the front door, she smelled brandy. That was ridiculous, she told herself, because no one had lived here for many months. Dust motes floated in weak sunlight, and beautiful wood panelling seemed to scream for beeswax. She unlocked the door to the cellars and went down below ground level. With just a vague idea of the location of the bodies, she sat on an old crate and talked to Denis. 'I didn't know where you were, sweetheart. All these years, I've been going to Morecambe, but you were here all the time. He's with you, isn't he? Never mind. They'll be getting you out soon, then you can go and have a decent burial in Tonge Cemetery.'

A slight breeze brushed her cheek. Where had that come from? Agnes stood up and walked towards the front of the house. She knew she was nearer to him. The cellars were made up of load-bearing walls that carried the pattern and shape of rooms above, yet the layout was slightly confusing for Agnes, who had never before descended to this level. Some areas were plastered, some were not. Several of the judge's wines rested on wooden racks, and the remains of Pop's model of Lambert House were jumbled in a corner.

Placing her hands against one of the plastered walls, she spoke again. 'I know you're inches away from me now,' she said. 'I think you're under the judge's study. There'll be police and all sorts of people around soon, but I had to do it, had to tell. Helen meant me to release you from here. You're not resting. Before you can rest, you have to become a crime scene.' The smell of brandy came again. 'Neither are you resting,' said Agnes, her voice louder, 'and you never will, you bad bugger. Helen did the right thing. Denis – you know she never meant to kill you.'

She left the house and stood outside for a while, remembering Kate, who had run the kitchen here for years. Gardens, neglected and overgrown now, had been cared for by Denis under the watchful eye of an Alsatian named Oscar. Louisa had breathed life into the place until her pregnancy; Helen, who had once believed herself to be in love with Denis, had matured and improved greatly under Louisa's protection.

All gone now, all ground to dust, but never forgotten by Agnes. A thought struck her and she picked her mobile phone from one pocket, Ian Harte's card from another.

He answered immediately. 'Hello?'

'There are blueprints with Granada TV,' said Agnes. 'My grandfather made a model of the house and, if you look at his drawings, you'll see where the original walls of the cellar were. The judge and Denis were still alive when Pop built that huge doll's house, so that should show you where any changes were made. He did the cellars as well as the upper part of the building, you see.'

He cleared his throat. 'I don't need the plans, Mrs Makepeace – I know exactly where the . . . the problem lies. I'm with the police now,' he said softly. 'They'll be up there soon.'

'I know.' She understood what was coming. Feeling strangely peaceful, she wandered back to her cottage and telephoned her son. He needed to know what was happening and he promised to travel up as soon as possible. Agnes smiled. Denis would have been so proud of David, who fought daily battles on behalf of sick children. 'You are proud, aren't you?' she asked a photograph on the mantelpiece. He was still here, would always be here.

Cars began to arrive, one stopping outside her house, others carrying on round the corner and up Skirlaugh Rise. There would be questions, of course, then inquests, then two funerals. Agnes would go to her husband's service and burial, but her father could be put out with the council's bins for all she cared.

She opened the door. A plain clothes officer who looked far too young for such responsibility entered the house. 'Mrs Makepeace.'

'Yes, that's me.'

And so it began.

Skirlaugh was packed with reporters, photographers and television crews. Whenever Agnes left the house, she was accosted by seekers of sensational headlines. One man, who had entered her rear garden without permission, was dealt with very tersely. 'Your sort may have chased Diana to her death, but pond life has no effect on me. Bugger off before I clock you with my poker.' She brandished the brass-handled fire iron. The man stood his ground until she raised the weapon, then scrambled up the wall, almost screaming when brambles bit into his flesh.

After that small event, life moved slightly closer to normal. When she walked to the village shop, a policeman accompanied her, and she was grateful for that small service. Shopping further afield involved Lucy and her car, but they almost always managed to outwit their pursuers.

David arrived with his wife and children. The youngsters had to sleep in their parents' room, but reporters melted into the ether as soon as they noticed a man in the cottage. David Makepeace, who was kindness itself when it came to his family and his job, had little time for tabloids or broadcasting journalists. Within twenty-four hours of his arrival, Agnes had the peace she had sought.

However, the story was front page news, not only in Lancashire, but throughout the whole of Britain. The nanny's letter was mentioned, as was the illegitimate status of Agnes, second daughter to a corrupt judge. One daily tabloid gave graphic details of the state of the two bodies – it seemed that they had mummified because of airbricks at the tops of walls and the proximity of a huge, oil-fired boiler that heated the house. There was no escape. Television and radio chipped in. Pop was there once more in all his glory, a wonderful, difficult old man showing off his doll's houses and his model of the then Lambert House. Tears flowed down Agnes's cheeks as she listened to him lecturing on the subject of retirement. 'You can retire when they put the last nail in your coffin lid,' he pronounced.

Lydia, too, wiped away a tear. 'Come on, Mum,' she said. 'Turn that damned thing off. David's taking us out for a meal.'

'People will stare,' said Agnes. Then she raised her head. 'Let them,' she whispered. 'There's enough of Pop in me to tell them to bog off.' So she went with her son, daughter-in-law and grandchildren to face the world.

'I'm not leaving my cottage,' she told David. 'I'm not running away like Helen did.'

'Nor should you,' said Lydia. 'But you know where we are if it gets too much. You could have your own flat in the basement.'

Agnes managed a smile. 'No, love. My Denis was nearly forty years in a cellar – I think I'll keep my head on the surface, thanks.'

The inquest was a nightmare. The police had gathered from Helen's script and from Agnes that Harry Timpson, whose name had been changed by Helen, had been working for the Spencers in 1965, so he was summoned to answer for his actions. His name was called, but he never entered the room. The meeting was adjourned until the next day, giving the police time to force Harry to obey the order commanding him to attend both inquests.

David and Lydia, having spent two weeks in the north, had to travel back to London. They would return for Denis's funeral, but David was needed by the sick. They made Agnes promise to visit as soon as the business was over, then left with their children to drive home to Islington.

Alone again, Agnes suddenly felt more isolated than ever. It had been an exhausting time for a woman no longer in the first flush of youth. 'I'm old,' she told a contestant on *Who Wants to be a Millionaire*. The Sky channels offered nothing better. There was a film named *What Lies Beneath* – she wasn't going to look at that. So she tuned into a shopping channel to learn the virtues of foam mattresses and American hand-sewn quilts.

Denis's body would be released for burial within days. She would be able to claim the watch he had worn and his mother's rosary, which he had always carried in a pocket. 'But you'll rest soon,' she promised. 'Away from him, you'll feel better.'

The evening dragged itself along on feet of lead. Agnes picked up some unopened mail, found an offer from a trashy newspaper whose editor wanted to publish Helen's script for a six-figure sum. They could ask Millie, she thought before tossing the letter into a bin. The police held chapter seven while she owned the rest, so they could all bugger off, because Millie had been left just money and property.

Ian Harte arrived at nine o'clock. Aware that Agnes's family had left for London, he wanted to check that Mrs Makepeace was safe and well.

'They were mummified,' she told him.

'Yes.'

'Did you see my Denis?'

He shook his head. 'No one was allowed in. But a young policeman said your husband didn't look as if he had been dead for long. They'll let you see him if you like.'

Agnes looked at all the photographs in the room. 'I can see him here,' she said. 'There's no need for me to look at his body. I have a few of what they called his effects. Soon, I'll get his watch and rosary – they're enough for me.'

She was all right, Ian decided. He finished his cup of tea, said goodbye, then left for home.

It was half past nine. Agnes, having endured many half past nines and beyond, wondered why time had suddenly started to drag to the point of stopping. She could go and live in London with David and Lydia, but London was not for her. It was full of people who knew no one. She glanced through her window – did she know these people? Hardly. But she was on nodding terms with plenty of trees and pathways, and had even been known to greet a neighbour in the street. During the police enquiry, three women had taken the trouble to come to her door with home-made scones, pies and casseroles. She could and would make a life again.

It had been like a football match with a very long half-time, she supposed. That was how Pop had described the twenty-one years between the Great War and the Second – time for a butty and a cuppa, he had named the interval. Since Denis had died, Agnes's life had been on hold. For a reason she failed to understand, the burial of his body would open a new chapter for her. 'But not a chapter seven,' she said aloud. 'Never a chapter seven.'

The doorbell sounded. It was a quarter to ten. 'Who is it?' she called.

'Me.'

'Who's me?'

'Mags.'

Agnes froze. Harry would be with her. Harry was the man who had moved Denis's body down to the cellar. He had also loved Helen and had betrayed poor Mags. 'Are you alone?' she managed eventually.

'Yes. Very much so.'

Agnes opened the door. Mags, in the company of a small suitcase, stepped into the house. She placed the case on the floor, righted herself and spoke again. 'He hanged himself, Agnes.'

'What?' A hand flew of its own accord to her throat. She swallowed hard. 'Harry's dead?'

Mags nodded.

'Bloody hell. Come in – sit yourself down. Oh, my God – whatever next? Why, Mags?'

'He knew he was guilty of helping to conceal the bodies – he was accessory after the crime. And Helen was his raison d'être. I must go back for the inquest, but I had to come and tell you myself. He won't be at the court tomorrow, Agnes. The police know what's happened. I am so tired.'

They sat for over an hour in a companionable silence that was familiar to both of them. Lucy had always been the noise-maker, Mags the quiet one, Agnes the go-between. Two elderly ladies gazed at a dwindling coal fire, each knowing what would happen next, neither needing to speak. Agnes knew that Mags wanted to come home; Mags knew that Agnes needed to share her living space with someone she knew and trusted.

'Shall I put a bottle in your bed?' Agnes asked finally.

'Please.'

'When everything's done and dusted, you can choose your own wallpaper.'

Mags's eyes filled with tears. 'Next door's selling up,' she said. 'I've seen the sign and you can put in an offer for me. We can knock through and make it one big house, or we can keep things as they are. But we'll be together, won't we?'

'Course we will, kiddo. One for all—'

'And all for one. With Lucy as our beloved nuisance, eh?'

That night, both slept well.

Visit **www.panmacmillan.com** to read more about all our books and to buy them. You will also find features, author interviews and news of any author events, and you can sign up for e-newsletters so that you're always first to hear about our new releases.